MW01277542

This book is, like, totally organic and gluten free. No actual desserts were harmed during its production.

Cover design by Krista Wallace, with added expertise from Jonathan Lyster and Brayden Fengler.

978-1-7773423-7-1

This book is dedicated to my stellar family:
Matt (BFF), Boy, DiL and Girl. *Lifting My Heart.*

Find the listen-along playlist here

https://tinyurl.com/GriffinsSpuriousSoundtrack

Griffin & the Spurious Correlations

1

Saturday, May 5

I squeezed my eyes shut and tried to become one with the concrete wall, sweaty hands clenched under my armpits. My guitar hung over my shoulders, and I had to take care not to knock it against the wall.

Calvin controlled his tension by tapping out rhythms on a table with his drumsticks. The others looked calmer than they probably felt, listening to the speeching through the double doors. Cameron wiped away a tear as the toast to the bride wrapped up.

"I love weddings," he said.

"You okay, Griffin?" Calvin asked, spinning his sticks through his fingers.

"Just nervous." A sudden undulation assailed my innards, and my mouth watered unpleasantly. I hastily handed Calvin my guitar and rushed down the blindingly white service corridor to the bathroom, nearly colliding with one of the servers on my way in. The stall door crashed against the wall, but I got there in time to throw up in the toilet and not all over the floor. I always think it's important to celebrate these little accomplishments. I rinsed my mouth and splashed water on my face. Bugger the makeup. Priorities, you know.

I ran my fingers through my short hair, begging it to respond anew to the mountains of hair product I had scrunched into it earlier, and patted down my skirt. Along with the sparkly T-shirt, I looked nice. Professional. At age twenty-seven, I wasn't interested in looking like a teenager.

When I got back, it was Pep Talk Time. "We've gotta be good tonight, you guys." Words failed me.

"We are good," Calvin assured me. "We just have to do what we do, and the rest will happen." I guess I looked doubtful because he stared at me with his brotherly brown eyes. "You're a good musician, Griffin." He touched my shoulder. I tried to feel confident.

"Where's Jason?" Andy said.

I looked around, gripped with a sudden panic. They were beginning the final speech, and I hadn't even noticed our lead guitarist hadn't joined us in the back hall. Was he still in the warm-up room? What the heck was he—?

Jason sauntered up, knocking into a cart filled with empty juice jugs, three of which clattered to the floor. "Don't fret your pretty little head, Andy-baby, I'm right here."

"Shh!" Cameron told him. "They're right through there." He pointed to the flimsy doors.

"What. Ever." Jason grabbed me around the waist. He swung me into the path of a busboy, who had to dodge with his armload of dirty plates. Jason didn't even notice. "I'm all set to play some shitty wedding music with my hot girl. Can we rock it up a little, Griff? I've gone over the set list, and it's totally fucked."

I stopped the twirling and grabbed his roving hands. "Be quiet," I insisted. "The set list is *fine*; it's made up of songs our *client* wants to hear."

"The client is fucked," Jason replied with no attempt at *sotto voce*. "Where's the Zep and Acka Dacka? I want to rock out with some hot solos."

Calvin came closer. "There are lots of nice solos in the set list."

"Shut the fuck up, Drummer Boy; just worry about keeping a steady tempo for a change."

An awful thought occurred to me, and I pulled Jason into the well-lit kitchen area. "What have you been doing?" I stared at him, searching for clues.

"Getting in the mood to play some lame-ass shit wedding music with my hot girl." He ground his hips into me and tried to kiss me with booze-smelling breath. I pushed him away.

"Don't you 'hot girl' me. You're not just hot, you're *fried*!"

His dilated red eyes confirmed it. Not only was he drunk, he was baked on I don't even know what. I thought I might throw up again.

"Come on, Jason, this is our big break! What are you doing?"

"Knock it off. You're such a fucking control freak."

"What? Just because I—"

Then it happened. The MC's voice said, "And now, Griffin Trowbridge and Dreamline."

Red haze billowed before my eyes. It was my big moment, and I didn't think I could walk let alone remember how to play a G chord. Calvin held the door, and as I passed, I took back my guitar.

He put a steadying hand on my arm. "It'll be fine, Griff."

I actually believed him.

Teryn and Quinn, the bride and groom, stood just below us on the parquet dance floor. Arms around each other's waists, they awaited the first glorious strains of *You're My Best Friend*. Their eager smiles said they intended to love us. Many cell phones waited to record the moment.

I plugged in, turned on my amp, adjusted my guitar strap on my shoulder, and strummed to make sure I had sound. The others got themselves set too, and I made a final tweak to the position of my microphone. I was about to give the nod to begin when I realised Jason had planted himself directly in front of his amp. Puzzled, I backed up and was about to ask him if there was a problem when he cranked his amp up to eleven, creating a mind-blowing blast of feedback.

Sound hurtled through the air, and I slapped my hands over my ears. Jason clamped his fingertips on the strings and struck the most dissonant chord I'd ever heard. He launched into an insanely obnoxious solo and thrashed at the strings as if they were a swarm of hornets. He stepped up to the microphone and screamed pseudo-melodic obscenities at the crowd.

"What the hell?" I gaped at Jason, who couldn't hear me over the sound of his tirade. A bunch of people stampeded to the doors of the banquet hall, causing a nasty bottleneck as too many people tried to push through at once, and a modern symphony of shrieking added to the cacophony. Some folks stayed at their tables with hands slapped over their ears, and a couple of die-hards with cell phones braved the noise to post us on social media.

Andy nearly knocked over his keyboard as he tried to get around to Jason. Cameron reached to clamp down on Jason's strings, but it was tricky while holding a bass, and Jason moved around too much. Calvin had leaped off the back of the stage.

"Shut it, Jason! What do you think you're doing?" Andy yelled and, having reached him, tried to wrestle his guitar out of his hands. It was as if it were tied to him with duct tape.

"Easy now, easy, come on, hold on," Cameron said in a lame effort to reason with him.

But there was no breaking through Jason's new El Screamo style, and he kept on. I could hardly understand a word, but it sounded like, "Fucking shit crap rich people can suck my balls," and any number of other charming phrases, mixed in with his grocery list.

I stormed across the stage and snatched the microphone away from him, just as Calvin unplugged Jason's amplifier. The high-pitched guitar squeal was replaced by horrified silence.

"What the hell do you think you're doing?" I screamed at him.

Jason shot insults at me as if I were a human silhouette at a rifle range. Then he crashed off the stage without a backward glance and bolted out the back door. Clatter upon smash of metal trays on the concrete floor receded down the corridor with him and faded away.

The entire episode had taken no more than about twenty seconds, but it was enough. I rotated on my feet to survey the results. The groom clutched his bride close as if protecting her from flying shrapnel. Her mascara had run so she resembled Alice Cooper.

Her father, high-powered businessman Carl Snifter, who had been comforting his wife, strode toward me shaking his finger, his face red and puckered with rage. I must have been in shock, or else I'd probably have reacted differently. I ignored him. The rest of my band waited for me to do something. I did the only thing I could.

With hands a-tremble, I picked up my acoustic and plugged it in. I strummed a chord and adjusted the tuning, vaguely aware of Snifter barking at me. I played the opening bars of *You're My Best Friend*. Calvin switched from sticks to brushes, Cameron plucked the root note on his bass, and Andy changed the setting from rock organ to acoustic piano. My voice was a bit tremulous, but we bluffed our way through an unrehearsed, unplugged version of the first dance.

Snifter's wife must have called him to attend her at some point because he stalked off. The bride and groom held each other in the middle of the floor. He tried to get her to dance; spoilt brat that she was, she had apparently decided we were pure evil and stamped her feet.

I thought we did okay, but I guess the evening had already been ruined for most people. We kept playing in a futile effort to placate the guests. The only reason we got through three songs was that the host and hostess were mollifying the crowd with free drinks. Teryn turned on the waterworks whenever her dad walked near her, and when he had a break from apologising to the guests, she wept openly in his arms. I heard her wail, "Make them go away, Dad!"

Snifter signalled to the DJ, who pressed *Play*, thereby ending our set a quarter of the way in. My heart sank. The DJ was supposed to play music just during our breaks. Snifter patted Teryn's back and turned to me again, exchanging his *There There* face for a *You Are Going to Rue the Day* face. He came right up on stage and towered over me. He smiled.

"If you do not have your gear packed up and removed from this stage in ten minutes, I will have my bodyguards remove it and *you*." He opened his suit jacket, and for a brief moment, I thought he was drawing a gun. It was a rectangular piece of paper. A cheque. "See this?" He held it up so I could see it was made out in my name. In the amount of $2,000.00. He tore it into tidy, narrow strips. A shredder wouldn't have done much more damage. "I am going to make damn sure that every person in my circle of acquaintance hears about this."

Despondent, I looked levelly at the buttons on his vest. "The only thing worse than being talked about is *not* being talked about."

Apparently Carl Snifter did not think better of me for my ability to quote Oscar Wilde. His pressed lips and widened eyes, not to mention the trembling and twitching of his entire torso, indicated a desire to slap me upside the head. "Ten minutes." He stormed off.

Even that might have been all right if it hadn't been for Teryn. She came up to me while I coiled microphone cable.

"I hope you're satisfied. You totally *destroyed* what was meant to be the happiest day of my life."

Without looking up—or thinking—I heard words come out of my mouth. "Geez, if we could ruin your wedding day, you'd better rethink your choice of husband."

She welled up. No shit. I would have too. Hiking up her skirts, she ran off.

An hour later, I said good night on the loading dock to Andy and Cameron, in whose truck we had loaded all the sound equipment for them to return to the rental place. I was taking the bus home, so I took my amp, backpack, and two guitar cases up in the elevator to the hotel lobby and plunked down on a cushy sofa to mope before leaving.

"Could have been worse." Calvin sat down beside me. It was quiet here, though I felt heartsick to know canned music was playing in the banquet hall upstairs.

"Could it?"

"There'll be other gigs, Griff."

"Not if Snifter has anything to say about it." The man was an arrogant jerk, but he had power in the business community. "I can't *believe* I told him off! Him and Teryn." I buried my face in Calvin's shoulder. "Why did I do that? Was that even me talking? What is wrong with me?" I pushed myself away from him and stared at the ceiling. "Not a *single* person asked for our business card. We're in debt to the eyeballs for sound equipment and rehearsal space." I held up my cell phone. "There are already a dozen terrifically unflattering shots of us online, with captions like, 'Band from Hell' and 'Wedding Band Banned from Wedding.' Not exactly what I was hoping for."

Calvin was silent. He knew when I needed to vent.

"Besides which, Teryn dances with my sister. She'll make Jillian's life miserable, even though Jillian's got nothing to do with this. Teryn's just that kind of person. *And* her mom was a regular in my mom's shop. I think she even bought her mother-of-the-bride dress there." My mom, in an uncharacteristic display of support for me, had told her about my band, which is how we got the gig. "She'll never go back to my mom's shop. She'll get all her little sheep friends to avoid it too. My mother's not going to speak to me for weeks."

Calvin threw his arm over my shoulder. "Give thanks for small mercies," he said with a crooked smile. I laughed a little at his valiant effort to cheer me up. And after all, I wasn't mad at him. I don't think I could be mad at Calvin if I grasped at the tiniest of straws.

"At least the wedding cake is beautiful. My dad's reputation should remain intact."

"Well, actually . . ."

"Oh no. What?"

"Jason pulled one more stunt before he left. He, uh, switched the little bride and groom on the top with a pair from the wedding next door."

"So?"

"It was a gay wedding."

My head dropped back onto the couch headrest, Calvin's arm in between. Could things possibly get worse?

"Hey, you're still coming to my sister's wedding in Victoria, right?"

"Of course."

"Good. I was worried you'd be put off weddings forever."

I couldn't help but smile. "I'll be there. I've had the May long weekend highlighted on my calendar for weeks." My spirits lifted a touch just thinking about it. "And it'll just be you and me playing. Two acoustics and two vocals, it's gonna sound great. I hope Teresa loves it."

"She will. No berserk guitar solos?"

"I promise."

Calvin gave my shoulder a squeeze. "You okay getting home?"

I nodded. "I think I need to just breathe for a few more minutes."

"Well, good night, Griff." He drew his black bomber jacket around him. "Don't hang around here too late now." I watched him walk away from me, cymbal case in one hand and drumsticks jutting out of his back pocket. He was whistling *Some Enchanted Evening* and I chuckled. I had never known Calvin to ever let anything get him down. His good cheer faded into the subdued hubbub of the hotel front desk and disappeared as the elevator door closed.

I stared at the carpet in front of me and pushed back tears. *I swear if I ever see Jason again, I'll skewer him.* When a pair of black boots at the end of black legs appeared in my vision and blocked the abstract pattern I'd been staring at, I didn't notice at first.

"Rough night, was it?" The accent was unidentifiably foreign.

I looked up and squinted at the figure silhouetted by the pot light behind him. I wasn't exactly startled—I was too drained for that—but curious. "Not stellar."

The figure stepped into my private pool of despair. Tallish, sharply dressed in black trousers and one of those long, full-skirted coats like men used to wear in Dickens' day. He even wore a top hat. I didn't recall seeing him among the wedding guests; he stood out too much to have missed him. He had the kind of face romance novels describe as "finely chiselled features," and might have been of mixed ethnic background, one Indian parent and one, say, Japanese. The guy was breathtakingly beautiful.

"My wedding was dreary beyond belief."

"You the groom?" I asked, eyeing his getup.

"No, a friend. I felt a need to leave, so I came to observe your 'stellar' event."

I got the sense he was laughing at me, so I declined to say anything.

He smiled apologetically. "Your wedding had thought-provoking entertainment."

"How much did you see?"

"I at least witnessed the beginning, the middle, and the end of your part in it." He peeled off his black leather gloves. "What will you do about a lead guitarist?"

I shrugged. "I don't know, advertise maybe."

He pocketed his gloves and sat next to me. He sat straight, on the edge of the couch with his feet just so and his hands on his knees.

"Guitarists, I am told, are a dime a dozen."

Was he trying to reassure me? "The average ones are." I knew I sounded defeatist. But why should a total stranger be so interested? "The good ones are harder to find."

"How about the brilliant ones?"

I laughed. "Rarer than diamonds."

He made an, "Ah," kind of sound.

"I suppose I don't even need a new guitarist," I went on. "Mr. Snifter'll make sure I never play in this city again."

"There are other cities."

He rose and a business card was in my fingers so smoothly, I still can't recall how it got there. "Come to the address on the back tomorrow night at nine. I'll have an opportunity waiting for you. I'm rather fond of diamonds."

He was gone so suddenly, I would have sworn he'd vanished like a soap bubble. I looked down at his card.

Rickenbacker Topiary
Salamander House of Music and Pudding
Finder of People and Things

2

Sunday, May 6

The first thing I did in the morning was log into *CAPPA*—the Conflict-Avoiding People-Pleasers Association—my online support group.

> *Hey gang. Bad night last night. Guitarist boyfriend had a freak-out and left the gig. I told off the bride and her dad . . . I am never going to get to play in this city again! I'm a mess.*
>
> *Weird man approached me afterward saying he knows a lead guitarist. I just have to go to his place tomorrow night. Should I do this?*
>
> *Big time stressing!*
>
> *~WingedLion*

There. Somebody would get back to me, and I would feel better.

I drifted into the music store around ten, in time to learn that my 10:30 student, Hon Jun, had cancelled.

"His bird has to go in for wing surgery," Brian, the store owner, explained as he rearranged small percussion instruments in the front display case, claves, shakers, and so forth.

Just as well. I didn't feel like I'd be any good to him.

"Wait. What?" I said. That was the most bizarre excuse I'd ever heard.

"I said, 'He got called into work,'" Brian said.

I stopped mid-jacket removal. "Hunh? That's not what you said." I wasn't angry, I was just confused.

"Certainly it was. Are you feeling okay?"

"Ye-es." I drew the word out because all of a sudden Brian was arranging toy furniture in the display case. I backed away and hung up my jacket on my office door.

"How was the gig?" Brian called.

I stuck my head back around the corner. To my relief, he had a cabasa in one hand and a tambourine in the other.

"I guess you haven't checked Twitter yet this morning." I looked around to make sure there were no customers in the store before I said anything rude. I could hear someone's trumpet lesson going on in a practice room, but that was all.

"Uh-oh. Didn't make a good impression on Ol' Snifty?"

"We made a very deep impression on him. Especially Jason with his drug-and-alcohol-induced thrasher solo."

"Uh-oh," Brian said again.

I gave him the rundown of events. "Is it too late to return the Telecaster? I don't suppose I'll ever need a guitar again."

"Aw, come on, Griffin, cheer up; there'll be other gigs."

Everyone seemed pretty sure of that. Easy for them to say. "Yeah well, I need a new lead guitarist before I can even think about other gigs."

"That shouldn't be too hard. Put up an ad on the store bulletin board," he suggested. "Seriously, Griffin, Jason isn't so good he's irreplaceable."

Fair enough.

Brian cocked his head. "Do I take it Jason is also no longer your significant other?"

I rolled my eyes. "Definitely an 'other.' No longer remotely significant. Not that I've told him yet."

"Aw, I'm sorry, really."

I shrugged. "I'm not. I should have done it a long time ago." I turned and stared at the office door, steeling myself. It was one thing to talk about it, and another thing altogether to do it. "Here goes."

I went into the office and tried not to think as I picked up the phone, palms sweating, and speed-dialled Jason's cell before I could talk myself out of it.

Phew! He didn't pick up—he almost never did. It went to his voice mail.

Not talkin' right now. Prob'ly hung over. Talk to me.

How could I ever have found that amusing?

"Jason, it's me," my voice trembled in my ears. "I want you to . . . get over to my apartment and get your shit out." The words rushed out like a waterfall. "Don't let the door hit you on the ass as you leave. Drop your key through the mail slot when you're through. Oh, and you'll need to find someone else to feed your fish when you go to your brother's next weekend." I hung up. Then I stood there and trembled for several minutes, tears welling. Golly, I really needed to talk to my support group. How could I abandon Jason's fish?

"Mrs. Osley left a message to see if she can change Dominic's lesson to four on Tuesday," Brian told me when I joined him back at the counter. He pretended not to notice me wiping my eyes on my sleeves. "He has a tournament game at six."

I thought it was a bit odd for a hockey tournament to carry over onto a Tuesday, but at least he hadn't cancelled his lesson altogether. I was grateful for Mrs. Osley's emphasis on the importance of Dominic's having music *and* sports in his life.

"And Jennifer won't be here today because she has a hair appointment."

A hair appointment? Well, it wasn't the lamest excuse the teen had given for missing a lesson. She never practised and she skipped at least every third week. Oh well, store policy was for people to pay in advance, so it was no skin off my nose.

But then Brian went on. "Yeah, she's totes getting extensions and blonde streaks? I tried to talk her into getting it bleached? And then getting, like, purple stripes, but just, like, underneath, y'know, so you can only see it when it's up?"

I stared at him. He was filing his nails as he chatted.

"But she was like, 'No, that's too much, and I don't like the way the bleach is, like, hard on your hair n'stuff,' and I was like, 'Okay, it'll look adorbs, anyways?'"

I needed coffee. Stat. I went to get my mug from my desk and came back.

"Are you sure you're okay, Griffin? You just walked away from me when I was giving you instructions."

He wasn't holding a nail file. He was holding a stack of sheet music. I shook my head.

"Geez, I'm sorry. I don't know what's up today." I gave a fake sort of chuckle. "Cobwebs in my brain."

Brian handed me a stack of sheet music to file then went off to the storeroom to work on instrument repairs. I set down the stack and grabbed coffee from the break room. Anything to help clear this crazy head.

I examined the stack of papers. He'd already sorted the sheets according to instrument and alphabetized them *(thanks, Brian)*, so I carried the stack over to the sheet music bins. Solo flute arrangements were on the top of the pile, so I leafed through until I had them all and carried the smaller bundle to the flute music section. I flipped through composers in the bin, looking for Bach, and discovered a bunch of trombone and alto sax parts. I kept flipping. Virtually everything had been misfiled. "Who screwed this all up?" Irritated as hell I started yarding out pieces of sheet music and trying to sort it all out again. The bell on the door jingled.

A young red-haired woman came into the store and headed straight for the books of pop songs arranged for piano and guitar. "Let me know if I can help you find anything," I called across the store in my usual friendly customer service voice. She thanked me and I went back to my project. I sorted and replaced, all the while aware of the young woman singing quietly to herself. As I filed, her volume rose until I could make out words.

> *The wedding was a bust. Jason wasn't very funny.*
> *And now you're in the hole. Gotta make some more money.*

I stared at her, but she seemed not to notice me. I crept closer, sort of hiding between the shelves of music.

You're not feeling satisfied, and I can understand.
You're looking for a chance to play with a great band.

"Griffin, what are you doing?" Brian stood over my filing mess with his arms wide. His quizzical expression featured eyebrows shaped like ski jumps, as he stared at me cowering behind the shelf. The woman left the store. I slunk sheepishly back to the shambles of music on the floor.

"Sorry, I was sorting all this, but that woman was singing something really weird."

"Umm, it sounded like Sarah McLachlan's *Fallen* to me."

"No, it was something else. The words were about—"

"And what the heck's all this?" Brian went on, gesturing at the floor. "You've pulled out every piece of flute music in the store." He was smiling as if he thought I were a bit goofy, but he also wanted an answer.

I looked over all the music. It was, indeed, all flute music. "But this is—I swear this was all misfiled trombone and alto sax stuff."

"Are you okay, Griffin? I dug some stuff out of here yesterday and it was all just fine. Please put it back in order?"

I nodded and knelt on the carpet, feeling stupid. I hadn't even been out as late last night as I expected, and yet my brain was just *not* functioning properly. I got all the music put away by the time my 1:30 lesson arrived.

Trevor and I sealed ourselves in a practice room, and I settled down to teaching him how to play a B7 chord. His hand was kind of small, so he had some trouble getting his first finger to hold down the entire second fret, but he'd get it. I gave him an E minor arpeggio progression to work on for a few minutes and went to the washroom. When I came back, I nearly dropped dead.

Trevor was finger-picking Bach's *Bourrée in E Minor* as if he were Lenny Breau. I stood in the doorway of the practice room staring, horror struck, at my ten-year-old student. When he finished, he looked up at me.

"What?"

I gulped air, swallowed, and said, "What . . . was that?"

He looked about ready to cry. "E minor, A minor, and B7. Isn't that what you wanted me to play?"

I counted to ten, took deep breaths, and wondered what had gone wrong with my brain today. I smiled at him. "It was great. Why don't you play it one more time for me?" I shut the door and sat down.

No more Bach. Just arpeggios. I finished up the rest of his half-hour lesson then told Brian I was done for the day. It was only fair.

Jason still hadn't come by my place while I was at work. I put the chain on the door so he couldn't burst in on me when I was home. I sat on the couch with my laptop and logged in to *CAPPA*, hopeful the sage advice of my group would help. To my relief there were some replies.

> **Iamworthy:** *Guitarist boyfriend freakout not your fault, WingedLion. You'll get through it.*

> **PowerofNo:** *Sounds exciting, WingedLion. Avoiding this opportunity would not promote growth.*

> **NerdBird27:** *You're not responsible for their feelings, WingedLion. Take a risk. Your self-worth is within.*

I nodded, and took a deep breath. They were right.

Feeling only marginally better about the wedding gig, but a lot better about meeting with this Rickenbacker fellow, I went for a nap. I hoped I would wake up with a clearer head that would not daydream odd things.

At 8:00 pm I caught the train to go downtown. The address was handwritten on the back of the card, so I wasn't sure if I was looking for a House of Music and Pudding or someplace else entirely. What on earth was a House of *Pudding*, anyway?

The street was more like an alley, narrow, dark. It being the beginning of May, it wasn't completely black at 8:52 pm, but there were swathes of shadow between the patches of light from the streetlamps. Dust and oil smells seeped out of the cracked concrete, and the hum of traffic a few blocks away faded into the distance as if someone had slowly closed a door on it.

"Why are you here, you moron?" I muttered. Even homeless people avoided this place. I spun around at a clatter of cardboard and plastic. A raccoon ambled out, apparently embarrassed, but at seeing me, he composed himself and blamed the garbage can with a disgusted look. Fixing his disdainful, beady eyes on me, he shrugged and sauntered across the street, his dignity intact.

I pulled out my cell to check the time: 8:54. Then the display light went out. *That's funny.* I pressed the button. Blank. I had just charged it at home. *Damn.* Seized with a clench of alarm, I felt like my lifeline had left me. I overcame my instinct to flee and went on down the street, realizing I must look peculiar, standing still like that, to someone watching from one of the black windows above. I checked the address again, compared it to the one across the street, and followed the raccoon. 1160 . . . 1156 . . . 1152.

The three-story brick building had no accoutrements. The list of tenants at the door indicated it was mostly an office building, with some apartments. With the businesses closed for the night, any residents would have it mighty peaceful.

The button next to #301 was simply labelled OCCUPIED. I crossed my fingers that I had the right place. Wiping my hands on my jacket, I wished I had told Calvin or Jillian or somebody that I was coming here. Heart hammering, I counted to three—no, make it five . . . how about ten?—and pressed the button. If it buzzed somewhere within, I couldn't hear it.

A tinny, fuzzy-edged voice popped out of the speaker. "Yes?"

"Uh, it's me—" I pushed the pitch of my voice back down to normal range. "—Griffin. I'm here to see, uh, Mr. Topiary?"

A pause.

"You sure?"

"What?"

"You sure you want to?"

A pause. Longer. "Umm, yeah. Why? Is there some reason I shouldn't?"

"I don't know. Come in, then. Elevator's round to the left."

"Thanks." The buzzer on the door echoed along the street like a train whistle in a tunnel. Nerves jangling, I went in.

It turned out to be a freight elevator, one of those square, girdered affairs with a nice view of the interior framing of the building. It creaked and groaned and scraped when I pressed the button, and I shielded my head from the monster descending upon me. The doors clanged and clattered open, and I tentatively stepped in, fearful that it would shudder and give up and plummet to the unknown depths of the building. By the time I was halfway up, I finally clued in that I could have taken the stairs. I might as well have brought a brass band with me; it would have been quieter. The lift jounced and shook and moaned like a banshee, and though, to be fair, it did deposit me on the third floor, it left me rattled and shaken. As it powered down, the silence that replaced it billowed like thick fog.

I leaned a hand on the nicotine-stained velvet-and-gold-foil wallpaper and wondered why I hadn't insisted this *Finder of People and Things* present his opportunity to me on neutral territory. Or I could at least have gone to his place of business; this sure didn't look like a House of Pudding. How was I supposed to be professionally aloof in my current state? I breathed and moved forward. My feet made *plocking* sounds as I stepped along the plastic carpet runner that preserved the flea-bitten red plush beneath. I peered around the corner, and there was room 301. You couldn't miss it.

The numbers were each a foot tall and arranged vertically next to the door in bright orange numerals. I stopped outside the door and checked the time. *Oh yeah, right. Not working.*

The door opened before I could knock. A tall, slim Mr. Darcy–esque figure greeted me, his 19th-century trousers and jacket not incongruous with the coat he was wearing when I met him. "Won't you come in?" Rickenbacker Topiary said.

"Should I take my shoes off?"

He regarded me with one puzzled eyebrow lifted. "That won't be necessary."

I followed him down the angled corridor and blinked at the bright colours. It was like the place was stuck back in the seventies, with sploshes of fiery red, orange, and yellow in angular rainbows up and down the walls. The hallway widened into a living-room space, where a white faux-fur rug obscured much of the red shag carpet. A mirrored desk sat just off centre, and an expansive leather couch with a plaid throw across the back and lots of cushions rested in one corner, a glass-topped coffee table in front of it. Funky.

"Love the fur," I said.

"You *could* remove your shoes if you wanted; the rug is very soft."

"So, do you live here alone, or with roommates?"

"Oh, we don't live here," he said. "We meet here. Please sit down. Would you care for a glass of wine?"

"Oh." I was still processing the 'we meet here' line. "Sure. Thanks."

He disappeared around the corner and left me alone with the faux fur. I sat gingerly on the couch, feeling just a little silly for having assumed he lived here. *Duh.* But who has their office hours at 9:00 at night? Out of habit, I checked my phone again and was surprised to see it read 9:03. *Weird.*

Part of me knew I ought to feel wary. I was, after all, a lone female in the presence of a man who was a complete stranger and in an unusual location. I kicked myself again for not having told at least my sister where I was going. But having said all that, I didn't feel uncomfortable. It was perhaps counterintuitive, especially given that my cell was acting up, but I felt safe. In control.

My host, or whatever you call him when you aren't at his home, returned with a tray bearing a wine glass and a stoneware decanter. He set it down on the coffee table and poured for me. The wine was purple. It gurgled and foamed as he poured.

"Wow, that's unusual."

"What is?" He set the decanter down and handed me the glass.

"Umm, the wine. I've never seen foaming wine before."

"Oh? It is by appointment to the king. Where do you come from?"

"Well, here."

"Do you want to meet him?"

Puzzled as hell, I said, "Who? The king?"

"I believe I promised you an opportunity?"

I sort of laughed, embarrassed and definitely confused. "Oh. Yeah."

"Come this way."

I took a hesitant sip of the wine as I got up. It was a little on the sweet side but not abominable. The weird thing was that the foam on top tasted like whipped cream.

I followed him through the doorway next to the couch and down a corridor. Several closed doors lined the hallway, and I half expected people to start coming out of them and criss-crossing the hall to enter other rooms. The red shag was no more. Here the walls were lime green and sky blue stripes, with pale orange carpet.

"What sort of business do you do here?"

"This," he paused before a heavy door at the end of the hall, "is where everything begins."

3

Still Sunday, May 6

Rickenbacker pushed the door, and the sounds bursting through it were nothing short of awe inspiring. Purple wine with whipped cream and seventies shag? Fine by me. I passed Rickenbacker into the theatre

—at least, that's what it felt like: a big, open studio with a high ceiling and subdued lighting. Band equipment waited—keyboard, deep red Ayotte drum kit, amplifiers. But at that moment, just one musician was present. The most gorgeous man I'd ever laid eyes on stood in a waterfall of light against an azure blue cyclorama. And he played.

I couldn't take my eyes off him as I sank into a cushy surface. He filled his jeans and T-shirt, leaving no surplus fabric, but although his body was attractive, it was not what seized my attention. Fingers flying effortlessly along the frets and tapping out harmonics, he played like he was channelling Steve Howe, Alex Lifeson, Jimi Hendrix, and Mark Knopfler combined.

I love watching a good musician lose himself in his playing. Nothing else exists in the world but that glorious ocean of sound. His eyes were one moment open, closed the next, looking at the instrument or at some image in his mind or the air in front of him. His shoulder-length hair swayed, and his mouth, eyes, and brows contorted in a kind of ecstasy. I recognised moment after moment from some of my favourite guitar solos, interspersed with passages I'd never heard before. There went the *Sultans of Swing*, right on its heels was *Starship Trooper*, segueing seamlessly into *Black Magic Woman*. Fast, slow, frenetic, sensual. I sat in awe.

His fingers tangled out one final riff, and his arm lifted into the air. The overtones floated to the ceiling and suspended there. I hardly noticed he'd stopped playing. I was in love. I could tell he didn't want to break the spell either, as he remained motionless, eyes closed. And when he finally opened them, lowered his hand, and searched for a reaction in the dim light, he grinned shyly and didn't even toss his hair around like someone else I knew. Here was a guy who deserved to be conceited as hell, yet I could tell he wasn't. He knew he was good—oh yes, he was no idiot—but he had the air of believing it was a gift he didn't have a right to. He was too good to be true, yet here he stood before me.

Ducking underneath the strap of his royal blue Variax 700, he set it on the stand.

At long last I found my voice. "Wow, that was ..." I searched for adequate words. "Really amazing," I finished before I'd found any.

"Thanks," he replied, both hands on the arms of the chair as he plopped into it. "I hear you're no slouch yourself."

I was stunned. "What?" God, I never knew I was capable of sounding so stupid.

He nodded in the direction of Mr. Topiary. "He tells me you played an entire set, unexpectedly without a lead. And you did it unplugged."

"Umm." I didn't know what to say. Would my brain ever join me again? "It was really only three and a half songs."

He stretched out his hand. "My name is Matteo."

"Griffin." Holy shit! I swear when I took his hand, there was an electrical shock. And no, I don't mean he'd rubbed his feet on the carpet. It was a . . . an energy surge, sort of a wave. Like when you're on an elevator that rapidly goes down. Or like that time we'd been hit with such wicked feedback during a gig, I'd nearly fallen over. Only this was more localized, flying up my arm rather than a full-body thing.

"Do you want to meet the guys?" the guitar god said. "The rest of the band?"

"I . . . uh . . . well . . . umm . . . if . . . where? This . . . hm . . . five." I'm sure that's what I said.

"Come on." He took a step, and he hadn't let go of my hand, so I was rising and following him over to the band's setup. "Grab a guitar; let's play something."

Next thing I knew, I had a twelve-string slung over my shoulders and I was surrounded by several other musicians who took position at their instruments, and Matteo was listing off names but I didn't hear a word he said, and he played a familiar lead guitar riff, and I strummed at exactly the right moment, nailing that tricky intro, which was instantly followed by Matteo's full, rich voice singing the lyrics, and the drum beat kicked in, and after a time, though I hardly knew what I was about, I came in with the harmony line and I was playing with this band as if it were the most natural thing in all the world.

Maybe it was just the foaming wine, but we rocked.

When we'd improvised an awesome ending to *Go Your Own Way*, a bunch of male voices congratulated me and made me feel better about playing music than I had in longer than I care to say. And then Matteo was pumping my hand and looking eagerly into my eyes with such clear blue ones that I felt I could dive in.

"Griffin, I—that was . . . Well, it was terrific."

How was it this beautiful man, this paragon of musicians, could be tongue-tied in talking to *me*? "Thanks." I think I may have even said it out loud.

"So, did Rick tell you—I mean, would you be into joining The Spurious Correlations?"

"The what?"

"The Spurious Correlations. That's the name of the band. Will you join us?"

My jaw went slack like I'd been given novocaine. He interpreted this as rejection.

"If not, that's okay; you're probably really busy." He looked disappointed.

No! Don't let him think you're not interested! But how to tell him? What to say? Say something!

"But why me?" *Not that, idiot.* "I mean, it sounds . . . I'm definitely interested." An improvement. "I just figure you could find someone way better."

I really needed to learn to kick myself *before* saying something stupid.

"Well," Matteo said, looking around at the other guys, "the recommendation of Rickenbacker Topiary counts for a lot around here. And I don't think I'm the only one in this room who noticed that you rather rocked, just now." Agreement murmured through the space. "You'd be a great fit."

"Let me interject a moment here." Rickenbacker stepped into the pool of light. "There is a slight catch, and it is unfair of Mr. MacCallum to leave it out of the discussion."

My heart caught in my throat. Just a bit. *Matteo MacCallum?* That was the dreamiest name I'd ever heard. Way more attractive than Jason Knowles. But Topiary had mentioned a catch. *Uh-oh.*

"Salamander is a restaurant, not merely a music hall."

"Oh yeah. Music and . . . pudding, was it?" I asked.

"Correct. All our staff, musicians included, also spend some time working the restaurant side of things. We need an individual who can not only play music but also be of use in the kitchen or as a server."

"Well, I do know a thing or two about catering. See, my dad's a caterer and a pastry chef, and I've worked for him on occasion. But I have to tell you"—it was insane, but I wished I didn't have to tell him—"I do have a job already."

Matteo and the rest of the band exchanged glances.

"I work in a music store. I teach and everything." Why did I feel a need to justify my job?

Topiary pursed his lips. "I'm afraid this position is full time."

"You mean, I'd have to quit my job?"

"Teaching music versus playing music."

"But also working in a *kitchen*. I haven't done that since I was seventeen. I've been proud to not be a musician whose day job requires her to say, 'Do you want fries with that?' I love my job."

"Your full-time commitment is a requirement." The figure in dress-up clothes had the nerve to apologise to the band. "I thought I had found just the person to fit your—and my—needs."

"Wait," I said. I knew there were all sorts of questions I should be asking, but I couldn't think of them. There was something wrong with this entire arrangement, but in my desperation to not miss a once-in-a-lifetime opportunity, I couldn't think what it was. I couldn't think of anything beyond how much I wanted to play with this band. With Matteo.

Matteo smiled kind of shyly. "I guess you need to think about it a bit, eh?"

"Yeah." I felt terrible, sick, like I'd let someone down. "I do." The answer should have been so easy to give. "And I have a friend's wedding to go to on the 19th. Well, it's not *his* wedding; it's his sister's, in Victoria. But he and I are going to be playing guitar and singing. During the ceremony. That's really important to me."

Rickenbacker bowed. "Of course. The 19th of May will not be problematic."

"All right, then." I looked at Matteo. "Can I get back to you? When do you need to know?"

He glanced at Rickenbacker, who said, "They're playing on Thursday night. Could you let me know by Wednesday?"

I gawked. "But—you mean you want me to play with you guys on *Thursday*? *This* Thursday?" How could I learn all their tunes in only four days? How could I decide so quickly and give Brian such short notice? "What if I don't; are you going to find someone else?"

"I don't want to pressure you, Griffin." Matteo put a hand on my shoulder, which sent another wave of energy shooting into me. "But we *do* want a good rhythm player who can sing. I'm so sure you're the one." Is this what it felt like to be a dish of ice cream left out in the sun? A sheet of paper was produced from someone's folder. "Here's a copy of our song list. This way if you decide you want to, you can get started on the tunes." I folded it up without looking at it. I wanted to keep a clear head to think about this.

What did I mean *keep* a clear head? That would imply I had one to begin with. "How do I get in touch with you?" I had a faint hope he would give me his phone number.

"Why don't I call you?"

Okay, that was a decent alternative. I gave him my number. He smiled down at me as he squeezed my hand. I breathed his tangy scent and wished I didn't have to go home.

I took my leave without finishing my wine that wasn't. This time I took the stairs. As I reached the ground floor, I wondered how to tell my band I had found a new one.

Out on the street, I checked the time on my phone as I hustled along. It was blank. I stopped walking. *Okay, that's really weird.* Working inside the building and not out? Maybe there was some equipment around here interfering with the signal. I'd check it again when I got to the train.

I hastened up the hill to Granville Street and headed north to the station. After about a block on the quiet street, I stopped and looked around. Something was off, but I couldn't put my finger on it right away. I stared around the way I'd come. Quiet. Wait a second.

Granville is *not* a quiet street.

It's lined with restaurants, coffee shops, trendy clothing stores, nightclubs, a bowling alley, a multiplex movie theatre, a huge mall, the Orpheum theatre where the orchestra plays. Not to mention that virtually every single city bus at some point comes down Granville Street. Even on a Sunday night, the place should be buzzing. But it was eerily dead. I counted only three other people, and they were all wearing long cloaks and hoods. *What the devil?*

When I turned north again, it was like someone had flipped a switch. People walked the streets, coming in and out of bars and the movie theatre. The doors of several coffee shops stood open and welcoming. An electric trolley bus whirred by, and a furry guy in a big ratty coat sitting in the doorway of a closed shop asked if I could spare any change. I couldn't. All my pockets contained was a paperclip, my decidamps, a guitar pick, an old Kleenex, and my transit fare card. Kind of spooked, I took several steps back the way I'd come, just to see if it all changed again. It was all as I would have expected. I pressed my lips together and frowned. Then I shrugged and went to the train, glancing over my shoulder every now and again.

On the underground platform, the LED readout hanging from the ceiling read *11:30pm*. I heard the hollow, windy sound of the train approaching, and the glow of its headlamps intensified on the concrete tunnel walls. The readout above read, *Expo Line to . . .* It flashed. *Griffin's house.* I did a double-take and looked again. *Expo Line to . . . King George.*

Okay. Good.

Cursing myself for stepping into insanity for a moment, I walked into the train car when it opened before me and sat in a front-facing seat at the back of the car. I'd have to change trains at Broadway, so I had a couple of stations to relax and consider my options. Obviously the strain was getting to me. *Griffin's house,* indeed. I didn't even live in a house.

There was no hockey game in town that night (and if there had been, the crowds would mostly have cleared away by this time). No big concert at the arena or stadium. So the train wasn't crowded. I didn't pay particular attention to the fact that all four of the occupants sharing my car sat ramrod straight, reading newspapers. The train left the tunnels of the downtown core and now rode along elevated tracks. I scrunched up in the seat, closed my eyes, and listened to the replay in my brain of Matteo's magical guitar playing.

Oh! To have exactly what I needed within my grasp. It struck me then what the problem was with what had happened this evening: Rickenbacker had promised I'd meet a lead guitarist, and he'd been true to his word. But I wasn't looking for a whole new band. I needed a lead guitarist in *my* band. Rickenbacker's proposition meant excluding the group of guys I'd been working with for two years. Including my best friend. And to have to quit the job I loved? It felt like an unforgivable betrayal to even think of it. But how could I not? Brian knew I wanted to play more, that I didn't want to teach and file music until my retirement. He'd understand, I was sure. But what about Calvin and the others?

Lots of people play in more than one band, right?

When the three-tone signal chimed and the voice announced our pending arrival at Broadway, I pulled out of my ponderings long enough to exit the train. I was aware of other passengers also walking the corridor and down the stairs to the other eastbound train. The train came along after a short time. I boarded and settled in to continue my deliberations. It wouldn't be my stop for ages, so I didn't even look up. But two stations later, the sense of presences crept in around me. Wondering at the number of passengers at this late hour, I drew myself out of my self-piteous wallowing to look around. I nearly fell off my seat. Why I didn't shriek, I'll never know —something about an instinct to not draw attention to myself in public, I guess. But I did sit bolt upright with unease.

The car was by no means full, yet every passenger in it, about a dozen, was seated at my end of the car. Two people directly in front of me, two more in front of them. Two across the aisle, two in front of them, one in each of the side-facing seats by the exit. One in the window seat at the very back of the car and one standing in the aisle as if it were rush hour instead of nigh on midnight. The rest of the car was empty.

In case their mere presence wasn't weird enough, they all wore hats of some kind, some ball caps, a cowboy hat, some toques, a 1920s cloche, and lots of other styles. And another subtle thing, which took me a few moments to pick up on, was that each and every one of my fellow passengers was reading a book. At first glance, it wasn't all that strange, but the more I thought about it, nobody was simply looking out the window, nobody played a game or read on a cell phone or even read a newspaper. They were reading actual books—some hardcover, some paperback, but books. How often do you see that nowadays?

"Jesus, is this some kind of midnight book club meeting?" I blurted.

The heads tilted, turned, twisted round to look at me. Even the guy in the cubby behind me peered round the corner. They all, male and female alike, had short, dark hair and dark eyes set in round faces.

"The name isn't Jesus," they said in unison, and they scattered, as though someone had picked up the train car and shaken it like a snow globe. The dark-capped, book-reading flakes settled all over the car, and most left the train at the next stop.

I think I am allowed to admit, at this time, that I was more than a little freaked out. Weird changes downtown, train instruction readouts with my name on them, and now the synchronized literary team. It was all just a bit surreal. *CAPPA's gonna have a heyday with this*, I thought as I stared out the window. We whirred through the swathe of city lights, but I didn't play my usual game of identifying neighbourhoods in the dark. I was too on edge.

The rest of the trip was normal. Then I got home.

I kicked off my shoes and hung my jacket in the closet. I'm pretty tidy. Just this once, I skipped a few of my bedtime rituals and flopped, fully clothed, onto the bed.

There was a familiar throaty moan, and an arm flung itself across me. I shrieked as I disentangled myself and leapt across the room to switch on the overhead light; it was the brightest and most obnoxious.

"What are you on that you could possibly imagine you are welcome here?" I yelled, adrenaline surging up and down my limbs. I flattened myself against the closet.

"Baby," Jason crooned, shielding his eyes from the glare. "Turn that off and come snuggle. I just wanna be close to you. I've missed your soft kisses."

"No!" I clutched my hair. "Damn it . . . just . . . *no!*" I paced along the wall, and banged my elbow on the closet door knob.

"Sweetheart, come here." He pushed himself toward the near edge of the bed. He was shirtless, exposing his muscular torso. He reached for my hand. "You're not still mad, are you? I know you're upset. I just wanna hold you. Make it all better. I missed you all day."

I paced like mad. Damn him! He knew just how to talk, how to make me feel like I mattered to him, to convince me he was hurting and I was the only one who could soothe him.

"No," I said, unsure of myself. "I—" I didn't know what I wanted to say. *Was* I still mad? What was I mad about, again?

"Come on, beautiful, you know how I feel about you."

Oh, God. He was a total asshole who could be so sweet. Which is how he finagled his way into my bed in the first place. I looked at his tousled hair and remembered his red eyes; heard him saying, *"You're such a control freak!"*

Not this time. "Get—get over yourself." I said it firmly, convincing myself as much as him. "You're out."

"Oh, lover," he said in the husky voice that always melted me. "I know you're mad. Come play with me and let me apologise."

He rose and moved toward me, his cotton pyjama trousers showing what he wanted. "Sweet thing," he murmured.

I stared at him, my resolve wavering.

"Baby," he whispered, sliding his hands up my back to my shoulders. He leaned down and kissed my neck. "Feel me," he breathed, "just feel how much I want you to forgive me."

My chest heaved. I fought against it, but he made me feel so wanted. He reached over and flipped off the light.

As he turned me around and tipped up my chin, I heard music in the background. Guitar music. It was like, by turning off the light, Jason had pushed *Play* on a recording of the entire evening at Rickenbacker Topiary's. It was Matteo's guitar playing. The same riffs and melodies, and it was just as magical. Stronger, more powerful magic than Jason's sexual wiles. I pulled away from my very *ex*-boyfriend.

"Baby, what is it?" Jason said in his boyish, pleading tone, but then the recording switched to a playback of a certain temper tantrum, the yelling and swearing, the shame and embarrassment, and the reaction of a crowd of influential businesspeople. I came to my senses.

"What is it? You really want to know?" I slapped his hands away. Somehow the darkness gave me courage. "You're finished, that's what. You burned me, you burned the band, and you think a little sexy talk is going to make me forgive you? Look, I don't need you. And I don't want you."

I heard his know-it-all smile in his voice. "I'm the best. You won't find anyone to match me."

"Oh yeah? I've already found someone who is leaps and bounds better than you." I poked Jason in the chest. "He's a masterful guitarist, with way better technique and finesse than you, *and* he's a super nice guy, not an arrogant prick like you."

Jason threw up his hands defensively. "If he's that good, he'd never play with such a mediocre musician as you."

I leaned forward. "He's the one who asked me to, and I've said yes." It was out before I could think about it. And just then, several things happened.

Every light in the room flashed on; Jason's trousers lost their elastic and fell to the floor; and to my utter astonishment, as if by magic, Matteo walked into my room.

"Can I help?" he said in his melodic, mild-mannered tone.

Gobsmacked, I did a good impression of Jason's fish before my throat unstuck. "As a matter of fact, yes," I answered, glaring triumphantly at Jason, too glad to see Matteo to freak out about his sudden arrival. "He needs to leave now."

To his credit, Jason would not give up without a fight. Too bad I didn't get the sense he was fighting for me. No, he was fighting for his misguided belief that he had any rights here. Matteo didn't flinch as Jason pulled up his trousers and stepped toward him, winding up a punch.

His fist darted out. I swear I saw it. I swear Matteo didn't make a move, but it was Jason who was laid flat out on the bed with a welt forming under his eye. It was a good, solid punch.

Okay, *now* was a good time to freak out just a little. I started shaking. "Where did you come from? What the *hell* just happened here?"

Matteo didn't answer but stuck out his hand and said, "Welcome to the team."

Interlude - Still May 6

Rickenbacker burst into his office, arms raised in triumphant *Ta dah!* fashion, amid simulated applause. "I am a genius!" he announced, the door closing behind him by an unvoiced command.

Meanwhile, his friend Phoenix, sitting in the guest chair in front of Rickenbacker's desk, was unmoved. His eyes flashed wildly out from under his straggly hair.

"I just read this note." Phoenix shook it in the air before him. "It's outrageous."

Rickenbacker bowed a couple of times to an invisible crowd of cheering fans then ended the recording with a snap of his fingers. The cheering stopped. This sort of thing was his specialty as instructor of Audio/Visual Arts at Salamander University. He removed his top hat and placed it on the hat shelf. His own hair was curly and not the least bit unruly.

"I'm glad you let yourself in," he said. "I apologise for the delay in my arrival; I was busy doing our first bit of homework." Rickenbacker had ever been the man of action, whereas his friend was the anxious type. Phoenix was an artist of a different variety: a highly respected clothing designer and manager of his own clothing store, Gobs of Togs.

"Without consulting me?" Phoenix slapped the paper down on the desk and stood up as Rickenbacker walked around to his chair.

"Mind the onion ring stand," Rickenbacker cautioned as Phoenix's hand narrowly missed bashing into said apparatus on the desk. Rickenbacker's floating chair lowered to the precise level of his bottom. He moved said bottom into it, and it adjusted its cushions in all his favourite places. He needn't have worried about the onion ring stand; the precious item shifted itself out of harm's way.

Phoenix paced, waving his arms about in their loose, winglike sleeves. "This is madness, I tell you." His left hand *whapped* the combination hole punch/pencil sharpener/drink dispenser that sat on the other corner of the desk and it tipped.

Rickenbacker said, "Careful. Family heirloom, that," and righted the device. His chair lowered again with him in it. "Some day those sleeves on your jacket will generate lift, and you'll be carried away by the slightest breeze."

Phoenix frowned and rubbed the back of his left hand with his right. "Why's it made of fecking *glass*, then?" He hadn't stopped pacing, and Rickenbacker wondered idly if his friend were wearing a pedometer to keep track of his daily exercise. Phoenix pointed at the document on the desk as he went by, and incredibly (to Rickenbacker) did *not* catch the papers in his air current and send them fluttering round the room. "What kind of ghastly rules are those supposed to be?"

Rickenbacker rearranged a few things on the desk and put his scissors away in a drawer. "Now, Phoenix, I am much more of a people person than you are, and since we're dealing with the Other World, I knew my delicate approach would be more effective. It's not *glass*; it's Bollerian crystal, and everyone knows the best pencil sharpeners are the Bollerian crystal ones."

Phoenix scowled. "What about the hole—?"

"And it's the sesquicentenary, after all. It makes sense to me that the rules would be more complicated this time."

The other man stopped walking and clutched his hair. "You are impossible to carry on a conversation with!"

"The hole punch too."

"What?"

"If you listen to the replay, I believe you'll find I have answered your questions in the order you asked them." He took an onion ring and dipped it in chipotle mayo. It crunched exquisitely as he bit into it. The mayo had the perfect spicy tang.

Phoenix flicked his finger a couple of times from left to right and said, "Go." The conversation replayed and Phoenix was forced to concede.

"Oh, fine." He let go of his hair and pressed his hands against the wall instead. "'Music and catering.' What's that supposed to mean, damn them!"

Rickenbacker tried to keep the *there there* tone to a minimum. He picked up the notice and read it with reverence.

> *The Sesquicentenary of the Quinquennial Live Action Role-Playing Tournament. This year's challenge: Participants must include an Other World person in a scenario involving music and catering. Your Other World participant must remain unaware of the circumstances of their involvement for the entire duration of the competition. In a timeframe of*

two weeks, ending on Fantlup the 83rd, this person must be inveigled to commit the Final Challenge.

And here was the part Rickenbacker liked best but would have to do some inveigling of his own with Phoenix to obtain his agreement.

"Now, Phoenix, you must agree that we should expect a sesquicentenary to have some interesting impediments. It can't just be the same as every other time. Besides, the vagueness of 'music and catering' is good. It gives us freedom to play."

"How can you just *sit* there? How are we going to get someone from the Other World?"

"This chair is extraordinarily comfortable; you should get one. I have already found someone, and she has committed. She will fit in nicely."

Phoenix slumped down into the guest armchair and rubbed his knees. "How did you manage it?"

Rickenbacker clasped his hands on his desk. "I am pretty much a genius, you know. You have simply to find a person who is ... impressionable, find out what she wants, and offer it to her in such a way that it is irresistible. I found just such a person. Here." He stuck out a finger. Phoenix leaned forward so Rickenbacker could tap him on the forehead. "Now, sit back."

Phoenix leaned back in his chair and closed his eyes. Rickenbacker could see the twitch in his eyes, indication that Phoenix's Intraspectroptivision™ had kicked in. He observed his friend's facial expressions alter as he watched the sped-up version of Rickenbacker's contact with Griffin Trowbridge to date.

He counted on Phoenix's lack of attention to detail. The fellow had skimmed the Tournament Challenge but usually relied on Rickenbacker to explain the fine print. Rickenbacker had made a habit of teasing out Phoenix's enthusiastic participation *before* giving him all the information. If he gave too much at the start, his friend might be frightened away.

Particularly this time, with *that* Final Challenge.

"Nice recovery on the street description," Phoenix said, absorbed in the audio/visual experience.

Rickenbacker paused the playback. "Yes, all I was able to find to aid with the creation of the setting were a few five-second video recordings of various areas in the Other World, and although they were high definition, they were too short to give me everything I needed. Hence the initial lack of detail on Granville Street. I had to improvise and fill in the gaps. If you look too closely, the people all look the same. They're extras, you see. It happened so fast, I didn't quite have time to set the scene properly, and it seemed to throw her off for a moment. The Reality Scan charm is a tad delayed, but it catches up eventually, which explains what you noticed: the description of Granville Street. I shall have to keep close track of that as we go along. Again, only short snippets of scanning are permitted by the tournament. But in the bit coming up on the train, you'll see that in truth, it enhances the storyline. Play."

Phoenix laughed out loud when it came to the train passengers, all looking somewhat similar, and reading books. "Nice touch," he said. "Is it intended to put her on edge like that?"

"Indeed, yes." Rickenbacker was surprised by this uncharacteristically perspicacious remark from Phoenix. "You see, the goal from the start is the Final Challenge, and we won't achieve it if she is completely at ease."

"Good thinking," Phoenix said vaguely. He was more interested in the audio/visual feast before him than in thinking ahead.

Rickenbacker felt hopeful that he had full buy-in from Phoenix.

When the playback was over, Phoenix opened his eyes. "Nicely done. But who is this Matteo person?"

Rickenbacker smiled and waggled his eyebrows. "Doris?" he called.

"Yes?" came her disembodied voice.

"Please send in our MGC."

"Certainly."

A moment later, there was a knock on the door, and in walked the character who would be known as Matteo MacCallum for the duration of the tournament. He stood in the middle of the room for observation. Phoenix got up and his pointy-toed boots made no sound on the carpet as he walked around him, scrutinizing the design.

"Wow, he turned out great."

Matteo blinked.

"He's based on your design," Rickenbacker said.

"I recognise him but I thought I had lost those blueprints. Wow. I had no idea he would turn out so well." He frowned at Rickenbacker. "Did you expand him?"

Rickenbacker swept his arm at the MGC. "As you see."

"No, I mean, add some details, give him backstory," Phoenix explained. "He wasn't complete; those were just blueprints, after all."

"Nonsense," Rickenbacker dismissed him with a wave. "He has plenty to get him through the one job he has to do; that won't matter at all."

"Well, if you're sure," Phoenix said. Then, "We've never been allowed to use MGCs before."

Rickenbacker picked up the tournament notice and instructions. "Maybe they changed the rules, or maybe they left off that rule in a stunning oversight. But nowhere on here does it say Magically Generated Characters are forbidden." Rickenbacker shrugged. "If they make an issue of it, so will I."

"Well. Good job. What else have you already taken care of?"

"The setting of the restaurant and rehearsal studio is complete and ready to be populated. I believe we shall be able to control other things as we go along. Griffin is a very intense person; her emotions and thoughts are easy to read, though as I said, I need to address the delay in the scanner. Have an onion ring." Rickenbacker took one. Pesto dip this time.

Phoenix declined. "She had better be the one we need. I *want that title* back, Rickenbacker. If I see those smug smirks on Blinky and Jethro's faces again—"

Rickenbacker waved a hand. "You must keep in mind that it was simply a matter of timing. They cleaned up their five natural disasters with greater efficiency than we did, that was all. We were well on the way. And frankly I believe whoever was in charge of doling out the herd animals had taken too much of the old blimlim oil."

Phoenix stormed about. "Yeah! Blinky and Jethro were so smug that they got their sheep under control so dang fast! We should have got bonus points for the way we dealt with ours. Mosquitoes were a way bigger challenge!" His eyes flashed and his face flushed. Rickenbacker smiled and nodded, encouraging him to sit. He didn't.

"And besides," Rickenbacker said, "that was five years ago. Since then, those two have done bugger all but gallivant around Salamander being guests on talk shows and waving on parade floats."

"Don't forget the ribbon-cutting ceremonies."

Rickenbacker bowed. "You see my point."

Phoenix leaned forward and squinted. "No?"

Rickenbacker smiled patiently. "They've become *complacent*, dear fellow. Worry not: with our Other World character as malleable as I believe she will be, and if we are on top of our reactions, the transitions should be smooth. I do believe it shall be . . ." He tasted the word as he applied it. *"Fun!"*

The MGC known as Matteo blinked.

Phoenix sat down eagerly. "What do I get to do?"

Rickenbacker seized this opening. "As I have already put in a great deal of effort to earn her trust, it makes sense I should carry on with that role. Alternatively, you get to be the Antagonist."

Phoenix frowned. He knew something was up. "What does that mean?"

Rickenbacker grinned and made his eyes twinkle. "You, my friend, have the greatest honour of all: the Pivotal Moment."

"You mean . . . the Final Challenge?"

"I do." Rickenbacker laid one hand on top of the other.

Phoenix grabbed the notice. Rickenbacker watched his eyes flit back and forth as he scanned it then widen as they found the line in question. Phoenix stared at him.

"With a *knife*?"

Rickenbacker grinned. "I do love this game."

"But—but—!"

"Now Phoenix—"

"But—!"

"All of Salamander will be watching via Intraspectroptivision™." Rickenbacker rose and his chair moved out of his way for him. He went around the desk to put his arm around Phoenix's shoulders. "There will be daily updates on the news. It is required viewing for all schoolchildren ages ten and up. My wife has already been in contact with yours and several others setting up an every-other-day fan club meeting to chat about the event and make predictions. Jordana is writing an article from the club's perspective for *The Semi-Daily Palpitator*. My friend, when we win, you will be the hero of the tournament. You will inspire future generations of LARPing competitors. Songs will be written about you. People will have your name embroidered on items of clothing and towels. In fact, you will be able to design your own egocentric-inspired line of clothing and charge exorbitant prices for it."

He watched Phoenix's eyes glaze over at the very dream of it.

"But—" Phoenix whispered. "But with a knife?"

Rickenbacker guided his friend toward the door and through it. "Trust me."

He closed the door, leaving Phoenix on the other side of it. He rubbed his hands with glee. He looked at Matteo, took him by the shoulders, and said, "You, handsome, are the key to our success. Now go and be everything our Griffin desires!"

Matteo nodded and left the room.

Rickenbacker tested the word again. "Ffffffffunnnn."

He liked it.

4

Incredibly, Still May 6

Matteo and I spent the next half hour removing Jason from my life, literally and figuratively. We dragged his sorry ass out into the hallway outside my apartment. Matteo guarded him while I gathered up Jason's clothes (after digging his key to my apartment out of the pocket of his jeans), his toothbrush and sundry items from my bathroom and the one drawer he'd occupied in my room. I snatched his jacket off the hanger in the front hall closet, recalling that I was the one who'd hung it there; Jason had left it on the couch. I was forever picking up after him, and he didn't even live here. *Bastard.* Why had I ever been—?

But there was no point in going there. I had come to my senses, and that's what was important. I dumped his stuff on top of him, and it tumbled all around, much as a shovelful of dirt would had I been burying him alive. We stood there, looking at him for a moment.

Matteo said, "This is a good look for him."

I laughed.

Then Matteo and I went back into my apartment and locked the door.

"Thanks," I said. "Do you want some tea or anything?"

"No, thanks. I should get going."

"Yeah, I guess."

"I'll call you tomorrow, okay?"

"Yes!" I felt suddenly frantic. I had committed now. What was I supposed to do? I had so many questions, not the least of which was, "How did you get in here? I don't remember even telling you where I live, and the door was most definitely—"

"Wow! Is it really 1:00 in the morning?"

I looked at the clock, and as if to confirm the time, a bloody great brick wall of fatigue slammed into me. I staggered, if you can believe it, and Matteo grabbed my elbow. Now, I am *not* a "helpless female"; it's not a role I am suited for at all. But when this man touched me, I was overcome with a desire to swoon and let him draw me into his arms.

He looked down into my eyes. "Come on, Griffin Girl. You've had quite a night." It was an attractively clumsy effort at an endearment, and I loved it. He led me to my room, where I lay down and was oblivious to his departure.

And Now It Is Monday, May 7

I was in the middle of an awesome dream when a horrible sound jarred me awake. The sound repeated a couple of times before I recognised it. I picked up the phone and cleared my throat.

"Hullo?"

"Griffin, it's Brian."

My heart jumped into my throat. Was I late for work? No, it was Monday. The store was closed.

"What's up?"

"Griffin, I have a favour to ask you. Liam broke his hand. He can't play for a few weeks. Can you take over his lessons for a while? He can take on some of your sales hours, which I think you'd prefer. Plus, you've said you'd like to take on more lessons."

I had? I was aware of a niggling little warning signal, but for the life of me, I couldn't think why. Brian went on.

"He only has five students, and four of them come on Saturday. The other we could move so it's right after Derek Sheffield on Thursday. Whaddya say?"

I got out of bed and went to the calendar on the fridge, rubbing the back of my head and thinking hard. Damn it. There was nothing on the calendar, no clue to what was bothering me. I should be excited at the prospect!

"I don't want to pressure you, but Alex is full and Sandra has already said she can't do it 'cause it won't work with her daughter's daycare. I really don't want to tick off a whole passel of parents."

"Yeah, no problem. I can do it."

Audible sigh of relief. "Great! Thanks *so* much. How about an extra fifty cents an hour too?"

My heart leapt. "Awesome. Thanks, Brian."

I hung up, flopped back down on the bed, and snuggled up with the down-filled quilt. Oh, to get back into that dream! The damn phone had been such a rude awakening, it had wiped the details of the dream from my mind. All I remembered was the feeling. I felt beautiful and appreciated. An image drifted before my eyes: a blue cyclorama, a waterfall of music, a godlike musician with great hair—

"Shit!" I sat bolt upright. "Oh no."

Rickenbacker had as good as told me I'd have to quit my job to be in the band, and here I'd done the exact opposite. Sweating like a hard-run horse and feeling sick to my stomach, I took myself to the kitchen. I rubbed my hair and paced around, seeking some form of direction.

Kettle. Where was it? If I were a kettle, where would I be? Cupboard next to the stove. Nope. Cupboard next to the fridge. Aha! I put the kettle on the counter and rubbed my hair some more. What the hell was I going to do? Water. I had trouble fitting the kettle under the tap, and a whole lot of water splashed all over the wall and counter, and some escaped down the drain before I got any into the spout.

Breathe, stupid.

I put the kettle on the counter again and gripped it with both hands. I glared at my reflection in the convex stainless steel. *Come off it. How hard can it be?* My chest rose and fell with a couple of steady breaths. I plugged the kettle in and grabbed a cloth to wipe up the water.

Brian would understand.

Oh sure he'd understand; then he'd be royally pissed off and hurt and he'd fire my ass—if I hadn't already quit—and never want to speak to me again. After all he'd done for me: the job, the break on the cost of renting equipment, the encouragement for my musical career, letting us rehearse in his studio sometimes. And most recently, the deferred-payment plan on a brand-new Fender Telecaster guitar.

No, there was not a chance in hell I was going to let Brian down.

I still had Rickenbacker's card. I could just call him and let him know I couldn't do it.

Matteo's guitar playing, the rest of his band, the tingle in my spine as we nailed those harmonies, his dreamy smile, his steady hand on my elbow, the tremor that shot through me when he touched me, his gentle voice calling me "Griffin Girl."

No, there was not a chance in hell I was going to turn this band down.

Rickenbacker had asked for my "full-time commitment." Did it have to mean I didn't work at the music store? I would just have to make it work, that's all. Try it for a while and see how it went, and then make a choice. It wasn't too much to ask to give it a shot for a couple of weeks, right?

Something came through the mail slot and made a soft *thud* on the carpeted floor. Despondently but with a sort of determination, I hung the cloth on the faucet and went to the entryway. A rectangular brown package sat there. Odd. It was early for the mail. But who doesn't find the arrival of a parcel exciting? I picked it up and turned it over. It was oblong, about two inches thick, and weighed about the same as a paperback.

A quick peek out the peep hole showed me Jason was gone. I stealthily opened the door in case he was hiding around the corner. Nope. There was a trail of his crap pointing the direction he'd taken: a running shoe, an old capo, a golf ball he'd peeled all the plastic off of, his toothbrush. I went back to the package. It was addressed in a flowery script to Griffin Trowbridge at this address, but the stamps were bizarre: colourful but not recognisable. The cancellation mark had obscured the city of origin, and the postmark was smudged. The guy upstairs had put on some music. I didn't recognise it, but it sounded like the soundtrack from a horror flick: mysterious enough to perfectly underscore this intriguing moment.

My tummy did a little flip as I tore off the paper and laid it on the table. I held a wooden box. I lifted the lid and found a folded-up piece of honey-coloured leather tied with a leather string. Once the string was untied, the unfolded leather flaps revealed a pocket, out of which I pulled a knife in a sheath.

Its four-inch blade was shiny steel and appeared to be all one piece with its handle, which was roughened by diamond-shaped carvings. It had a nice weight to it and felt good in my hand, the way a nice wine glass feels good. In the diffuse natural light from the window, the knife seemed to glow.

"Quaint," I said aloud, a little tremor fluttering in my chest. What did this mean? Who had sent it and why?

I stuck the blade back into its tight covering, tucked the thing back into its pouch, and folded and tied it with a shudder. Uncertain what to do with it, I stuck it on the shelf in the closet and shut the door. I folded up the brown paper covering and put it in the recycling tub. I went back into the bedroom and sat on the edge of the bed, contemplating what to do today, on my day off. Vacuum, maybe. Yippee.

My cell phone rang.

"Griffin, where are you?" said a vaguely familiar voice.

"Uh, it's my day off, so . . . at home?" I rubbed my still-bleary eyes.

"You realise, do you not, that you are supposed to be working in our kitchens right now," Rickenbacker said. I leapt to my feet. How had I missed this? "Your supervisor is already less than impressed, and he hasn't even met you."

I felt sick again and paced the hall, racking my brain. "But—I don't remember anyone telling me what my schedule would be. I hadn't even decided to take this when I left last night—"

"We're off to a poor start if you're going to invent excuses. Please get here as soon as you can." He rang off.

I screamed into the phone. "I don't even know where it is! I have to take transit!" I tossed it on the couch. I waved my arms wildly as I tried to get things straight in my head. Pacing back and forth between my TV and the kitchen table, I clutched tufts of my hair. "In through the nose, out through the mouth. In through the nose, out through the mouth."

I picked up the phone and pressed the buttons to search through the call history. Brian's call was there, but the one that had just come in was not. Great. Now my phone wasn't working properly, again, on top of everything else. The phone beeped as I turned it off. I dropped it back onto the couch.

My feet kept moving me back and forth across the living room floor. I stopped in the middle of the room and spoke with conviction to the poster of Van Gogh's *Starry Night* on the wall above the couch. "It's okay. We'll make it work. It'll all be *fine*. It's about the music."

I showered and dressed in record time. I threw a peanut butter and banana sandwich together—I had no idea what to expect at this place— grabbed a granola bar and an apple and tossed them in my backpack. Hair uncombed and still wet, I grabbed my jacket, my guitars—one on my back, one in my hand—and my small rehearsal amp. Awkward on the bus, but I didn't know what sort of equipment they might already have. Ordinarily I would have a chance to ask these types of questions. I locked the door behind me.

It hit me then that the apartment had been decidedly . . . moist. Moreso than after a shower. *Shit.* I'd left the kettle plugged in. I set my amp down, unlocked the door, bashed the neck of my acoustic case on the doorframe as I hurried in, unplugged the kettle, and rushed off again. I ran down the stairs —faster than waiting for the elevator. I figured I'd take the train downtown and head to Rickenbacker's. It obviously wasn't a restaurant, but it was the only address I had. It was a place to start. I stepped out of the building, and my left foot went into a puddle. It was pouring rain.

"Damn."

No umbrella and no time to go back for it—and no spare hand to carry it if I did. I set down my amp to pull out my cell phone; it wasn't there. I had left it on the damn couch. Still no time to go back for it. The bus was due any minute. Hunching against the weather, I started for the bus stop.

When a car pulled up alongside, I ignored it until it honked at me. I nearly dropped dead when I saw Matteo at the wheel of a stunning, bright blue Mini convertible (top up in the rain, of course). It was not the car I'd have imagined a guy like Matteo driving, but then, Matteo was not like any guy I'd ever imagined. The passenger-side window lowered.

"Rick said you might need a lift." He grinned. "Put your gear in the back."

"That's . . . that's great!" I opened the hatch. With the seats down, this little thing had tons of room for stuff. I laid my acoustic guitar case alongside Matteo's, the electric on top of that, shoved the amp in at the side, then went around to climb in. "This is gorgeous." I settled into the heated leather seats and ran my hand along the pristine dash. "So, do you live near here or something?"

"No." He seemed puzzled. As a result, so was I, so I didn't pursue it.

I tapped my foot to Tracy Chapman playing on his car stereo. "So. Where are we going?"

"To Salamander's."

"Where is it?"

"Powell Street."

"How come Rickenbacker thought I would be in today when nobody told me?"

Matteo shrugged. "Don't worry about it, Griff." He gave me a sidelong half grin, and I stopped worrying instantly. "I think he's probably just excited about your being involved. I know I am."

I felt myself blushing, so I concentrated on the trees swishing by out the window. "You sure know how to make a girl feel welcome."

"I hope I do. And I hope *you* do. We're gonna be great, Griff."

There was something about the way he called me "Griff" that was so different from when Calvin used that name. Calvin was my best friend, and it was a nice feeling to be called a nickname by a good friend. But there was an almost magical tone to the way Matteo said it. I was grinning all over, inside and out, and felt warm and fuzzy to go along with it. I knew I had better pull myself together or I'd be a mushy mess and not good for making music at all.

Besides, I was grateful for the lift, and didn't want Matteo to think I wasn't. Conversation was called for.

"How long has the band been together?"

"Not too long."

Was he a lousy conversationalist, or was he just shy? I preferred to think the latter.

"What're your favourite bands?" I ventured.

Excellent choice of question. There followed a stream of names, everything from AC/DC to Zeppelin, and I responded with equal enthusiasm. I especially approved of his appreciation for Rush, Yes, and Kate Bush.

"Now that you're in the band, it would be neat if we could do some Kate," he said, sending my heart through the roof of the Mini. "Female vocal is going to really help us be more versatile."

"Sweet," I said with equal parts buzz and lameness.

Salamander's, as it turned out, was located in a crummy area of Vancouver in the downtown East Side. Let's just say I was glad to have a ride. Matteo pulled into the parkade entrance and flipped on the headlights. I had never seen such a dark underground parking lot.

"Cripes, this is scary."

"How do you mean?" He steered the car expertly around the tight corners—tight, even in a Mini—and down the steep slopes. The headlights didn't penetrate the darkness one iota. They didn't even shine on the walls. What was the point of them? How could Matteo see a thing?

"Umm. Well, it's awfully dark."

He smiled, which is why I noticed it wasn't pitch black within the car. "You afraid of the dark?"

I hesitated because it seemed like he didn't know what I meant. "Well, no. But parkades are usually lit up. I mean, I wouldn't want to walk through here alone."

"I'm driving," he said, as though that answered all my problems.

"I meant—"

He rounded a corner, and suddenly the place lit up like a football stadium. I twisted around to see behind me. The darkness from which we'd just emerged appeared to me to be a wall painted black. A gaping square of dark that shrank as we pulled farther from it. Judging by my vast experience driving in underground parkades, we had come down about three levels. The parking level we were now on was occupied by a smattering of cars with a few clustered round a central entrance to the building.

Matteo pulled the little car into a spot next to a hearse-like vehicle. We got our guitars out of the trunk, and I followed him to a green door with a sign that read *Salamander's House of Music and Pudding This Way.*

The door opened into a hallway not unlike any other hotel or restaurant service corridor. A service elevator lifted us and deposited us on the first floor, where I followed Matteo to a well-appointed rehearsal studio. A drum kit, a keyboard, microphones, guitar stands, and amplifiers were all set up on a dais at the far end of the room, which was about four times the size of my living room. Nice place. Sound baffles hung on the walls and ceiling. Stacks of chairs up against the wall indicated that the space was at least sometimes used for larger groups or maybe performances. A rack of music stands in the corner would be handy for other types of bands too. What a cool place that would provide such a great rehearsal space for its own musicians! It must mean the restaurant was noteworthy as well. Why had I never heard of it? I couldn't wait to start filling this room with music.

"You can leave your gear here, and I guess you'd better go find Rickenbacker."

"Where would I find him?" I reluctantly set my guitar cases on the hardwood floor up against the oak-panelled wall. I wished we could start playing right away. "I may need you to give me a tour."

Matteo laughed. "I can understand why. This place can be a little confusing. But don't worry, I'll take care of you."

I couldn't hope for anything more.

He locked the studio door, which was a relief because I'd have worried about the safety of my guitars, and led me down a bizarre hallway with so many twists and turns, I wondered why we hadn't criss-crossed our own path. The walls were papered in the diamond style of a colourful harlequin, and the textured pattern hurt the eyes. Moreover, it did not supply any landmarks. I was hopelessly lost and cursed the architect who designed this structure. And the interior designer too.

"A little confusing?" I said. "That's a bit of an understatement, don't you think?"

He took my hand and gave it a squeeze. "You'll get used to it. Here we are."

We emerged from the narrower corridor into an entryway of sorts with a set of industrial metal double-swinging doors, the kind with round windows in them. Matteo pushed on the right-hand door, and I went past him into a swirl of mayhem worthy of Kitchen Stadium. Multiplied by ten. Complete with underscoring. Seriously. The music playing through the speaker system was *The Flight of the Bumblebee*. The kitchen staff wove in and around each other, wielding wooden spoons and spatulas, mixers and stainless-steel bowls of what might have been batter, and cookie sheets of dough like dancers in a musical about baking.

Matteo walked me over to an egg-shaped man in a black jacket and apron. "Chef, I'd like you to meet our newest acquisition. Griffin here is a very experienced pastry chef."

"What? No, I'm not; my dad—"

Chef pumped my hand. "Griffin, it's great to finally meet you."

"You too, but really, I'm *not*—"

"Come now, there's no need to be so modest." He mock-punched me on the jaw, the way my grandad used to do to me when I was four.

I turned to Matteo to protest but he'd vanished. I was not beginning to get used to that sort of thing. Chef put his arm around me and led me over to a workstation, complete with a large island table surrounded by ovens, a couple of fridges, and more counters with cupboards and drawers. Filled with equipment and utensils? That's where I'd start looking anyway.

"What we really need for this evening are 150 servings of crème brûlée. Can you do that?" He started to walk away.

I wondered if there were some exercises I could do to keep my heart down in my chest where it was supposed to be. I chased after Chef and touched his elbow, trying to sound urgent but not contrary. "Honestly, I have never—"

"Steven here can be your assistant." He gestured to a tall, pimply, brown-skinned youth in kitchen whites, who stepped out from where he may have been hiding in a corner. He approached like a bunny who had been instructed to pet the Dangerous Animal. And with that, Chef bolted. I looked at my new assistant and grinned reassuringly, though there was no way he could have seen me with his head tipped down like that, not to mention all that hair.

The swinging doors crashed as another man burst into the room like an explosion. The entire kitchen staff stood at attention. I don't know how the music knew to stop, but the kitchen was as silent as a cave, except for the *flup-flup-flup* of the doors as they swung back and forth and finally stopped. I glanced around at my new colleagues and waited. The man was not much taller than I am and was sorta scrawny with a mosh of black matted hair, but he had an air of self-importance. He wore what looked like coils of gold springs all around his torso and each limb, with—was that a unitard?— underneath. His gaze didn't wander around the room, that sounds too random. His gaze surveyed the room and ultimately rested on me. I tried not to blush, but there's only so much you can do about that.

"And you are?"

"I—*ahem*—" Damn it, why did my throat have to constrict just when I was trying to sound confident? "I'm Griffin."

He didn't respond.

"Trowbridge."

No response.

"I'm new. I'm—"

"I figured *that* much."

"—in the band?"

Nothing.

"You know? The band? With Matteo?"

That got a reaction. His face bloomed into a sunny grin, and he clapped his hands together. "Oh, Matteo! He's marvellous, isn't he?"

This seemed to be directed at the kitchen staff as a whole, and they all nodded and smiled in appreciative agreement. I allowed myself to breathe again, relieved we apparently had found some common ground.

"Yes, our Matteo is practically what holds this place together, wouldn't you say?"

I shrugged and smiled a little. "Uh, yeah, well, I hardly know him, but so far he sure seems great."

"Seems? *Seems?* He is great! He's a musical genius."

"Yes, yes, he's wonderful."

"Well, GriffinTrowbridgeI'mnewI'mintheband, I am Phoenix Reysing." He pronounced it "rising," as in bread dough. As in, well, a phoenix out of the ashes.

"Oh. Nice to meet you." I stuck out my hand.

He didn't take it. In fact, he seemed put out.

"Do you not know who I am?"

I definitely couldn't stop the blush this time. Nor the sweat. "Umm. Well, you just said you are Phoenix Rising, so I have to assume you're Phoenix Rising."

He rolled his eyes. "It's Reysing, not Rising, and I am the owner of this establishment."

"Ohhh!" A revelation. "Sorry, I didn't know. Nobody mentioned—I thought Rickenbacker—"

"No, no, no." The man was beaming again, and I felt unaccountably relieved. "He's my partner, but he takes on the managerial duties. So, you're

Griffin?"

I nodded, glad everything was clear now. "Yes, I'm Griffin."

His grin became a glare. "You're late."

Taken aback, I swallowed. "I'm sorry. You see, I didn't know—"

"We don't tolerate lateness around here."

I was interested in playing music. I hadn't signed on for *this*. "Well, maybe it would be a good idea if you told me my schedule so I'd know when to come in."

He huffed and pivoted like a musician in a marching band with a dismissive wave of his hand. "Never mind that now. I want crème brûlée as our feature, this evening. Understand? *Crème brûlée.*"

And he was gone, the doors hardly even swinging as they closed behind him. The kitchen staff had already gone back to their tasks, and I hadn't even noticed the music starting up again. This time it was jolly fiddle music.

Was this some kind of a joke? Steven stood there, hands behind his back, awaiting instructions. His stare, between his bangs, rested on the counter behind me, as if it would have been considered rude to meet the eyes of his superior. The armpits of my shirt dampened.

"Is there a recipe book somewhere?" I asked Steven. "I have never made crème brûlée. I don't know why Matteo said I'm a pastry chef; I'm not. It's my dad."

Steven turned around, walked two steps, and fetched a book from high on a bookshelf I hadn't noticed before. It wasn't so much a book as a tome, complete with leather cover and gold-leaf writing on the front and spine. It was about six inches thick and dusty as a Saskatchewan dirt road in drought season. The book was titled *My Seventeen Years as a Fort Steele Madam*.

"Umm, Steven, I need a recipe, not a memoir."

He thrust the book into my hands with an insistent nod. The damn thing weighed a ton, and it dropped onto the worktable with a resounding thud. I opened it at random. Dust flew everywhere. Great. Now I'd have to clean the work surface before I could do anything. The page on the left was a list of items one might take on a camping trip. The page on the right, however, was, oddly enough, a recipe for crème brûlée. "How do you figure that?" I asked of no one.

I tied on an apron I found hanging in the corner and read through the recipe; it didn't look all that hard. And who knew? Maybe some of my dad's genes would turn up. The recipe was for only a dozen servings, though, so we'd have to do it over and over. We got started, Steven following my instructions as I recited them out of the book and still never looking at me. We were a quiet team. The blending of the milk, cream, vanilla, and sugar, the separating of the eggs, all seemed to go well. I brought the mixture to a boil on the gas stove then set it aside to cool.

Then it came time to pour the milk mixture over the eggs. As I stirred, a funny thing happened. "Ach!" I cried. The mixture turned scarlet. I reread the recipe. I saw nothing in the ingredients which could account for the transformation. Maybe it was a special brand of vanilla or something. I checked the bottle but it gave me no clue. It was bizarre, but I kept going. Steven got out the little ramekin dishes to make individual servings and set them on the counter before he began the second batch. I poured the cream into the dishes. Given the size of them, the recipe made twenty-one servings instead of twelve, so that was handy. I put them in the oven inside a large roasting pan of water, as the recipe instructed.

"This is going well."

Steven and I cracked eggs, poured cream, measured sugar, over and over, with increased confidence. Each batch turned a different colour. There was lime green, Kelly green, royal purple, mauve, lemon yellow, orange, and magenta. It was during the third batch that I noticed the music coming through the speaker. It was a song from a musical about the biblical story of Joseph and his coat of many colours. The singers were reciting a list of colours, which made me wonder how they could memorize lyrics like that. I chuckled at the coincidence.

"That's kind of funny, hunh?" I said to Steven.

He looked surprised and without moving his head, focussed his eyeballs somewhere to his left. He didn't say anything.

"The music, I mean," I explained.

Steven's eyes turned to his right.

I decided it would be best to drop it.

Each time a batch came out of the oven, it went on the rack to cool. Then we filled the refrigerator with our little cups of brightly coloured heaven. They had to refrigerate for several hours before I could torch them, so I asked Chef, who was working with the other cooks, what I should work on in between.

Just then Matteo reappeared to say I was needed at rehearsal. Chef rolled his eyes but waved me off.

"I have to be back in three or four hours to caramelize the brûlée."

Matteo smiled at me. "No problem."

I felt as wobbly as the crème brûlée.

Matteo and I retraced our earlier steps along the winding, blinding corridor. The route seemed less complicated this time. Maybe it was just because I had been so nervous on our way to the kitchen, and I was already getting used to the place. Or maybe it was that Matteo walked beside me and smelled sweet, kind of like he was wearing vanilla-scented deodorant. Or it could have been that I was so excited to play guitar and sing with him that everything in my life made more sense just then. In any event, we made it to the rehearsal studio. The drummer and bass and keyboard players were already there.

Matteo pointed to a microphone where two guitar stands had been set up, alongside an amp, which meant I could take mine home. One never knows. I got out my guitars and set them on the stands.

"What do you want to start with?" I needed to know which guitar to tune first.

"How about we warm up with *Take it Easy*?"

We discussed harmony parts between me and the other band members as I adjusted my mic height and tuned my acoustic. While the other guys finished getting set up, I noodled with *Gotta Have You*, the song Calvin and I would be playing at Teresa's wedding on the 19th. After a minute or two, I looked up and instantly felt a feverish blush. Matteo was watching me, wearing a crooked smile that triggered a roller coaster in my belly. I pulled myself together as best I could, which wasn't very well at all, and said, "Ready?"

Matteo just nodded, his blue eyes still connected to mine like the sun through a magnifying glass, igniting my substratal region as if it were a dry leaf. A breath gusted out of me as I broke eye contact and turned to the mic, awaiting the count-in.

Matteo's voice was rich and gorgeous, and when I joined in with the harmony, the blend made me giddy with pleasure. Afterward we tweaked a couple of things then decided to move on to *Bring Me Some Water*, and boy, could I sing that song like a method actor! Some of the lyrics drew warmth to my cheeks again, but I like to think I maintained a professional demeanour.

The guys applauded when the song was over.

It was such a rush to play with a band who treated me like I was the best thing they'd ever heard. I mean, maybe it was a little over the top that they high-fived each other, but in my other band, the highest praise anyone gave was, "Sounded cool." It probably didn't help that I was the leader there, so I always felt a bit uptight and responsible. This . . . this was like the lid had been taken off a pressure cooker.

We played a mind-blowing variety of tunes, and it's funny, but it felt like I had never played better than I did opposite Matteo. I don't know; there was just a *vibe* between us. A connection. It sounds all airy-fairy to say it, but that's how it was. I felt more confident with my playing and with my singing. The drummer and I were locked in, the bass player too, which made the rhythm perfectly solid. It probably also had to do with not having to worry about whether the lead guitarist was going to take over and change the arrangement in the middle of the song or go off on some wacko, unplanned solo. There's a certain level of trust necessary in the relationship between musicians, and Matteo and I had it in spades.

Not to exclude the rest of the band, mind you. Matteo had introduced them, only I guess I was nervous because as we played, I realised I had forgotten their names, the way details of a dream slip away as you wake up. Then I was embarrassed to ask. Still, they were sharp as nails. Tight. Solid. I was certain these guys knew their stuff so well, nothing would go wrong. But if it did? We would get it back together in moments; the audience would never notice a thing.

Rehearsal was, in short, awwwwessssooooommme!

After three hours of it (with a short break for some lunch in the middle), I was ready to go home. I had the exhausted-but-buzzing feeling that comes from an exhilarating rehearsal. Then again, were I at home already, I'd be too wired to sleep. It was just as well I had dessert to deal with. Overall I felt better about the entire arrangement. Making great music made up for a lot. Still, it was with an ache of regret in my heart and soul that I turned my amp off and put my guitars in their cases.

"What else do you and the others do here?" I asked Matteo.

"We wait tables."

Good. Rickenbacker had said everyone was expected to help with the restaurant, and this meant there was the chance I'd run into Matteo occasionally.

By the time I returned to the kitchen, I was way less nervous about having our first gig on Thursday. In fact, I could have played that very night with a high degree of intestinal fortitude.

The one thing I was a tad bit miffed about was that Rickenbacker had promised me a lead guitarist, not a whole new band. Don't get me wrong; he had come through. But how had he misunderstood I wanted someone for *my* band? I hadn't wanted to join a new band myself. *Griffin, you're so lame.* I'd sorta let myself be railroaded. Should I speak to him about it? If I played the gig on Thursday, would it be too late to change my mind? Was there a statute of limitations on stuff like this?

Then again, after I had given The Spurious Correlations a try, maybe I could invite Matteo to meet the guys in my band, and maybe he'd like to play with us.

Yeah. That's what I'd do. At this point I was only just beginning to make music with Matteo MacCallum.

In the kitchen, I found my apron and tied it around my waist. I'd been at work for, like, six hours already, so I hoped it wouldn't be much longer. Still, I didn't mind seeing my crème brûlée through to the end.

Chef was chomping at the bit to get the feature dessert started. I grabbed Steven, who had just finished up slicing date squares—how come the experienced chef got date squares and I was stuck with crème brûlée?—so he could help me get the desserts out of the refrigerator. We moved tray after tray onto the counters. Then I checked the recipe. After I put on the sugar mixture, I knew they needed to be fired. I mean, that's the *brûlée* part. It seemed you could either broil a bunch of them at a time or use a little blowtorch specific for the purpose. I asked Steven how it had been done in the past.

Steven, with his terrific energy, enthusiasm, and helpfulness, looked at the floor and shrugged like a guilty child.

"Is there a blowtorch thingy?"

He pointed to a drawer. I found it and turned it on. It worked, to my great relief, since I'd never used one before. I approached the table of custardy desserts, took one in hand (a green one), and prepared to aim and fire at it.

The double doors burst open again, as they had in the morning, and I jumped. However, I was focussed on the cup of creamy goodness in my hand and didn't turn around.

"Hey, new kid."

"Yeah?" I made the blowtorch approach the ramekin.

"What are these?" Phoenix waved at the trays of rainbow-coloured desserts, and his gold coils swung on his arm.

Ulp. "Crème brûlée." I chortled. "We could say we're celebrating diversity and inclusiveness!" No reaction. "I mean, I know they're kinda—"

"They're not just 'kinda' anything. I hate crème brûlée."

"But." Had I lost my mind? "You asked me to make it. One hundred fifty of them." The blowtorch was still flaming, and I shut it off.

"Now, dear . . ."

I have to say, I hate terms of endearment from people in authority, especially ones I don't know. Especially ones who are being assholes.

"I hate crème brûlée. Do you understand me? *Hate* it. So why would I have asked you to make it?"

Maybe if you have a split personality? I thought. *Or maybe are just an asshole.*

"Brownies, now *there's* a treat. Make brownies next time."

"But I—"

"Just do it, new kid."

"It's Griffin."

He ignored me and abruptly gave me the back of his coil outfit. Pausing only to snick a crumb of brown sugar onto the floor, he stalked out of the kitchen.

I noticed I was trembling and took some deep breaths to steady myself. As the swinging doors slowed their flapping, I became aware of something else too: I looked down, raising both clenched fists at the same time. Clutched in my left hand was the little leather sheath I thought I'd stuck on the shelf in my front hall closet. And in my right?

Instead of the blowtorch I thought I held, my knuckles were white surrounding the handle of the knife that lived in the sheath. It might have been my imagination, but I could have sworn its pointy tip *twinkled* like in a movie. The hair on my neck rose.

One more oddity creeping into my consciousness was the theme from *The Good, The Bad and The Ugly* coming through the speakers.

5

May 7 Was a Long Day

I forced deep breaths through my constricted throat. If they helped the trembling, I didn't notice. It may have helped the first set of trembles, but I was being bombarded by a whole new orchestration.

Rickenbacker walked in and his face lit up. "Oooh! Is that crème brûlée?" He picked one up and thrust his face into it.

"I'm so sorry! I thought that's what—Wait a minute. What?"

He spoke around a mouthful of pudding with untorched sugary topping. "I love this stuff. And this," he pointed at it, "is particularly good. Our patrons will be very happy."

"But Phoenix said—" I pointed back at the door then noticed the knife was still in my hand and scrambled to put the damn thing back in the sheath before I hurt myself with it.

"Our patrons," Rickenbacker said, "are sophisticated. They expect a wide selection of desserts, and crème brûlée is . . ." His eyes searched the kitchen for just the right descriptor. "One of them."

Grateful for the chance to explain myself, I rushed to say, "Phoenix was the one who told me to make it, and then he suddenly changed his mind."

Rickenbacker darted a sharp look at me. "Are you . . . accusing Phoenix of something?"

He sorta sounded . . . gleeful. I had to be wrong about that. In any event, maybe it was a good time to let it go. "No." I jammed the damn knife into my hip pocket. "Listen, I'd better get moving." I indicated the rainbow of puddings with a vague wave.

He nodded, licking out his dish, and handed it to me then left.

Matteo walked in. "I have six orders for crème brûlée. I didn't know we had it on the menu."

"I guess it's a special or something," I replied, uncertain what to do with Rickenbacker's dish. "Steven and I made it this afternoon."

Admiration poured out of his eyes. "Wow. You're a really amazing person."

If anything could obliterate Phoenix's loathsome contradictory behaviour, well, a comment like that from this man did it. That gaze of his was like an infrared light for keeping food warm, and I couldn't help but react accordingly. I also couldn't meet it. I smiled, probably like an idiot. "I'll get torching six of them for you."

He continued to watch me while I set aside six of the ramekins. I struggled not to wither under his scrutiny but rather to take his admiration as a vote of confidence. I'm just not used to anyone paying that kind of attention to me.

"I'll be back for it," he said and went back into the dining room.

Something weird happened when I aimed the torch at the first dish. I guess you're becoming less and less surprised each time I refer to "something weird," but anyway it did, and if I'm going to tell this story, I want to be accurate. The flame met the sugar, and instead of melting it and making it crumble into that crunchy, sugary topping characteristic of traditional crème brûlée—well, this was already not traditional given that the table of dessert resembled the wall of swatches at a paint store—the flame touched the sugar, and the sugar leapt up in the dish, squeezed and twisted itself, until it formed a sculpture of a mermaid on a rock, just like the one in the harbour of Copenhagen.

I stared at it, open mouthed. I instinctively withdrew the torch before it could burn the crap out of the mermaid. *What the fuck?* I turned the torch over, careful not to set my hair aflame. I couldn't see anything about it that would cause this effect, but then again, I'd never used one before.

I set that ramekin down and picked up the next, tentatively aiming the flame at it. With my nose wrinkled in determination, I went in. This one lifted and stretched and became a dragon's head, complete with coloured flame snorting out its nose. I attacked the next with more confidence. It was a castle with turrets as perky as meerkats. And a moat. Another was a leaping dolphin. Each and every dish of pudding had a crunchy, sugary topping of a unique, dramatic design. What with the wacky colours and the peculiar shapes, I was at the same time puzzled, delighted, and terrified.

Matteo came in to get a tray of them. "Wow, those are amazing! How did you do that?"

"That's the thing," I said. "I don't actually know how I'm doing it. Have you ever seen anything like this here before?"

"I don't know. Rickenbacker is committed to having nothing but the best in his restaurant."

That didn't really explain it for me, but I shrugged. Lots of things about this restaurant were unusual. I could ask my dad if he'd seen crème brûlée do this sort of thing. Meanwhile, I had more dessert to torch.

When Matteo took the tray into the dining room, balanced on his hand and shoulder, he was met with a round of applause.

Several more orders for my creation came within the next half hour. I torched each one, and the sculptures got stranger and more impressive, never repeating themselves.

Shortly before the end of my shift, a call came from the dining room: one of the servers said her table wanted to applaud the creator of the amazing crème brûlée. Blushing, palms sweating, I stepped through the doors into the dining room with its deep red floral carpet and dark wood furniture and approached her table. I smiled as they stood and applauded. My heart beat with a pride I had never experienced before.

Then I stopped walking. They weren't looking at me.

Phoenix stood before them, bowing and modestly brushing off the applause.

Kind of as if he didn't deserve it.

Furious, I reached behind my back to untie my apron, and my hand brushed against the knife in my hip pocket. *Bloody hell.* Never had I felt so much like pulling a weapon on somebody. I ignored it and bashed through the swinging doors back into the kitchen. I took off my apron and flung it on the counter and stalked to the other door.

I stopped myself, hands clenching and unclenching, and went back to hang my apron up properly where it lived. I hated that something so stupid as an apron would have eaten at me all night, but it would have. *That* sent me pounding through the doors.

In my fury, I made a couple of wrong turns in the maze of funky, eye-jarring wallpaper and had to backtrack but eventually found my way to the rehearsal studio to get my gear.

I shrugged into my jacket, slung my Tele across my shoulders and picked up my amp and acoustic. Matteo was nowhere to be seen. Probably still waiting tables.

Back through the maze again; we'd come in through the parkade entrance, so I wasn't sure where to find the front door, but finally I found myself back in the dining room. Most of the tables still had patrons, so I kept my head down so as to not draw attention to myself as I snuck past the stage at the end of the room to the front door. I was out on the street, and it was dark and it was raining and I was cold and I was mad and, damn it, somewhere someone was playing Roy Orbison singing *Crying*. I brushed tears and raindrops off my face and headed south toward Hastings Street, where I felt reasonably sure I would find a bus route.

My first day had gone so well. Too bad it had ended so poorly. Something about walking to the bus stop in the rain seemed to help me a bit. Phoenix had told me he was the owner of the restaurant. Was it that much of a surprise for him to take at least some credit for the creations served in his establishment? Even though he'd given me mixed messages about the crème brûlée, I conceded that it wasn't too far out of the scope of possibility.

At any rate, it was a healthier outlook than the resentment I had hitherto been dwelling on.

It was a good thing Matteo was involved in all this; if Phoenix were the only person I had to deal with, I wouldn't last long in this place.

By the time I got off the elevator in my apartment, it was 10:30. What a long bloody day. I was utterly spent. My few snacks had run out long ago, and my weary feet dragged along the carpet.

A few stray bits of Jason's stuff still sprinkled the hall outside my door. I went in, locked the deadbolt, tossed my keys on the stand in the entryway, and stood my guitar cases up in the corner by the closet. I didn't have the energy to even put my jacket on a hanger but hooked the neck on the closet door handle. I made a quick peanut butter and honey sandwich and a gin and tonic. I gave my cell phone an evil eye where it lay so relaxed and undisturbed on the couch. I picked it up. So many notifications! Maybe it had been busier today than I assumed, poor thing. Slumping in the armchair, I punched all the right buttons to access my voice mail. Seven messages? Yikes.

Something was digging into my bum. I pulled out the knife just as Jason started screaming at me through the tinny speaker.

"You fucking bitch! You cow. Who the hell do you think you are? After all I've done for you, you get some pretty boy to come and throw me out. Who is he anyway?"

Pretty boy? Well, he is that. I tossed the knife onto the couch.

"D'ja meet at that piece-of-shit wedding? Did you screw him right away?" Jason paused, apparently to think of some more witticisms to throw at me. "Well, you must have, for him to want to come home with someone as ugly as you." Jason seemed unaware of his own irony.

"Well . . . Have a shitty life."

Seriously?

The thing beeped, introducing Jason again.

"Hey. Griffin. Babe."

Seriously?

"Hey. I miss you already. I—I don't know what to do! I'm like, totally lost without you. Griff . . . I know I messed up. I totally know it, and I'm really sorry. Just . . . can I come over? Okay, well. Call me, babe."

Beep.

"Griffin?" came my mother's scolding tone. "It's your mother"—*Duh*—"if you choose to remember. Are you there? I suppose you're screening your calls. I imagine I'll never see you again since you're so ashamed of what you did on Saturday night."

What *I* did?

"Well, I'm going to continue to call you and keep you up to date on this little saga you initiated. You'll no doubt be happy to hear that Mrs. Price was in the shop today. She bought a dress for her anniversary dinner. She told me she had heard about the 'incident' from Helen Deacon, who was actually there, and *she* said that one of the other ladies at her table actually said that the mother of the bride bought her dress at *my* shop. This is all your fault, Griffin, if my business suffers as a result of this.

"Now. See? I hope you're satisfied. I'm going to have to have a glass of sherry, I'm so worked up. Sleep well in your guilt-free, happy world."

Bloody hell. It was my fault if the business suffered, but guaranteed, if business picked up, I wouldn't get credit for it.

Beep.

"Griff, it's me." Jillian. "God, where are you, honey? You don't usually wait this long to call me. Anyway, I just wanted to warn you that mom's really pissed. She's pissed at the world—no clue why—but I have a feeling you're the scapegoat. Sorry, but I just wanted to warn you. Don't take it personally, okay? She's just, well, just being *her*. She'll get over it. Anyway, see ya. Call me, okay?"

My younger sister was forever my dearest friend. She was right. I usually talked to her every day. She sounded a bit down; Mom must be really getting to her.

Beep.

"Griff?" A throat clearing. "It's me—" *ahem* "—Calvin." As if I wouldn't recognise his voice! I heard music in the background, so I knew he was calling me from work. He worked at a really cool used record store.

Lucky him getting to listen to records all day. Sometimes I went there and hung out, and we would take turns closing our eyes and picking an album to listen to. That's how I'd discovered Jean Michel Jarre. Calvin went on.

"Listen, are we going to rehearse on Wednesday night? I mean, it's Tuesday tomorrow, and I kind of thought we should, you know, keep things going. Get back on that horse, so to speak. So we don't lose momentum. I mean, it's just one gig; it doesn't matter all that much. I mean, it matters, yeah, but I mean, we kept playing, and, well, I think for the short time we played, we sounded pretty damn good. In fact, when you picked up your acoustic and started playing, I was like . . . Wow. You sounded really good, honestly. I was kinda proud. Anyway, I know you were pretty upset. Don't let it get you down too much. The rest of us are still here, and we want to play. Don't let Snifter win." He paused. "Don't let Jason win." A sort of throat-clearing sound. "Call me, okay?"

Calvin. The voice of reason in a crazy world. Without him, I would probably be a puddle on the floor somewhere. That was really nice of him. And he was right too. About everything. Which was probably why my conscience chose this moment to start singing like Jiminy Cricket in my ear. *Dang it.* It was probably too late to call him now, but I'd for sure call him first thing in the morning. I took a gulp of G and T.

Beep. Bloody hell! I never get this many messages.

"Griffin, if you don't call me back, I don't know what I'll do!" Jason was crying this time—or pretending to. "I'll probably kill myself. Do you want that on your head? Well . . . good-bye." The phone rattled and there was one more tiny sob, to make his big finish as dramatic as possible.

Nice try, jerkoff.

Beep.

"Hey, Griffin Girl." I sat up and adjusted the phone on my ear. I did not want to risk missing a single word spoken by the caramel tone of that voice. "I have to tell you, today was one of the best rehearsals I've ever had. One of the best days, in fact. I really enjoy making music with you. You're super talented and I think the band'll go far. I—well, I can't tell you how glad I am that you joined us. Anyway, I'll see you tomorrow. G'night."

How I managed to get up and go to bed after that message, I don't know. I pretty much floated around my apartment. I forgot all about being scolded for my lateness in the morning. I forgot about my mother's berating, and I completely forgot the sting of Phoenix Riesling, or whatever the hell his name was, taking credit for my success.

I absolutely did *not* forget to set my alarm for 7:00 in the morning. There was no way I wanted to miss a single moment of potential work alongside Matteo.

The other thing I forgot about altogether was my intention to phone Calvin first thing in the morning.

6

Tuesday, May 8

Matteo didn't magically appear to drive me to work on Tuesday. He hadn't told me where he lived, so it was still a wonder to me that he had appeared the day before. I ate some cereal and rushed out the door, one guitar on my back and the others in my hands—I figured my twelve-string would add versatility—and yes, my cell phone made it into my jacket pocket this time, and my lunch went into the pouch in my guitar case. I tried not to bemoan the fact that a ride today would have been even better than a ride yesterday. I caught the bus to the train with all the other rush-hour commuters, a hazard to them with guitar cases pointing in all directions at once, but I did my best not to clock anyone. Several people glared at me on the train for having the nerve to take up more space than they felt I deserved, despite the care I was taking.

"Glad I don't have a double bass," I remarked with a friendly smile.

A woman crinkled her nose at me as if I smelled bad. I let it go.

The plan was to be at Salamander's way ahead of time because I'd have to cut out early to be at the music store by 4:00 for Dominic's lesson. (It was rebellious of me, and I felt sort of sick at the thought of it, but I felt less guilty than I would have if I hadn't been cheated out of my crème brûlée glory the day before.) I wondered what awesome dessert I'd come up with today and kind of looked forward to telling my dad about it. I bet he'd never have imagined one of his daughters—least of all me—would take after him. I lugged my gear off the bus and arrived at the restaurant at 8:30. It was dark and locked up.

I felt a little silly. Was the place open just for dinner? When a restaurant is open only in the evening, do people usually arrive this early in the morning? Perhaps not. What did I know? Was the restaurant open for lunch? I couldn't have told you what time Matteo and I had arrived the day before; I had stopped paying attention to anything but him, and you don't have to tell me how high school that sounds. I decided it was evidence of how icky Jason had been.

I went around the corner in search of a back door, but all I found was the parkade entrance. I peered in. It was pitch black. But that's how it had been when Matteo and I drove into it. *How is this even allowed?* I thought. *Aren't there, like, codes and bylaws about this sort of thing?* I braced myself and headed down the passageway, carefully sliding one guitar along the wall as a guide. It was like descending into a mine shaft, only darker. I looked behind me and could no longer see the light of day from the entrance. How far had I walked in such a short time?

I set my acoustic down and pulled out my cell phone and turned on its torch feature. The bright light was unable to pierce the blackness. I couldn't carry the phone and the guitar, so I left my guitar on the ground and went on a scouting mission, hoping a car wouldn't come along and crush it. As I crept deeper and deeper, the wall became damp and I heard a *drip-drip* which made me think of a cave. It smelled like wet stone too. I bashed my knee into something sticking out of the ground and almost tripped. I shone the torch closely along the thing I'd bumped into. It was about three feet high and narrow, a sort of cylindrical shape, growing out of the ground. It was rough to the touch, and even the ground no longer felt like concrete, but like stone. Oh, for crying out loud, a *stalagmite*?

In the utter blackness, I reached up above the thing and shone the meagre light from my phone on a similar structure hanging from the ceiling, dangling to about four feet above its lower partner. A drip of moisture let go of the stalactite and fell, splashing gently.

I am so done with this. I turned, went back, snatched up my guitar, and raced as fast as I could in the freakin' dark back to the entrance. When I reached it, I burst through the wall of black into the daylight as if I'd come through a curtain.

The place still looked locked up like a prison. I sat on the front step to wait for somebody.

By nine, I was still alone, and chilly, so I decided to grab a coffee. I wandered the streets a bit, heaving my guitars the whole way. I had a brief chat with a grizzled fellow sitting on a mangy-looking sleeping bag. He thought I should give him some money. Instead I bought him a coffee and a muffin and an apple, for which he thanked me, though I then had to convince him I wasn't after his shopping cart of treasures.

I found my way back to Salamander's. It was lit up like a Christmas display, and when I hurried inside, several heads attached to bodies sitting at a dining table turned to greet me. Rickenbacker rose, still in top hat and tail coat, and gave me a bow. I started to ask him about the torch thingie, but he interrupted me. "We've been missing you this morning, Miss Trowbridge."

I indicated the front of the restaurant. "But I got here early—"

"Never mind, off you go. I believe Chef has another delectable item he'd like our master pastry chef to create."

I didn't bother trying to protest, but soon got lost in the insane back corridor, finally found my destination, put my guitars in the rehearsal studio, and ran back to the kitchen.

Chef was making shortbread. He asked me to make mille-feuilles.

"What is that?" I asked.

Chef laughed as if I'd told an Eddie Izzard joke.

"No, seriously. I have no idea what that is."

But Chef's attention was back on other things.

Steven appeared at my side with a book entitled *The Origin and Signification of Scottish Surnames*. Ah yes, definitely a book that was sure to help. He plonked it on the work surface, opened it in the middle and flipped a few pages. On the left was a recipe for dog biscuits. On the right, mille-feuilles, a multi-layered dessert, kind of like napoleons. I took a deep breath. I thanked Steven and thought, *Yay*. My first experience with French puff pastry was bound to be an eventful one.

I read through the recipe. It didn't look too complicated, but it sure was going to take a long time. The dough needed to be folded over and over and refrigerated for two hours, folded again and refrigerated for another two hours. That had to happen a total of *four times*. There weren't enough hours in the day. How in hell could I get it done in time to leave *late* today, let alone early? I started calculating how long it would take me to get to the music store, teach a lesson, and come back. Could I fit it into one of the two-hour refrigeration periods?

My stomach already felt as if it had been folded over and over. I took another deep breath, pressed my lips together, and started hauling out ingredients and equipment.

"There is no way; there's just no way." Had I been able to enter the building when I'd first arrived, I might have stood a better chance.

By the time I'd finished getting stuff out, Steven had measured out all the dry ingredients. I added the butter, and he worked the dough with his hands as I poured ice water and lemon juice. I bent over the book to check the recipe. When I looked back, Steven had already begun rolling out the dough.

"Wow, you're quick. Have you made this before?"

Steven shook his head.

The music from the radio filtered through into my brain. It was *Yackety Sax*, the frenetic theme from *Benny Hill*. The other kitchen staff still looked like they'd been choreographed; today was just a new routine. It did not help my stress level.

"Could we change the radio station to hear something calmer?" I called out to anyone who would listen.

Two people stopped what they were doing and eyed me quizzically. "We don't have a radio," the short one said, and the taller one agreed.

I pointed to the air. "Can't you hear that?"

"Hear what?"

"What do you mean, you don't hear it?" I asked. "It's so loud. And all of you are—" I stopped as more of my coworkers stared at me and peered at me from behind each other. I decided it would be best if I didn't finish the sentence to point out that they were all moving like the "Toot Sweet" dancers in *Chitty Chitty Bang Bang*.

Steven looked sidelong at me (from under his longish bangs). I gleaned from this near-eye contact that I should not carry on.

I shrugged and stopped, but it was . . . yes, it was weird.

Beating the butter in the mixer was next on my list, so when Steven had rolled the dough to the right thickness and wrapped it in plastic, I could easily flatten the butter to the correct size. Both went into the fridge.

I got busy separating eggs for the cream filling. It had to completely cool before I could assemble the dessert, and I had two hours to kill before it would be time to fold it over and roll it out again. Steven put the milk onto the stove to heat. It was all going very well—surprisingly well—and I felt confident, like I might even be able to do this.

With the pastry cream in the refrigerator to cool, I decided to pop down to the rehearsal studio to see if the guys were ready to go through set one. Tension eased from my muscles as I moved farther away from the kitchen and closer to the studio. It was like going on vacation, driving away from the city out to some rural campground. With a bit of the thrill about playing music thrown in. The others were all set up and ready to go, and I wondered fleetingly what their other jobs in the restaurant were. But I didn't want to waste good playing time with a discussion about the restaurant, so I plugged in and tuned, and the drummer—I think his name was Bernard?—counted us in for the first song.

A short time later, Steven interrupted the rehearsal, which felt a bit like stepping on a LEGO, to say the dough was ready for folding and rolling.

That couldn't be right. "But it's supposed to be in there for two hours."

"We used the fast fridge," Steven said, which were the first words I had heard him say aloud.

"Oh." I'd heard of those, only I thought they were called something else. And I thought I'd put the trays in the regular fridge. Maybe it had a special setting?

The band looked at me with a question in their eyes.

"I'll be right back." I put my guitar on its stand and jogged with Steven down the hall to the kitchen. I don't know if I was just getting used to the place or what, but there seemed to be fewer twists and turns in the route. Anyhow we made it. Steven had pulled out the dough and the butter, and I followed the instructions on the recipe. I folded the dough around the butter and rolled it, folded it, rolled it, wrapped it up and put it back in the fridge. It sure looked like a regular fridge. Oh well. I had time to rehearse more while it chilled. The clock on the wall said 10:00.

Wait a minute, 10:00? I hadn't even gotten into the building until 9:30. How could it be only 10:00? I checked my watch. 10:00. My cell phone showed the same thing. Mystified, I went back to the rehearsal room.

"What time is it?" I asked.

Matteo looked at his watch. "Oh yeah, you have to leave a bit early today, right? Don't worry, it's only ten."

"Hunh. Well." I picked up my guitar warily, a little afraid it might, I dunno, turn into a flamingo or something. I forgot all about it, though, as we played through set two with such a level of perfection I was nearly bursting with the thrill of it. We took a few moments to work out some harmonies in *Walk of Life* and *Rocket Man*. Matteo's and my voices blended so well together the overtones made my spine tingle.

"Wow, that sounds great, you two," the drummer—I think his name was Shawn—said. Matteo was smiling sorta shyly at me, and I felt a glow like I'd had a glass of red wine. Music does that.

There was a knock on the door: Steven, returning to tell me the dough had chilled to the right temperature again. I looked at my watch. 10:30.

"How is it we just played through a forty-five-minute set, plus stopping to fix things and arrange harmony parts, in only half an hour? Is this place part of some loop in the space-time continuum?" I chuckled at my humour, though I was afraid I might sound a little hysterical.

The guys all looked at me, baffled.

"Griff," Matteo said in that caramel voice of his. "We've been in here for two hours."

I laughed, though all the hairs on my arms were standing at attention. "You're hilarious. Remember when I came back from the kitchen and asked what time it was, and you said it was only ten? Remember that? And why did the—the fast fridge take two hours this time?" I looked around for the hidden cameras. My voice was rising with my annoyance. I do *not* like being made fun of or made to look stupid, and this was pushing my limits.

The band shuffled their feet and cast glances around the room. Steven rocked back and forth in the doorway. Maybe they knew where the hidden cameras were. I was about ready to scream at somebody. Matteo came over to me, put his hands on my upper arms, and gazed down at me with his dreamy blue eyes.

"You must have had a late night or something. It was shortly after eight when you asked what time it was."

When Matteo touched me and looked at me like that, he could tell me we were in a castle floating through the air, and I'd believe him. I shivered and blushed, damn it, both because I felt a bit silly over my mistake and also because, god, I was in love with him. A little voice in the back of my mind said, *No no no, this is all wrong!* but I couldn't make sense of it, so I forced a laugh.

"Heh, okay, well, thanks for your patience, you guys. I'll just . . . go deal with this dough thing and be right back." I ducked under my guitar strap.

Matteo brushed my hair with his fingertips and said, "You're gonna knock this one out of the park again, babe."

Babe? He called me "babe." I could hardly breathe. How my legs-of-jelly carried me to the kitchen, I am not sure, but I got there, folded and rolled the pastry again, and returned.

The rest of the rehearsal was terrific, especially the part where we worked on the electrifying five-part harmony in *Lovin' Touchin' Squeezin'*. The keyboard player—was it Quentin?—was brilliant on those bluesy lines. I sang lead and when we got to the "nah-nah" bit, the guys joined in one at a time, adding another layer of sound with each repeat of the phrase. It sounded so glorious, I signalled to sing through the section a couple of times with all five voices before we finally sang the last few bars a capella. The sound ended abruptly, and the vibrations hovered in the space for what seemed like ages, bouncing off the walls and ceiling. Then there were hoots and cheers from everyone, and we grinned at each other like clowns and Matteo hugged me, carefully so we didn't smash guitars, and I didn't think I had ever been so happy. Tears filled my eyes, and I laughed with glee and felt as high as the space station.

When Steven showed up, I didn't even resent him, though it was tough to tear myself away. I was on top of the world, and after two more sets of half-hour-two-hour blocks, my pastry was ready to be turned into a gigantic sheet of mille-feuilles. I rolled it onto parchment paper, baked it, and cut it, and Steven helped me assemble it into three layers of pastry with two layers of cream in between. Then it could chill until it was time to be served.

It was 2:30 (if time was to be believed on this day), nearly time for me to catch the bus if I was to be at the music store for a 4:00 lesson. I spoke in a low voice to my invaluable assistant. "Steven, can I put you in charge of cutting this into serving sizes?" I asked. "I have to leave early today."

The swinging doors banged open, and Phoenix walked in dressed like a cross between Robin Hood and a leopard. I happened, just then, to notice that the music through the radio changed to *Tubular Bells*, also known as the theme from *The Exorcist*.

"What did you just say?" He yelled it quietly, if you can imagine what that sounds like.

He was, apparently, my boss. But yesterday he had taken credit for the dessert I had made, which he had previously criticized me for. Today I was determined to not be intimidated by him. Besides, I was still riding the wave of an amazing rehearsal. My determination did not, however, neutralize the tremolo effect in my voice.

"I have to help a friend by teaching his guitar students because he broke his hand. It just came up, and he really needs my—"

"You have a commitment to Salamander's."

Maintaining my composure admirably, I pulled my voice into a deliberate, calm state, though my hands were shoved in my pockets to hide their shaking. "I know and I have already finished what I needed to do for Salamander's today. Not only have I rehearsed with the band, but I made the dessert Chef asked—"

Phoenix put his hands on his hips like a petulant eight-year-old. "Oh yes? And what is this creation you've produced?"

"Mille-feuilles," I said. "With puff pastry and everything."

He looked doubtful. "Show me."

Wondering why he had to be such an ass and wishing Rickenbacker were my immediate supervisor, I opened the fridge door to reveal my masterpiece.

"What. Is. That?" Phoenix didn't look angry. He looked shocked.

I followed his gaze into the fridge. Where previously the sheets of pastry had taken up three individual shelves of the industrial-sized refrigerator, they now took up the entire appliance. The pastries now were models of jagged mountains, with layer upon layer of colours, depicting the way the earth's surface had been formed by massive earthquakes at the dawn of time. The layers of pastry cream Steven and I had so painstakingly spread were no longer horizontal, but thrust up into accurate representations of the layers of sediment that settled throughout evolutionary history. I had a strange notion that if I were to bite into it, I would find fossils of ancient shellfish and bugs.

Phoenix's voice was breathless with awe. "Steven, these are amazing."

"Steven?" My jaw, which had dropped to my chest, snapped shut. This jerk took all the credit last night, and today he was giving it all to my assistant? "Sure he helped, but . . ." I looked around; Steven was nowhere to be seen, which meant . . .

"Can we get these out on the counter and take photos for our poster board out front, Steven?"

"Uh, my name's *Griffin*. Remember, we went through this yesterday?"

"Yeah, whatever. Why are you here again?"

Asshole. "Rickenbacker hired me to be in the band. And to make dessert, even though—"

"So why aren't you?"

"What?" Ire was about to get the better of me. It caused me to say things I wouldn't otherwise say. "I am! I just finished a rehearsal with the band, and I made the pastry in between."

"Why aren't you getting it out of the fridge like I asked you?"

I stared for a moment. Was he for real? My mouth opened then closed again. I stepped toward the fridge, but something lumpy was pressing into my ankle, my sock maybe. I reached down to adjust it. Instead, the leather sheath and the knife found themselves in my hand again. I gasped, and half dropped, half flung them to the floor and kicked them under the counter. My hands were shaking when I straightened up to pull out the pastry mountains. I nearly let the first tray slide to the floor as I turned from the fridge to the work surface. Phoenix, the moron, kept getting in my way and didn't offer to help. The bloody trays were enormous, and puff pastry was, today at least, as heavy as devil's food cake.

Finally I had all eight trays—How did three trays become eight? And how had they all fit in the fridge?—spread out on the huge worktable.

"Who normally takes the photos?" I asked.

"I do." A large camera suddenly appeared in his hand, one of those old-fashioned ones with an accordion for a lens. "How about you stand behind the table and be in the photo too?"

Well, this was a welcome change from yesterday, although I was getting a little anxious to catch my bus. I positioned myself and made myself smile as he set up the shot.

Without warning, he pulled out a hose from exactly nowhere and squeezed the nozzle, sending a high-powered jet of water right through all the mountains of pastry, spraying it all onto me. I shrieked and tried to both duck and save the dessert. In the same moment, the flash went *pop* and the shutter made a loud *click*. He continued to spray the mille-feuilles and me, all the while squealing with maniacal laughter.

When the hose finally stopped, I found myself on the table kneeling amongst the pastry and cream. I was covered in it. In my right hand, I was brandishing the knife, the very sharp point aimed for Phoenix Reysing's left eye. Fear squeezed my throat as I stared at it, glued to my shaking hand. Where the hell had it come from? A terrible squealing growl issued from my throat.

The other kitchen staff had frozen still, staring at the wall away from me. Phoenix, on the other hand, was smirking.

"What's that you've got there?" he asked as if it wasn't obvious.

"I don't know where it came from!" My whole body shook and the knife slipped out of my hand into the mess of puff pastry.

"What the bloody hell did you do that for?" I crawled off the table. I was covered in flaky, creamy muck and very close to tears. Wet pastry and cream dripped from my hair. I had to blink it out of my eyes. It stuck my shirt to my torso, and my underpants felt like I'd peed myself. I unconsciously licked the back of my hand; the stuff was delicious.

He snorted. "You should've seen your face!" He fucking-well *giggled* and walked out of the kitchen.

Was this his idea of initiation? A hazing ritual? What was the best way to take it? I sure as hell didn't feel like laughing.

"I'm not doing anything about this!" I screamed after him, indicating the mess of my culinary efforts. I dug through the muck for the knife so whoever did clean it up wouldn't impale themself on it. It was nowhere to be found. My pulse pounded in my throat, and I struggled to regain control of my breathing. Where was it? In my rage had I imagined it? A dollop of cream dropped off my hair onto my shoulder. I whipped a towel off a hanger and wiped my face and hair, clawing back tears of fury and fear for my sanity. What on earth did this psycho have against me? The towel saturated, I looked in every cupboard in the kitchen for more.

"Where are the towels?" I asked the room at large. The staff turned to me as if it made no sense at all that I should need a towel.

"In the laundry." They spoke in unison, like a Greek chorus.

"Every single towel this restaurant owns is in the laundry?" What kind of insane place was this? "Oh, never mind. I have to go." I quaked with anger as I pushed the door into the back hallway.

Part of me hoped I would run into Matteo so I could tell him how horrible Phoenix had treated me—again. The other part figured just seeing Matteo would make me bawl my eyes out. The maze of the back hall with its staggeringly garish diamond patterns did nothing to improve my mood, but I finally slopped my way to the rehearsal room. Nobody was there. Where had they all gone off to? Working in the restaurant, I supposed. Whatever. It was just as well Matteo wasn't there as I grabbed my guitar. But looking around that terrific, well-equipped rehearsal space was nearly as good as a shower and a nap. I imagined I could still hear the reverberations of those five-part "nah-nahs," which effectively smoothed the peaks and valleys of my rattled emotions. I was more at home in this room than I was, well, at home. The drum kit, the guitars on stands with the steel pickups reflecting the mood lighting, the microphone stands, one of which was mine . . .

"It's all. About. The *music*," I insisted aloud.

I didn't see my bandmates in the restaurant as I passed through, but that didn't mean anything. Having made my way to the entrance, I stepped outside into the cool spring afternoon air. On the pavement stood a sandwich board, inviting patrons to come to Salamander's for yummy desserts and lots of fun. There was a photo.

To my shock and horror, the photo was the very one Phoenix had just taken of me. I looked like a cross between a Pekingese dog and a hairless cat, with a crown of cream and a flaky pastry cape. My expression resembled Shelley Duvall with an axe smashing through her door. I supposed it *might* look like a fun place, worthy of a great laugh, even—if you weren't the one in the photo who'd had it done to you. I had no idea what I could possibly have done to Phoenix to prompt him to be so awful.

But then, it wouldn't do to look like I was a person who took stuff too seriously. I remembered a coworker I'd had in a restaurant when I was sixteen. A manager had come into the kitchen one day when we were running off our feet and stressed because it was so busy. This manager popped a balloon, surprising the crap out of the entire kitchen staff. We were startled as hell, but then we all laughed. All but this one fellow who got pissy and took the incident as a personal affront. The laugh had broken the tension, but he piled it back on. It wasn't the only time he insisted on assuming the role of victim, and the result was that people generally didn't respect him. I couldn't afford to develop a reputation like that.

Fine. I could laugh.

Wet, sticky, and still dripping with pastry and cream, I gripped the handle of my acoustic guitar case and headed for the bus. When it pulled up and the doors opened, I stepped onto the bottom step. The bus driver said, "Nope. Get off. You're too mucky." In shock, I backed off wordlessly. He pulled away and my body sagged beneath the unfairness of the whole wide world.

I put my guitar down and rolled around on the grassy boulevard. The homeless dude watching me looked hungry, and I wished I could offer him some excess mille-feuille, but I didn't think he'd take it the way I meant it. He looked nervous and staggered away, poor fellow.

When the next bus came, I was wet and mucky but not dripping. This driver let me on without a word. I vowed to drink a toast to her next time I had a beverage, which would likely be as soon as possible. I stood so as not to muck up the seats, and when I switched onto the train, I found a stray newspaper and spread it out so I could sit on it. I'm just that thoughtful.

I arrived at the music store by a quarter to four. I was dry but crusty and sticky.

"I like what you've done with your hair," Brian said. He sounded almost sincere.

"Ha," I said moodily. "Very funny."

His eyes widened. "I mean it, it looks really good."

"You're crazy." But I peeked into a mirrored sign on the wall. It didn't look half bad.

"Oh," I said.

"You're touchy today. What's up?"

I tried to explain how I'd taken on another part-time job and the boss was irksome, but then a customer needed his attention, so I didn't get to finish. I was kind of hoping I'd be able to hint that I'd like to take some time off, but no, I couldn't do that to him.

My 4:00-changed-from-6:00-because-of-a-tournament-game lesson, Dominic, arrived and we secluded ourselves in my room. Things went well, except when he said,

"You smell like sour milk."

At home I logged in to my support group forum before I did anything else. I reminded them about Rickenbacker, and told them about the band and the restaurant. I hesitated before the next part.

> *This is going to sound really strange. I made crème brûlée*
> *that turned into castles and dragons. I made puff pastry*
> *that turned into models of the Thompson Canyon, and then*

my boss wanted to take my picture with it, but sprayed me with a hose. Am I out of my mind? I really want to play with this band, but I don't know if I can handle working for this jerk. Oh, and there's this knife that keeps appearing, even though I'm really sure I put it away. Thoughts?

~WingedLion

Let's see if they'd be able to help with all that.

Interlude - May 8

"It was terrifying! Don't make me do it again," Phoenix pleaded.

Rickenbacker stopped mid-pace, hands clasped behind his tailcoat, and squished his stockinged toes in the faux fur. He pivoted and planted his scrutiny on his friend. Had he just heard what he thought he heard?

"Please do repeat that."

Phoenix dropped his head into the cradle of his arms. He was curled up in the armchair, one knee up by his shoulder. He looked like a grasshopper who had lost an argument with a brick wall.

"Yes? Go ahead," Rickenbacker said as if drawing a confession from a child, which was very close to what he was doing. "I'm listening."

"Mm mmbmhm," Phoenix whimpered from within his elbows.

Rickenbacker took a couple of steps toward the cowering form and bent down, hands on his knees.

"Try again. Out loud this time."

Phoenix raised his head, and a wail issued forth from his throat. "I'm sca-ared!" He flung his arms wide within the confines of his curled-up leopard-print legs. "It's so easy for you to stalk back and forth and be all excited about our progress and so forth, all pleased with yourself. You're not the one staring at the point of a knife, wondering when it's going to skewer you and hang you over a fire for the fat to drop and make the flames flare up, thereby bringing your exterior to an overzealous crisp."

Rickenbacker straightened. "Is that what this is about? My dear fellow, this is perfectly safe. Do you think the Tournament would make us do anything that was actually life threatening?"

Phoenix's glower forced Rickenbacker backward to sink into the sofa on the other side of the room.

When Phoenix spoke, it was barely above a whisper, and the intensity was life threatening. "What about the dandelions?"

Rickenbacker waved a hand. "Oh, pish tosh. The dandelions were never a real threat."

Phoenix unfolded himself and his feet landed on the floor with a thud that was dampened by the red shag and faux fur. "Says you, the one of us who didn't have to face down a whole field of them! They were in bloom, and some of them had *gone to seed*." His white-knuckled hands gripped the arms of the chair.

"All you had to do was run through the field to the other side and grab the goat. What was so difficult about that?" Rickenbacker couldn't believe his ears.

Phoenix pouted. "I might have got my trousers dirty."

A bad, bad feeling had crept into Rickenbacker's consciousness. "What?"

Phoenix shrank under Rickenbacker's stare. "And I don't like those seeds blowing around."

"What?"

"They make me skittish!"

Rickenbacker pushed himself forward to sit on the edge of the cushiony couch. "Do you mean to tell me we lost the Tournament because of a few *dandelions*?"

Phoenix withered and whimpered. "I felt my life was in danger."

Rickenbacker widened his eyes to express his incredulity.

Phoenix couldn't retreat any further into his chair. "I want that title back," he whinged.

"Then you, my friend, have to do what is necessary."

Phoenix nodded meekly.

Rickenbacker slapped his palms on his lap. "Let me hear no more of this."

"All right."

Rickenbacker rose and in the few strides it took him to get to the wine decanter on the mirrored desk, his ire had dwindled. He poured himself some of the purple froth and didn't offer any to Phoenix. The twit could get his own wine.

"That was a nice touch, using the hose," Rickenbacker said by way of showing forgiveness.

Phoenix accepted the opening and perked up. He even giggled a little with a self-congratulatory tone. "The look on her face was priceless. I thought we had won at that very moment. Any second she was about to come at me." He shuddered at the thought.

"You have set up the relationship perfectly." Rickenbacker dipped his finger in the creamy foam at the top of his cup.

"She's a very nice person. I really wish we could just be friends."

Just then a figure appeared in the doorway. The MGC came in and sat down on the floor by the desk.

"Come to think of it, that she is such a nice person may work in our favour." Rickenbacker saw the danger of letting Phoenix become sentimental and insisted on keeping the discussion on track. "I believe we earn bonus points for our choice of candidate, given the inherent challenges. And if you continue to push her, she's sure to break at just the right moment, if not before. Early would be all right; I believe bonus points are awarded for that too." He pointed at Phoenix. "You just be sure to be in the right place at the right time. We don't want her using it on a table or something."

Phoenix threw his head back and laughed, evidence that he was feeling more positive. "Have no fear; she hates me."

"Matteo" scrunched his fingers in the faux-fur rug.

Phoenix instantly sobered. "Though I still don't know why it has to be me and not you."

If Rickenbacker hadn't been looking right at him, he would have rolled his eyes. But he wanted to show he was a compassionate fellow, so he held off. "I told you, dear chap. My role, set up from the start, was of the kind one, the *fatherly* figure, if you like, the one she could come to if she needed to talk about . . . the way she's being treated at work, for instance. It would be far too much to get her to turn on me so abruptly. Besides," and Rickenbacker knew well how to time his little bits of flattery, "you are so well suited to the role you have taken on. I could never pull it off the way you are. You're, well, you are a genius if I ever met one."

Phoenix shrugged and nodded ever so modestly. "I do have a certain style. And hey, if it means I get to spray our Other World partner with a hose, I have much to be thankful for."

The MGC had fixed his gaze on the spot where the sofa met the carpet. Perhaps a crawling insect had caught his eye. Rickenbacker wondered what went through his Magically Generated mind when he wasn't playing music.

"I should think we would not employ the same tack again," he suggested gently.

Phoenix stared a *duh* at him.

"My personal favourite detail," Rickenbacker poured himself more wine, "is the 'Scorific' I applied. The soundtrack of her life is how I think of it. You've heard it said there is a song for everything? That is the Scorific. Music to suit her every mood, music to accompany her experience."

"Did you invent the spell?"

Rickenbacker struck a pose and raised his cup. "Indeed." He bowed. "Just a little something I've been working on. It was an idea I had, you know, back in the day, as it were. It had been percolating in my mind, and I've been tweaking it for the last few months. I had no idea I would be able to use it to such advantage in this Tournament."

"How lucky."

"And it was a simple thing to apply." He half-shrugged with extraordinary modesty. "I gave it to our MGC to pass onto our OWP once we had her agreement. He simply shook her hand, and the spell was triggered."

"How do you generate its energy, though? You can't follow her around."

"True, and very perceptive of you, my friend. It feeds off—and I think this is very clever, indeed—her own stress and anxiety. Which it is, of course, designed to increase."

"You mean it causes stress and anxiety, which then give it energy to continue to do it?"

"Exactly." Now was a good time to stroll about the room and look impressive. Rickenbacker did so. "I have a theory on how to create a perpetual-motion machine using this very principle, but so far I haven't figured out how to manage it without the separate recipient/source. A true perpetual-motion machine would give off its own energy, which it would also feed off of, and would not require a living creature to feel the anxiety which would feed it. I am close to it and would like to acquire a—

"But never mind." He waved a hand and turned his attention back to Phoenix. "I do so wish I *could* follow her around, as you suggested. To see if it has the desired effect." Certainly not so that Rickenbacker could congratulate himself or celebrate his own success.

"Can we at least do a Mood Check?" Phoenix said.

Rickenbacker cocked his head to the side. "Yes, good idea." He was feeling generous enough to give Phoenix credit for *something*. The Mood Check was a useful, if limited, tool similar to taking a person's temperature. "I should be able to tune in fairly frequently and take a reading. It won't tell me any details about what is happening to her or why she is feeling a certain way, but it will identify her mood. It should give us a small hint of our progress."

Phoenix nodded. "I have to say the Scorific is a clever touch."

Rickenbacker bowed again, raised his cup in a toast, and drank. "I have also unleashed a Prankster on her, which I hid in the business card I handed to her when we met. It is a tournament-sanctioned spell, which will last only for the duration of this tournament, and will take care of adding a few trifling Salamanderian delights in her vicinity, some oddities, if you will, that will cause her some confusion. Keep her questioning her soundness of mind. I cannot keep track of it, any more than I can keep track of the Scorific's music in her head, but I am certain we will witness the results. Just another little thing that I hope will add to her discomfort and edginess."

"Which is good for our purposes."

"Exactly."

Phoenix squirmed. "But I still don't completely like it. What will happen to me?"

Rickenbacker had no idea. For the sake of simplification, he brushed his friend's concern off as he lowered himself onto the couch. "Oh, the implement will probably just disappear . . . or something."

Phoenix said, "Ulp. 'Probably'?"

"Yes, yes. But consider how much work I have put into our team's effort. The Prankster, the Scorific, setting up the periodic Reality Scans, not to mention our MGC. Why, I even found our Other World Partner! It's only right you should take on your fair share, and with your role, I believe we achieve balance."

Phoenix grunted. He pointed to the MGC. "And him?"

Rickenbacker raised his cup again. "He," —he paused for dramatic effect—" *He* is everything I could have hoped for. He is a marvellous musician, and it's obvious our candidate loves being in the band as a result. The juxtaposition with the kitchen work gives us much to congratulate ourselves for."

"Don't you think it would have been better if she didn't like playing with the band quite so much? Maybe we would have won already."

Rickenbacker shook his head with utter certainty. "No, no, my friend. If she didn't like the band, she would simply quit and leave altogether. The music is what keeps her here."

"Won't she be surprised at the end of it all!" Phoenix got up and paced the room, rubbing his hands, his face an illustration of "eagerness" perfect for a picture dictionary.

"All we need to do is stay on track. Our candidate is primed. Or at least, she's getting there. So long as we make the deadline—"

"—and don't break any rules."

"—and do not break any rules, we stand a very good chance. A very good chance, indeed. You must make sure you're always nearby in those moments of tension, of course—"

"Of course!" Phoenix interjected with bravado.

"—and that cup and title will be ours. We could not have planned it better."

7

Wednesday, May 9

On Wednesday morning I felt so wiped out, I had to drag myself out of bed and did not feel motivated to go to Salamander's at all.

I checked for responses from my support group.

PowerofNo: *Remember to practise self-care, WingedLion. Stay balanced.*

KeepSmiling: *What colour was the hose?*

NerdBird27: *You made puff pastry? That's amazing,*

WingedLion!

These were not as helpful as I'd hoped for, but PowerofNo was right. *Stay balanced.* That's what I needed to do.

The guy upstairs was playing Johnny Cash's version of *Hurt* on a loop. What was going on in his life to drive him to listen to that over and over? Poor fellow. In the end, that's what got me moving because obviously he was worse off than me. After all, I was doing what I loved: playing music with a terrific band. Once I reminded myself it was all about the music, I was able leave the apartment. See? Balance.

I left *Hurt* behind, but on the bus, someone's iPod, or phone or other music listening device, must have been cranked because I could hear *Every Breath You Take* as clear as day. I looked all around but couldn't see where it was coming from. Good thing I like the song, or I'd have gotten mad. As it was, it was mildly weird, but weird was becoming more or less my new normal. I think it was a bit much that whoever was playing it followed me to the train and listened to the song over and over about 437 times, so that by the time I arrived at work, my limbs were jittery and I kept glancing over my shoulder.

As I turned the corner, I saw the sandwich board outside the restaurant and almost wished I still had the knife on me; I would slash the shit out of that damned photo. But Phoenix was lucky because the photo had been removed. I walked in—I had chosen the correct arrival time today. Go me!— to be greeted by Rickenbacker hastening toward me through the empty dining room, his coattails flying behind him.

"Griffin, my dear!" He took me by the upper arms and kissed both cheeks, kind of European style.

"Hello, Rickenbacker?" I said with cheerful uncertainty.

"You culinary genius, you. I knew you were the right choice."

"Umm, what?"

"The dessert you created yesterday was an absolute *hit* with our patrons. It sold out in two hours, even the vast quantity you made. And such an amazing sculpted delight it was! Many of our customers recognised certain sections as particular mountain ranges they've passed in their travels throughout our province. I have to say, my favourite portion was the one resembling that section of the Fraser Canyon between Lytton and Skihist, you know, on the far side of the river from the highway? Well, of course you know. You created it, after all!" He bowed at me.

It was too much. "But Rickenbacker, Phoenix destroyed the dessert!"

"Nonsense."

"But he did! He sprayed it with a hose, and me too, for that matter. When I left here, my pastry was an enormous, slathery mess all over the worktable, and my bus driver didn't let me on until I'd rolled around in the grass like a dog."

Rickenbacker smiled, shaking his head in a kind, patronizing manner that put me off. He curled his arm across my shoulders and guided me through the darkened dining room with its red-upholstered wooden chairs and dark wood tables. It smelled like burned soup. "Ah, Griffin. Quite a cutup is our Phoenix. Doesn't he just have the nuttiest sense of humour? It's such a delight. He's always pulling stunts and causing mayhem. You must have heard the story that circulated for months about Phoenix turning up at William and Kate's engagement party . . . by jumping out of a giant cake, wearing nothing but a fig leaf!"

Rickenbacker chuckled and fake-slapped his thigh in a mechanical way. "But I do believe that story is apocryphal."

I was so confused. I would have sworn upon my life that the day before I had been the knife-wielding cake top on a disaster of dessert. I had *not* dreamt it. There was no way I had imagined that nasty bus ride, nor the way my guitar student turned his nose up at the smell. And yet apparently my creation had elicited high praise from the customers. Phoenix's behaviour baffled me, and Rickenbacker's inconsistent dialogue confused the hell out of me . . .

"It was too bad you weren't here to receive the ovation from the crowd," Rickenbacker went on. He patted my shoulder. "They cried out 'Chef! Chef!' for quite some time and were disappointed that you had gone."

I rolled my eyes. "Why didn't Phoenix just take the credit like he did on Monday?"

"How can you say such a thing? Phoenix has a cabin in the Kootenays."

With which unrelated remark Rickenbacker deposited me near the kitchen and took his leave, disappearing into the unlit gloom. I stared after him and blinked with my bitterness and bewilderment. What was going on in this place? Were they trying to make me question my reason?

I dropped my guitar and jacket off, and my heels dragged as I took the last few steps to the kitchen door. What would it be today? I took a preparatory deep breath and pushed on the door. The kitchen was a bevy of activity. They seemed to be training new kitchen staff; a few of the cooks were shadowing younger folk, making the space feel quite a bit smaller than usual. Cramped, in fact. Standard kitchen sorts of sounds issued forth, instructions and requests of cooks to each other, the clanging and clattering of dishes and tools. Everything as one would expect. *Hmm.*

My instruction was Black Forest cake. Two of them. Great. Another thing I had never made. My pal Steven already had the recipe out on the counter (a single sheet of regular paper, printed on a regular printer, double-sided), for which I thanked him as I gave it a study. We would double the recipe.

"Uh-oh," I said. "This says to soak the cherries in the kirsch overnight." I turned to Steven, who was staring at the floor, his hair hanging over his forehead like a curtain. In his hands he held out a jar of something that looked an awful lot like cherries. I took it and opened it. The sweet aroma of the cherry brandy was stunning. "Wow! That smells awesome."

"I did it last night."

I set the jar on the counter. "Wait—what? You vanished last night."

Steven nodded silently.

What was I thinking? What was the point of questioning him? Did it matter? We had our kirsch-soaked cherries, and that was the main thing. Fine. Cool.

Steven sifted dry ingredients while I creamed the butter and sugar and added the eggs and vanilla. I put Steven in charge of prepping the cherry filling while I mixed the cake batter and poured it into pans. It needed to bake for only twenty minutes.

"Steven, can I please leave you in charge of taking the cakes out when they're done?" I washed my hands and hung up my apron. "They need to be removed from the pans, then poke holes in them with a toothpick, and pour the kirsch on top so it can soak in. We can assemble them this afternoon."

It was with profound relief that I took my leave of the kitchen and braved the labyrinthine service corridor. The rehearsal studio was my haven, the only place I felt safe in this building. Matteo was there, practising a tricky riff over and over. His face lit up like a rock concert stage when he saw me. Stress melted off of me like candle wax. I didn't even feel like telling him about what had happened yesterday. I was less annoyed, so why bring it all back up and ruin the current mood?

I warmed up playing the opening of *Mood for a Day* just quietly. It was a good finger workout, but I didn't want to be, you know, show-offy. When the others were ready, I switched to my twelve-string, and like magic the last vestiges of my anger and discombobulation evaporated when I strummed the opening of *Give a Little Bit*. The bright, jangling chords were always a mood-lifter, as was the message of the song, but with this band? When the drums came in and Matteo joined me in unison on the lyrics, it was a rush like I imagined bungee jumping would be. And then from out of nowhere, the keyboard player—Victor?—pulled out a sax and blew me away with his solo.

Rehearsal was breathtaking. Even the minor slips we had tweaked the day before went flawlessly. We tightened up the segues between songs, where we didn't plan to say anything but move seamlessly from one song into the next. It's surprising how tricky that can be sometimes, to get your brain to change style and tempo smoothly. Kind of like changing gears in a car with manual transmission, you don't want the transition to lurch. My brain seemed to have decided to play nicely today. It helped that the bass player—Dwayne?—was able to communicate with me so clearly that, well, it was like he was right inside my head with me, we were so in sync.

I had never looked forward to a gig so much! I was less nervous than ever before because I had so much confidence in us as a band. On the other hand, I was more nervous than ever before because I wanted so much for this to go perfectly, to prove to the band—and to myself—that their choice was the right one. I worried Thursday night would be replete with all the mistakes and screw-ups I hadn't made in rehearsal.

On the whole, though, I was feeling pretty confident about everything when I tore myself away to go back to the kitchen.

The swinging door made a satisfying *thunk* as I bashed it open. All the cooks and Chef hovered over a dish of something, like medical students examining a patient. Steven was whipping cream. What a swell guy he turned out to be. I watched momentarily while the cooks all laughed about whatever it was they were doing, and Steven actually looked right up at me. He looked away again, but I celebrated the fact that he'd made real eye contact. It's the little things, you know.

"All right, Steven, let's get building some Black Forest cakes."

We spread cherry filling and placed layers of chocolaty goodness and spread more filling and dolloped whipped cream until we had two impressive cakes. Nothing had gone wrong, and I proudly patted my assistant on the shoulder.

The other kitchen staff rushed about working on their own creations, stirring and slicing things. The tunes were cranked through the speaker system, as usual, with songs like *Sugar Sugar* and *Pour Some Sugar on Me* featuring prominently.

"If we don't get some new subject matter in the tunes, I'm gonna cry!" I said with a laugh.

Candy Man came to an end as I finished washing my hands, and the next song on the playlist was, coincidentally, Elvis singing *I'm Gonna Sit Right Down and Cry*.

A severe case of the willies rippled through me.

At least this time I wasn't the only one who could hear the music. To my surprise, my hitherto quiet and shy assistant, Steven, stopped what he was doing and hopped up onto the work table, where he launched into a terrific impression of the King. My instinct was to move the cakes to a different counter, so I did. The entire staff, myself included, got a huge kick out of watching him, right up until Steven jumped down, dropped to the floor and started breakdancing. Legs flew in all directions, knocking people over and sending carts, trays, and equipment flying.

"Steven, cut it out!" I yelled as I placed my body like a shield in front of the precious cakes to prevent any utensils from damaging them.

"I can't help it!" he cried. "I have to break to Elvis." I dodged a ladle that came perilously close to the side of my head and managed to deflect it away from the cake. Then the song stopped, and Steven righted himself and backed into me. I lost my balance. My foot slipped out from under me, and with one arm, I grabbed Steven to right myself. That arm pulled Steven into one cake, and my free arm knocked into the other. Now we were both covered in chocolate cake, cream, and cherry goo.

"Damn it all to hell!" I yelled. "No more Elvis through those speakers!" Steven sheepishly helped me to my feet and handed me a towel. I groaned in dismay when I examined the cakes just as Phoenix entered. The man's timing was disturbing.

He took one look at the mess and rolled his eyes, making little scoffing noises. "This is the brilliant creation you've come up with today? I have to say you are the most careless, irresponsible individual I have ever met."

"It was an accident," I said in Steven's defence.

Phoenix threw up his hands. "Oh! And there you go, blaming it on your subordinate. How typical!"

"I'm *not* blaming him, that's the—" I wiped my hand on the towel, and when I pulled it out, my fingers were clenched around the knife that I had dropped into a mound of ooey gooey flakiness the day before. "What the *hell*?" Incredulity came out in a shriek.

Phoenix's eyebrow rose. "Clean up this mess." He walked out.

I slapped the towel onto the floor with a new understanding of what it means to "throw in the towel," and slammed the knife into a drawer. "Stay," I told it, my hand quivering.

In another uncharacteristic move, I heeded my instinct.

"Steven? I am going back to rehearsal. You are going to clean this up and fix those." I pointed at the cakes. "Got it?"

My assistant nodded sheepishly and I left.

"Nervous?" Matteo put his arm across my shoulders, resulting in a very different effect from when Rickenbacker began my day the same way. Whereas I had wanted to shrink away from Rickenbacker's suspect kindness, Matteo's arm was warm like a hot water bottle and fit like a toque, but a toque that sent giddiness fluttering around my shoulders, down my arms, and into my belly. Matteo's arm coaxed a goofball sort of smile out of me. It was evening and we'd spent the afternoon going over minute details and perfecting entrances and song endings. We walked through the dining room toward the door.

"A little."

"Don't be."

I shrugged but only a little because I didn't want him to think I wanted him to move his arm. "I can't help it. I want to be perfect, and I'm afraid everything's going to go wrong."

He laughed a little, and I didn't feel like he was laughing at me. "I know what you mean."

"You do?" How could this god of music be nervous?

"Of course. I'm not perfect."

"Coulda fooled me."

"You're funny. No, I'm pretty confident and I feel great about what we're doing, but I always get nervous before a gig. That I'll mess up the lyrics, or I'll play the wrong chord right in the middle of a song, or I'll play the wrong ending . . ."

As Matteo listed all the possible things that could go wrong, I got to giggling because he was right: all musicians feel this way before a gig, and by the time we reached the door, we were both laughing our heads off.

I told him about the fateful night—only four nights ago—when Jason had launched into his feedback-ridden thrasher solo. "The look on the bride's face was priceless," I said. "I mean, what Jason did was awful, and I'm still plenty mad at him, but in retrospect, it was kinda funny." In that moment, it was true.

We leaned against the wall by the door, facing each other, wiping away tears of mirth.

"But you know, Griff?"

God, I loved it when he called me that. "What?"

He smiled sorta shyly, his eyes downcast but peering at me. "I'm glad it happened."

My heart skipped a beat, which sounds cliché, but sorry, that's what it did. "Yeah?"

He ran his hand down the length of my arm and took my hand in his very soft, warm one. "Because if that gig had gone well, I wouldn't be standing here with you right now." He caressed the back of my hand with his thumb. It was like being mildly electrocuted.

"And you know something else? I know this gig isn't going to be like that. This gig is going to be awesome." He ran a feather-touch fingertip down my cheek, and the ripple effect carried on all the way through my body. Oh god, he was about to kiss me. He leaned down and whispered conspiratorially, "I know this gig is going to be awesome because I'll be playing with you. And you and I . . . we're terrific together." He smiled again, warmly this time. "Don't you think so?"

I tried to nod but didn't seem to have control of my muscles. I managed to whisper, "Yeah."

He kissed me on the cheek, ever so softly, like the breath of a butterfly, stroked my hair again, and was gone.

I swear I stood there for a full five minutes before I found the energy to push myself away from the wall. I swear I floated all the way home and didn't even need the bus. I also swear my cheek was still tingling from the feather-light touch of his lips by the time I got home. I swear I ate something before flopping into bed, but I couldn't tell you what it was.

I swear it was 3:00 in the morning when I awoke, bolt upright in bed, upon realising that not only had I missed rehearsal with my own band, but I hadn't even returned Calvin's phone call the day before.

8

Thursday, May 10

I tossed the blankets aside and wearily dug my cell phone out of my jacket pocket, where it had been for a couple of days. The battery was almost dead, so I plugged it in and flopped into the armchair, pressing a gajillion buttons. Sure enough, there he was.

"Hey, Griff. It's me. You know, just wondering, since I didn't hear from you, are you coming to rehearsal or what? The guys are coming over here, and it's just gonna be casual, so . . . hope to see you."

Then was another guilt-laden message from my mother: "Griffin. You'll want to know that Mrs. Beckett brought two friends into the store; they were buying dresses for a tea they're going to next weekend. Mrs. Beckett heard about your little escapade through her sister, whose next-door neighbour's mother-in-law was actually *at* that wedding. Unbelievable, the stories that are circulating about your behaviour. I hope you're satisfied that people are staying away in droves. Are you coming for dinner on Sunday?"

Eye roll from me.

Then I heard Calvin's voice and my heart sank. He sounded tired.

"Well, we had a good time. It would have been better if you'd been here because we need to decide what to do. But . . . we played some tunes, talked about shit . . . For what it's worth, the rest of us want to keep going. The guys were all asking about you, and well, I didn't know what to tell them. I don't want to sound like I'm mad or anything, but . . . And, thing is, it's kinda more fun with you there, so . . . Come on, Griffin, call me."

There were several text messages saying pretty much the same thing.

The ball was definitely in my court. He wasn't the one being a jerk.

I went back to bed by about 3:20 but didn't sleep well for the rest of the night. I lay awake with my overactive mind alternating between Matteo's lips like rose petals on my cheek and stewing over having fucked up with Calvin. Calvin didn't deserve this kind of treatment. He was genuinely one of the nicest people on the planet, and he had every right to be mad as hell at me. Yet not one of his messages contained anything stronger than, "Come on, Griffin, call me." Now, big coward that I am, I dreaded ever talking to him. I wished I could vow to never speak to him again and just pretend those guys didn't even exist. Yeah, right. I wished I could wash my hands of him and not feel guilt, regret, some more guilt, and let's face it, profound sadness at losing my best friend.

That was the thing: Calvin was my best friend, and I'd royally let him down, not to mention the others in the band. With friends, you know you can trust them to understand if you make a mistake. Goodness knew I'd made plenty in all the years I'd known him. And so had he, though probably not as many as me, so I was glad we weren't keeping score. But I was also well aware that there must be a limit to his patience. I didn't want to find out what that looked like. For all that I dreaded talking to him, *not* talking to him wasn't an option.

But when? Oh crap! because that was the other thing keeping me awake. It was early hours on Thursday morning, and my first gig with The Spurious Correlations was that night. I had a full day of work to get through first. I'd be seeing Matteo again in just a few hours. Too few hours considering I was awake instead of getting my beauty sleep, yet too many when I thought of the shiver running down my back with the touch of his fingers on my hair.

Somewhere—I think in the apartment next door—someone was listening to *In the Wee Small Hours of the Morning*. Such a melancholy song did nothing to improve my frame of mind. And why were people listening to music so damn loud at this time of the night? I didn't remember the walls being this thin. Maybe I'd just never noticed it before. Or maybe it was a new tenant or something.

I must have drifted off because the time went by too quickly for me to have stayed awake the whole time. But I swear I spent the rest of the dark time dreaming I was lying awake fretting.

When my alarm jolted me out of restless sleep, I had to hustle. It was still too early to call Calvin. I would call him when I was on the train. We had discussed, as a band, what to wear for the gig, but I hadn't pulled out anything. I sure wasn't going to wear my gig clothes to work. I was a little choked to still have to work in the kitchen on gig day, but it shouldn't be bad. I hoped my task would be as easy as the day before. I wondered if I had any choice? What if I were to say, "No, I don't want to make that. I'd rather make shortbread." I could try.

I showered, pounded back a piece of toast with chocolaty hazelnut spread (my eating habits had been shameful these past few days), shoved my gigging clothes (the kind that don't need to be ironed), some makeup, a hairbrush, and hair product into my backpack. I could really use a coffee, but I had neither time nor enough hands. I had to carry my small backpack on my front, my electric guitar in its backpack-style case on my back, my acoustic in the hand-held case, and my amp. I always prefer to use my own amp for gigs. My twelve-string was still at Salamander's, thank goodness. One smart decision I had made. Yay. A peek outside told me it was misty but not pouring. Good. I could get away with not wearing a raincoat or adding an umbrella to my load.

I hefted my amp and guitars to the bus stop, eyeing the bench hungrily.

An elderly lady sat on one end, and the other was occupied by a pimply youth wearing a pale blue shirt and an argyle sweater vest. There were no spectacles to complete his stereotypical nerd ensemble, but my guess was that he wore very thick contact lenses. You'd have thought someone so obviously smart would think to shift over so I could more readily access a seat on the bench and keep my gear out of anyone's way, but no. I've learned over time that often the smartest people have the least common sense. I didn't recognise either of these people, though I'd lived in the neighbourhood for years.

I had to step down into the road to get around the kid but plunked my amp down and sat in the centre of the bench, careful not to lean back against the electric guitar case. My acoustic case I rested on its butt end, the neck pointing skyward to avoid poking anyone's eye out. The elderly lady *humphed* as if I'd sat in her lap.

The kid said, "What's that? Is it a guitar?"

"No, it's a turtle," I told the kid. *Duh.* I wasn't responsible for his self-esteem. Damn, but I was in a bad mood.

"You're a liar," the old woman said in a snotty tone.

"He's an idiot," I replied.

"I can recite pi up to the ninety-fifth decimal point." The kid's pride filled me with dismay.

Oh dear. "Hmm." Maybe if I sounded like I didn't fucking care, he'd leave me alone.

"3.14..." he began, and I shut my eyes, preparing for the pain. The more fool me for arriving early to catch the bus.

"...1592653589793..."

I stared straight ahead and tried to think of England.

"It's not a turtle," the old bag huffed. "It looks like a musical instrument of some description."

"...238462643383279502..."

"In point of fact, I think it looks like a trombone."

"Are you familiar with a trombone that requires amplification?" I had to ask.

"…88419716939…"

"If Kingdom Animalia were to be represented, I would say more like a kangaroo than a turtle."

"What?"

"…937510582097494…"

"Or a great blue heron."

"…459230781…"

"What the hell is great blue heron- or kangaroo-like about my guitar?"

The old scrag leapt to her feet and brandished an umbrella at me, which I could have sworn just materialized in her hand. *"See?! See?!"* She waved the umbrella at me and danced around shouting to all and sundry (of whom there were none). "Perfidy!"

"…640628620…"

"Witness the skulduggery inherent in the young!"

She sounded for all the world like an evangelical preacher. I wondered why she didn't climb up on the bus stop bench.

"…89986280…"

"It is a guitar, *not* a turtle! May you shrivel and waste away for your chicanery!"

For my part, I looked at the sky and wondered what had become of my world.

"…348253."

They both stopped talking at the same time, and all was silent. It was like switching off the music in the middle of a song I didn't like. A leaf dropped off a tree across the street and floated to the ground, where it touched with a soft *fff*. A car several blocks away revved its engine as it pulled away from the curb. Some black-capped chickadees twittered. The bus came around the corner.

I rose, waiting till the last minute to lug my acoustic and amp. Just as the bus lurched to a stop, diesel fumes billowing round it, an insistent honk blared from its rear.

Bloody hell.

Matteo waved out the window of the Mini, which had come to a halt behind the bus.

Billy Graham climbed aboard the bus, followed by Mensa Twit Boy, who had rudely pushed past me, nearly knocking me into the side of the bus, and only then did I head over to Matteo's car.

"You couldn't possibly have arrived five minutes earlier, eh?"

"Trouble?"

I laughed. "Just some fellow transit users who were a little more entertaining than I needed this morning." I hoisted my gear into the trunk of the car and climbed in next to him, then becoming aware of sitting very close to the very hot young man who had sent me to Cloud 9 with a kiss on the cheek. That very cheek and its partner turned warm. Had he spent the entire evening thinking about it too? Was he thinking of it even now? Could he read my mind or see on my face that I desired more than anything for him to repeat the gesture or take it just a couple of inches to the left . . . .

He was speaking and I wasn't paying any attention. How embarrassing!

". . . probably'll need a new clutch next year, but that's not bad for it being five years old—"

"Where do you live, anyway? Sorry for interrupting but I didn't think you lived around here."

He turned and grinned a secret sort of grin. "I don't."

"Well then?"

"Some things are worth going out of one's way for."

I kept my mouth shut because I was in danger of babbling.

We somehow missed all the traffic. Matteo seemed to know all the back routes to avoid all the accidents, stalls, and heavy volume. We made excellent time getting to the restaurant. He pulled into the parkade entrance. Which was well-lit with LED lighting that was evenly distributed to illuminate both vertically and horizontally, and to eliminate dark areas, thereby ensuring user safety.

"They got it fixed, that's great!"

He looked at me while expertly negotiating his car around the tight driveway. "What do you mean?"

I waved behind us. "Well, the darkness."

"Where?"

I chuckled. Was he kidding? "I mean the lighting that was—" I stopped.

He grinned at me. My chuckle held a note of hysteria. It was like he had no memory of the dark parkade of just the other day. Had I dreamt that?

"Do you have anyone coming tonight?" he asked.

My heart sank. What an idiot! Why hadn't I invited Jillian? Or Cal— No, that would be a bad idea. *Hi, Calvin, it's me, remember? Griffin? I was your friend who vanished and never spoke to you, and now I'm cheating on you with another band. Why don't you come out and hear us play?* He would not exactly respond favourably.

It was true. I did feel like I was cheating on my band.

I mentally slapped my wrist. Damn it, today of all days I could not think like that. I had baking to do and a gig to play tonight. *It's just for a while*, I lied to myself. *You're just seeing how this goes.* Then I'd decide what to do about my band. Maybe after trying this out, I would invite Matteo to meet the guys.

Oh, Griffin, you ought to be ashamed of yourself.

Who was I kidding? I wanted this band with Matteo to be my band forever and always. I was set to marry Matteo and make beautiful music with him until death do us part.

Great. I was in a foul mood, and we hadn't even parked the car yet.

After depositing my guitars and amp in the rehearsal studio, I pulled out my cell phone as I headed to the kitchen. There were two calls I had to make —to my mother and to Calvin, who I had intended to call from the train but then hadn't taken the train. I feared the sarcastic wrath my mother would baste me with if I neglected to return her call to confirm I would be at Sunday dinner. Faced with that, you might think it would be easier to call

Calvin, but the truth was I feared his calm sensitivity even more. The phone beeped as I clicked numbers.

"Mom?"

"Yes?"

"It's me. Griffin."

"Oh, *Griffin*! You mean the long-lost daughter who I never thought I'd hear from again? That Griffin?"

"Well, I don't know why you would think that," I murmured.

"You know I'm at my wits' end here, with all these women coming into my shop *specifically* to embarrass me about the behaviour of *one* of my daughters. Which one, do you suppose? Well, certainly not *Jillian*. You know, why can't you pay closer attention to what Jillian does and how she behaves? A true professional. It's so exotic that she is a dancer—"

"You want Jillian to be an exotic dancer? How quaint."

Mother carried on as if she hadn't heard me, which she likely hadn't because that would mean tuning out the sound of her own voice for a millisecond. "—It's so classy! Not like being a—a—what do you call yourself?"

"A musician, Mom."

"—A *rock* guitarist. That just has so many implications."

"It does?"

"You're probably surrounded by *drugs*, which would explain your behaviour of the other night."

"It certainly explains someone's behaviour, not mine." I was just too tired of this kind of talk and too used to it to rise to her challenges.

"When my friends ask about Jillian, I am thrilled to talk about her, but with you, I have to swallow my pride and tell them *what you do*—"

She said "what you do" as if she were playing with a mouthful of tapioca pudding on her tongue, or bad seafood.

"And now I have to defend the family as these women talk about your awful, awful wedding fiasco."

"Look, Mom, are you finished? I have to get to work. I don't know if you can hear me or not over the sound of your voice, but I am coming over on Sunday, so . . . Bye."

I hung up with a sigh and accompanying eye roll and leaned against the wall outside the kitchen. I called up Calvin's name in my phone and hit the button.

The person who picked up the phone was definitely not Calvin. She was speaking in a foreign language I couldn't identify. She used a lot of words. I interrupted her.

"Hello? Who is this? I'm looking for Calvin. Calvin Sheeley?"

The woman on the other end sounded upset, so I said, "Sorry, I'll try him again," for some reason and hung up. I double-checked the button and the number and tried again.

A different woman answered, but she spoke in the same language as the previous one. I hung up and examined my phone. How was it possible to dial a wrong number when I was using a programmed cell phone? I looked at the clock and regrettably realised I didn't have time to figure it out. I would just have to try again later.

I pushed on the door into the kitchen.

When Chef told me I had to make something called dacquoise, I decided to test a theory. With a deep breath, I shut my eyes and opened them again.

"I'd rather do something simple today because of the band playing tonight. How about I make shortbread?"

"No."

"All right." Face hot, I backed away. How silly of me to have suggested it.

Steven had already pulled out *The Day of the Luminous Laundry*, ostensibly a science-fiction murder mystery, but Steven knew better. On page 47 was the recipe for dacquoise, which was described as "a fluffy and crunchy cake of hazelnutty-chocolaty goodness that proves the existence of Heaven."

If anything, I was learning all kinds of things about dessert, and maybe I'd be helpful to my dad one day. See? I'm a glass-half-full kind of person.

As we dug out ingredients and equipment, my cell phone buzzed in my pocket. It was a text from Brian reminding me I had two guitar lessons to teach at 5:00 and 6:00.

Shit shit shit.

If I left here at four, I'd be able to get to the store in time to teach Derek Sheffield at five. I hoped Liam's student would be early, and I could get her in, say, 5:45. I'd be finished by 6:15 and back to Salamander's by . . . 7:15? I'd be basically warmed up already after teaching. We wouldn't start playing until eight.

No problem.

I left Steven to grind hazelnuts and beat egg whites while I went to find Matteo. I told him about having to teach. A crease appeared in his forehead.

"It *sounds* like you have plenty of time." He shook his head doubtfully. "I hope so."

I half-hoped he would offer to drive me in that hot little Mini of his, but I wasn't about to ask him. "I'll be here in time. Definitely."

He squeezed my arm. "Anyway, really? This isn't the gig to worry about. The really big gig is a week from Sunday."

"Oh yeah? What's big about it?"

"It's some festival or other. There's apparently going to be tons of bigwigs here."

"Wait a minute," I gasped. "What's the date of that gig?"

"Sunday, May 20th." Matteo hurried off to . . . whatever it was he spent his time doing.

I wilted against the wall in relief. Saturday the 19th of May was Calvin's sister's wedding. In Victoria. I had made it clear to Rickenbacker I was absolutely unavailable that day. This big gig being on Sunday meant something was going right for a change. It was a drag to have to leave Victoria and come home early on Sunday when the plan had been to spend the weekend, but it was better than the alternative.

I have got to get ahold of Calvin. If only because we needed to practise our song together.

But not right then. Later. Instead, I phoned Jillian and got her voice mail.

"Hey, Jill. I know it's kind of last minute, and I'm really sorry I haven't called earlier. Listen, the reason I've been so busy is that I—I'm sorta . . . *guest*-playing with this band, and we've been cramming in rehearsals. Anyway, we're playing this little gig tonight at eight at this restaurant downtown on Powell Street. It's called Salamander's. I wondered if you wanted to come hear us."

There. I'd made a little bit of an effort, anyway. The chances of her coming were pretty slim, but at least I'd told her.

The dacquoise included butter cream and chocolate ganache and all sorts of layers of meringue. It was complicated and took hours and virtually all my sanity. Steven deserved a medal, not only for his proficiency as a pastry chef, but for his calm, silent nature that kept me from cowering in a ball in a dark cupboard. When the dessert was finished, it did, indeed, look like something inspired by Heaven. It had turned out beautifully, I had to say. I was reluctant to leave the kitchen. Would something happen to destroy our creation this time?

"Steven, I beg of you to protect this today."

Steven looked at his shoes—orange sneakers—and nodded. I had to trust that the work he had put in today meant as much to him as it did to me.

The band had decided not to have a full-on rehearsal today, but we did get together to tweak and tighten a couple of things. When I said I had to go, Matteo gave me an encouraging wave and said, "See you soon, Griff."

With heavy trepidation about my dessert and my timing of things, I pulled my arms through the sleeves of my jacket and hustled out the door, breathing a sigh of relief that I hadn't run into Phoenix or Rickenbacker. I was excited about the gig and wished the lessons were over so I could get back. As I walked to the bus stop, I replayed some of my favourite moments from the band's repertoire in my head, which gave me goosebumps, which made me chuckle. Given how great the band's harmonies sounded, I had started making a list of potential new songs we could learn after the gig was over. I wouldn't bring it up today, though. We needed to get through the gig first.

To my great annoyance and increased stress, my bus was late, so I was late for my 5:00 lesson. Derek didn't seem to care, but the father was like, "I don't appreciate this, you know. We have to bolt from here and go straight to soccer, so you can't run late at the end; you'll have to make up the time on another day."

I assured him I'd be happy to do so and that I didn't want to waste any more of today's lesson talking about it. I ushered the kid into a practice room. By the time we emerged, Brian was waiting to speak to me after the kid and his dad left.

I was about to explain the situation from my side, but Brian said, "Did you *really* tell Derek's father his kid was as dumb as a sack of hammers?"

Shocked, I said, "No, of course not! I would never say anything like that." *What an asshole!*

"I don't need to tell you—"

"No," I agreed vehemently. "You don't."

Riled as I was, the next lesson, although it started on time, was not very beneficial to Liam's student. I kept messing up. For starters I didn't know what Liam had assigned her to practise, and then I didn't recognize the song when she began to play. Davinder let me know, as teenaged girls often took pride in doing.

"It was *Heart*."

The "duh" was implied.

In that half hour, she played better than I did, and as a result, I was more nervous than ever for my gig.

Her mother, whom I had never met, her daughter not really being my student, wanted to talk to me after the lesson, which never happens unless I'm in a hurry to get out the door.

"So will there be a recital at the end of term?"

I tried to look in a hurry while I put my guitar away and folded the strap. "Brian usually puts one on in the early summer, yeah."

"Because I think it's important to share what they're learning with their peers."

I nodded. "Yes, so do we."

"The older kids provide mentorship for the younger ones. I remember when Davinder was little, she used to love hearing the older kids play, and she'd say, 'I want to learn to play like that!' You know? It was really good for her. It pushed her."

Frustration crept into my voice, in spite of all my efforts. I shoved my arms into my jacket. "Yes, we agree."

"So do you think Davinder will be ready to play *La Villa Strangiato* by then?"

"What? Had she talked to Liam about wanting to learn that?" I tried not to sound scornful. "It's only one of the most difficult guitar tunes there is."

Davinder had already gone out into the front room. I picked up my guitar and tried to sort of push past the woman, who said, "Well, it's a shame, really, that you haven't taught it to her because I think she would play it very well, and it would do a lot to inspire other students if they saw—"

"Well, I haven't thought of it because I'm just filling in for Liam, but maybe she's talked to him about it. Listen, I've got to run," I said with a fake smile. "I encourage you to bring it up with Davinder. If she wants to learn it, we can start, though I doubt she'd be ready by June." I made my way by even though she didn't budge out of the doorway. "See you next time."

She said, "Oh!" in a startled pitch, and I had a feeling I'd hear from Brian about this one. But it couldn't be helped. I had a gig.

I rushed to the bus stop just as the bus was pulling up. A close call I don't care to experience ever again. Nothing had gone terribly wrong, but I was nervous because of the gig, anyway, never mind the added urgency of almost missing the bus. It wasn't the first time I questioned my insane decision to tackle both jobs, but when I thought of the music we made . . .

"It's all about the *music*."

By 7:23, I got back to Salamander's, where Phoenix, dressed much like the Ghost of Christmas Present this time, pinioned me in the dining room.

"Well? Did you make it?"

"Obviously. I'm here, aren't I?"

He gave me a puzzled sort of squint.

"Listen, Phoenix, I have to go get ready?"

"Oh!" The light bulb went on behind his empty eyes. "No, I didn't mean did you make it here for the gig. I meant did you make the trifle?"

"What? No, I didn't make trifle." My jacket pocket suddenly felt . . . weighty. "I made that dacquoise thing Chef asked for. It was really tricky and took hours." I stuck my hand in, and sure enough, there was the damn knife and my heart rate leapt a couple of octaves.

"For cryin' out loud! Why does this keep happening?" I pulled it out and turned it over and over. It had abandoned its sheath.

"What the hell's dacquoise? It sounds . . . *French*." He screwed up his nose as if French pastries were the most distasteful thing you could ever suggest to him. I hesitated to point out that the French had quite a history with pastries.

"I don't know what nationality it is, to be honest, but I made what I was asked to make, now if you'll excuse me." I pushed by him less gently than I had manoeuvred past Davinder's mom. Hot pokers of anxiety were stabbing me in the back, and molten lava was under severe pressure in my gut. Something was about to explode if I didn't get the hell into that back room to prepare. Anyhow, since I had also made mille-feuilles and crème brûlée, I didn't think he ought to suddenly have a strong opinion about French desserts.

I heard Phoenix holler something after me, but I ignored him, tears stinging my eyes. I held the knife in front of my face and glared at it in supreme confusion and frustration. "Go. Away. And never. Come. Back." I tossed it in the garbage bin on my way out.

I smashed my elbow on the corner of the wall in my haste, dumped my stuff in the rehearsal room, and ran to the washroom to change. Sure enough, a nice new bruise decorated my left elbow like a tattoo of a plum. I did some humming to warm and relax my throat while I changed and rubbed some mousse into my hair. I finally joined the others back in the rehearsal room. Matteo looked incredibly handsome in black jeans and a red plaid shirt with a few buttons undone and a black vest. He looked me up and down in my gigging outfit—just a funky black skirt and dark red top and some cool boots with a bit of a heel. Of course, the minor attention I'd paid to my hair helped too, as did the teensy dab of makeup I'd put on for a change.

He grinned at me like a fool. "Wow, Griffin, you look really nice!"

Who knew such simple little words could have such a big effect? I was on air.

As if by magic, all my anxiety fled, as though I'd been there all afternoon and hadn't just survived mayhem. I didn't even feel like barfing. I did a decent vocal and guitar warmup and ignored a stab of angst that we hadn't had a proper sound check. It was a matter of supreme luck that I had a brief moment to take a deep breath before the opening strums. We went out to the stage.

Rickenbacker Topiary announced us.

"Ladies and gentlemen, you're in for a treat this evening. This is the inaugural performance of the house band's new lineup. Please enjoy The Spurious Correlations!"

Matteo gazed across the stage at me, and we counted in the first song together. We opened with *Wild Wild Life*, which struck me as funny, given what I'd been through these past few days. I laughed as I sang, and it felt great.

The audience loved us. I loved us. Matteo loved us too. Performing with him was even better than rehearsing with him. We were in sync like I'd never felt with any other musician. We sounded great together. Our voices blended beautifully. This was all so good, I could hardly believe it was true. The entire band played pretty much flawlessly, and we had lots of laughs on stage. Matteo and I related to each other and had a great rapport. The audience, just a blur in the dim light beyond the stage, couldn't stay seated.

The thing about our set list was there was so much variety that if someone didn't like one song, chances were they'd like the next one. Consequently, when one group sat, another one got up. The dance floor was full for pretty much the entire evening. Rickenbacker lurked in the corner, but he looked happy enough. I didn't see Phoenix.

Jillian didn't come, but then, I hadn't really expected her to with such short notice.

The one thing that was odd was the way the audience behaved. I didn't notice it until later in the evening because I was having such fun. From up on stage, they looked sort of funny, as if they were a CG audience. When they clapped along, they always seemed to be just behind the beat. A few times I saw people laughing, but the sound didn't come out until a fraction of a moment later. It was kind of like watching a video when the audio track is out of sync. And the clapping and cheering seemed fuller than was possible for the size of the crowd.

It was sort of a strange thing for me to notice, but I've played enough live gigs to know what it feels like. At one point between songs, I stepped over to Matteo.

"Have you noticed the audience?"

He grinned, a brightness in his eyes I only ever see when someone is doing something they're passionate about. "Yeah, they're fabulous! They're really enjoying us, don't you think?"

I didn't want to waste any more time on it, and clearly he hadn't noticed.

Maybe it was time to get my eyes tested.

Oh yeah, the other thing that happened was this: In our break between sets, I went into the kitchen to grab a refill on my water. I checked to see how well my dacquoise was selling. I couldn't find it. I grabbed one of the waiters, a plain-looking fellow with brown hair.

"Did the dacquoise sell out already?"

"That chocolate-hazelnut-cake thing?"

"Yeah, that's it."

"Oh, Phoenix took it home."

What? I thought, and then said it aloud. "What? All of it?"

The waiter balanced about seven small plates of . . . something . . . on his arm. "Yep, he was having a birthday party for his three-year-old and needed a cake." The doors swung behind the waiter and his plates.

A little kid's birthday party? What the hell was wrong with Dairy Queen ice cream cake for little kids? Since when did a bunch of preschoolers need French fucking dacquoise, for cryin' out loud? I felt cheated. And yes, hurt. Again. My chest ached.

But I couldn't feel down for long, not when Matteo flew into the kitchen and grabbed me around the waist and swung me around so my skirt flared out and nearly caught on some pot handles on the equipment shelf.

"Griffin, they love us! We are awesome together, you and I."

"The rest of the band too!" I was laughing my head off as I corrected him. Frankly, I couldn't even remember what the other guys looked like. My head was full of Matteo only.

"Yes, of course, they rock, but you and I . . . we *sizzle!*"

We stopped spinning abruptly. The kitchen was empty except for us. He hadn't taken his hands off my waist. My whole body trembled.

"Your eyes . . ." he whispered. "They're so . . ."

I reached up and tucked his wavy hair behind his ears, never disconnecting from his deep blue gaze. He leaned down. I reached up. When our lips met . . . *sizzle*, indeed. The tingle in the small of my back nearly made me lose my balance. His lips were soft and just a little moist. The tip of his tongue flicked ever so lightly, and then it was done. He took my hands, and we pulled apart. My neck and shoulders had tightened with expectation; my breathing was so shallow, I thought I might hyperventilate.

"Oh, Griffin . . ." He ran his fingers through my hair in that way of his.

I licked my lips and failed to produce words.

"We have to start the next set." He seemed to be having trouble breathing, too.

I nodded and finally managed an airy, "Uh-hunh."

He went out.

Oh, this won't do at all. I went to the sink and splashed some cool water on the back of my neck. How could I play *now*? How could I ever have thought Jason was attractive? How could I ever have thought he cared for me? No, this was brand new.

I sang *At Last* with more heartfelt energy than I ever had in my career.

Voice mail from Jillian on my cell phone after the gig:

"Hey, Griff. I got your message. I'm sorry I didn't make it to hear you play. It's too bad you didn't give me an address. I looked it up online, and I couldn't find the place. I know you said it was on Powell, but I didn't know the cross street, and obviously I couldn't drive around every street looking for it. 'Course, I'd have been listening for great music, and that would have drawn me to the right place, I guess!" She laughed. "Anyway, sorry, honey. Let me know when your next one is."

She always said such nice things. And she meant them too, which is why I wonder how she can be the daughter of our mother.

As we said good night, I reminded Rickenbacker about my trip to Victoria a week from Saturday.

"I'd cancel but it's my best friend's sister's wedding and we're singing. It was planned months ago."

Rickenbacker bowed. "Yes, of course. I would not expect you to alter a long-laid plan, especially one which will bring about the joy of another." He told us we had Friday and Saturday off, placed his top hat on his head, and made his exit.

The man I was most definitely in love with took my hand and kissed it. It was so hard to part, I felt like Juliet must have. Standing at the bus stop, the mere memory of his hand on my cheek kept me warm. I wondered at his not offering me a ride home since it was late at night and I had my guitars and amp as I had in the morning. But I had no right to expect it of him, and I still didn't know where he lived or what brought him near enough to my place to pick me up. Not to mention how he knew I'd be there, in that place, at that time. Those odd things occurred to me, but I guess I chose to simply set them aside in favour of closing my eyes and allowing my recollection of the way he smelled—sweet and . . . kind of . . . nutty—to carry me home.

9

Friday, May 11

Though it pained me to be apart from Matteo, I recognised the pathetic nature of this and shoved it aside. In truth I was relieved to have a couple of days away from the restaurant. I could have benefited from some time at home, but I really did need to make an appearance at the music store, and I had four lessons to teach on Saturday. So although I was exhausted from lack of sleep and the expending of more energy than I typically did in a week, I went to my music store job on Friday.

Brian was serving a customer when I walked in. He did a double-take then finished ringing up the book of piano music and said good-bye.

"Well, hello stranger. You haven't worked here for days. Apart from teaching."

"You sort of indicated I could back off on my hours if I took on the extra teaching. And to be honest, it's been—"

"I don't really mind. This week it has been quiet. Lessons going well?"

His words sounded clipped. Stilted.

"Yeah, apart from being a bit late yesterday, and that kid's—"

"That was yesterday? I don't even recall that. I didn't notice."

My mouth opened and shut again before I could say, "Oh." I decided not to go into it. "Liam's students are nice kids. Davinder has really good tone."

A customer stepped up to ask Brian a question, so I went and hung up my jacket. I saw there was a shipment of music, so I opened up a box and started sorting. Brian's conversation with the customer went on in the background.

"Yes, we can do that," said Brian. "I can order it for you. It will take a week."

Brian was definitely speaking oddly. He didn't sound like himself. I paid closer attention.

"That would be super," she replied. "It is no problem to wait. She will be happy."

"That's so exciting. Anything else you need here? How 'bout guitar picks?"

I counted on my fingers.

"No, that will be all. I guess I'll hear from you soon?"

"I'll call when it's in."

She left and I approached the front counter.

"Uh, Brian, I think—"

"Yes, Griffin? What's going on?"

I nodded. "I figured it out."

"You figured what out? Let me guess: You now know who . . . wrote the book of love!"

I stared at him to see if his eyes were swirling. Had he been hypnotized? No, because the customer had been caught in it too. "I only wish. No. It's that you and that lady spoke all in haiku."

Brian laughed. "Ha! Look who's talking! You're doing it too, Griffin!"

Horrified, I thought back to what I'd said and counted the syllables.

Everything we had said could be divided into smaller sections of five, seven, then five syllables. "Oh, damn it, you're right."

Matilda, the flute teacher, came in.

"Hey, Brian, Griffin.
Haven't seen you in a while.
Where you been hangin'?"

I backed away warily. Perhaps if I stayed far enough away, I wouldn't get caught too deeply.

"This is outrageous.
I thought things were weird enough.
This was my safe zone."

"Safe zone?" Matilda asked. "Safe from what?
What's she talking about, Bri?
I don't understand."

"You just called him 'Bri,'" I cried, hands jumping up to my cheeks.
"You have never called him that.
This can't just be me."

"Can't I call him that?
What's wrong with calling him Bri?
Is there something wrong?"

"Gen'rally, nothing.
But you only shortened it
to make a haiku."

"She's going nutty," Matilda said to Brian.
"I think she's under a great
deal of stress lately."

I nodded. "I believe you're right.
Maybe I should go home now."

"That sounds like a plan," Brian finished for me.

"Stop it! Say nothing.
Wait until I've left the store.
Call me when you've stopped."

I went for a coffee. I made a conscious effort to use more than the allotted number of syllables when I ordered. "Just a small coffee please." There. Six syllables, not five or seven. The barista looked at me funny because I seemed to be studying my own words. Which I was. But never mind. I had evidently broken the cycle. I sat at a little table by the window and pulled out my cell phone.

I stared at it. Afraid of aggravating the irate people who had usurped Calvin's cell number, I texted him.

I am so sorry. I've been trying to call you, but my phone is acting weird and giving me a wrong number. If you get this, I have time to talk right now.

I drank coffee and watched people park their cars crookedly in stalls, watched them back out without looking and narrowly miss hitting other drivers.

My phone *pinged* and my belly jumped as if the message had been sent via trebuchet. It was the right number but had some weird name made of numbers and symbols. Also, the message itself was a dick pic with a clown nose on the tip. I know you don't know Calvin, so let me assure you there was no way in hell Calvin had sent me that. I hastily deleted it. A split second later, it rang. It said it was Calvin. I tried to sound as apologetic as I felt when I answered.

"Hey."

"This is a warning from the CRA. Records show that you owe $1,422 for current or back taxes, and an arrest warrant has been issued. Do not hang up, or the police will come and arrest you—"

"Fuck off," I told the scammer, and hung up.

Nerves like a squall, I watched a dog owner let her dog poop in the middle of the sidewalk and not clean it up. I was appalled. I banged on the window at her, and when she looked at me, I gave her a stern look and pointed down at the sidewalk. She glared at me as if to say, "What the hell do *you* want, weirdo?" To my horror and dismay, she barged into the coffee shop, dog in tow.

"What is your problem?" Her dog licked crumbs up off the floor.

"Nothing, apart from my not wanting to have to watch my step on the sidewalk, doe-si-doeing around your dog's crap."

The other patrons of the coffee shop stared at me. The room fell silent. When I say "silent," I mean *silent*, with zero sounds of coffee makers or talking or fans, nothing. There was a dearth of ambient noise. Was I in a vacuum?

The woman's voice was like a razor cutting through the silence with a hiss. "I have never, *never*—You understand me?—let my dog have a bowel movement on a sidewalk. You with your *coffee* and your *cell phone* and your *hair*—"

My hair?

"—are a disgrace!"

My face burned and my innards wanted to purge. "Look, I don't know what you have against people with coffee and cell phones and—*ahem*—hair. But I would sure appreciate it if you would clean up after your dog."

Her dog barked and vomited all over the cafe floor.

"Geez," I said, sinking onto the stool. I looked around at the people in the coffee shop and the ambient noise returned. The woman and her dog vanished, along with the vomit. I took a chance and checked out the dog's poop. In yet another of a series of situations that were becoming less and less surprising to me, the poop revealed itself to be no longer poop, but a chalk drawing of the Sydney Opera House.

I closed my eyes, took a few gasping breaths, and tried to remember my own name.

Pulling out my cell phone, which mere moments ago had been so offensive, I took a risk and called my sister. I had never been so thankful to hear her voice at the other end. I invited her to join me for lunch after the lessons I had to teach the next day. She was delighted. Her tone sounded pinched, almost like she was holding back from crying. I asked her about it.

"Oh nothing, no not at all, Griff." The tone was gone, and she sounded like herself again. I chalked it up to more of the same kind of madness I had just experienced with a dog. "See you tomorrow at noon!"

Taking a chance, I went back to the store afterward. The truth was I didn't feel like going home and being alone. Nor did I want to stare at the phone, trying to make myself phone Calvin again. Later.

I stuck my head in the door of the store. Brian was pulling stuff out of the very box I had started to work on earlier. He turned his head and saw me.

"Hey, Griffin? How's it going? We haven't seen much of you." He looked happy to see me. Moreover, it was as if it were the first time he'd seen me today. I waited just a moment longer to make sure he added more than three syllables. "Are you coming in or what?"

When I got home I grabbed my laptop and slumped onto the couch. I logged in.

> *Hey gang, Holy cow, I seriously think I'm losing my mind. Today people started talking in haiku all around me, and then I got caught up in it, too, and I had to go for coffee, where a woman yelled at me about my hair and let her dog puke on the floor..*
>
> *Has anything super weird like this ever happened to any of you? I'm freaking out a little, here.*
>
> *I had a gig with my new band, though, and it was amazing!*
>
> *~WingedLion*

There. Someone would either assure me I was crazy, or come up with a decent explanation.

I pulled out my phone.

I put it down.

I made myself a half-decent supper of bacon and eggs with baked beans and a salad. I washed and dried the dishes and even showered.

I checked *CAPPA*. Thank goodness! There were a couple of replies.

> *I'msorry: Wow, WingedLion, it sounds like you've re-evaluated your priorities. Great job!*
>
> *Can'tSayNo: They say if you can't stand the heat get out of the kitchen. You're on track.*
>
> *NerdBird27: Your focus needs to be on you, WingedLion. Trust that all will be ok.*

If I were completely honest, a lot of that was only marginally helpful, but it felt good to have told someone. Everything felt a little less heavy on my shoulders. Well, not everything.

I wracked my brain but could not come up with a single other thing to do to put off calling Calvin. "Later" was now. The one thing I hadn't tried was actually punching in his phone number and bypassing the auto-dial. Sweat soaked my armpits as I pressed the numbers. I paced as I listened to it ring, and my mind raced, half-hoping I would get his voice mail. My heart nearly stopped when I heard the click.

"Hello?" It was actually him.

"—" No sound came out of my mouth. I cleared my throat. "Hey, Calvin, it's me."

Pause. "It's alive!" he said in his best impression of Dr. Frankenstein.

I chuckled, not quite allowing myself to be totally at ease, not yet. "I'm so sorry it's taken me so long, I've been, like, ridiculously busy."

"Yeah?"

"I honestly tried to call you back when I finally had time. For some reason I kept getting wrong numbers, even when I used the programmed buttons."

"Yeah?"

"Yeah, and then—" It occurred to me that I sounded like I was trying too hard so I stopped.

Calvin said, "I've been sorta worried because you hadn't called since the . . . event. You okay?"

"Umm, yeah, I'm okay. I guess I took it pretty hard." I cringed at my exaggeration and felt unworthy of his friendship. "How're the others?"

"They're good. Everybody wants to know when we're going to rehearse again. The other night wasn't really a rehearsal; we just jammed. We need to talk about what we're going to do about the band."

Oh, no. I paced rapidly around my living room. I knew I'd have to answer to this at some point, yet all the lead time hadn't helped me formulate a response. "I—well. I don't know . . ."

"Come on, Griffin, it wasn't that big of a deal. It was one gig. And you know what? We were bloody good, when all is said and done."

My frustration and anger from that evening came flooding back in an instant. "I don't know how you can say it wasn't that big of a deal. It was the biggest wedding of the year."

"Pah," he snorted. "In some circles, maybe, but who cares? Snifter is one guy. And he doesn't have as much pull in the city as he thinks. Besides, nobody out in the suburbs cares about him. There are plenty of gigs out there." He meant in the world, not just out in the suburbs. This level of understanding is what comes of being close friends for a long time. "And anyway, isn't it just about making good music?"

Great, now he was using my own words.

"Yeah, I guess."

"So . . . do you want to get together?"

Stall for time. "Umm, yeah, maybe, but . . . can we wait a bit longer?"

I heard him sigh, even though he was trying to cover it up. "To be honest, I don't know what we're waiting *for*, but whatever. Are you still in to help me at Teresa's wedding?"

"Yes! Yes, absolutely." I hustled to the calendar. "It's next Saturday, eh? In Victoria."

"Yeah, the ceremony starts at 3:30, so we'll play around ten to four. I'm catching the 7:00 ferry on Friday night. Do you want to come with me? I'm crashing at my cousin's, and you could too. We can order pizza and have some laughs. It'll be fun."

How sad was it that my best friend was trying to convince me that we would have fun? He was right and I truly wished I could say yes.

I pounded my forehead with my fist. *Shit!* "Actually, this is going to be a bit tricky."

"How so?"

"I'm covering some lessons on Saturday morning." *Shit. Fuck.*

"But . . . wouldn't Brian give you the day? He's pretty understanding."

"I know but I only just took it on, and I feel bad if I—" Then I got a bright idea. "Don't worry. If I catch the harbour-to-harbour flight, I can fit everything in. I've always wanted to try that, and it'll be worth it."

"Are you sure? It sounds tight. And expensive." He sounded doubtful, which was reasonable.

"It shouldn't be a problem."

"Okay, well, maybe we should get together to go over the song?"

My gut was churning by this time. The knot twisted a little tighter. But he was right. "Yeah, I guess we ought to."

"Just iron out the wrinkles."

"Yeah, totally."

"When would be good?"

I looked at the calendar. It was packed. "How 'bout now?"

"Now? It's 9:00."

"Just for a couple hours. I wouldn't go to bed before then, anyway."

"I suppose not. I'll come over."

Alarmed, I looked around my apartment at all the evidence that I was not being completely honest with him: guitars out (not a big deal), twelve-string not here, copies of set lists, not to mention the calendar with both gig dates and an attempt at a work schedule scrawled onto it. I could tidy, but no, it was too risky; I'd end up missing something.

"Naw, I'll come to your place."

"Are you sure?"

"Yeah, no problem. It was my idea to get together now; I don't want to inconvenience you. Besides, you've been waiting patiently for me. I'll be there in half an hour."

"Aw, that's great, Griff. I'll make sure there's a cold beer for you."

He rang off and I felt like absolute poo.

In the interest of time, I called a cab, grabbed my acoustic and fretted all the way to Calvin's.

I knew I should tell him. I wanted to tell him. But it had all happened so fast. He would never believe that I hadn't known Matteo longer than a week. Besides, the whole thing might fall through, anyway. Plus, I had set out to find a new lead guitarist for my own band, not to find a new band to play with. How would the guys feel to learn I'd hooked up so instantly with another group—one that was already gigging—and that the new guys didn't want my old mates?

I remembered a time an old bandmate told me he'd started playing with another group; I remembered the feeling of betrayal, the thought that we weren't good enough for him. He hadn't said so, of course, but all I could think was if he loved our band as much as I did, then he'd be getting what he needed and wouldn't need to join another band. And it was worse, since he'd sought them out; it wasn't as if they needed someone and recruited him.

He had eventually quit us, and I did not want my friends to think that's what this was about. No, I'd wait for things to settle. Maybe after I had this big gig behind me.

On the other hand, as I had thought before, I knew other people who played in more than one band, and it wasn't a problem at all. So it *could* work fine, but the longer I took to tell Calvin, the more it would sound like something I didn't want to tell him, and that would cause all kinds of mistrust and awkwardness.

By the time I arrived at Calvin's, I had changed my mind about seven times. This was Calvin Sheeley, a guy I'd been friends with since we were six. He'd moved away and come back years later, and it had been as if no time had passed. We'd seen each other through the inelegance of puberty, for cryin' out loud. Who better to talk to about it all? He'd understand and even be just as excited as I was! The sooner I told him, the better.

And anyway, I could downplay it: say this guy was a friend of a friend and had invited me to come jam with them. Save saying it was a full-on gigging band until later. That would soften it a bit. Besides, I might not be able to handle this working-two-jobs thing. The Spurious Correlations might fall through.

Yeah, right.

He opened the door and handed me a beer before I'd even crossed the threshold. It was really good to see him. Comfortable. We knew each other, we *trusted* each other. It was a profound relief from the craziness, the unpredictability. We played guitar and sang *Gotta Have You*, our song for the wedding. Calvin was our—my—drummer, but he was also a more-than-decent guitarist. We went over the song a few times. We sounded really good, if I do say so. He told me about the procedure for the wedding.

"Teresa wants us to sing between the vows and the rings. So there'll be a reading and some talking then the vows and then us."

"Cool," I said.

We played some more and had some laughs. It was just like always, no awkwardness, as if nothing kooky were going on in my life. Like a holiday. I felt so good, I was about to blurt out: "I have to tell you what's been going on!" when he spoke.

"So ... my dad's been assessed." Calvin's face drooped. Where a moment before he'd been smiling, all of a sudden he looked lower than a snake's belly. I didn't say anything, just waited.

"He's got to go into a care facility." He exhaled deeply, as if he'd been gearing up to tell me this for days and was profoundly relieved to have let it go.

My heart broke and tears filled my eyes. "Oh, Cal. I had no idea things were that bad."

"Neither did I." Calvin's dad had Parkinson's disease, and his particular version was accompanied by dementia. I'd been alongside Calvin, watching his dad deteriorate over the past few years. I'd known them almost forever, so I could sincerely share his grief. "My mom's just been coping and dealing with it. I don't think *she* even realised how bad things were. You know when you're in the middle of something and everything's fine, and you don't even sense that it's getting harder and harder to deal with it because it's happened so gradually?"

I nodded, even though I didn't really know; I could only imagine.

"I had no idea he was getting her up, like, six times a night, having to go to the bathroom or imagining people were breaking into the house or thinking he had to go to work and actually starting to get dressed, but putting his pants on backward. He started turning the stove on for no reason. Shit like that."

My eyes overflowed and I wiped my cheeks. "Oh my god, Cal. And he's so young." The man was older than my own folks—Calvin had another sister, older than Teresa—but it had hit him awfully early.

"Why didn't she tell me?" He wasn't angry, just heartbroken. "I could have helped her."

"Oh, Calvin, what could you have done? Stayed at the house with her? You already gave her lots of breaks, taking him for coffee and to movies and stuff over the years, when you could. You told me ages ago you'd been encouraging her to get him assessed."

He nodded dismally.

"Don't they have home care and stuff like that?" I went on. "She ought to have done this a long time ago, but you know what? She wasn't ready, pal." I reached over and touched his knee. "She wasn't ready."

He gently strummed his guitar. "Yeah, I guess."

"You did what you could; you can't blame yourself. It would still have come to this point eventually."

He nodded and sighed again.

"Have you told the others?" I asked.

"No. I wanted to talk to you."

Fuck. "Calvin, I am so sorry." Impulsively I set my guitar down and went over and put my arms around him. He returned my hug with a kind of urgency. His shoulders shook, and I couldn't dam up my tears. It was awful that this was happening right at the time of Teresa's wedding. The family must be clinging to each other like crazy. He had needed to talk about this. I had made him wait, and I wracked my brain for a way to punish myself.

We wrapped it up soon after. Obviously I didn't dump on him further by telling him my "news." I gave him another hug as we said good night. I was so glad I had made this happen, finally, but felt shitty that I had been so unaware.

On my ride home, I felt like my heart had been ripped out of my chest, spun around three times, and stuck back in again.

10

Saturday, May 12

Dragging my tired arse out of bed on Saturday morning was tough. It had been a late night after an exhausting week. Having said that, I felt refreshed after a long-overdue get-together with Calvin, despite his bad news. It was great to play with him again. And it was great to just hang out and be friends. Hanging out with Calvin never felt like work. We knew each other so well that I never had to guess what he was thinking, and we could joke around without hurting each other's feelings. I was surprised to realise it had been less than a week since our "stellar" event. It seemed like way longer.

Playing great tunes with a friend is what it must be like when people go for a run or a long swim. I don't do those things, but I imagine it's the same mental break, the change of focus to something other than the everyday, that they bring the same kind of clarity.

Last night had unfortunately brought with it a whole new set of emotions to work through. I was deeply saddened by Calvin's dad's condition. I had always been close to him and had fond memories of going to Calvin's and getting told off—pretending of course—for not wearing a dress, or for not leaving my shoes neatly enough, or ringing the doorbell instead of coming right in. The day he told me I was now old enough, at age fourteen, to call him Rob instead of Mr. Sheeley, was the best coming-of-age ceremony a girl could ask for. I had a bad habit of clumsily knocking stuff over and breaking things at their place too, and Calvin's folks were always so sweet about it. Their relationship was so different from what I could perceive of my own parents'. This must be hell for Calvin's mom. It gave me pause.

I resolved to tackle the upcoming day, and the week, with a new attitude. You have to live life to the fullest and appreciate what you have, right? I started my new outlook by phoning and booking a harbour to harbour flight for the following Saturday at 12:30. It would be a bit of a push after my last lesson ended at 11:30, but if I was organized, I could do it. I just wouldn't be as early for the flight as I'd prefer. I would be nice and early for the 3:30 wedding, which was more important. The next flight wasn't until 2:30, which would put the stress at the other end of things, so all in all, this was better. In any event, the idea of the little flight was exciting. A new experience that fit right in with my new philosophy.

I got myself ready for work, brushed my teeth, and grabbed my hairbrush out of the drawer. Only it wasn't my hairbrush. I nearly stabbed myself in the head with the knife. I jumped a mile and dropped it on the floor as if it were fiery hot.

Why did this keep happening? How the hell did it keep appearing, ignoring all the laws of all the sciences? It made absolutely zero sense. What was it trying to tell me? Did it have a problem with my new philosophy? It showed up in my hand during moments of high anxiety. Was it telling me to avoid those moments? Pressing my hands on the counter, I glared at myself in the mirror.

What are you doing, you fool? Is this what you really want? Was it worth all the complication I was putting on myself? Then I thought again of Calvin and his dad, which instantly put things back into perspective. These were all opportunities: to make music, to share my knowledge through teaching, to learn. Even the dessert making. But especially to play music. Isn't this what I'd always wanted? I nodded to my mirror self. *I've been given opportunities, and I appreciate them.*

I left, forgetting to brush my hair.

Before locking the door, though, I made sure the damn knife was on the bottom shelf of a bookcase, underneath a massive, illustrated and annotated —and therefore, thick—volume of the *Complete Works of Shakespeare*. The book weighed about seven hundred pounds, so there was no way the knife could accidentally fall off the shelf and find its way into my backpack or my pocket or my shoe.

I maintained my new philosophy all the way to the music store. The best part of this day would be meeting Jillian for lunch, so no matter what occurred during the four lessons I had to teach, I vowed to appreciate what I had and look forward to: the reward of lunch with my sister.

I should never even think stuff like that.

I arrived at the music store by 8:30, so I had plenty of time to mentally prepare. As I opened the entrance door, though, I knew something was wrong. It was quiet. Too quiet. I walked through the door at my regular speed and nearly tripped over a prostrate form. It was on a mat. It was inhaling to a count of eight which was the only reason I knew it wasn't dead.

"What the hell?" I searched for Brian in the aisles of the store.

The form in front of me was duplicated so many times throughout the store, I couldn't count them in a single glance. They were dressed in stretchy outfits with multicoloured tops. The one in the doorway put its hands by its shoulders and pushed its torso up into an impressive cobra. So did all the others. At last I clued in to what was going on.

There was some kind of yoga gathering in my place of employment.

Brian emerged from the back hall. "Oh, hey, Griffin!" he called in a murmur as the forms pushed up into downward dogs. As I stood there, gaping, they went into lunges, then forward bends, which swooped up into majestic tall mountains, all accompanied by well-timed, deep inhalations and exhalations.

"What the devil is this?" I stepped between back bends toward the front desk.

"Looks to me like about thirty sun salutations."

The leader of the group was progressing through her poses on a mat that covered a sheet of plywood, which lay precariously on top of the bins of music I had tried to organize just the other day. A tinge of worry crept into my face, but I decided if she wasn't concerned, then why should I be?

"How 'bout some tuneage?" she called.

Brian obliged.

Instead of what I would have considered normal, relaxing yoga music, with soft strains of flute or saxophone over quiet, ambient chords, he chose *Aqualung*. The instructor didn't object. I shrugged. What else could I do? Brian didn't think any of this was odd. In fact, it occurred to me that maybe they were renting the space from him. Was the business not doing as well as it appeared? It always seemed busy, but what did I know? I owed Brian a lot; I resolved to redouble my effort to not let him down.

I appreciate all I have.

"Are we still open for customers?" I searched for any place patrons could safely step as they browsed the store. All I saw were hands and feet that could be trod on. But it wasn't my problem, ultimately. I was there to teach today, and that was it. I meandered through to my little practice room and got set up for my first lesson of the day.

I altered the tuning on my guitar and started experimenting with *A Case of You* by Joni Mitchell. I had an "out there" idea that if I could get it sounding good enough, I would play it for Matteo, just to see what his reaction might be. I'd be lying if I didn't admit that my ultimate desired reaction would be for him to propose marriage. Or something along those lines.

I had thought about learning *Help Me* but thought it too obvious and that might turn him right off.

Melissa, a solid-looking girl of fourteen, clattered and banged through the door, which explained the dents and scrapes on her guitar case. She let it *thunk* on the floor near her chair.

"Hi," I said. "I hope Brian told you I'll be filling in for Liam for a bit." I twisted the pegs on my guitar to get it back to standard tuning—Joni had polio as a kid, and it affected her fingers, so she created her own tunings— while Melissa crouched on the floor and clicked the clasps on her guitar case. She didn't respond. I changed focus from my tuning pegs to her face. She had that ashen greenish pallor that meant just one thing.

"You not feeling well this morning?"

She shook her head and closed her eyes with regret at the movement. "Uh-uh."

Having felt that way myself—haven't we all?—I said, "Hey, you don't need to be here if you're not up to it."

Her voice sounded hoarse, ragged. "Mom says I have to 'cause she paid for it." She pulled out her guitar and, head hanging, pushed herself up to sit on the chair.

I rolled my eyes. "We do make exceptions for illness," I said gently. "This is no good."

"She said it's my own fault 'cause I drank a litre of bourbon last night."

Stunned, I said, "Oh."

"Oh," she said, and vomited all over the floor.

There is something about the smell of someone else's vomit that inspires one to add one's own vomit to the mix. Motivated to avoid turning this concept into reality, I set my guitar on the stand and dashed from the room, ostensibly to get paper towels or something, but I leaned against the wall in the hallway, gasping for air. The acoustic guitar section of *Aqualung* still played in the front of the store. Did Brian have the song on a loop? How irritating.

I went to find him, since my music teaching skills did not extend to cleaning up hazardous materials. The yoga people were rolling up their mats and pulling on sweaters and saying "Namaste" to each other. I found Brian dealing with a customer who had brought in a flute that needed the pads replaced. Brian was standing on his head, and the customer had leaned over to talk to him. What the hell was going on around here?

"Umm," I said. Then, rather than disturb him, I looked up Melissa's file and found her mother's cell number. She was annoyed as hell.

"It's her own fault. What she did was inexcusable. She made her bed; now she can lie in it."

Before she could come up with any more clichés, I explained how Melissa's being sick to her stomach may very well be her own fault but unfortunately it wasn't the best use of her time, nor mine, and could mom please come pick up her daughter right away?

"Couldn't you just make her keep playing?" Melissa's mom asked.

Frustrated by this lack of compassion from the woman, both for her daughter and for me, I said, "Well, the trouble is that the room we practise in is now filled with puke, and by the time we either clean it or even move to a different room, Melissa's lesson time will be over, and I have to teach someone else at 9:30."

"This is the lousiest customer service I have ever encountered. I am going to consider taking Melissa somewhere else for lessons."

Really?

I counted to ten. "That is your prerogative, certainly. Meanwhile, your daughter is producing toxic waste in my practice room, so would you be so kind as to come round and take her away?" I was starting to sound like

Rickenbacker. I hung up.

Brian, now the right way up, asked what was going on.

"Melissa just purged a litre of bourbon into my practice room."

"Again?"

What? "You mean she's done this before?"

"Oh, you know how kids are," he said, as if talking about the way four-year-olds like to sometimes bring stuffed animals to listen to their lessons.

"Not really," I mumbled, not having discovered my love of gin and tonic until I was twenty-four, and even now I rarely drank more than what it took to elicit a teeny buzz.

Brian told me where to fetch a wet/dry shop vacuum.

"I don't think this is part of my job description." Even with my raise, I wasn't getting paid enough to clean up teenager puke. Melissa took off without offering an apology, which added to my exasperation. I scrubbed the carpet and sprayed stuff down to remove the smell, all the while repeating my mantra for the day: *I appreciate all I have.*

I was a few minutes late for the 9:30 lesson, which ticked me off, because Brian, or one of the other shop employees could have helped me. Oh, well. After scrubbing my hands with ridiculous thoroughness, I finally joined Markus in a different, vomitless practice room.

Markus, eleven, was here at his very first lesson.

"So, Markus, do you know any chords?"

He sat with his arms crossed, pouting. He shook his head.

"Okay," I said, "We'll start with a couple of easy ones. I'll teach you three chords today, and you'll be able to play quite a few songs with those. How does that sound?"

He sat there, his face stormy, and did not pick up his guitar.

"What's up, Markus?"

"Wanna play *Stairway to Heaven.*

I nodded slowly. "Okay, that's a great goal. Have you practised it?"

He shook his head.

I swallowed my desire to kick him. "See, the thing is, most people don't just pick up a guitar and play one of the most iconic songs of all time without ever having learned a single chord." I might have let a little bit of sarcasm creep in, there.

He kicked his feet the way a three-year-old might.

I appreciate all I have.

I adjusted the tuning on my guitar, a process I hadn't completed at the point when Melissa shared her purge with me. Then I just talked through the A chord. I'd eventually get to the numbers of the strings and their names, but I find it's easier to keep students engaged if they come away able to actually play a song.

"See? I put these three fingers on these strings here, one, two, three, in this fret. You have to press down hard, or it sounds like this." I demonstrated the dull, clunky sound that occurs when the strings can't resonate.

Markus sat there and did nothing but sulk as I went through and showed him D and E7. For the entire half hour, he did bugger all. It didn't matter to me; I was getting paid anyway. A crummy attitude, I suppose, but what would anyone else have done? I was teaching him. I couldn't help it if he refused to learn. You can lead a horse to water, and all that, speaking of clichés.

Keeping up a friendly demeanour was the hardest part. I was more than ready for a half-hour break before my 10:30 student. Markus skipped out into the front of the store as cheerful as if I'd fed him cake.

"Guess what?" he said to his dad, "I can play *Stairway to Heaven*!"

I chuckled, all nice and friendly, as I followed him. "Well, not quite, but you'll get there!"

Markus's dad put a hand on the boy's shoulder as they headed out of the store. "When we get home, you can show me, and if it's not true, we'll have this woman's ass on a plate for lying, right, son?"

My jaw dropped open. Markus turned and sneered at me over his shoulder as he walked.

Dread filled my innards like wet clay as I headed to the back room to grab a coffee. I intended to sit and work on *A Case of You* for a few meditative, mind-clearing minutes.

As I emerged from the break room, coffee in hand, the front door of the store banged open, and a throng of people filed in, carrying placards and chanting, "We're very busy! No more interruptions!" They turned left then right, and marched all the way around the store, up and down the aisles. Their placards had interesting slogans that made it tough to tell what it was they wanted. *Free time is free!* read one. *Down with marshmallows!* read another. *A daisy a day!* and *I like ham!*

Should I call someone? Like the police?

Or a shrink.

Brian had disappeared. So had Tony, the other employee working the front. I had no idea where they were, but frankly, I was there to teach today, not to operate the front. In spite of my previous conviction, I did something kind of irresponsible: I hastened to the back and into my practice room and pretended I hadn't noticed anything. The protesters could wipe the store clean of merchandise if they wanted to; I didn't freaking care at that point.

I couldn't focus on my song, though. I sipped my coffee and stared at the poster of guitar chords on the beige wall. What was happening to my world? I could pinpoint when it had all started, of course. It was pretty much right after I had met Rickenbacker Topiary a week ago. I rubbed my eyes with the heel of my hand. He was a different sort of person, without question, but that didn't offer any explanation for the strange things happening. Maybe the things in his restaurant, though I blamed most of that on Phoenix, but here in the music store? So much of the past few days didn't make sense at all. I considered myself to be a relatively intelligent person, and yet I was baffled. I mean, really. Haiku?

And the knife that poked its ugly head out like a whack-a-mole no matter how deeply I stuffed it at home. I didn't know where it had come from, but it obviously liked being with me.

Nevertheless, the bottom line was the music I was making with Matteo. I smiled. I had absolutely no recollection of ever being affected this way by Jason. What had I ever seen in that jerk? In retrospect, Jason had always been an arrogant asshole, and for some reason I hadn't noticed. To be fair, he was pretty good looking and even had a decent sense of humour when he felt like it. He was a good guitarist, and well, I guess it always felt good to make music with someone. He'd complimented me on my singing and my harmonies too, at the beginning anyway, and who could deny that being complimented is a draw?

But the guy was no Matteo. Not in his guitar playing, not in the way he made me feel. The disparity between the two men was astonishing. I had never imagined anyone like Matteo existed. I don't mean in the sense of his being a brilliant musician. I mean in being a brilliant musician who is *kind* and *generous*. Who gave back as much as he was given. Who could be so caring. Who could care that way . . . about, well, let's face it: about me.

I had Calvin, of course, but he was different.

My sister was amazing, and I loved her like crazy. My dad was a cool guy, and as I'd gotten older, we'd had some good conversations and some laughs. He appreciated my music, which was nice. Then there was my mother. How had we become so distant? So adversarial? She had been fun once in a while. We played board games as a family on occasion, back when I was younger. She had a good sense of humour sometimes. Now that I thought of it, though, I couldn't remember the last time she had told a good joke or laughed at one. Maybe running the dress shop was more stressful than I bothered to think about.

Which only made me feel worse about my band's failure to impress the Snifter family and all the resulting ramifications.

I no longer cared about teaching. I had two more lessons to get through today, and then I'd be having lunch with Jillian. That was the light at the end of the Lessons From Hell tunnel. I picked up my guitar and tried *A Case of You* again. Joni originally played it on dulcimer, so I was worried I wouldn't be able to get it sounding quite right, but I had some success with it, which cheered me up a little. I started to feel excited about playing it for Matteo.

I was struck by a memory so powerful and vivid, it was as if it had just taken place: Matteo's lips on mine, the sizzle, the softness, the little flick of his tongue, his hand on my hair, his deep blue eyes drowning me . . .

As my next student walked through the door, a silly grin had overtaken my face, and he asked if he was in the right room. I floated through the next two lessons.

About 11:45, I pulled open the door of the restaurant and stepped up to the hosting station.

"For one?" she asked.

"No, there'll be two of us."

She grabbed two menus and indicated that I should follow her. We passed several empty tables for two before she seated me way at the back, and carried both menus off with her. My chair was so close to the men's washroom that my short hair got caught in the door when it opened and closed. The man who had just exited turned and looked at me like it was my fault for being in the way.

"Sorry," I said, as if it were my fault for being in the way. I kicked myself for it, and then tried to get the attention of the server. Her eyes passed in my direction twice, but she didn't notice me.

Finally Jillian rushed in. "Hey, honey!" She gave me a breathless hug. "Sorry to keep you waiting." She hung her purse on the back of her chair and began to take off her jacket. "Hang on. This is a terrible table." She turned and caught the server's attention instantly.

"What can I get you?" The server pulled out her pad.

"How 'bout a better table?" Jillian suggested politely. "My sister is in danger of being swept into the men's washroom."

The server's eyes widened as if seeing me for the first time. I smiled tiredly, saving my eye roll for inside my head. The server tossed me a glare, as if I had demanded this table and was now showing a fickle nature.

"Of course," she said, with a kind smile at Jillian, probably feeling sorry for her having to hang out with the likes of me. She moved us to one of the prime tables we'd passed on my way in. We seated ourselves and she placed a menu in front of Jillian and walked away.

"Umm, excuse me?" I said.

She turned around and snapped, "Yes?"

I smiled sweetly at her. "May I have a menu, please?"

She sighed as if I'd asked her to turn our table around six times and light ritual candles. She slapped a menu down in front of me and dashed away before I could ask anything else of her.

"What was that all about?" Jillian asked.

"You're asking me?"

We had a good laugh over it. I ordered coffee and cream of mushroom soup, and Jillian ordered herbal tea and a Cobb salad. The server brought our beverages, and I told Jillian all about the morning I'd had: the yoga, the vomit, the pouty kid, the protesters . . . Somehow talking about it with her made it all seem less strange. I don't know how protesters in the music store could avoid being strange, but that pretty much summed up my relationship with Jillian. She made everything seem all right.

I noticed that although she was laughing, her eyes weren't as sparkly as usual. We drank and laughed about the server not noticing when I raised my hand to ask for a refill. As soon as Jillian gestured in her direction, she approached.

"Would you like more hot water for your tea?"

"No, but my sister would like a refill on her coffee, or don't you do that here?"

The woman looked snarky. "Of course we do." She said it with a *tone*, as my mother would say.

Our food arrived and we dug in.

"Enough about my goofy day, Jill. How about yours? How're rehearsals going?" The dance studio's production of *Faust* was coming up in about eight weeks.

A shadow passed over Jillian's face and she shrugged. Alarm jolted through me like the sizzle of Matteo's kiss.

"What? Jillian, what's wrong?"

She smiled and waved her hand. "Nothing is wrong. Truly. Rehearsals have just started, so there isn't much to report. But seriously, it's same ol' same ol'. I'm more interested in what's up with you. Sorry I missed your gig. I drove down there but couldn't find the place. Tell me about this new band of yours. When do I get another chance to hear you?" Jillian's eyes sparkled with glee.

I love her. Her interest in what I'm doing is always genuine. She's my biggest supporter. Part of me thought I ought to press her a bit more, but she had made it clear that she didn't want to talk about whatever it was that might be affecting her.

So instead I told her about the strange meeting with Rickenbacker and how when I met Matteo, it was like something had gone *click* and we'd connected. "Musically, I mean."

"Oh yeah?" she twinkled at me.

They say it's impossible to refrain from blushing. "He is awfully gorgeous. And so talented! I mean, I don't know why he's in this city and playing with the likes of me."

She rolled her eyes at me. "I wish you wouldn't say stupid stuff like that, Griffin! You're fantastic, and it's about time somebody else noticed it."

"Yeah, well, he's just . . . 'amazing' sounds lame but it's true. And man, I have never met anyone like him: he has every right to be an arrogant bastard, but he's just not. And he's such a gentleman. I think if he asked me to marry him this moment, I'd say yes!" I was exaggerating, of course, but this was Jillian. I could be over the top with her, and she'd get it.

"And are there others in the band, or is it just the two of you?"

It was a perfectly normal question, of course, but for some reason, my mind went blank. I chuckled, perplexed. "You know, there are a couple or three other guys in the band. I mean, keyboard, drums, and bass, of course, but—" I thought hard but wound up shaking my head and feeling embarrassed. "Geez, I can't remember—Carlos? Sergei? Maybe Tim?" I bit a lip and thought. "I think one of them has dark hair."

Jillian snorted. "Wow, this Matteo guy must have quite a hold on you if you don't have eyes for anyone else!"

My face flamed like the crème brûlée torch thingy. "He is . . . out of this world."

"Wow, that's so cool. I'm excited for you!" Jillian rested her chin on her hand and grinned at me. "When are you playing next?"

I shrugged. "We sort of have this gig next week."

She sat up straight. "Next week? Wow, two gigs so soon. That's madness! How do you learn enough material to play a gig in under two weeks of knowing each other?"

She's a dancer, not a musician, but she gets it.

I shrugged again. "The band is really good, Jill. I mean, yeah, the set list is a lot of songs I've been playing for years, and other ones I know pretty well. Still, it's different. These guys are so tight! We don't struggle over transitions and endings. We really connect. There's a level of communication while we're playing that I've never had with the other band. It's like Matteo and I can look at each other and each of us can read what the other wants to do. It's . . . cool."

"And it isn't like that with Calvin?"

I didn't want to automatically say no, so I thought about it for a moment. I shook my head slowly. "It's different somehow. Calvin and Andy and Cameron are all solid musicians, and they're great guys. Jason is chucked out, of course, but even if we had a new lead player, we'd have to work harder to get to this point, you know? We'd still get pretty close, but it would take a lot more time and effort. Honestly? I'm not sure we would get to the same level. Yet with Matteo, we're there already. It's unbelievable. Playing with them is like . . . magic."

"Wow. Awesome. So can I come?"

"Of course! I'd love it." I gave her the date and the address. "I should also tell you about Calvin's dad."

"Oh no! What's happened?"

I filled her in briefly. We'd known the family for years, of course, so the news was hard for her to hear.

"He's so young, too. Poor Mrs. Sheeley."

We talked some more about it. Then I said, "Now it's your turn. Tell me about this new ballet of yours."

She filled me in with as much, if not more enthusiasm than I'd used to tell her about the band. Her eyes clouded over just briefly when the poor, wretched bride's name came up. "Teryn's a spoiled brat, but I'm not letting her give me grief. This is what I love to do, and if she can't share the stage, it tells us all something about her, right?"

"Hell yeah. What happened at her wedding had absolutely nothing to do with you, so you don't deserve to be given any grief about it. If she does, I'll be royally pissed off."

Jillian put her hand over mine. "She's capable of anything. But not to worry. I've got this."

As if to emphasize her point, Jillian picked up the bill too. She paid it and we went outside to the parking lot.

"See you tomorrow at dinner," I said.

"Yes. And hey, don't let Mom get you down."

"Naw." I scrubbed my hair with my hand. "I don't get why she has to be so . . . *mean* about things. But I'm trying not to let her get to me."

Jillian grinned at me. "Easier said than done, I know. But none of what she's complaining about is your fault. She'll be over it soon enough."

I chuckled. "I bet she knows it and that's why she's getting as much mileage out of it as she can before it blows over."

"Probably keeping it going so it doesn't blow over until she's done with it!" Jillian laughed.

"Like the time with the ice cream," I reminded her.

She just about lost it, laughing. "Stop it! Oh my god, that was hilarious!"

And there followed an uproar of hysterical laughter as we recalled the time my dad had given us two little girls the last of mom's maple walnut ice cream. People walking by looked at us like we were crazy. But there was no point explaining it. Nobody could possibly appreciate an inside story as much as two sisters.

Finally we wiped our mirthful tears off our cheeks, and I gave her a big hug.

"Thanks," I said. "That was the best lunch date ever."

"Yeah." She looked kind of sad for some reason. "I love you, Griffin."

"Me too, Jill."

"Take care now," she warned me as I walked away. "Don't fall too hard."

I waved. "Yeah, gravity's a bitch."

On my way home, I grinned to myself. *I appreciate all I have.*

Interlude - Still May 12, evening

"This will not do. This will not do at all." Rickenbacker scolded no one in particular while rocking back and forth on his heels next to the desk in his office. The Mood Check screen went dark, but he didn't fold it away yet. Phoenix sat in the armchair, his cheeks and hair drooping dejectedly, and shook his head in disbelief.

Rickenbacker reached absently for an onion ring and dipped it in peanut butter anchovy garlic sauce. He didn't like peanut butter anchovy garlic sauce, which was why he chose it. He believed it was a suitable punishment for his lack of attention to Griffin's too-pleasant day. A mild form of self-flagellation, to be sure, but he approved it, and since his approval was the only approval he needed, he carried out this necessary action.

"Blech," he said. Once he'd swallowed the entire onion ring, he added, "There, that's done," and chose another, using a nicer flavour.

"How can this have happened?" Phoenix said. "We've more or less allowed all our efforts to be undone."

On the viewscreen they watched again the six-second looping playback of Griffin's view of her sister's laughter. Griffin's laughter could also be heard, and the view jiggled as she laughed.

"I agree that this day came to a positive conclusion, which is unacceptable. Laughter, so I have heard, is an effective remedy for the very type of stress with which we have been burdening our Other World participant. I fear she will approach tomorrow with a New Outlook."

Phoenix banged the arms of the chair. "See? I told you she was having too much fun!"

Rickenbacker would not stand for that. "No, Phoenix. I stand by what I said before. The snippets we are seeing of her enjoyment of the band are crucial. Watch this."

He poked his finger in the air a few times, opening up the screen showing the list of snippets. He chose one and flicked *Play*. The viewscreen dutifully played a snippet from the band's rehearsal. It was from the MGC's point of view this time, so it showed Griffin smiling like the sun as they worked through a tricky bit of music. A different snippet showed her working on one of her desserts in the kitchen. In this instance, her whole manner was wound up like a coiled spring.

"Like I said, if she experienced nothing but stress, she would walk away from Salamander's altogether. Don't you see? Is that what you want?"

"No, but—"

"Then trust me on this."

"I've trusted you all along," Phoenix muttered.

Rickenbacker held his arms out. "Come now, come now, my friend. Where, exactly, is the flaw in my reasoning?" Phoenix pouted and opened his mouth to reply, but Rickenbacker overrode him. "I concede our neglect of her today. Clearly the incidents in the music store were not enough. And the unexpected mirthful exchange with the other young woman was . . . unexpected." He paused to catch on to a thought that had just sparked in his mind. "But! It is a mere minor drawback. You cannot have thought our plan would develop so smoothly there would not be a single setback?"

"Why are you putting this on me?"

Rickenbacker ignored him. "Certainly not!" He stalked about the confined space as though it were a vast hall. "You see? Everything is fine."

The breakable items on his desk were wary and did not allow themselves to be knocked aside by the man's enthusiastically flailing arms. Phoenix ducked.

"We simply have to step things up. I will turn up the Prankster a couple of notches. A few more unusual circumstances will twiddle with her frame of mind. Tomorrow is a new day, my friend."

"But what about the knife? She can't use it if she's not even at the restaurant! It was madcap to give her those days off." Phoenix dropped his face into the crook of his elbow in despair.

"You worry too much." Rickenbacker rubbed the bottom of his chin with the back of his hand.

"Can I go now?"

Rickenbacker pointed at him dramatically. "What's the plan for tomorrow?"

"Don't you worry so much," Phoenix Reysing said, rising. "I'll come up with something." Hand on the doorknob, he turned back and added, "I want that title."

As the door closed behind his friend, Rickenbacker said, "Good. Good."

He wished the Tournament rules allowed for more constant Mood Checks. He had a small concern that there might be more moments like the laughter one. Was their OWP deceiving them in some way? But he was not willing to jeopardize their chances by cheating. He scowled and crunched another onion ring. Plain, this time, which was delightful, for they were delicately spiced.

11

Sunday, May 13

My lunch with Jillian, followed by a nice, quiet evening, had rejuvenated me so I felt quite generous toward Salamander's on Sunday morning. Despite Liam's taking over my store hours, I still had lessons to teach, so I had a crazy day ahead of me. In a moment of clarity, I had come up with a plan.

I didn't own a car; however, I did have a membership in the car co-op. I rarely used it but figured today I could justify the cost because of my necessary back-and-forthing to the music store. It was Sunday and the bus schedule was weird, which would make all my travelling too chaotic. Plus, I had the dubious pleasure of looking forward to dinner at my parents'. Access to a car to get there and back would ease the tension of the evening. I had reserved a car, so I took a bus to the mall near my apartment to pick it up. At the same time, I wisely thought to book a car for the day of Teresa's wedding, next Saturday, May 19th. Go me.

Congratulating myself on my organization, I drove to the restaurant through a surprising volume of traffic for a Sunday. Still, I made decent time and pulled into the parkade—still nicely lit—by 8:30. I deposited my gear in the rehearsal studio as usual and wondered when Matteo would be in. Having had Friday and Saturday off, I assumed we would rehearse as usual today, though I needed to talk to him about my lesson situation. The plan was to find out my baking task for the day and get it started. Then I would dash back to the music store to teach lessons at 10:30 and 11:00, go back to the restaurant, then back to the store for Trevor's lesson at 1:30, then back to the restaurant. We could squeeze in rehearsals here and there—we had lots of days before the Big Gig, so I wasn't worried. It would be an insane day, but I could do it.

It was times like these when I wondered if I was giving too much to this pastry job.

Also, it occurred to me that I had no idea how much this job was paying me per hour. Another thing to feel dumb about. If I told my dad I'd taken on a job without finding out my schedule or my level of pay, he would be ashamed of his failure to educate me. Well, I wouldn't burden him with the knowledge. This was all on me. As I stood in the middle of the kitchen, tying my apron, I was almost convinced I was nuts.

On the other hand, nobody seemed to mind my coming and going at will, despite Rickenbacker telling me I was expected to work full-time hours. Maybe other jobs would be less flexible. See? Always something to be positive about.

Sunday was Chef's day off. To my joy, Phoenix himself was my immediate supervisor (and I hope you've picked up on my use of irony). I quickly learned that this meant Phoenix could adopt Chef's persona in some sort of exaggerated role-playing game, which, in Phoenix's mind, gave him the power to boss us all around, even though it was plain he didn't know what he was doing. He was, however, wearing a chef's hat, so . . .

Phoenix told me to make shortbread.

I have said before that I am not my dad. I have never claimed to be a chef, or a baker, or even a caterer. But I do know how to make shortbread. Finally, here was a task I could be excited about. Not only that, but it fit in perfectly with my broken-up schedule. My lovely assistant, Steven, was off, but I wasn't worried. If there was one baking project I could handle on my own, it was shortbread.

I got out flour, berry sugar, and butter—lots of it. Christmas music was playing, although it was May. I didn't even notice right away; it just seemed right to listen to Christmas music while making shortbread.

I was already in the kneading phase, and my hands were buried in creamy, buttery, sugary goodness and dusty with flour when Phoenix came into the kitchen with a group of about half a dozen tourists. I'd have thought there would be some regulations against that sort of thing but . . . whatever. The tourists had cameras and excitedly dashed about, taking billions of shots of . . . odd stuff. Like, not the things I and the other cooks were working on, but of light switches, nesting stacks of mixing bowls, the ceiling fan, the fridge handle, a burner on the stove. Phoenix was giving some sort of schpiel about how efficiently his kitchen ran and what a terrific manager he was. His speech was upstaged by his bright floral pullover.

As he came by my workstation, he decided to do his Gordon Ramsay impression. He slapped his hand on my table, making me jump.

"What the bloody hell is this?" He adopted a really bad English accent. "Is that *butter*?"

I looked askance at him. "Of course."

"What the fuck do you think you're doing? Bloody hell." He stuck his finger in my dough and took a taste. "Fuckin' 'ell. That's putrid."

Now, as I mentioned, I am *good* at making shortbread. I tasted it myself, and it was wonderful. Ire tightened my chest. "With all due respect, Phoenix, I've made shortbread dozens of times, and this is how it is supposed to taste."

"Hot shot, are you? Are you the boss?"

I carried on kneading. With patience that deserved a frickin' medal, I said, "No, Phoenix, I am not." My sternum was taking a pounding from my heartbeat.

"Then why the hell are you giving me such attitude?"

Sweat ran down my sides, sourced from my armpits. I didn't know if the tremor in my voice was audible to anyone else, but I sure felt it. "I don't understand why you think I'm giving you attitude, Phoenix. I've been doing my best here all week. Shortbread is the one thing I've been asked to do that I know I'm good at."

The tourists took my photo. I tried not to scowl at them.

Phoenix glared at me for a moment before his expression changed ever so slightly. There was a twitch in the corner of his mouth, and his eyes narrowed just a touch. "Time will tell." With the same petulant dispatch as a selfish child who doesn't want to let anyone play with his ball anymore,

Phoenix gathered up his little tour and left.

I swore a blue streak under my breath while giving the dough a pummelling it did not deserve, but it seemed to understand.

The dough mixed, I left it in several large bowls in the refrigerator, washed my hands, and took off my apron.

"I'll be back to roll that out; nobody touch it, please," I called to my coworkers. Somebody acknowledged me; I don't know who. I was in a hurry.

I ran down the silent corridor to the rehearsal room. Nobody was there. I stood in the middle of the room, tapping my thighs with the low rumblings of panic in my core. Had I missed a call or a text or something? I checked my phone, but there was nothing. Maybe everyone always had Sunday off, and they just forgot to tell me. Assumed I would know. I kicked myself again for not being more assertive about needing a proper work schedule.

"Okay," I said to myself. This was not a problem. I was a bit downcast not to see Matteo, but hey. As an adult, I would make myself get over it. Like I said, I wasn't worried about next weekend's performance, and this way I would be early to the music store. I could help out a bit and make up for not having been around very much.

However, traffic was even heavier now, with nothing in the radio traffic report to account for it, and I got to the store with only seven minutes to spare. Hon Jun, sixteen, was already there, plucking away in the practice room. Miraculously, the room didn't smell like Melissa's bourbon vomit. It smelled more like toasted marshmallows.

"Did you have something sweet for breakfast?" I asked him.

"Hunh?"

"Never mind. Maybe the cleaners have changed products."

"Bacon and eggs and sausages all the way, baby!"

This was quite the outburst from the usually soft-spoken boy. "Oh."

Carrying on with the lesson was the best way past this awkward moment. "So how're you doing with *Aerial Boundaries*?" Hon Jun was my best student, and I was always kind of excited about lessons with him. He'd really gotten into Michael Hedges, so together we'd been playing around with some of Hedges' unusual techniques, the hammer-on, pull-off, and slap harmonics. It wouldn't be perfect today—Michael Hedges' music was insanely tough; he had always sounded like there were more than one of him playing at once. Frankly I was not qualified to teach amazing stuff like that. But I saw my job as guiding and helping my students to figure stuff out on their own. Besides, every teacher dreams of having a student who challenges themself and strives to be *that* good. That Hon Jun had the desire was a gift unto itself.

Hon Jun started to play some of those amazingly cool harmonics with the hammer-on, and it sounded really good for a learner.

"Holy wow, Hon. That sounds terrific."

He burst into tears.

Uh-oh. I swallowed and shifted to the very edge of my seat. "What is it?" I wanted to touch him. He sobbed. "Hon Jun? What's up?"

"I—" *sob* "—made—" *sob* "—a—" *sob* "—mistake!"

I rocked back and forth, my mouth opening and shutting repeatedly. I could have argued with him, told him that no, he hadn't, at least not so I'd noticed anyway, but I didn't want to trivialize his feelings. Besides, it didn't really matter what I thought at this point.

There followed a counselling session, wherein I assured him he sounded great and his playing perfectly was not part of my expectations but I was incredibly proud of him for his hard work and dedication.

"Do you know what inspired Michael Hedges to play guitar?"

Hon Jun sniffed. "No."

"*Puff the Magic Dragon*," I told him. "So if he got that good as a result of *Puff*, how good could you be as a result of Michael Hedges?"

I didn't know if my reasoning made any sense. I tried my best, but I don't know how helpful I was to him, being a bit of a mess myself. We mucked about together a bit more. Then I had him play something simpler, and he felt pretty good about that just in time to leave.

I took a moment to take a deep breath and a drink of water. I was already exhausted, and the day wasn't even half over. All I really wanted to do was crawl into a corner somewhere and sleep for six days. No such luck.

My next student's hair was significantly shorter than it had been the last time I'd seen her. I indicated it. "I missed you last week."

My grin should have let Jennifer know it was fine; instead, her lip quivered.

"I was really sick."

"I thought you were getting your hair cut."

"Is that what my mom told you?"

"Well, she told Brian, but yeah."

She rolled her eyes. I left it there.

"Let's go in and see how you're doing with the étude."

Jennifer hadn't practised; it was obvious. In fact, it was as if she had *un*practised. Her playing was a knitted sweater that had come halfway unravelled.

"Okay," I said in a patient, kind voice, "you're having a bit of trouble there, hunh? Let's go back to—"

"No, I didn't." She looked at me, sincerely puzzled.

I smiled, more *pretending* to be patient than actually *being* patient. "What do you mean? Sure you did. I heard quite a bit of stumbling but it's okay. I'll help you work—"

She sat up straighter and jutted her jaw at me. "It was perfect! I practised for hours. That's how *you told* me to play it last time."

I wanted to yell, *Why on earth would I tell you to play it like crap, you little turd?* but reason prevailed, and I took a deep breath instead.

"Jennifer, let's try it again, just the melody line, a bit slower."

"That *does* it!" she leapt to her feet. Guitar in hand, she stormed out the door of the practice room. I set my guitar on its stand and followed her. She was already up at the front desk, screaming at Brian.

"I want a new teacher! One who has her shit together would be nice."

Brian, with the patience of . . . a person or thing with a lot of patience, said, "What's the trouble?"

Jennifer wheeled around, pointing at me as if we were in the Big Reveal scene in a murder mystery and I was the killer. *"She is a fraud!"*

I had come here today in an enormous rush. I had told myself I could get through it. I had shoved aside the incredible stress I was under as a result of the emotional elevator that morning, not to mention the week I had just been through; shoved it into a little box labelled *That Other Thing*, and sealed it tight so I could let it go for the time I was dealing with teenagers. But the Week That Was seemed to have found some cracks in the box. My desire to smash the glass case displaying the selection of tuners and guitar capos manifested in my clenched fists. The words *Your haircut looks like ass!* came to my lips but didn't manage to pass through. The fingernails digging into my palms kept me together. I closed my eyes. I opened them and just shrugged in disbelief. "I don't know what to say, Brian. I don't know what the problem is. But if she wants another teacher, then fine."

Brian pressed the air with his palms. "I'm sure there's a way we can talk this through. But for now, let's maybe just leave it. Jennifer, when your mom gets here, we can sort it out. I won't charge you for this time—"

I opened my mouth to protest. "This—!"

"—Griffin, you'll still get paid; don't worry."

I shut my mouth and stabbed figurative red-hot pokers at Jennifer with my eyes.

Brian continued to talk to her. I told him I'd be back later for my 1:30 lesson, annoyed as hell at having wasted time with Jennifer when I needed to get back to Salamander's to roll out my shortbread. I gathered up my stuff and went outside to gulp some fresh air while I loaded my gear into the car, still hoping that perhaps the guys would be there for a little rehearsal.

The air and the drive shallowed the furrow in my brow, and I felt a bit better by the time I got to the restaurant. Matteo still wasn't there, so I came to the conclusion there would be no rehearsal today. Regret battled for supremacy with Relief, along with its sidekick, Exclusion. *Why didn't anybody tell me?* I bit my lip and set that aside.

There was no evidence that anyone had tampered with my dough, but I tasted it for quality control. Just in case. It was divine. As I rolled it out, I considered which shape to go with. Past experience in this venue told me it didn't really matter what shape I chose; the dough would probably take on the shapes of famous literary figures or something. With that in mind, I decided to just go with fingers. I poked it all over with a fork then cut the dough.

Phoenix and his tour group came through the kitchen again. Was it a new tour group? The same one? I couldn't fathom what he might have done with them over the past couple of hours I had been absent. A meal, perhaps? But really, what was so extraordinary about this place that anyone would want to come on tour? Nevertheless, they took photos as I transferred the cookies onto baking sheets. (No, they didn't change shape.) Several dozen of the beauties would soon be ready to be snapped up by the patrons. I checked the clock. Not enough time to bake them now, so I stacked the trays in the fridge, each layer perpendicular to the one below. I snuck out to the car.

I got to the store in record time. Brian looked at me funny until I noticed I was still wearing my apron. I shoved it in my backpack.

Trevor was a good kid, keen on learning. For the duration of his lesson, I fidgeted, waiting for him to break into something out-of-this-world magnificent, like last week when he'd played Bach's *Bourrée*. He started his newest tune. He'd wanted to learn *Rainy Day People* for his mum's birthday, so I'd given him a simplified version. He played it so well, I felt the hairs on the back of my neck stand up. I didn't want to overreact and accuse him of something like I did last week.

"You must really like that one, hunh?"

I braced myself to hear him say, *What do you mean?* He didn't. Instead, he blushed in a charming way and grinned. "Yeah."

"Great job," I told him.

I relaxed after that, convinced I might even get through the rest of this day without anything unexpected coming along to ruin it.

Silly me. I had done it again.

Back at the restaurant, I took the raw cookies out of the fridge while the ovens heated. They baked until they were perfect. I ate one—for quality control purposes, of course. Melt-on-the-tongue perfect, as I'd planned.

A little later, Phoenix called all the cooks and kitchen staff into the dining room, where he had assembled his tourists. *Really? Still?* They were taking photos of cracks in the floor and towels. Very artsy.

"Ladies and gentlemen, we're going to have a Taste Test Fest!"

All the kitchen staff cheered and clapped and jumped up and down. Except me. I didn't know what he was talking about.

From out of nowhere, several servers appeared with plates of each of the desserts we'd been creating all day—wait, who? I had never seen these people before. Who were they and where had they come from? Was I really so unaware of my fellow staff? I felt rather small just then, shrinking under the blanket of guilt I'd pulled over myself. The servers placed the plates of dessert on the tables in front of the tourists and other customers. Another three servers passed out forms and pencils.

"Now, dear guests, we will introduce each delight, along with its creator. You may taste it and tell the chef your thoughts, and then give it a score. The winner will get a day off with double pay."

How fantastic would that be? Why hadn't Phoenix chosen to do this on a day when I'd made puff pastry? Or crème brûlée? No matter; my shortbread was damn good.

"First up is Jeff. Tell us about your item, Jeff." Phoenix sounded like the host of a cooking competition as he gestured to a dish of what looked like green jelly with a large chunk of something purple in it.

Jeff stepped forward, his chest puffed up with pride. "The dessert I have created is lime jelly with zip. It is not the simple bowl of gelatine you might expect. It has a secret ingredient, which I think you will find gives it an unusual punch."

The guests eagerly tucked in. They squealed with delight.

"What did you use to make such wonderful zip?" asked a blonde woman.

"Red onion."

Holy crap. Green jelly with red onion. *Yum.*

More irony, just in case you weren't sure.

To my amazement, the prevailing comment seemed to be, "This is marvellous."

There's no accounting for taste.

Samuel presented a basic ginger snap. Tamara brought forth something that looked like a dish of shredded lettuce and called it green delight. Farhad unveiled sliced bananas in a bowl of milk. Carly's dessert was a jelly roll made of bread and a jar of store-bought jam. Zhang boasted about using store-brand Neapolitan ice cream and a box of Fig Newtons.

Throughout this you may have noticed I knew all their names. Please don't ask me when or how I learned them. I vowed to stop questioning that sort of thing.

Then it was my turn. In all honesty, I was *not* feeling cocky. I was ambivalent to the proceedings, truly, because I just didn't understand them. The rules were odd, to say the least. However, I was able to proffer my contribution with confidence.

"I made traditional shortbread, from scratch." I tried not to emphasize the last bit.

The guests took sizeable bites. They almost instantly spat it out, saying things like, "Good lord!" and "Ecchh!" and "That is awful!" and "Khlah khlah."

Cripes, what was wrong?

Phoenix sneered. "Griffin, did you *taste* your dough?"

"Of course!" My face was turning red and hot and numb. "I tasted the dough before I rolled it out, and I even tasted a cookie when they came out of the oven."

Phoenix sniffed. He looked around at the patrons, and his tourists, chuckling. "What do you say, folks? Shall we get Griffin, our self-proclaimed Expert Pastry Chef to taste her own baking?"

"I never said that!"

My protestations were drowned out by howls and cheers of Witch Hunt proportions; they sounded fuller and louder than could be produced by a gathering of this size. I felt like a gladiator in the Colosseum.

Phoenix offered me a plate of my own shortbread. I bit into one.

It was ghastly. Try mixing some dish soap into play-dough and baking it, and you'll be close to what this tasted like.

The entire crowd, including the kitchen staff, roared with laughter at my reaction. They took pictures of the ceiling and the undersides of tables. I could only hope there was gum there.

I turned on Phoenix. "Damn it, I don't know what you did, Phoenix, but you did something. That shortbread—*my* shortbread—was wonderful." I wiped my mouth on a napkin. He wiggled his eyebrows at me, which gave me the idea that he confirmed my accusation.

I loathed him.

"The Expert Pastry Chef, ladies and gentlemen!" Phoenix clapped and instigated hateful laughter and moblike applause from the room. "She's also in the house band, believe it or not. Let's hope she plays and sings better than she bakes."

My body had gone so rigid my hair hurt, and I wanted nothing more than to scream at him and cry. But the tourists would have loved that. As I pulled the napkin away from my mouth, the knife was in my hand. The knife I had left at home underneath a massive seven hundred–pound volume of Shakespeare. The hairs on my neck stood as straight as flagpoles. Phoenix had planted himself right next to me, and he clapped and laughed. The knife had a really nice weight to it. The tip *twinkled* in the dim light. I gasped as my hand lifted of its own volition, the knife coming terrifyingly close to Phoenix's ribcage.

I had to get out of there before I did something I'd regret. The crowd noise accompanied me as I pelted from the dining room, flinging the knife into a dusty corner on the floor.

Back in the kitchen, I rinsed out my mouth. The last tray of my shortbread still lay on the worktable. I picked one up and sniffed it. I bit it hesitantly. It melted on my tongue. I grabbed the tray and ran with it into the dining room.

"Try these ones!" I cried.

To an empty room.

"Where did everyone go?" I asked Phoenix, who sat at a table facing me, his hands folded before him as if he'd called a meeting.

"They left after you tried to poison them."

"There was a mistake. *This* is my shortbread. I don't know what that other stuff was."

He merely smiled.

I was just so tired. I had had two days off, but you'd never know it. And I hadn't seen Matteo in three days, which sounded ridiculously pitiful, but he generally was a highlight of a day spent at Salamander's. As if to rub salt in my already raw wounds, I was expected at my parents' house for dinner. I had to commit to it, on pain of hearing comments like: "Is it too much to ask to have you over every *second* Sunday, since *every* Sunday seems to be too hard for you? Can you spare one evening out of fourteen for the woman who sacrificed so much to raise you to be a *responsible* young woman?" Seriously, it's just not worth it.

So in spite of the day—the week—I'd had, I put yet another measure of my sanity on the line and drove to my folks' house. I patted myself on the back about having a car, since this allowed me to make a hasty retreat if necessary. I made one stop along the way and drove through the damp twilight along the old, familiar road. I looked forward to seeing Jillian, and to be honest, my dad and I had always had a pretty strong connection. On the other hand, the thought of my mother kept my esophagus constricted with trepidation. It's important to note that I arrived on time.

Seemingly feeling ripped off for not being able to complain, my mother said, "Well, look who's on time for a change. What did you forget?"

Ha! I had her, regardless of the sting of her comment.

"I didn't forget anything. Look, I even brought a bottle of wine." I held it out triumphantly, glad I had taken the time to stop on the way.

She took it and untwisted the bag from around the neck of the bottle. "You know, they have such charming gift bags for wine these days, so one doesn't have to present a bottle in the brown paper bag from the liquor store."

She'd probably have preferred that I forgot the wine so her criticism would have been easier. But I had to admire her creativity in still being able to come up with something. *Sigh.* With Phoenix's smarmy voice fresh in my memory, I was near to snapping. I'm surprised my tongue didn't bleed, I was biting it so hard. I deserved a medal for all the things I managed *not* to say.

After a breath of a pause, I asked, "And what did people do before gift bags were invented?" I tried to mask the sarcasm. You'd have to ask her if I was successful.

"Honestly, Griffin, you're as aware of the real world as a badger."

That didn't make any sense at all. "What?"

Mother rolled her eyes and sighed as she stuck my contribution in the back of a kitchen cupboard where it would be easy to forget to ever serve it until it turned to vinegar, whereupon she could blame me for buying bad wine. Picking up her wooden spoon, she stirred the gravy. Yup, my mom really knows how to make a person feel good.

Plus, I was freezing. My folks believed in keeping the house several degrees below what penguins would consider room temperature, and I'd forgotten a sweater. That alone was enough to make me cranky.

Jillian walked in with a familiar polystyrene container. Our mom tapped the spoon on the edge of the pot and set it on the spoon rest. She gave my sister a big hug.

"Jillian, dear, what a marvellous surprise. Gelato!" Mom took the little box and gave her a kiss on the cheek. She continued to look at Jillian as she talked to me. "Here's a girl who knows how to attend Sunday dinner."

When she'd been released, Jillian gave my arm a squeeze.

"You could just leave that on the counter, and it would be fine," I said with a massive shiver. She scrunched her nose in a silent giggle then put her contribution in the freezer.

I'd hate her if she weren't such a damn lovely person. Besides, it didn't matter: If I'd brought gelato, I would have heard, "Oh, store-bought ice cream. You know, sometimes people bring homemade things to dinner." It wasn't Jillian's fault our mother had a clear favourite.

Dad walked in wearing khakis and a golf shirt. He'd had a haircut since I last saw him. "Hey, what kind of luck to find three beautiful women in the same room at once!" He put an arm around each of us girls and gave us a hug and kiss. Dad never made me feel less than I was. Then there was mom.

"Did you ask your daughter if she saw the news this week?"

"No, I didn't, Adele, and I wish you wouldn't make such a big issue out of it." Dad took the dish of potatoes from her hands. He swung around and carried it to the table. I spooned broccoli into a stoneware bowl and handed it to Jillian, who also grabbed the butter dish and set both on the table.

"I'm not making 'an issue' out of it. But she should be aware of these things."

"Why should she?" Dad said, returning to the kitchen. "It has nothing to do with her." He picked up the carving knife. Instinctively, I checked my pockets. No knife.

"Oh, Henry, it does so." Mom whisked gravy with vigour.

"*She* is standing right here," I pointed out. Jillian had sat on a kitchen stool, and her eyebrows were raised in an 'Oh brother' expression. "Look, you might as well just tell me what you're talking about."

Dad sliced into the meat, shaking his head. "It's nothing, Griff. Paul Webb on the *Society Report* made a big thing over the gay cake top on Teryn Snifter's wedding cake." To be clear, it wasn't a problem that such a thing as a gay cake top should exist; it was a problem that it looked like this caterer put one on the top of this *particular* cake.

"But that was Jason!" I cried. "Calvin told me it was. The guy could have said it was a . . . a prank. Or a mistake."

"Nope."

"Did he actually use your name?" I was aghast.

Dad sighed. "'Fraid so."

"Oh, bloody hell." My mood was getting darker and darker.

Mom saved the coup de grace until we were sitting down to eat. She served us wine that I hadn't brought. It was red and a much cheaper one than the brand I had chosen. Typical. I doused my potato in gravy and took a bite, and cut into my meat. Overcooked. How surprising.

"Well, Jillian," Mom said with an innocent smile that frightened me. She took a dainty bite of broccoli. "We haven't heard much from you. How about you tell us how *your* week has been?"

I looked at my sister in alarm. She rolled her eyes, finishing the act with a dagger-look at our mother.

"My week has been *fine*, Mom."

I didn't believe her, which is exactly what my mother wanted when she replied, "Oh, now someone's telling fish stories!" She glanced sidelong at me.

"Mom, I was absolutely *not* going to bring it up, and I recall asking you not to."

Mom shrugged her shoulders disingenuously and gave a long-suffering look to Jillian.

"There's no sense protecting her, Jillian, dear; I mean, the rest of us are all suffering the consequences of her poor choices. Why should she be spared?"

I ignored the remark and placed my fork down on the green placemat. "You might as well tell me, Jill; you can't make my Sunday dinner any less enjoyable."

"Griffin!" Mother looked positively wounded.

Dad ate meat.

Jillian looked as if someone had told her her dog had died. "You know Markie, the artistic director of the dance studio? Well, she came to me on Friday and said Carl Snifter has threatened to pull his funding if I get the principle role in *Faust*."

A giant fist constricted my chest. I had to take an enormous gulp of cheap wine. "On Friday? So that's what was bothering you yesterday. I knew there was some—"

"I didn't want to tell you. I didn't want you worrying about it or beating yourself up since *I* don't blame you—"

"But that's extortion! Snifter can't do that."

"Who's going to stop him?"

"Well. Markie, for one! The board of directors! Markie just told you last month it was yours."

"I know but Teryn made a scene, and it's too late to change the budget, and if Snifter pulls his funding, the show will fall through."

"Oh god." I dropped my forehead into my hand.

"Griffin, I hope you're not blaming yourself. This is not your fault; it's Teryn being a scrag."

That was the worst thing I'd ever heard my sister say about anyone.

"This tells everyone who she really is," Jillian said. "The other dancers aren't idiots; they'll know what this is all about. I don't blame you, and I'll betcha nobody else will either."

A medley of emotions running through my digestive tract made my food taste like cardboard. Outrage at Carl Snifter and hatred for his spoiled, undeserving daughter; dismay at the artistic director's reaction, even though she was in a very difficult position. Most of all, the love I felt from Jillian preemptively protecting me.

I lifted my eyes to her with what I hoped she could see was sincere gratitude. Mother, however, wasn't finished.

"Jillian, you are a kind, forgiving girl. But you mark my words: everyone still knows who was really behind this." As if her words weren't direct enough, she pointed her fork at me.

That was it. Why was I here? Why subject myself to this kind of abuse? Weren't families supposed to, I don't know, *love* each other? Stick up for one another? Be there for each other in times of need? Why did she always make me feel like moving to the Arctic? I almost wished I had brought some of the shortbread Phoenix had tampered with to poison her. Words spilled out of my mouth and tumbled all over the table.

"You're the fucking Master of Subtlety, aren't you?" I said. "I have *so* had it." My knife and fork met the table with a loud clatter and echoed through the carpetless dining room. I pushed my chair back with a loud scrape, which I knew would horrify my mother, who was ridiculously overprotective of her hardwood floors. "Just in case anyone is interested, I've had one hell of a week too, and you, *Mom*, have a bizarre way of showing that you want me at Sunday dinner. I swear, if Paul Webb doesn't keep blaming me for shit in the *Society Report*, you'll be the one phoning him to give him more dirt on me." I picked up a slice of meat. As if to punctuate my point, I said, "This meat is *overcooked*! And why don't you ever turn on the god damn *heat* in this place?" I glared at her. "I'm outta here."

Mom burst into what I now knew were pretend-hurt tears as I stormed out of the dining room. I got as far as the top of the stairs and stopped. Turning around, I went to the kitchen cupboard where Mom had tucked the bottle of wine she had received with such scorn. I snatched it and bolted down the stairs to the back door. All the raised voices didn't stop me. I shoved my feet into my boots as I heard thumping feet pursuing me down the stairs. Not waiting for them, I went out and slammed the door behind me.

"Griffin!" Jillian. "Griff, please." I stopped, hand on the car door handle. My sister had run outside in the rain with no footwear. She grabbed me and forced me to face her.

"Don't listen to her. Don't you *dare* listen to her. Dad is up there lambasting her this minute, and you'll never hear me make excuses for her. Griffin, I promise you: I didn't want to tell you. I wanted to wait until it all blew over."

I couldn't meet her gaze.

"It *will* blow over, Griffin. And all this about the dance studio, just never mind; it'll work out somehow. Markie isn't happy about it either. No cultural organization is interested in pandering. It's just that this is so last minute. Now, Griffin?"

She waited until I said, "Yeah?"

"Something nobody has bothered to say all evening: How are *you*?"

I nearly lost it. I hugged her a long time.

In the car, every radio station was playing *Oh What a World* by Rufus Wainwright.

Once I got home, I put a Michael Hedges album on the turntable, cranked up the heat, and opened the bottle of wine. I settled in my armchair and warned my sorrows they were facing their doom.

12

Monday, May 14

In the middle of the night, I got up and drank a couple of glasses of water, adding to the ones I'd drunk at bedtime. This would counteract the effects of the copious amounts of wine I had drunk all by myself. But heck, I'd started early, having cut out of Sunday dinner, and it had been worth it. My head was a bit wobbly as I went back to bed, but I was confident I would feel better in the morning. I grabbed my pillow to fluff it up and felt a stab of frustration to see the god-damned knife under it.

"What the—" I pulled it out. "Grrrrrr!" I said to it.

There was absolutely nothing special about it. It was shiny. And it had a nice weight to it. Why did it keep showing up? I snatched it up and stomped into the kitchen, opened the drawer, and mixed it in with all the other knives. Maybe they'd develop a friendship, and it wouldn't desire my company so damn much.

I stormed back to bed and managed to fall asleep after punching my pillow with a hand I now noticed was tingling.

I'd been involved with the band and Salamander's for an entire week. The previous Monday I had been expected at the restaurant first thing in the morning, so I assumed this week would be the same. This was, as I've said, the first time I'd had a job where I didn't get a weekly schedule letting me know my shifts. Salamander's seemed to do a lot of things differently.

By 8:00 Monday morning, as I left to catch the bus, I felt fine thanks to all the water. The tune being played by the guy upstairs—and oddly enough, some other residents in the neighbourhood whose windows must have been open since I could hear it loud and clear—was *Good Day Sunshine*. I wondered which radio station was so popular. I decided this was a good omen and boded well for a good day at work, yesterday's nonsense by Phoenix notwithstanding.

And to be sure, he pretty much stayed out of my way at first. I caught glimpses of his red suit flashing around, but he didn't venture near me. Perhaps he knew he'd gone too far with the cookie-swapping escapade (that had to have been what happened), and he was afraid I might pull a knife on him or something if he came too close. Heh.

Matteo had not yet arrived in the rehearsal room when I dumped my stuff, though one of the other guys was there. I said, "Good morning," but did not allow myself to ask where they had all been yesterday or if Matteo would be there today.

There. Look look. See Griffin manage her emotions. See Griffin walk fast. See Griffin walk to the kitchen with her nose slightly elevated. See Griffin exhibit professional detachment.

As per Chef's instructions, I set out to make apple strudel. Steven—I told him how happy I was to see him—found the recipe in a book called *The Treasure of Mortal Mindlessness*. Who comes up with these ideas? But there, on page twenty-three, was what we needed. We'd already mastered the puff pastry part, so we dove in with the mixing and buttering and folding. At an appropriate time, I left to join rehearsal for a while.

To my great, albeit restrained, delight, Matteo was there. I took a risk: I had worked on *A Case of You* between records while drinking wine and had pretty much mastered it, even with Joni's unconventional tuning. While everyone was setting up, I started playing it . . . just for a lark, avoiding eye contact with Matteo. It was the first time we'd been in the same room since our little . . . encounter in the kitchen. I was embarrassed as hell, a bit because I felt like I was showing off a little, but also because the lyrics meant a lot to me, especially with him in the room.

I hadn't heard him approach. When I felt his hand on my shoulder as I played, I felt a swoop like when a fast-moving elevator comes to a sudden stop. A fiery blush overtook my face and neck like a nasty case of hives, and my voice faltered a little, but I kept going. Having him stand over me like that while I played—while I played for *him*—was intimidating, to say the least. If anyone was worthy of judging my guitar playing, it was Matteo. When I finished, he didn't say anything for several moments of eternity.

At long last, he said, "Wow. That was . . . gorgeous." He entered my peripheral vision and came around in front of me. He sat on the chair opposite, leaning toward me. "Griffin, you are so talented. That is a tough song to play, and you did it, well, it was perfect."

I'm sure I was smiling like a clown. "Well, I don't know about *that*. Thanks."

His deep blue eyes seemed to drink me in, and I wanted nothing more than to drown in them. My whole body tingled, right down to my nethers, and the way he looked at me sparked a flame in my depths. He smiled and slowly licked his lips. The flame in my depths reacted to his smile and lip-licking as if they were a bellows. My desire for him, and his apparent desire for me, made me tremble all over as if I'd been wrapped in bubble wrap where each bubble was a popcorn maker.

He stood up. I stood up and put down my guitar. He stepped forward. I stepped forward.

"I've missed you," he said.

"Really?" I squeaked. Could he hear the throbbing of my heart? He smelled like cinnamon and almonds. He reached over and his hand was warm and soft on my cheek. I closed my eyes involuntarily. I opened them, not wanting to miss a thing. Our lips met, soft and moist, and my loins responded instantly. I parted my lips, and his tongue played lightly with mine. Oh, how I wanted him! But here? Now? Not the place or the time.

Reason took over. "I guess we have to rehearse." His voice was hoarse with desire, and his eyes dim with disappointment, which I'm dead certain was mirrored in mine.

I could hardly speak. "Yeah."

"Do you wanna, maybe, go out somewhere together? Maybe after work tomorrow?"

Had I heard him correctly? "Umm, what?" Oh no, I had done it again: flipped the 'brainless' switch. "Go out? With me?"

Matteo chuckled softly and smiled, like he was kind of confused. "Yes, with you. Why is that so strange?"

Pulling myself together, I dredged up some self-confidence and said, "Yeah, that'd be great."

"Great," he said, taking my hand and stroking the back of it with his thumb. "I'd like that more than just about anything."

With mental acuity I had not possessed in days, I recalled my responsibilities. "I have to teach a lesson at six, though." I was fearful he might say, "Never mind, then," but he didn't.

He said, "Why don't I drive you there and wait for you?"

"Great! Cool."

We pulled apart and a chill shivered through the room as if the air conditioning had turned on and poured through a vent right above us. I even looked up. There was no vent. When I looked down again, Matteo had headed across the room. I was about six feet in the air. I think I even giggled during rehearsal.

I kept on giggling, internally at least, as I returned to the kitchen to take the next steps in the strudel process. Phoenix butted his nose in at one point and found nothing positive to say. He merely sniffed.

"Do you ever even *try* to find something positive to say?" I asked him cheerfully. I didn't bother hiding the fact that I did not hold him in very high regard.

He looked me up and down as if I were dressed in a dragon costume.

"Oh, believe me, I'm trying," he sneered.

God, I hated him. If it weren't for the band, I would *so* be out of here.

Despite Phoenix's best efforts to throw Steven and me off, the strudel turned out well. The apple mixture was easy to make, with cinnamon and ground almonds, and it made a lot, so I scooped it liberally onto the rolled-out pastry. When I baked the strudel, the apples seemed to multiply, and the pastry puffed up until it was as tall as a layer cake. It was the biggest, puffiest strudel I'd ever seen and delicately flaky like gold leaf. I hoped it would taste as good as it looked.

When he saw it, Phoenix said, "I guess if our patrons find something that looks like puke *appetizing*, we may sell some of it."

Nice guy. I guess that might actually pass for a positive comment in some circles.

I hurried back to rehearsal, not even caring what became of the strudel. I figured I had done my job, which was making it. Whether or not it found its way to tables was someone else's responsibility. I wasn't getting paid enough to— Oh. Wait. I still didn't know about that, dang it. Never mind. I was there for the music.

We worked through almost the entire first set, fixing chords and riffs and making sure the kick drum and I were totally locked in. We called it a night, and I put my guitar away, feeling more thrilled about my own playing and more excited about the upcoming gig than I'd ever felt before.

"So, I was thinking about other tunes we could learn," I said.

"Oh yeah? We're always up for learning new songs," Matteo said.

"With our harmonies, I was thinking we could do *Suite: Judy Blue Eyes* and maybe *Galileo*."

Matteo's face lit up like a streetlight at dusk. "Those are great suggestions. Anything else?"

I chuckled, hoping it wasn't too much of a stretch to suggest it. "With both of our guitars and with—" for the life of me I couldn't remember the bass player's name, "—such a solid bass player, I thought we might try *Starship Trooper*. Not for this next gig, of course, but to work on for the future."

In a couple of strides, Matteo was near enough to lay his hand on my cheek. "That's an awesome idea."

I leaned just slightly into his hand. I loved that he hadn't argued with me or doubted that either of us, well, especially me, would be able to handle the duelling guitar solos in the last section of the song. Matteo believed in me as I had never allowed myself to do, even when I was studying with my private instructor. This is what comes of maturity.

I said good night to the guys, half-hoping Matteo would offer me a ride home, but he didn't. No worries. I had tomorrow to look forward to. Where would we go? What would we do?

The weather had changed. The rain was out to rival Niagara Falls, and I had no umbrella. *It's Raining Again* was playing as I walked by the bar on the corner. In the convenience store near the bus stop, the radio played *Here Comes the Rain Again* and *Standin' in the Rain*. I was soaked by the time I boarded the bus. Six blocks from the train station, the bus broke down. I waited for a bit because I figured it was just the trolley poles getting disconnected from the wires, which was not an uncommon occurrence. The driver got off the bus and appeared to be trying to reconnect them, but then she didn't get back on board. I cupped my hands to the window, trying to see where she'd gone. I couldn't see anything in the murk. I was alone.

After about ten minutes, I got off the bus, rather than waiting. I didn't see another bus coming, so I hoofed it along the six blocks to the station, a song about raindrops continuing to fall on my head playing somewhere. Drenched by this time, I caught the train, and it wasn't until we got to Main Street Station that we were told the train couldn't get to the next station because of a "police incident," whatever that meant. The bugger about the timing was that the next station was where I had to change trains, and if I'd known I couldn't get there, I'd have taken a different route home.

I trudged down the station stairs and found a relevant bus stop. The bus I boarded took me partway to the next station, but I had to transfer on the corner of Main and Broadway. I watched the river of water course along the road, the storm drains having a time of sucking it all down. Large pools had formed along the curb, and street corners were beaches extending into lakes of water. Dunderhead that I was, I missed the significance of this until a car came by. The driver made no effort to avoid the puddle. An icy wall of water splashed up over my head and doused the entire length of my body like a tsunami. I gasped with shock as water went down the front and back of my jacket, the front and back of my pants, and filled both shoes. My hair flattened against my head. I could scarcely breathe and shook uncontrollably. I was almost sure my heart had stopped for a moment.

The driver did a U-turn and came back the other way. I could almost have sworn it was Phoenix in the driver's seat.

I didn't scream. I didn't cry. I couldn't even find it in myself to swear. I just stood there and whimpered for a little while as the wind ensured that I experienced every millimetre of wet fabric on my person. Eventually I was able to take a very deep breath and let it out in a controlled manner. I was fucking freezing, but I had made it through the initial blast.

"Oh no!" Teeth chattering, I not only realized my left hand gripped the handle of my acoustic guitar case, but I remembered the case on my back containing my Telecaster. "Oh no, oh no, oh no." Panic was another icy puddle, and I hastened to a dry-ish spot under the awning of a shop a few steps back from the sidewalk. I gently set the acoustic case down and used my right hand to pry my frozen left hand open. My fingers hardly worked on the clasps. All was good in there, the plush not even damp. Trembling, I shrugged the backpack straps off and swung that case around, my chest tight with worry. I laid it on top of the other case and unzipped it. A short sob of relief escaped my throat upon confirming that my beloved guitar was dry. I re-covered and zipped it up again before another car could come along.

Someone, somewhere was playing the Carpenters' song about Mondays and rainy days. How frickin' appropriate.

And that's another thing. This damn music I kept hearing, even when there wasn't any obvious source. And nobody seemed to hear it but me. Once this gig on Sunday was over, I'd need to see my doctor; there were quite a few bizarre things on the list to make me think I was losing my mind. I mean seriously losing my mind. It was starting to scare me.

A bus finally came to take me the rest of the way to the station. As I boarded, the driver yelled at me to "Stop dripping." *Yeah sure, dude. I'll get right on that.* The bus ride was even less pleasant than you are probably imagining since it wasn't long enough for me to dry out even a little bit. I was soaked through, and I huddled in my seat, shivering. The train ride that followed was no improvement, and I never did get warm that whole damn trip.

I'd left the restaurant at 5:30 and didn't get home until 7:45. In that time I had heard tons of songs about frickin' rain. They were playing everywhere. They suggested I sing in the rain, that the rain was in the early morning, and that it was purple. They asked if I had seen it, and asked who will stop it, and told me they would carry on crying in it, even that somebody with blue eyes would do said crying. It was suggested I blame the rain, and more than one person *wished* it would rain, for fuck's sake. I was starting to think the music was somehow in my head. As I boarded the bus to head up the hill to my apartment, Ella sang to me about how into each life some precipitation must fall, and I wanted to yell at her that I had had quite enough, thank you very fucking much.

I had to wring streams of water out of everything, and I mean *everything*, into the bathtub, and then I had a great long, hot shower to try to warm up. It took ages. Especially since I found myself thinking about the soft moistness of Matteo's lips . . . and his eyes, . . . and his tongue, and . . . well.

After, I spent the evening playing guitar. I played and sang through *Gotta Have You* for Teresa's wedding and then worked through a few trouble spots in the songs on the list for Sunday. I was irritated, though, because no matter what I played, I was distracted by music from other apartments. All songs about rain, which didn't even surprise me anymore. Beatles and Dylan and Billie Holiday and Eddie Rabbitt. I gave in and started playing along with them.

Later I lay in bed, listening to the buckets of rain slapping my windows and among it, hearing a familiar bass line from the apartment behind mine. I couldn't hear the melody or anything, so it took me a while to figure out what the song was, but I always take that on as a challenge. I figured it out. It was *Riders on the Storm*.

13

Tuesday, May 15

I awoke clenching my teeth so hard, my jaw ached. When the phone rang, I jumped as if someone had popped a balloon right behind my head and hesitated to pick it up because lately the phone had meant bad news. But the call display showed it was Brian, so this time I picked it up with a tentative, "Hello?" He reminded me Dominic's lesson was at its normal time of 6:00 this week. I recalled that the previous week his lesson had been at four. I told

Brian I remembered, thanked him, and hung up the phone with a sense of a tiny weight, akin to that of a goldfish, having been lifted, which resulted in my relishing a cup of tea with my morning toast with honey and cinnamon.

It was Matteo's kiss that had stayed with me through the night, not the trauma of the soaking-wet bus ride. I was almost excited about going to Salamander's. Almost but not quite.

The weather was considerably drier, if not lots warmer, so my trip into town wasn't utterly horrible.

As I walked to the restaurant from the bus, I saw the same homeless fellow who had watched me roll on the grass the previous week. He looked kind of alarmed, and I figured I owed it to him to be friendly. I pointed out the entrance to Salamander's.

"Hey, if you come in there sometime, I'll give you some lunch, okay?"

He looked at me warily and stepped back as I passed him.

I succeeded in making it to the kitchen without running into anyone I didn't want to see. I didn't run into anyone I *did* want to see either, but that was all right. The kitchen was vacant of people, too, and I checked the clock to see if I was inordinately early. I was not, but since other people's schedules were not my responsibility, I didn't worry about it. Maybe Tuesdays were Chef's other day off.

A note handwritten in thick, green marker was on my table: *Cinnamon buns.*

Really? They thought I was an expert pastry chef, and they asked me to make . . . bread?

Well, all right. I'd be able to go rehearse for a decent chunk of time while the dough rose, so this would work out well. It was kind of the perfect scenario as there was absolutely nothing on this earth I wanted more than to go and be in the same room with Matteo. I hoped I didn't drool with the desire to pick up where we'd left off last night.

My phone rang. It was Calvin. I stared at it, frozen, unable to press the Talk button with my head still full of Matteo. It went to voice mail. A filament of guilt wound round my hand and up my arm, and I kept staring at the phone until the little icon appeared in the corner of the screen, indicating that he had hung up. Only then could I press buttons through the sequence that would allow me to hear what he had said.

"Hey, Griffin." He sounded way more uplifted than he had on Friday night. Excited, even. "Do you ever pick up your phone these days? Or is it just when I call?" He chuckled and couldn't know how close to home he'd come. "So listen, Andy's cousin knows a guy who lives not too far from here, and he's apparently a half-decent lead player. So we were talking and thinking we could get together on Wednesday night, well, tomorrow, and have a jam session. Y'know, like an audition kind of thing. Can you make it? And if we find anybody else, they can come too and take turns or something. Anyway, give me a call and let me know. It doesn't make sense for us to do it without you, so . . . I hope you can."

The message ended with a beep, and I stood still, with the phone in my hand, stunned and perplexed.

Well, of course the rest of the band should be looking for a new lead player! Of course they should. Why would I think it was up to me? My head knew this to be true, but for some reason, my heart felt like a needle was stuck in it. And now I had to make a choice.

On the one hand, it was the perfect opportunity to introduce Matteo to my band, to clarify what I should have clarified days ago: that I needed a lead guitarist for *my* band, not a new band for myself. He could come and audition. He would blow them away and voila! We'd get to make fabulous music together twice. Or he could come and audition, and he'd spill the beans about the Spurious Correlations, and I would have some explaining to do.

On the other hand, there was a childish part of me that wanted to keep Matteo to myself. What if he didn't think we were very good? Good enough for him? What if he realised that I'm a complete fraud? Maybe he wasn't interested in playing with another band anyhow?

Maybe I was overthinking it, as usual, and I needed to just ask him.

The other person I did not see anywhere was Steven. Without him to find the recipe for me, I stepped over to the bookshelf with the eager determination of an archaeologist. Where would one begin to look for a recipe for bread among a shelf of titles such as *Flossy the Multi-Lingual Fungus* and *I Shipped My Parcel to Bolivia*? Excitement and suspicion took hold of my nerves in equal measure with their anemone-like tendrils when I saw a narrow-spined book entitled *Bread*. It turned out to be a treatise on the auto industry in Belize. (There pretty much isn't one, in case you were interested. After revealing this illuminating fact within the first two paragraphs, the book was filled with the word *codswallop* over and over.)

I won't bore you with details of the search. Suffice it to say I eventually found the recipe in a book called *Fourteen Times I Called My Cat*, which was sitting on the counter by the large mixer, which was a very convenient place and would have saved me twenty minutes of searching had I seen it there. Why couldn't whoever had placed it there have placed it with the *Cinnamon buns* instruction sign?

But never mind. I opened to the recipe and determined that for the number of cinnamon buns I needed to make, I'd better double, or even triple, it. I found all the ingredients I needed and got started. I measured flour and yeast and other things and dumped them in the large mixer, which folded and mixed and kneaded the dough. It was probably the easiest thing I'd ever made since I didn't have to do all the kneading by hand. All the while, I wondered what Matteo was doing and if he was thinking about me. The speakers were playing *Rise Again*, but I was humming *At Last*.

When the mixer had kneaded the dough enough, I turned the machine off and released the bowl to place it in a suitable location for rising. I rubbed the massive ball of dough with butter so it wouldn't dry out and lay a sizeable cloth over it. By this time, several of the kitchen staff had arrived, and I left them to their devices while I washed up.

On my way to the rehearsal room, I thought how convenient it was that, apart from Sunday, all of us band members seemed to always be available at the same time. My pace slowed. It dawned on me that I hadn't seen any of the guys working in the dining room, or anywhere else for that matter, not since Matteo served crème brûlée on my very first shift. Yet whatever jobs they did outside of rehearsal, it was darned convenient that we didn't seem to ever say, "Oh shucks, we have to rehearse without Dennis this time because he's waiting tables over the lunch rush." Nobody was ever missing. I always was the last one to arrive.

Come to think of it, was there a guy in the band called Dennis?

I banished these confusing thoughts from my mind as I pulled open the studio door.

The others were there but Matteo wasn't.

"He's going to be late," the bass player—I think his name was Bjorn—said.

That was a surprise. "How come?"

"He said something about needing some new guitar picks," said the drummer—Thor, I think his name was.

"Well, that's goofy," I said. "I work at a music store; he knows that. I'm going there later. I could easily have brought him some."

"He wouldn't have wanted to trouble you," the keyboard player—Darcy? or was that Dennis?—said.

A niggle of disappointment wiggled up the back of my neck. Not only was it kind of a lame excuse to be late, but he had squandered an opportunity for me to do him a favour. I imagined him asking me to grab some guitar picks for him on my next trip to the music store. I imagined myself saying, "Sure, no problem," with cool, yet warm, disinterest. I imagined myself returning, completely self-possessed, downplaying my triumph as I handed him the little paper bag. I would have received the warmth of his smile; the tenderness in those deep, blue eyes; and the caramel of his voice saying, "Thanks, Griffin."

Wait a minute. Matteo had said he would drive me to my lesson after work. He could have picked up guitar picks then. Had he forgotten he was going to drive me? Had he forgotten about our date as well?

Whoa. What the hell was this reaction about? I was disappointed not to see him, that was all. It was a small thing I could have done for him. It was not horrifying news that he'd been in a car crash or something. Good heavens, I was reacting like a junior high school girl over her first crush. *Pull yourself together, muttonhead.*

"Okay," I said. "What can we work on until he gets here?" There is always stuff a band can work on when there are people missing. Which this band had never had to do before. See above.

We worked on a few songs, but I couldn't keep from glancing over at the door, awaiting his arrival. I was so distracted, I just couldn't focus on the music. As a result, I felt utterly feeble on top of everything else.

After about an hour, I excused myself. "I have to go to turn bread dough into cinnamon buns." I hesitated a moment, waiting for someone else to say, "Oh yes, it's Clean the Vinegar Bottles day in the dining room," or something to indicate that the others did anything around here but play music. Nope. Nothing.

Disappointment was a knife in my side, and I stumbled down the hall to the kitchen. So dispirited was I, so entrenched in over-reactive melancholy, with thoughts like *Why didn't he show up? Where could he be? Does he remember our date? Why am I the only one that seems to work in the restaurant?* that it took quite a few moments for my senses to catch up. At long last the mantra turned to *What the devil is that smell?*

Have you ever entered a building and observed the familiar aroma of chlorine and instantly known there was a swimming pool somewhere? Imagine that, rather than smelling chlorine, you are assailed by the warm, acid-and-alcohol aroma of yeast.

My bread dough had risen.

The bowl it had been in was no longer visible, buried under a mountain of dough. A goodly portion of it had spilled over onto the floor, and it resembled the Matterhorn towering over my head. The cloth I had used to cover the dough fluttered at the top like a flag. The song coming through the speaker system was *Rise Up*.

"Not funny," I told it.

Even if I punched it down, there was no way the counter, albeit the size of a pool table, was large enough to roll out all the dough at once. I would have to pick off and bin all the surfaces that had touched the floor, which was tragic, not to mention a royal pain in the ass. I sighed as loud as a jet engine and grabbed my apron, then washed my hands and approached the puddinglike monster that wanted to swallow the kitchen.

If you've ever made bread from scratch, and by hand, you'll know the way the dough behaves, for the most part easily pulling away from the sides of the bowl. This was not like that. This was more like Oobleck, and I don't mean the kind you make out of corn starch for kids to play with. I mean like Bartholomew's, sticky and bubbly and threatening to take over the world. And it continued to burgeon.

I had complained about the rain; of course I had. But not once during my harrowing journey home last night had I complained like King Derwin in Dr. Seuss's *Bartholomew* story, that rain, in and of itself, was *boring*. I didn't know which magic words I had used to summon this mess, nor could I guess what would make it stop.

I tried the obvious. *"Stop!"*

Exactly nothing happened. Until a brief moment later, it did. The dough mushroomed. Fast. I had to back away.

"God damn it!" I yelled. "I did not sign on for this." I was being *Punked*. That was it. Any second now a TV host would waltz through the door. *Please!*

I placed myself before the mass, making myself as large as possible, as if I were facing a leopard. It slammed into me and I staggered. *Do not fall over!* I told myself. If I fell, that would be the end of me.

"Help!" I yelled, but of course there was no one else around. Where were all the dancing chefs when I needed them? I pressed my whole self against the onslaught, bracing my feet against the cupboards.

I wracked my brain and recalled that in the story, the king had finally said, "I'm sorry."

It caused me pain to apologise for something that was not my fault. This was exactly the kind of thing my support group would tell me *not* to do.

(What was I even apologising *for*?) Especially when I seemed to be apologising to Phoenix bloody Rising. Remembering his name felt like being stabbed between my eyes. Believe me, I considered my options carefully. What I really wanted to do was walk out. But I knew that would spell the end of playing with the Spurious Correlations, and that was simply not a choice I was capable of making. I might be free of baking hell, but there would be a hole in my heart that would drain me of my life force.

"Fine!" Tipping my head back to avoid the suffocating blob approaching my face, I looked around for the camera I was certain existed somewhere. "Fine." I raised my doughy hands in supplication, swallowed my pride and dignity, and said, "I'm sorry?"

It took a moment, but at last the dough stopped its growth and even subsided like a falling soufflé, leaving little moraines of dough here and there. I dropped my head and squeezed my eyes to prevent tears from even forming, let alone falling. I had humbled myself to a mass of dough, which was an all-time low. What had I done to deserve this? Why me?

When the dough was a manageable size, and I had picked off any obviously dirty bits, I pushed and punched and rolled it in on itself, taking out all my frustrations on it. It deserved the beating more than I did. I found several large bowls and moved quantities of it to other surfaces, leaving a wieldy amount on my worktable. The original bowl I had used revealed itself the way a statue emerges from the sculptor's stone.

Picking bits of dough off my clothes and out from under my fingernails, I took stock of the room.

About five cooks puttered away in their corners of the kitchen, oblivious to my antics. These were all new cooks. Whose names I didn't know. Who had not been in the room for the past forty-five minutes. My jaw relaxed and I just stood there, shaking my head. In all honesty, this place was starting to feel unreal to me. Every day some bizarre thing occurred, to me and me alone, and each one was a dose of anaesthetic, benumbing me to the point where it was all becoming commonplace. Any moment now, somebody would come along and tell me I was the hilarious victim of a prank show and wasn't I such a good sport?

"I am not even surprised by this, honestly," I said to no one in particular, flicking dough into a tub. "This whole dough thing just kind of sums up my life of the last ten days or so."

The other cooks smiled and nodded and kept about their business.

"That's another thing." I pushed dough into a shape I could roll with a rolling pin. "Who are all you people? Where do you come from? Where do you live? Do you speak English?" I found the rolling pin under the counter. "Not that it's a problem if you don't. It's just that I've worked here for over a week, and I don't know any of your names and you're awfully quiet."

I rolled dough and chattered and spread butter and a mixture of cinnamon and brown sugar. The song had moved on to *Cinnamon Girl*. I took the next couple of hours gathering up the rest of the dough, punching it, shaping it, rolling it out so I could swamp it with cinnamon bun filling, roll it into a spiral, and slice it. I lay the coils of sticky-sweet goodness on baking sheets and lined them up on every possible surface to rise.

I washed my hands and excitedly reached behind myself to untie my apron, looking forward to the rest of rehearsal more than I had ever looked forward to anything in my life. Including the time I met Alex Lifeson. Only playing guitar and singing had charms to soothe the savage breast, as Congreve sort of said. It was what I needed right then if I were to regain any composure. I stepped toward the hook to hang my apron. Just then, the door burst open and Phoenix, wearing a royal blue cape over a white-and-blue-striped onesie, filled the doorway. I froze.

I clutched the apron and stared at him. He stared at the cinnamon buns. I swallowed and waited for the disparagement. None came. He spun around and the door swung *fwoop-fwoop* behind him.

My urgent need to make music just then became overshadowed by my even more urgent need to stay and guard my project as it rose. I did not wish to come back in an hour and find they'd piled themselves up and hardened into giant snowmen. Missing a chance to play hurt like the time I had to miss the Peter Gabriel concert to attend the funeral of some uncle I didn't know.

My heart ached with desire to run down and see if Matteo had turned up, but there was no damn way I was leaving those buns unattended. I put my apron back on in a kind of *None shall pass!* declaration.

After an hour of reading *Tales from the Potter's Wheel*—not one of which had anything to do with pottery, getting bored and instead sitting on the counter miming finger-picking patterns and humming through solo sections and wishing I had a guitar in my hands, I turned on every oven in the place. The baking took ages with so many pans of cinnamon buns, but finally, eventually, at long last, in the fullness of time, they were done. The heavenly aroma coaxed drool onto my tongue. I was hanging up the oven mitts when Phoenix blew in like a gale-force wind.

I braced myself.

"Wow. Those look amazing."

I squinted at him, suspicion overwhelming me like vertigo. "What?"

He turned to me and shrugged. "What what? I said they look amazing and it's true."

"Why are you saying that?" He was mocking me, for sure.

He threw his hands in the air. "Must I have a reason? Other than the truth?"

"Oh, come off it, Phoenix. This is exactly what I was talking about yesterday. You never say nice things."

"And so today I am saying something nice."

"Why don't I believe you?"

"I cannot imagine. Look," he said, pointing to one of the cinnamon buns in the middle of the table. "That one is particularly extraordinary. You should eat it."

My heart pounded like I'd run a marathon. "I should do what?"

"Eat it. You know, in the name of quality control."

Why that one? What had he done to it? My knees quaked. "Why don't *you* eat it?"

His eyes widened and he straightened. "Why, I think I will!" He reached over and separated the bun in question from its friends. "But I don't like to eat alone; why don't you eat . . ." he ran his gaze over the table, ". . . that one?"

I studied him, suspicion cranking up my heartbeat. And now why *that* one? The man hid his intentions well, but I wasn't buying it. On the other hand, I hadn't eaten since breakfast, so my needs got the better of my intellect. "Fine." I snatched the bun in question and took a tiny bite. It was mouth watering. I pretty much crammed the rest of the bun in at once, the whole time staring at my hitherto-and-probably-still-but-pretending-not-to-be tormentor.

"I do hope you're going to make icing for these." He licked his fingertips. "They would be positively *divine* with icing. Cream cheese icing."

My chest puffed with shallow breaths. The cinnamon bun was delicious. But I didn't trust it for a moment. All right, so what had he done to the ones *next* to those ones?

"You there!" he called to two other chefs on the other side of the kitchen. "Come and try these!" They tottered over curiously.

Phoenix pointed. "Try that one and you try that one. No, not that one, *that* one."

They picked up the buns that had been selected for them and took a bite. My usually silent coworkers found their voices.

"Oh my, this is the best thing I have *ever* tasted!" said one. "My compliments to the chef."

"It is delicious," said the other. "Very tasty. You're a fantastic cook!"

I frowned, incapable of politely accepting compliments that sounded rehearsed. After they had orated their lines, the two chefs retreated to the side of the kitchen.

"See? Told you." Phoenix spun around with a wave of his cape. "Beautiful work today." He ducked through the door to the dining room. "Oh my word, you would not *believe* these cinnamon buns in here!" he pronounced to persons unknown. "You simply *must* . . ." His voice faded as the door *flupped* behind him.

I stared after him and waited for the cinnamon buns to turn into fireworks and explode. Or to fizzle and dry up. Or shoot jets of water like a water park. There had to be something wrong with the rest of them; there *had* to be. There was absolutely no way on earth Phoenix would be encouraging. He had somehow set this up with the other two chefs without my noticing. Something was up; that's all there was to it, and I imagined him waiting on the other side of the door for whatever it was to happen so he could come back in and laugh his fool head off at me.

They were delicious. They were *too* delicious.

Somebody's Watching Me taunted me through the speakers. The other chefs had vanished. Probably hiding in cupboards, waiting to pop out at me.

"No," I said to the room. "I am not going to let it happen."

Trembling like a wet chihuahua, with near-hysteria tightening my throat, I dragged all the huge garbage bins over to the table and swept row after row of suspiciously "perfect," and therefore entirely suspect, cinnamon buns into them. I pressed them down and squashed more in until not a single crumb remained on any of the counters. I backed up and cowered against the fridge, cringing, awaiting the massive volcanic eruption from the bins.

When it didn't come, I whipped off my apron, flung it on the floor, and flew to the door, where I stopped and turned around. I stalked back to the apron, picked it up, and deliberately hung it on the hook, my back as tense as a guitar string. I ran from the kitchen.

I raced to the rehearsal room. Would Matteo be there yet? He had to be. We had a gig in just a few days. Not to mention a date that evening.

I ran down the hall and burst through the door.

"Is he back?" I panted.

"You just missed him," Bjorn? Thor? No, that one was Dennis. No! Darcy, said.

"What?" My anguished disappointment at missing him was so pathetic, my mother would have had good reason to turn her nose up at me. "Where has he gone now? He was supposed to give me a ride—" I was highly strung out from cinnamon bun panic.

"Doctor's appointment," either Darcy or Thor or Bjorn said. "He has a —"

"No!" I put up my hand as a stop sign. I did *not* need to hear any details of what physiological ailment had taken the man of my dreams to the doctor. I was despondent enough not having seen him all day, and I did not need to add to my discombobulation by worrying about something that was either, well, worrisome or not any of my business. He wasn't officially my boyfriend. I didn't think it right to have too much personal knowledge yet.

But I wished he had popped his head into the kitchen to let me know he was leaving and when he would be back. Or if he would be back. I also wished I hadn't stayed in the kitchen guarding bread while it rose instead of going to rehearsal. Why hadn't someone come and asked after me? A spoiled child–like pang of feeling left out again was yet another reason to be ashamed of myself.

I wasn't sure what to do. We had already worked through things we could work through without lead guitar. I mucked about with *Power of Two* and kept checking the door until it got to be time to leave if I were to make it to the store by bus. I gathered my belongings and headed out to the street.

Where Matteo's blue Mini sat waiting, and the man himself stood next to the car. He smiled and waved as soon as he saw me. After the insane thoughts that had been going through my head all day, I was supremely frustrated and felt like saying, "What the hell are you doing out here?" (And believe me, I thought this with full knowledge that it was a stunning betrayal on my part to harbour such a thing as a negative thought about this man.) But his smile was sheepish, and he said, "I was afraid to come inside lest I get roped into something."

That was a decent enough excuse.

And now I would make it to the music store early, which would be a nice surprise for Brian.

"One of the guys said you had to buy guitar picks," I said. "How come you didn't just wait until we got to my store?"

"Guitar picks?" He seemed puzzled. "No, I had to pick up a parcel from the post office."

"Oh. And your doctor's appointment? Not that it's any of my business."

"That's okay. I had a bit of a fever."

"Really?" I said with some alarm. "Are you okay?" If he had to cancel tonight, I would be disappointed, but I'd totally understand.

"Yeah. Turns out I just need more cowbell."

"Ha!" I laughed but he looked at me unsmilingly, and I shrank, uncertain. Surely he wasn't serious. "Are you sure you're okay? Like, for this evening and stuff?"

He turned his beaming smile onto me again. "Yeah, I'm fine."

Now it was my turn to feel like I had a fever.

We decided to go to the pub for a drink and some food after my lesson, and he dropped me off outside the store. He didn't want to come in, which I thought was weird, but he said he wanted to sit in the car and read. He showed me his copy of *The Secret World of Og*, and I couldn't blame him for his choice.

My lesson with Dominic went well; he'd been practising. I liked that kid.

Afterward, Matteo and I went to my favourite pub and sat across from each other in the corner near the fireplace. Could this be any more perfect for a first date? (Was this a first date?) I didn't want to leave my guitar in the car, so I stood it up in the corner next to me. I also turned my cell phone off. The server came and I ordered a gin and tonic. Matteo ordered cake-flavoured vodka with Dr. Pepper. I thought my eyes would drop out of my head. Can you say, "Sweeeeeet?"

Oh well, it was not for me to judge.

I also ordered some hot wings and yam fries. Matteo said, "Do you guys have deep fried kohlrabi?"

"Pardon?" asked the server.

"Kohlrabi," he repeated. "It's like a turnip in appearance but like cabbage or broccoli stems in crunch and flavour."

She stared at him. "No," she said.

"All right, then. I'll just have yam fries too. Do you have a raspberry vinaigrette I can dip them in?"

"I . . . don't . . . think . . . so . . ."

"Never mind, then. Just the fries."

The server looked relieved as she went to the next table.

I decided to launch into the conversation I knew I had to have but was causing me some anxiety.

"So do you remember the night we met?" I was instantly aware of how lame that sounded. Like a line out of a crummy movie.

He said, "Yeah, how could I forget?" which sounded like a response from a crummy movie, and I am ashamed to say it still made me blush.

"Heh. Well, see . . . when Rickenbacker told me he knew a guitarist, I was interested because I needed someone to replace Jason. You met Jason."

Matteo rolled his eyes. "Yeah, what a rotter."

"Yeah. So you see . . ." Reticence held my words back like a mother preventing her toddler from running into the street. "I wasn't actually. . . looking for a new band to play in—"

Alarm lit his face. "Are you quitting The Spurious Correlations?"

"No! No no no. *God* no! I love The Spurious Correlations, though Phoenix is an awfully big deterrent—"

Matteo leaned forward suddenly. "Yes. He is."

"Umm, yeah. So."

Our drinks arrived and we *clinked*. I watched Matteo's face to see if it went funny after he sipped his strange choice of highball. It didn't. "But you see, my other band is still looking for a lead guitarist." I got all stammery then, for whatever reason. "I—I—I don't know if you would be interested, but we're auditioning another fellow tomorrow night, and I wondered if you —"

"Yes."

"—might be open to coming and play— Wait. What?"

Matteo put his hand on top of mine, taking my breath away. "Yes. I would really like to audition for you."

"That's great. Cool."

Our food arrived, necessitating the lifting of his hand. It had rested upon mine for only a moment, but it was an intimate gesture, and I liked it.

Now it was imperative for me to bring up the only awkward part.

I picked up a wing. "I kind of have to ask you a favour."

He said, "Oh yeah?" through about six fries jammed in his mouth. *Umm* . . .

This was the tricky part. I hoped he wouldn't think I was immature or, even worse, a conniving sort who could not be trusted.

"So I haven't actually told Calvin and the others about playing with you." Oh, lordy, this sounded so high school! I hastily added, "I *will*, I mean, I have every intention, but I wanted to just give it a try, and we had just come off an awful gig. I know this sounds lame." I took a bite of wing. It was plump and juicy and doused in hot sauce, so it was kind of sloopy. Just the way I like them.

He swallowed fries. "I get it. You don't want them to think you have betrayed them by leaving them for another band when you aren't even sure if things are going to work out with us."

It sounded like I was having an affair or something, which is exactly what it felt like. On the other hand, I was pleased that he grasped the situation. "Yeah, you've pretty much hit the nail on the head. Sorry."

"Lots of people play in more than one band."

Was the man right inside my head, sifting through all my arguments with myself?

"I know, which is why I *will* tell them; I just don't feel ready to tell them *yet*. So if it doesn't go against your integrity, would you be willing to . . ." Wow, this sounded so childish. "Could you pretend you don't know me very well? We could say you're a friend of a friend."

"A friend of a friend."

"Yeah. Just for the audition. After our gig on Sunday, I'll feel more confident and I'll sit down with Calvin and tell him all about it."

"Who's Calvin?"

"Calvin's my best friend, and he's our drummer. We met in elementary school and were really good friends as little kids. Then he moved away for a few years and came back when we were in high school. It was really neat seeing each other in band and choir at school and saying, "Wait a minute. Hey, I know you!" We've been super good friends ever since. He's a terrific drummer, and it just made sense that when I wanted to start a band, it would be with him. Like, I think he'd have been hurt if I hadn't asked him first." I was grinning like a madwoman. Talking about Calvin was like talking about music. I nearly changed my mind right then and there. *Never mind. I'll introduce you and tell him all about The Spurious Correlations* was on the tip of my tongue.

"It all sounds very congenial."

What a strange choice of words. Was he being sarcastic? "Yeah, he is, but he's just a friend, I mean, Jason was my boyfriend. I was really slow on picking up that he's an arrogant jerk."

Matteo smiled that boyish smile of his. "Of course I'll do it. I'll say whatever you want me to say. I wouldn't want anything to be awkward for you, Griff."

"Oh wow, thanks so much." I loved the way he called me "Griff."

"I care about you."

Was that the hot sauce making me feel sweaty and flushed? "I . . . care about you too. And I really appreciate this. I promise I won't let it go on. Like, if they decide they want you in the band, then it's a nonissue, right? And I'll explain everything."

"Cool," Matteo said and stuffed six more fries in his mouth.

We ate and sipped our drinks and chatted about music, brainstorming songs we could add to our repertoire. I offered him a couple of my hot wings, and the one bite he took nearly blew his head off. I had to laugh, but I also felt bad.

"Wow, not much for spicy, eh?"

"I guess not," he said. "I've never had those before."

"What?" I couldn't believe my ears. "Have you been living under a rock?"

"No, just at the base of a mountain."

"Heh." That was kind of funny. Wasn't it? "Where do you live? Did you grow up here?"

"Not exactly. Listen, what time is it? I can't stay too late."

"It's only eight," I reassured him.

"Oh, wow. I have to get going."

"Why? Is it past your bedtime?" I chuckled, but I was also a wee bit annoyed. This going out for a drink thing had been his idea. Why would he suggest it on an evening when he had other things going on?

"I'm sorry." He took my hand. "I've really enjoyed spending this time with you. But I have to go."

I was not sure I was able to keep the disappointment from my voice as I said, "Okay."

The server brought our bills upon request. I was relieved to just pay for my own and avoid that "who is paying for whom" awkwardness that always makes me feel like I have to keep track of whose turn it is. Perfectly fine for a first—was this a "date"? I couldn't be sure.

I slung my guitar over one shoulder, and we went out to the car.

Matteo opened the passenger door for me in a gentlemanly way. "Your carriage, miss."

He took my guitar to deposit in the back for me, and I climbed in. We drove the short distance to my apartment, where I was tempted to invite him in, only he had said he had to get going, so I didn't. I reached to unbuckle my seatbelt.

He turned to me and said, "Thank you, Griffin, for a lovely evening."

"Heh," I said. "Thank *you*. I had a good time too. Thanks for the rides."

He was staring deeply into my eyes like he was trying to hypnotize me. "It was my pleasure. I look forward to many more opportunities of this nature."

Okay, so obviously he really wished he didn't have to leave this early. Naturally I forgave him instantly.

"I guess I'll see you tomorrow, then," I said.

He brushed my cheek with his fingers. "I look forward to it. And the audition too. I promise I won't spoil anything for you."

"I'm sure you'll be amazing."

He moved his hand so it was under my chin, and I leaned forward in anticipation.

His lips brushed mine like kitten whiskers. "I don't want to start something I can't finish," he whispered, his breath on my cheek. *Too late, truth be told.*

I agreed, with a massive reluctant sigh. The moment over, I said, "Good night," got out of the car, and retrieved my guitar from the back. I went to the door of my apartment with leaden feet. I turned and waved as he drove off.

Our first date had been short but very sweet. The first of what I hoped would be many. I watched his little blue Mini until he had disappeared around the corner.

Inside, I made myself a massive gin and tonic (I had had only one at the pub) and turned on my phone to check my voice mail.

"Griffin?" said my mother, as if she weren't sure which number she'd called. "You brought a bottle of wine over the other night, and I want to know what you've done with it. Where did you hide it? I want to serve it to my Bunco club because whatever it is, it's good enough for *them*. If you were so childish as to take it away, well, you're not the daughter *I* brought up."

I fell asleep thinking of Matteo while my brain played Les Paul and Mary Ford's recording of *I'm a Fool to Care*.

14

Wednesday, May 16

Wednesday I had the pleasure of taking transit to work in the sunshine for a change. I had slept well, but my head felt woolly, and in truth, I wanted nothing more than to just stay in bed and sleep all day. I hadn't had a day off, a complete break from everything, in ten days. Longer if you count the Snifter wedding, for which we'd had rehearsals for days beforehand. Exhaustion was an overcoat with chains sewn into the lining. Its weight pulled me closer to the ground and filled me with a yearning to become one with the earth, or the carpet, or the sidewalk—really, every horizontal surface I encountered. The tiny thought of my other band added a guilty ingot of lead to one of the pockets of the overcoat, and I fervently hoped I could be relieved of it soon.

The sunshine was an elixir, bringing warmth to my very core. It didn't warm me enough to remove the overcoat, but it allowed me to open a few buttons.

The question as I boarded the bus on my street, piece of toast with peanut butter in hand, which the bus driver ignored, bless her heart, was *Would the rest of my band like Matteo at tonight's audition?*

The very thought of it coaxed a smile to my lips, not to mention the breakdancing elves in my belly. I got off the bus and climbed up the stairs to the train platform. The train journey was fine except for the guy with nasty body odour sitting next to me, followed by a packed bus ride where a woman kept bumping into me while gripping an overhead strap and coughing into her elbow with poor aim. Once I pushed through and popped out of the bus doors, anticipation of rehearsal gave my feet buoyancy as I walked to the restaurant. I was mentally figuring out the fingering for *Señor Mouse* and getting excited about trying it.

I passed my homeless friend on the corner and reminded him to come and see me sometime. As soon as the words were out of my mouth, I realized the offer sounded like something other than lunch, so I hastened to the door.

My hand grasped the door pull but I hesitated.

Would anyone mention the bins of cinnamon buns? I frowned and told myself I could just lie my way out of any responsibility. *They were intact when I left the kitchen*, I would say if questioned. I would feign outrage, and all would be exactly the same as it had been every other day my work had been sabotaged. Truth be told, the waste hurt me deep inside, but the threat to my dignity and pride was a greater risk. Having talked myself through that issue, I crossed my fingers that my baking task for the day would be something simple. I wasn't terribly hopeful, though, considering yesterday's fiasco wasn't even a complicated task.

I steeled myself and entered. My heels dragged as I meandered between the dark wood tables of the dining room and approached the kitchen door. What would greet me on the other side? I pushed through and the doors made a quiet *flup-flup* behind me.

Not a trace of cinnamon or brown sugar or bread remained. The bins, I saw with blessed relief, were empty. *Phew.*

"Griffin, you doll!" Chef fluttered over like a dancer in *Swan Lake*. "I have a special request for you today. I am sure with your skill—nay, your *genius*—you will be up for the task."

"I'll do my best."

"That's good enough for me. After all, *your* 'mediocrity' is far beyond anyone else's 'best.'" He gave me his instruction and twirled off.

My task for the day was to make sugar cookies. I figured Phoenix must have been tired of testing my mettle. I didn't even need Steven's help, which was good because he was nowhere to be seen. I went and dropped off my gear then returned to the kitchen, where I scooped, dumped, mixed, tasted. Not bad.

The simplicity of my task was an unfamiliar juxtaposition with the frantic carrying on of the other chefs. They scurried like pigeons, circling around each other, moving dishes from one counter to another, stirring things, setting pots on stoves, sliding roasting dishes into ovens, pulling heated pans out. I had stuck my cookie dough in the fridge to chill for a while, so I hesitantly approached the other section of the kitchen. I didn't want to get in the way, but I was super curious. I hadn't thought of it before, being over-my-head busy with my own responsibilities, but I had no idea what else was on the menu at this restaurant. I had continued to bring my own lunch from day one since I'd never been offered a meal or anything. It seemed to me I had never actually laid eyes on a plate of food going out of the kitchen into the dining room. How airheaded was I that I hadn't noticed?

The cooks seemed to still be able to manoeuvre around the kitchen without bashing into me. They were all very aware, which was neat. When I got close enough to see right into the saucepans and dishes coming out of the oven, I stopped short. It was as if I had found myself in a black and white film. Except food in a black-and-white film still looks, well, like food. This was all just . . . masses of grey. In that moment I also noticed I couldn't smell anything. No meat cooking, no sauces simmering, no brightly coloured vegetables steaming, no large bowls of salad greens. That thing there looked like a massive bowl of what might be grey playdough but without the weight: a cook picked it up one-handed and passed it to another cook with the same ease as if she had passed a paper plate with one lettuce leaf.

I backed away very slowly, every inch of skin on my body crinkling with horror. My throat constricted and I fought an urge to flee. I opened my mouth to say, "What the hell is going on?" to a cook named . . . Wait, come to think of it, I still didn't know any of their names. And *that* is when I fled into the dining room.

Which was still dark and empty. It was 11:00. Shouldn't there be a few customers there for early lunch? The restaurant was on the edge of downtown. Surely there were businesses nearby that would have people who needed a coffee break? And certainly there ought to have been servers rolling cutlery in serviettes, making sure condiment bottles and salt and pepper shakers were full, or placing water glasses on tables. I had never worked in a restaurant, but I had eaten at a few, and I was pretty sure these things would have to take place. In fact, shouldn't my bandmates have been in there getting the place ready for customers?

I stalked through the dining room and burst through the front door onto Powell Street. It looked like it always did. It was one-way westbound, and several cars moved along it as I would have expected. Not busy.

Seeing the spot where I'd last spoken to the homeless fellow, I glanced up and down the road. I didn't see him, and I hoped he was all right. It was just as well because if he did come by, what on earth would I have given him to eat? *Here, dude, have this dish of ashes.*

I went back inside and saw Phoenix heading through the dim dining room to a door at the far, dark end—a door I hadn't noticed before. I hunkered back against the wall, so he wouldn't notice me. Once he had passed through the door, I almost ran toward it, weaving through the dark chairs and tables. I hoped it was an office and that Rickenbacker would be there. I had no interest in talking to Phoenix—he was a nutbar—but Rickenbacker had gotten me into this. He owed me an explanation.

Through the door, I found myself in a hallway so brightly lit in contrast with the dimness of the dining room, I raised my arm to shade my eyes. Bright colours glared at me. This hallway was familiar. The lime green walls with sky blue stripes, the pale orange carpet, the closed doors on either side, of which, I observed, the door I had come through was one. Either Rickenbacker was so fond of his choice of decor that he used it everywhere or—and this just didn't make sense at all—I was now standing in the very hallway I had followed the night I met Matteo for the first time.

But *that* was impossible because that hallway had been in a completely different part of town, blocks and blocks away. If I were to follow this hallway to that archway down there, would it open up into a sort of foyer with a cushiony couch, a mirrored desk, and a faux-fur rug? The place was quiet as a cave. Eerie.

I moved farther down the hall, stopping short when I heard hushed voices from around the corner where I was sure I would see the place where I had been served foaming wine. My breath coming in tiny puffs, I tiptoed along the corridor until I could press myself against the corner. I recognised the voices.

"He's an MGC; can he even *do* that?" That was Phoenix.

"I believe he must." Rickenbacker. "It would be extremely out of character for him to refuse."

I had to see what was happening. I simply *had* to. I got down on hands and knees so when I peered around the corner, my head was less likely to be seen.

"What say you, MGC?" Rickenbacker went on. "Do you think you can do this?"

I slowly, slowly let just one eye see past the edge of the wall. The hair on the back of my head rose to attention.

Matteo stood there in silence. Both of my employers had their backs to me, thank goodness, but Matteo faced me. His jaw was slack and his eyes . . .

You know that spinning spiral image they use in cartoons to show that somebody's been hypnotized? Well, that's what Matteo's eyes looked like.

The man I was in love with was behaving like a zombie.

"I give you permission," said Rickenbacker. "Continue to show your mastery."

Matteo's eyes focussed and he gave Rickenbacker a tiny bow before turning around like a wobbly dancer in a music box and heading to where I believed there to be a door that, at least when I went through it more than a week ago, led to a dingy hallway with plush carpet and foil wallpaper.

My spine overtaken by the willies, I pulled my head back before the other two noticed me. I leapt to my feet and turned back the way I'd come. I saw the door at the end of the hallway; the one that had been the entrance into the theatre-like space just last week. I took a step toward it, and then every scary movie wherein the camera slowly approaches a doorway at the end of a hallway came to my mind and I froze.

The icy fingers of terror clawed up my chest and throat, threatening to squeeze the life out of me. I'm not ashamed to say my heart pounded on the bars of my ribcage to be let out, and I fled back into the dining room.

Where there were now several patrons, and servers milling about, rolling cutlery in serviettes, filling condiment bottles, and placing water glasses. A strange, high-pitched hum began in my chest along with a squeezy feeling, and it grew as it climbed up my esophagus. Looking over my shoulder to see if Phoenix or Rickenbacker were following me to punish me for whatever it was I had witnessed—they weren't—I ran and didn't stop running until I was back in the kitchen, and by the time I got there, the humming was nearly a scream, but I gasped it out as I burst through the doors. I leaned my back against the door, shaking and sweating, panting as if I'd just run a marathon. My heart hammered so hard, it could have kneaded bread dough. I allowed myself a few moments in that meditative pose until I could shrug off my supreme perturbation, shove it down into an abyss at the back of my mind, and get back to work.

The song on the radio was the tinkly piano of *Music Box Dancer*, only a wonky, out-of-tune *Music Box Dancer* that made me cringe.

What had all that been about? "MGC" they had said. What did that mean? Matteo's initials? No, his last name was MacCallum. I took several deep breaths and pressed my palms to my eyes. So much about this place and this job and this whole experience was just plain freakishly bizarre. Would I have the nerve to ask Rickenbacker about it next time I saw him? I doubted it, and it was better for my stress level to lower my expectations of myself.

I pulled the sugar cookie dough out of the fridge and started rolling it out, thereby exorcising the fierce panic that had gripped me. My mouth watered as glorious aromas of fried chicken and cream of mushroom soup wafted in my direction. I stopped dead. I did *not* head over to the other kitchen area. Just—no.

My mind had been taken over by aliens, I was sure of it. Maybe I was coming down with a cold, and my sinuses were plugged up. Yeah. Yeah, that could be it.

I focussed on the task at hand. I found a simple round cookie cutter, which I used. As I lifted them onto baking sheets, the cookies morphed into high-relief tomb effigies of various monarchs and fairy tale characters, all recumbent and peaceful. From then on, I closed my eyes as I worked. I flung them into the ovens and sat on the worktable with my back to them while they baked, air-guitaring through *Gotta Have You* and a couple of other tunes. I had never looked forward to a break more than after those cookies were done so I could go to rehearsal.

The vibrations that flowed through the room when we created beautiful harmonies were a sound bath, more relaxing than any massage. More soothing to my nerves, more effective at sloughing off anxieties and negativity. I knew that a session of making music was all I needed to get me through anything. Look how it had helped this whole time I had been working at Salamander's! Despite all the crap my boss had put me through, there was still no place I would rather be than here. Well, not *here*, in the kitchen, in the rehearsal studio. Speaking of which, I wanted to be there *now*.

With oven mitts on, I pulled the trays out and set them on cooling racks. They looked like a bird's-eye view of a massive parking lot. I looked about warily for anyone, or any *thing*, that could sabotage this project, but by that time I had almost convinced myself that nothing I did here in the kitchen was fully in my control, no matter how hard I tried. What I *could* control was the music. And since that was the real reason I was here, I put the oven mitts away and left the kitchen.

I heard Matteo's guitar playing before I got to the door of the rehearsal room, and I slowed my pace. Should I walk into the room and ask where he had been? Should I ask him about the scene I had witnessed? Should I ask him what "MGC" meant?

It took me all of a split second to answer "no" to every one of those questions. I didn't think he had seen me, and obviously I was not meant to overhear any of it, and now was not the time to add complexity to the already complicated situation I was in. I would maintain the status quo.

I walked in with an air of "cool and collected."

He stopped playing, his blue eyes brightening and his face lighting up as he saw me.

"Hey, beautiful."

Had he really just said that? The rush of elation was like a sudden wave *whooshing* me into the room, grinning like the Cheshire Cat. I blushed way too much like an idiot to be described as "cool and collected." I know, I'm pathetic. I decided I didn't care. I didn't need to know about something that was between Matteo and our employers. I pulled out my guitar and slipped the strap around my shoulders. My bandmates poked around with tuning and plucking out riffs. The drummer played a fill over and over. The keyboard player stared at himself in the mirror and swung his hair around. Good bunch of guys, these bandmates of mine. These entirely unruffled bandmates.

None of them looked stressed; none of them looked rushed. Not a one of them looked like he'd suffered through any kind of confrontation in recent history. And I had a bad feeling.

"Say, Matteo, how come I haven't seen you guys working in the dining room the last few days? I was told at the start of this how important it is to work in the restaurant end of things as well."

He plucked notes and adjusted his tuning. He shrugged and shone his blue eyes on me. "Phoenix told us to take some days off, what with the big gig coming up and all."

Had he clocked me on the side of the head with a two-by-six, I'd have been able to write a paper comparing the two experiences.

"But. . . I have a 'big gig' coming up too. How come he doesn't give me any time off?" Now I was cross. I had been riding a wave of elation, which had opened my weighty overcoat, but now indignation filled the pockets.

Matteo put his hand on my shoulder. "Griffin Girl, I really enjoyed last night." He gazed down at me with admiration.

The endearment didn't work today. How could he stand there and blatantly ignore the fact that Phoenix was incontrovertibly an asshole to me? "I did too," I said with a frown. "But that doesn't make this okay." *CAPPA* would be proud of me for that response.

"Of course not."

Was that the best he could do? How irksome that he couldn't bring himself to defend me.

He smelled sweetish today. I found myself very interested in the abstract design that played across the front of his T-shirt and admired anew, with a racing pulse, the way it fit perfectly on his perfect chest. I gave it an A+. But I was still irked.

We played a song about continuing to believe, which I sang with less conviction than usual. My voice caught on some of the high notes because I wasn't relaxed. I tried to lose myself in the harmony, but it lacked potency. After a few more songs, it was time for me to go ice sugar cookies, and I figured I would leave after that.

"So I'll see you at the school tonight?" I asked.

Matteo nodded. "Definitely. 8:30?"

"Yup." I confirmed the directions and we parted ways, and for the first time, I didn't feel like I was tearing myself away, which made me feel worse.

I hoped Phoenix would be in the kitchen so I could confront him, and the thought of it made my palms sweat. But when I pushed through the swinging doors into the kitchen, he wasn't there. Part of me said, "Yay," because the confrontation could be put off. The other part of me was mad because I had started to gear myself up for it. Why should it take so much effort for me to stand up for myself? I walked through the heady aroma of deliciousness that the kitchen had become, to my side where the tiny sarcophaguses sat in tidy rows.

Steven was there, stirring something in a large mixing bowl. His head tipped in my direction, but he didn't show me his eyes. He held out the bowl and a spatula.

"Thanks." I scooped a bit of the glaze he had created and began to gently smear it on a cookie that looked like Mary Queen of Scots, complete with the hands pointing up in prayer position. Though the glaze was beige, it turned the cookie into a colourized version. Steven helped and by the time we were finished, we had tray upon tray of gorgeous sculptures. I would have been proud of them if I had believed they were actually my own creation. Instead I felt a measure of relief that they hadn't exploded as I picked them up, and how twisted was my life that *that* was even something to cross my mind?

On the bus ride home, I decided to forgive Matteo. It wasn't his fault, any more than it was Jillian's fault that our mother was a jerk to me. It would have been nice for him to notice I had been treated differently, but really, it was all on Phoenix. I pushed my anger at that douchcanoe aside, so I could look forward to the auditions in the evening. I really hoped the man I loved would make a good impression on Calvin and the others. If Matteo could join my band, we could still make music together without Phoenix breathing down my neck. If Matteo could join my band, my life would be complete.

15

It Is Still Wednesday, May 16

We usually rented rehearsal space. Occasionally we rehearsed at my music store, but sometimes, like tonight, we rehearsed in the high school band room where our bass player, Cameron, taught. Convenient, well equipped (the amps and stuff were kind of old, but they were serviceable, and it meant I didn't have to carry my own); and most important, it was free.

The door of the school was open, which told me that Cameron had to be around somewhere, though all was quiet as I stepped inside. The music rooms were on one side of the hall, and the theatre was on the other. My footsteps made little sound as I walked along between photos of school theatrical productions and music concerts. There was one with Cameron lying on his side with a few of his students holding him up in the air and the other students doing jazz hands all around him. I only ever taught one on one, of course, so the concept of having so many students at once was kind of neat—only *kind* of.

I hesitated outside the band room, feeling like I had just come off a roller coaster. I wasn't sure what would greet me on the other side of the door. These were guys I knew and had been playing with for years, but also guys I had neglected for more than a week and at times had wished would disappear. Would they call me out? Would it be just like before, as if nothing had happened? Would we talk about Jason and the wedding fiasco? Would I be able to relax and be myself? Or would I feel self-conscious the whole time, overthink everything I said, and be compelled to leave out pieces of information, thereby making myself feel like a complete tool? I suspected the latter, but only time would tell.

We had agreed that we, the band, would get together and play for a bit, kind of loosen up our chops, and then have the two auditionees arrive an hour apart from each other. That way we'd have time to get a real feel for how they each played and maybe even a brief discussion in between. We didn't want a situation where they were showing off in front of each other; we wanted to get to know each on his own.

Todd was expected at 7:30, and Matteo, at 8:30.

I pulled open the door at 6:30. There was nobody else there. I walked about three steps into the room and stopped, my breaths coming hard and fast as if I'd been jogging. My fight-or-flight response was clicking in. Like Wesley Crusher punching in coordinates on the starship *Enterprise*, all I needed was for Captain Picard to say, "Engage," and I'd be outta that room so fast, you'd think I had jumped into warp speed.

At the same time, a morsel of sadness planted itself inside me, kind of like the dollop of chocolate inside certain ice cream treats, only this was the opposite of the feeling brought on by chocolate. Since when did walking into a rehearsal studio to play music give me the urge to run away?

"Hey, stranger!"

A cheerful voice behind me startled me into movement. I turned around.

"Move on in or you'll get ploughed under," Calvin said with a chuckle. He was smiling at me, and I let out an enormous breath of relief. That was the only clue that I had actually been afraid of how he'd react to my being here. When had I ever been *afraid* of Calvin in any way? I realised then that I was blocking the path of anybody else getting into the room. Andy and Cameron were behind him, and I was the dam.

"Oh, geez, sorry," I said lamely and nearly tripped over my own feet as I moved the rest of the way in. I gravitated to the same corner I usually stand in and slid my guitar off my back, mentally bracing myself for the onslaught of accusations and questions. *Where had I been? Why wasn't I interested in playing anymore? Who else had I been playing with?*

"Decided not to take it back?" Andy said.

"What?" I didn't have a clue what he was talking about.

"The Tele," he clarified. "You had thought of taking it back after the wedding."

What? Oh! "Oh, right," I laughed. "Yeah, no, I figured I'd regret that." I unzipped the case, revealing the Telecaster in its sunburst splendour.

"Well, good," Andy said, wheeling his folding hand truck over to his favourite keyboard-playing corner, between my stuff and the drum kit. Calvin had already shucked off his jacket and was making hi-hat noises and adjusting the position of toms and cymbals, while Cameron had plonked his bass amp down on the other side of the drum kit. I liked being across from the bass and drums in rehearsal.

"So you've got someone coming tonight too, hunh?" Andy went on. "My guy is a friend of my cousin; no idea if he's any good. Who's yours?" He opened up his X-shaped stand with a *thud* on the floor.

I looked down at the guitar across my belly, ostensibly to tune it. "He's a friend of a friend," I said, going with the story Matteo and I had agreed upon. "Pretty good, from what I hear," I added with a vagueness that would, I hoped, not inspire further questions. My fingers trembled on the tuning peg. I needn't have worried.

"Hey, do you notice that it's a lot quieter here without Jason?" Andy said.

"Tell me again why we put up with that guy for so long?" Cameron added as he grabbed microphone stands from the corner of the room.

Andy laughed. "Ask Griffin why we put up with that guy for so long."

"Hey, none of you complained to me." I set up a stand for myself. "How was I supposed to know he was so universally repellent?"

"We were too polite," Cameron threw back. "How could you, of all people, not have *noticed* he was so universally repellent?"

"Ugh, I don't even know, it's kind of embarrassing."

Andy said, "A *lot* embarrassing."

Calvin piped up. "Leave her alone. Can't you see she feels bad enough?" He seemed unusually chipper.

"So our first bit of criteria tonight," Cameron said, grabbing coils of mic cable off the hooks on the wall, "needs to be to find out whether these guys have a sense of humour."

"How would *you* notice if someone had a sense of humour?" Andy pulled mics out of the box.

Cameron hung cable on each stand for us to plug in ourselves. "Ask them to tell us a drummer joke."

"Naw, that's way too easy," I said.

And just like that, we fell back into our old camaraderie.

The quips flew around the room as we finished setting up and warmed up, and I became aware of a gap in my music psyche. Well, first I became aware that I had a music psyche; *then* I noticed it had a gap in it. And as the chatter and laughter swirled around the room, bouncing off the sound baffles and the awful carpet and the posters of famous people playing their instruments to inspire the youth who used this room during the day, that gap slowly filled itself in, as if with Polyfilla. I listened to these guys, my pals, toss playful insults around and realised that if there was one thing missing from rehearsals with The Spurious Correlations, it was the banter. But before I could really take note, we got down to business.

"So what should we get them to play?" Cameron noodled and tapped harmonics on his bass. "Let them choose something from our list?"

Calvin said, "That makes sense. Griffin?"

I looked up from tuning. "What?"

Calvin smiled at me with a kind of patience. "You're the leader of the band. How do you want to handle this?"

I took a deep breath as a flush spread to the roots of my hair. When words finally came to me, they rushed out as if I were ejecting a mouthful of bees. "That sounds good let them pick something that way they can choose a song they know and will do well on." I went back to tuning.

Next thing I knew, Calvin's shadow appeared on the floor below the neck of my guitar. He spoke quietly. "You seem nervous. Everything okay?"

I looked up at him. "Umm, yeah, I'm good. I dunno. I guess it's important. I hope M—" I caught myself and quickly turned the initial into a thoughtful hum, "—mmm one of these guys will work out."

Calvin didn't seem to notice my little flub. "And if they don't? No big deal. The right person will come along." He kept looking at me, and I tried to think of a response, but before I did, he shrugged his shoulders, gave me a grin, and went back to his drum kit.

For some reason, that small encounter left me feeling like I had been bumped while standing on one foot. It was an odd feeling, but I steadied myself as we warmed up by jamming on a bass riff Cameron started. We played around on a few tunes, and after a bit, our first auditionee came into the room.

Todd was about twenty, and he seemed nice enough, but it was tricky to find a song he knew. He scanned the list I handed him and said, "I don't really know these."

I *ulped* inwardly. "No? Like *Bad Moon Rising*?"

"Uh, no, I've never heard of it." Who on earth didn't know *Bad Moon Rising*?

"How about *I'm a Believer*?"

"I think I've heard that one . . ."

Seriously?

"How about—" I threw out the one suggestion I would stake my life on every guitarist knowing, "*Smoke on the Water*?"

He shook his head, and I thought Andy was going to tip his keyboard over.

"I'm more of a Beatles guy," Todd said.

"Okay, great! We can do the Beatles. What do you feel like playing?"

We finally settled on *Taxman*, and I was impressed with his choosing one of my favourite Harrison tunes. His singing was decent, but he didn't do all that well in the guitar solo and didn't handle our improvised ending too well either. He fared a bit better in *I Feel Fine*. A bit. We discovered he knew *All the Small Things*, and that was his best performance. But it was too little too late.

Andy said, "So, Todd, are you a Whovian?" This was a clever test to see if Todd liked our collective favourite science fiction show.

"Oh, I know them," Todd said. "They play *Teenage Wasteland*, right?"

I nearly burst out laughing, and I thought the other three guys would keel over. Poor Todd had not only failed Andy's test, but he'd failed a second test we'd had no intention of giving him. I smiled at Todd ferociously as I restrained myself from correcting him on the actual title of that famous song by The Who.

After we thanked him and he left, Cameron said, "Sorry, Andy, but if you're auditioning to be a lead guitarist and you only know two songs, hadn't you better actually be able to play them?"

"Hey, don't blame me. I told you I didn't know the guy!" Andy protested.

"I hope you're going to poke your cousin in the eye," Calvin said.

"Or put glue in her shoes," Cameron suggested.

"Geez, you guys, I don't think she even heard him before. She just said, 'Hey, I know a guy who says he plays guitar,' and that was that."

"You're officially on New Person probation," I said.

Don't get me wrong. Nobody was mad; we were actually killing ourselves laughing the whole time. He had been a nice enough kid, just not for us.

"Your guy had better show more promise, Griffin," Calvin said with a wink.

"Or what? You're going to poke me in the eye?"

"Oh, I'll come up with something way worse." Calvin grinned.

"Yeah, because you ought to know better than Andy's cousin—" Cameron started but was interrupted by a knock on the door. He was closest so he raised the neck of his bass and opened it.

My heart rate skyrocketed, and I tried desperately not to care who came in but failed as miserably as poor Todd.

Matteo stepped in, clad in a leather bomber jacket and carrying his guitar and amp. His smile beamed around the room, and I felt myself relax. No zombie swirling eyes.

"Hey, guys, I'm Matteo." He quickly scanned the gathering before settling on me. "Hi, Griffin." I felt all melty again. This guy was definitely not normal. Was there anybody else who could step into a room and simply introduce himself and have that kind of effect? He didn't pay any special attention to me, which allowed me to release a bit of tension. The others greeted him graciously. Cameron showed Matteo where to set up, and Andy plugged in his amp for him while Matteo opened his guitar case.

Calvin watched him as though he'd never seen someone pull out a guitar. "So how do you two know each other?" He asked as if just needing a reminder.

Matteo looked at him and smiled. "I'm a friend of a friend." He sounded oddly rehearsed, and it worried me. Would he have trouble pretending we didn't know each other?

"Oh yeah, which friend?"

Annoyance flashed through my mind. Why did Calvin sound so mistrusting? It didn't help that Matteo didn't respond right away.

"My sister," I said, hastily covering up what Matteo and I had failed to discuss. "Jillian," I added for Matteo's benefit.

Matteo slipped his strap over his head and grinned at Calvin. "Jillian."

"I know Jillian," Calvin said with an uncharacteristic lukewarm . . . ness. "Good friend?"

"Anyway, thanks for coming, Matteo," I said in an effort to put an end to . . . whatever that was. "This is Cameron, Andy, and Calvin on drums." A weird vibe was floating through the space like a nasty fart, and I needed to dissipate it. "Cameron, do you want to hand Matteo our list? See if there's anything on there you'd like to play."

Cameron set the list on Matteo's music stand. Matteo looked it over while checking his tuning. "How about we start with *Go Your Own Way*?"

"Good one," I said in an *I have never played that song with this man before, not ever!* sort of tone.

"Oh, sure." Calvin sounded like he didn't believe it possible that this guy could hope to get the tricky opening of the song without practice.

"I don't have a twelve-string here," I said apologetically, "but we can do it anyway."

We had a quick discussion about vocals, and then Calvin counted us in. Now, the opening is tricky because the lead guitar sets up the rhythm and then it's tricky for me, as rhythm guitarist, to find beat one for my entrance, and then it's tricky for the lead vocal for the same reason. It's less tricky after that for the drummer to find beat one for his entrance but still tricky. I locked eyes with Matteo to get our respective entrances, and then turned to Calvin so we could hit that sixth bar together.

I am pretty sure I saw Calvin's eyes pop out when the timing of the beginning was flawless. His eyebrows definitely went up—because I was watching him—when Matteo's voice rang out so clearly on the high notes. We all sang the harmony in the chorus, and the other guys were grinning like we'd just signed a record deal. Nobody had expected this to go so well.

Except Matteo and me, of course. Shh.

Hoots and hollers helped to make the Big Finish to the song, and I knew that my band was impressed with my potential recruit. Then I remembered I had to look pleasantly surprised too.

"That was awesome," I said. "Good solo."

The others threw in their compliments as well, and Matteo smiled in that shy sort of way of his.

"Thanks," he said.

"Is there another one you'd like to do?" Calvin said.

Matteo suggested *Rock and Roll*, and I have to say I was kind of pleased to show off my Robert Plant impression. Calvin went over the opening a bit, and then said, "Okay, let's go." The drums have the intro, so he didn't bother counting in but began. Two bars in, he messed up the timing, stopped, said, "Hang on, hang on," started again, messed up again, did a little frustrated-at-himself shriek, and stopped.

"Been a while." He laughed.

Matteo stood with his fingers poised and ready. He smiled. "Do you need to take a minute?"

"Naw," I reassured him as Calvin started again. "It's just a grey matter hiccup."

"Ah," said Matteo, raising his eyebrows almost doubtfully. I thought I detected a bit of a tone, but then Calvin nailed the bit and the guitars had to come in, and then I had to sing, and I remembered that I hoped Matteo would be impressed with my Robert Plant impression. It had been a mere moment, but it left an infinitesimal mark.

At the end of the song, Matteo smiled at me. "That was awesome."

I couldn't help but be pleased and resolved to dismiss the glimpse of passive aggression. But it still didn't sit well. Especially given it was a comment on Calvin.

We got him to pick a couple of other tunes, and we basically had a terrific jam session. I was blown away when I saw it was already 10:00.

Calvin came out from behind his drum kit to shake Matteo's hand, amid enthusiastic responses from the other two. "Thanks for coming out."

"Oh hey, no problem. It was fun."

As he packed up his guitar, Matteo said, "You guys—and gal—are really good." He glanced at me only briefly.

"We'll be in touch," I said, truly relieved that it had gone so well. I shook his warm, firm hand and allowed myself to look into those clear azure eyes of his, all the while putting massive effort into *not* showing my true feelings for this man for the rest of my band to see.

He left and the rest of us looked wordlessly at each other for a few seconds. When we heard the outside door of the school shut, Cameron broke the silence.

"Holy *shit*! Who *was* that guy?"

"Some sort of superhero," Andy said. "Like, he comes outta nowhere, does this amazing thing, and then he's gone."

Cameron turned to Andy. "You didn't even bother asking him if he's a *Doctor Who* fan."

"Who cares? If he can play like that, we can *train* him to be a *Doctor Who* fan."

Cameron grinned at me. "Looks like we've found our replacement for Jason."

"In more ways than one," Calvin said in an undertone.

Andy and Cameron chattered away as they packed up their gear.

"What do you mean by that?" I looked at Calvin with kind of mixed feelings, hoping I looked neutral. But he was already looking at me, and that didn't help the blush situation.

He shrugged and started back to gather his drumstick case. "Nothing." He didn't look at me as he slid sticks into the leather sheath. Then he seemed to change his mind. "Just be careful, that's all. Dumping Jason was good for you. But that was only, like, ten days ago. And this guy is obviously someone you would be attracted to."

Pause while two cars collided inside my chest with a crunch. And then, "I'm not at all sure how I feel about that remark."

"I'm sorry," he said defensively. "It just seems . . . *soon*, that's all."

"Soon for what?" I demanded.

Calvin put up his hands in surrender. "I saw the way you—he looked at you." He turned away. "Look, never mind. I'm sorry. I was obviously mistaken."

When had Calvin started noticing how other guys looked at me? The bubbling anger in my gut was not at all calmed by the fact that Calvin was right on point. I could think of nothing to say that I could be confident wouldn't come out sounding super snarky, so I packed up my stuff in silence.

"Okay, guys, talk soon," I said and left.

"See you Saturday!" I heard Calvin holler behind me.

I was propelled to the bus stop by a strange jet-pack sort of emotion. Calvin had never been one to voice his opinion on any guy I was attracted to. Jason turned out to be a jerk in the end, but Calvin never said word one during all the time Jason and I were a couple. He had supported; he hadn't judged. Any time I was crabby about Jason, Calvin had been there for me to lean on. He had never said, "I told you so," or even suggested I break up with him. He allowed me to make my choices. So what was this sudden commentary on my hypothetical relationship with a guy Calvin had just met and didn't even know I already knew? It pissed me off.

I boarded the bus feeling cross and frowny.

16

Thursday, May 17

Thursday. One week since my first gig with The Spurious Correlations. One week since Matteo had kissed me in the kitchen. Two days since our first date. Only one since things had become complicated.

Weird vibes between the two men notwithstanding, last night had been amazing. I was thrilled at the prospect of having Matteo in my band. I needed to talk further with the guys, but I was certain they wanted him in. Even Calvin.

I had been bothered all night about Calvin. Why did he have to wreck the evening with a comment like that? I mean, sure, Jason had been my boyfriend for a couple of years, but was there some sort of "appropriate" mourning period for a guy who was obviously a jerk? I ought to have dumped him ages ago. Maybe that was why I had fallen for Matteo so easily. From the get-go, Matteo had treated me better than Jason ever had. Did that mean I was on the rebound? Or did it just mean I now knew how I wanted to be treated?

Having said that, what was with Matteo's oddly uncool reaction to Calvin? His comment hadn't been an obvious slight, but the more I thought about it, the more I defined his tone as an indirect put-down of Calvin's capability as a drummer. On the one hand, it sounded like a comment a supportive fellow musician would make. But on the other hand, Matteo had been the guest. Had Andy or Cameron said it, it would have been welcome, even unnoticeable.

As I boarded the bus, I worked to convince myself that maybe I was reading too much into it. Funny how I felt so protective of Calvin all of a sudden. Jason had been a jerk to him more than once, but I'd ignored it. I don't know why. We all had. Maybe we all just accepted that he was like that. We knew it said more about him than it did about Calvin. With Matteo, it was a different story for some reason.

I was kind of pissed off at Calvin, but I also knew he wasn't really *wrong*. In fact, he had no idea how right he was. Damn it, I had to tell him about The Spurious Correlations. This not-full-truth thing did not sit well.

But what was it he had said? He saw the way Matteo looked at me. I smiled. Matteo had been looking at me in such a way that Calvin had noticed? Heh.

I was pretty sure I was in love—or at least infatuated—with my lead guitarist, and he obviously had feelings for me. But he did not have my permission to be rude. I couldn't—no, I wouldn't—put up with Matteo being a jerk to Calvin even a tiny little bit. I would have to have a talk with him.

Already in a bit of a mood, as soon as I entered the dining room, my fury at Phoenix from the day before was renewed. I had managed to shove it all aside to get through the auditions, but just the old-soup smell of the dark restaurant reminded me that Matteo and the rest of the band had been given time off and I had not. Phoenix was a complete bastard. Well, I was damned sure I would let him know I was no fool. The grubby carpet cushioned my angry stomps. With my new revelation that Calvin had seen Matteo looking at me in a certain way, I walked into the kitchen, feeling like I could take on the world. The room was devoid of cooks.

I heard the *foomp* of the door from the dining room and whirled around to see Phoenix. How had he come so close behind me without my noticing?

Before he could open his mouth, I said, "What's the big idea giving the other band members this week off?"

"They deserve it. You don't."

I had begun by feeling relatively calm, but this comment drew my ire, and heat spread up my neck to my face. I couldn't argue that Matteo deserved it; I wouldn't have been able to stomach such disloyalty. But *I* deserved it too, and I was dead tired of being toyed with. I glared at him, eyebrows drawing together.

"Today you will make baklava!" he boomed.

I stared at him. Matteo got time off, and I was being asked to make yet another of the trickiest desserts there is?

An unexpected thing happened. "No," I said.

He stared back at me, his mouth imitating a train tunnel.

Before he could even reply, I said, "Don't even think about arguing with me." My breaths came short and shallow. My hand curled around the knife that had materialized as easily as if I'd grabbed it out of the drawer I'd tossed it in. I gripped it. Its weight felt good in my hand. My fingers twitched. It was like the knife *wanted* me to use it.

He found his voice. "I could fire you. Then you won't get to play in the band!" he said triumphantly, his explosion of hair like a forest of exclamation points sticking out of his head.

My brain was going places I never expected it was capable of. Apparently I was fed up. "I could quit. And then you'd have to find a new dessert-making rhythm guitarist by Sunday." It was a battle of who would call whose bluff. I sure as hell needed the band like a heart attack victim needed a defibrillator. Did Phoenix know that? Did he need me as desperately as I needed the band? Who was this person who was speaking in my voice?

Phoenix closed his mouth. He opened it again. His face suddenly drained of all colour, and he looked positively stricken.

Wow. I did not expect that.

"What will you make, then?" he asked in an oddly respectful tone.

I trained laser eyes on him and decided that what was good enough for Matteo was good enough for me.

"Nothing," I said. "I am making nothing."

"Okay," he said almost meekly.

Wow. I had braced myself for way more of a fight. What was up with that reaction?

The dining room door went *foomp*, and in walked Matteo.

"Hey, Griffin Girl, whatcha doing?" He leaned on the worktable and gazed at me with puppy eyes. "Are you coming to rehearsal?"

My eyes still on Phoenix, I said, "I was about to head there."

Matteo turned to where Phoenix stood, basically right next to him. "Oh hey, Phoenix. I didn't see you there."

Didn't see him there? One of those "I only have eyes for you" kind of moments? Well, *that* was a little bit thrilling. My body quaked with the adrenaline of confronting Phoenix and the antithetical emotions that came along with Matteo's entrance.

Still glaring at Phoenix, I grabbed a random book off the shelf. It was called *Bobbing Blobs and Bulbs* by Bob Loblaw. "I'm sure you'll find a recipe for baklava in there, and I can come back later and see how you're doing with it."

A hand gently grabbed my arm and spun me around. Matteo had walked around the table and now cupped my face in his hands and kissed me. Golly, had someone cranked up the temperature in the room? Either that or we'd been transported to a tropical paradise.

His voice low and rich, he said, "You are really something, Griffin. I'm so glad—"

I thought he might kiss me again. I'd be omitting pertinent information if I didn't say I *hoped* for it. Now, it wouldn't do for him to be the only one taking charge of the situation, so in spite of Phoenix standing there—maybe because of him—I reached my hand up to Matteo's cheek and pulled his face down to mine. Let Phoenix see that it was possible for someone to love me. Like hot liquid running through the body on a cold day, heat from Matteo's soft lips traipsed through my every limb so I might have been standing in a very small room with lots of fireplaces. When our lips parted, I was surprised to observe I was still standing on the floor. I couldn't feel it beneath my feet; I felt cotton candy.

He put his strong arms around me and rested his chin on the top of my head in a hug that would protect me from anything that could possibly harm me, including Big Bad Wolves, Bad Guys, and Dragons. Maybe even Phoenixes and magical knives.

With extreme reluctance, I pulled away from him, sure I'd left my heart stuck to his chest, and let his warmth and security envelop me as I noticed the knife still in my fist. I opened an oven door and tossed it in.

Phoenix hadn't said anything since Matteo had come in. He stood there, wearing a wordless frown, as if pissed off he hadn't succeeded in . . . whatever he was trying to do. Then he left the kitchen, and the door swung behind him.

Matteo held my hand all the way to the rehearsal studio. I tried to shake off the hodgepodge of emotions. I was a complete mess. I could hardly wait to share this with my support group. I told him off! I could imagine their congratulations.

Way to go, WingedLion! they'd say. *Honour your needs!*

I let myself sink into the music, and slowly but surely, I recovered.

Rehearsal was less about practising today than it was about the joy of making music. For a band who'd been together for just ten days, we were really damn good. The drummer, bass player, and I were the tightest rhythm team I'd ever been part of. Matteo played like a fucking god, and I swear I played the best I ever had. Our voices blended and we harmonized so well, I had shivers up my spine and goosebumps almost constantly. We went over changes in tempo, tweaked transitions and segues, and talked about our between-song patter. I left most of the talking up to him since I've never been comfortable with that part, and he was more or less the leader of the band, anyway. This band was going to blow the audience away on Sunday. And I was completely and wholly thrilled to be a part of it, no matter what other weird shit the universe could throw at me.

At the end of the day, I said, "Hey, Matteo, thanks for coming out to audition last night. I think the guys were really impressed."

"It was fun. Although that drummer was a bit . . . How long has he been with you guys?"

My back went up like a flag. A red flag. "I told you about Calvin when we were at the pub. He's the one who started the band with me."

Matteo said, "Hmp," in an *I'm not impressed* kind of way.

Confused, and suddenly unsure of myself, I said, "'That drummer' is my best friend."

"Really?" Matteo said doubtfully. He shrugged. "Okay."

I did not know what that was supposed to mean. And all of a sudden, the roiling mass of conflicting emotions became more than I could cope with. Plus, I noticed the time.

"I gotta go. I have lessons to teach." My voice came out like a rusty hinge. I packed up my guitars, hands shaking. "I'll see you tomorrow."

Matteo insulting Calvin was *not* the kind of weird shit I had been referring to.

My bus was late, so I was late for my 5:00 lesson. The kid didn't seem to care, but the father was like, "I don't appreciate this, you know. We have to bolt from here and go straight to soccer, so you can't run late at the end; you'll have to make up the time on another day."

I assured him I'd be happy to do so, and that I didn't want to waste any more of today's lesson talking about it. I ushered the kid into a practice room. By the time we emerged, Brian was waiting to speak to me after the kid and his dad left.

I was about to explain the situation from my side, but Brian said, "Did you *really* tell Derek's father his kid was as dumb as a sack of hammers?"

Shocked, I said, "No, of course not! I would never say anything like that." *What an asshole!*

"I don't need to tell you—"

"No," I agreed vehemently. "You don't."

And if you're finding that scene to be a bit familiar, you aren't alone.

It was at the point when Brian mentioned the sack of hammers that something went *click* in my head. None of this felt real. It wasn't just your basic déjà vu; I had lived through the *exact same* sequence of events just last week. In fact, the more I thought about it, the more I recognized that if I were honest, it hadn't felt real then either. Who would accuse me of saying such a nasty thing to his kid? Nobody, that's who. Just like nobody would so blatantly say one band member didn't deserve a day off when the rest of the band did. This was about me. Phoenix and me. I didn't know why, or how, but I was determined to find out before we wound up facing each other twenty paces apart amid dust and tumbleweeds.

Somehow my mind was being messed with in a big way. Somebody was trying to give me a mental breakdown by—it sounded ridiculous to even think it—*replaying* last Thursday afternoon. *Breathe*, I told myself. *Breathe*.

For lack of another option in the moment, I allowed the scene to play out as it had last week, then I retreated to my practice room, where I tried to recall what came next.

Ah, yes. Davinder, who played Heart, arrived. I said, "How about you play your Heart tune for me?"

Suspicion in her eyes, she sat down and started to play.

I also remembered that the week before I had been nervous about my first Spurious Correlations gig, which had thrown me off. Today I had Phoenix's assoholery and Matteo's off-putting comments about Calvin. But! I also had Matteo's arms around me and his lips sending hot chocolate through every fibre of my body. I think I had become numb to being riled. When my student's mother arrived, I forestalled her question about the recital by saying, "You know, Davinder's playing so well, I'd love for her to learn something even more difficult. I don't know if she'd be ready to play it at the recital, but it's something to work toward."

"All right," she said with a puzzled expression.

And because I wasn't in a hurry to get out the door, the woman had nothing more to say.

I had taken control of my day. It was an unfamiliar sensation, yet one I was prepared to get used to.

When I got home and found the knife on my dining room table, I picked it up. It had a very, very nice weight to it. It was the same knife I had tossed into the oven in the restaurant kitchen. The same knife I had not only chucked into the back of the closet but hidden on a shelf with a volume of

Shakespeare on top of it. This, I decided, was no ordinary knife. It vibrated in my hand the way my cell phone does when a text comes in. It twinkled on occasion and often made my hand feel tingly, like I'd been electrocuted. It either had a message for me, or it *was* the message. This time I didn't get startled and drop it, nor did frustration surge through my veins. I peered at it with determination.

"What. Do you want. From me?"

Interlude - The Tail End of May 17

Rickenbacker selected an onion ring and dipped it in spicy dipping sauce. As he leaned back in his chair, the chair moulded itself into its occupant's favourite reclining position. He breathed a self-congratulatory sigh and crossed his ankles on the built-in footrest. He noticed, with delight, that he was wearing his salmony pink and mustard yellow plaid socks, a gift from his mother last Fenugreek Gratitude Day. She would be tickled he was wearing them when he arrived at her place for dinner after his meeting with Phoenix. He hoped she would make noodles. Rickenbacker loved noodles.

He pictured the large plate of curly blue-green slimy deliciousness topped with his mom's delectable cherry-pumpkin-squid sauce, and his mouth watered. Or maybe that was the onion ring.

Phoenix burst into the office, interrupting Rickenbacker's reverie.

"What is the matter with Matteo?"

"What do you mean?" He snapped his mind away from noodles and onion rings and sifted through recent events to try to guess what his friend was talking about. In fact, Rickenbacker was so very pleased with the way things were progressing, especially the buildup of Griffin's frustration with Phoenix, that he was at a complete loss as to what his friend was talking about.

Phoenix slapped his hands down on the desk. "He's gone haywire. He's behaving strangely."

"What do you mean?" Rickenbacker said again.

Phoenix squinted at him. "Don't you see? The way he looks at her, the little touches—"

"Wait. Looks at whom?"

"At *Griffin*! Haven't you seen it? He's behaving as if he's . . . you know . . ."

Rickenbacker tilted his head to one side and regarded his friend. Was the man nuts? With an instant answer to the question not forthcoming, he stroked his chin with his thumb, and thought. Finally he shook his head. "No. I can't think what you're referring to."

Phoenix leaned almost all the way across the desk.

"Mind the onion ring stand," Rickenbacker cautioned.

Phoenix whispered, "You know, like he has Other World kind of . . . *feelings* for her!"

Rickenbacker was puzzled. Baffled, even. His chair tipped him upward to a less recumbent pose. "Feelings? Like . . . as in . . . *love*?" Surely not. The very idea was synonymous with "flapdoodle."

"Yes, that's it." Phoenix's eyes were wide, and every muscle in his body was rigid like a statue. "And what's more," he said with a tight throat, his whole body quivering, "it is plain that *she* returns those feelings!"

Rickenbacker simply could not believe it. It made no sense at all. He dismissed it with a wave. "Preposterous. Impossible. It was not part of his instructions."

"What instructions did you give him?"

Rickenbacker was not at all used to Phoenix being this contrary. Rickenbacker would say *Today, red is blue,* and Phoenix would say, *Yes, of course it is.* This Phoenix was displaying an unpleasant tendency to . . . *question* Rickenbacker, and it made him not happy at all.

"Obviously," Rickenbacker said with impatience, "I told him to be an exceptional lead guitarist. He was to be an excellent Band Mate, so the Other

World Partner would feel welcome in the band. I told him to be nicer to her than that other fellow was." He waggled his fingers as if it would help him remember the name, which it did not. "The one who messed things up at the wedding. Nothing more. The most important thing was to make certain she would want more than anything to be in *this band* and not go back to those others." He suddenly realized his voice had raised in volume. He closed his mouth into a pout, and lifted his nose just a touch as if to say, *The very idea!*

"Yes, yes," Phoenix said. "Oh dear, oh dear, I was worried about this from the start." He wrung his hands. "But what *else* did you say to him?"

"Nothing! What else would I have said?"

"Play the recording."

Taken aback at this effrontery, Rickenbacker's torso pressed into his chair as if he were on a very fast train. "I beg your pardon?"

Phoenix stood straight and tall, and in Rickenbacker's seated attitude, he saw the little tuft of hair on the underside of Phoenix's chin for the first time.

"Play. The. Recording," Phoenix said and sat down.

Rickenbacker clamped his jaw and pressed his lips together stubbornly, but he reached through the audio files until he found the correct date of the conversation with Matteo twelve days ago. He flicked his finger to make it play and listened.

Phoenix: *Why's it made of fecking glass then?* Pause. *What kind of ghastly rules are those supposed to be?*

Rickenbacker: *Now, Phoenix, I am much more of a people person than you are—*

"Discussing the competition, yes, yes." Rickenbacker flicked his finger to pass through all of that. He had no liking for the recorded sound of his own voice. *Play.* The sound of a knock on the door and said door opening to allow the entry of their Magically Generated Character.

Phoenix: *Wow, he turned out great.*

Rickenbacker: *He's based on your design.*

And on and so forth through Phoenix's concern: *He wasn't complete; those were just blueprints, after all.*

Rickenbacker: *Nonsense. He has plenty to get him through the one job he has to do; that won't matter at all.*

To Phoenix's plaintive whining about Blinky and Jethro, Rickenbacker's unfailing reassurance of his friend. Phoenix's departure from the room.

Phoenix rose to pay close attention to what happened next. Rickenbacker closed his eyes nonchalantly. There was nothing in here to worry about.

"There you have it, you s—?"

But then he heard his own voice again.

Rickenbacker: *You, handsome, are the key to our success. Now go and be everything our Griffin desires!* The quiet *click* of the door closing behind Matteo. Rickenbacker savouring the word, *Ffffffunnnn.*

The recording stopped. The room was utterly silent. Rickenbacker shifted uncomfortably. His chair lowered and righted itself to a standard office chair position. He lifted his unaccountably damp palms from its arms. He reversed the recording a wee bit and played it again.

Now go and be everything our Griffin desires!

Rickenbacker said, "Oh."

Phoenix glared at him. "Why did you say that?"

Rickenbacker shuddered and shook off the nasty, unfamiliar feeling of *guilt.* "Clearly I meant *musically—*"

"Perhaps not so clear."

Rickenbacker slapped the desk petulantly. "But she wants to be a musician!"

Phoenix rolled his eyes and strode across the room, arms wide to embrace all the air. "That's the trouble with you, Rickenbacker. You see people as two-dimensional. That is why so many of our secondary characters aren't developed well enough and Griffin can't even remember what they look like from one moment to the next. That is why I was worried about the

MGC being no more than a blueprint!"

"But she was adamant that she wanted to have a successful band. She said that businessman fellow would 'make sure they never played in this city again!' and such like. It was incontrovertible!"

Phoenix stopped and held his arms out in front of Rickenbacker. "I'm not saying you're wrong about that. Yes, of course she wants to be a musician. What I'm saying is she wants *other things* as well. Most people do."

Rickenbacker squinted. He grabbed an onion ring and chewed it. It was a bit soggy. Mouth full, he said, "So, wha- yo- saying is . . ." He swallowed and worked onion ring bits out of his teeth. "Griffin wants . . ." He tried to find the word, and failed. He blinked at Phoenix. "I—I don't know. I give up."

Phoenix's body sagged in disgust. "*Love*, you moron. She wants to be appreciated and *loved*."

Rickenbacker stared at him, white noise buzzing through his mind. "Love?"

"Yes."

"As in . . . a boyfriend?"

Phoenix nodded. "In this case, yes. A boyfriend."

"Nonsense! She is feeling all sorts of frustrations; we have her just where we want her!"

"Think again, genius. Did you not see what happened this morning?"

Rickenbacker raised both hands dismissively. "I'm a busy man. I don't have time to keep checking in over and over—" He stopped, puzzled by Phoenix's impatient glare. Hastily accessing the recording from that morning, he watched as the MGC took Griffin's hand tenderly and walked her out of the kitchen. Rickenbacker was so shocked, he had fewer words to say than usual.

"But, but . . . *how*?"

"Back. It. Up."

Rickenbacker did so, to a point in the kitchen that was one of the recorded bits Rickenbacker hadn't bothered to go through because he had been assuming, due to overconfidence, it was all boring. When he saw his target locked in an embrace with his MGC, he leapt to his feet, breathing as if he'd just run up twenty flights of stairs, which he would never have done, and struggling to hold back a howl of rage, dismay, and horror, much as he had howled when he was first paired up with Phoenix for a project in Salamander History back in their boyhoods. He whimpered a little, and when he had breathed enough times, he calmed down to the point of just being confused.

"But—but—But Phoenix, she was happy to be rid of that other chap."

"That other chap was a complete bastard."

Rickenbacker felt the penny drop. "Oh. I see."

Phoenix nodded.

"So when I told Matteo to be *everything* she desires, he took my words to heart."

Phoenix nodded.

"This is unbelievable."

Shame poked Rickenbacker in the gut, and he was reminded of that time in his youth when he'd— Hm. No, wait, he'd never felt shame before.

"Now," Phoenix said, sitting down again, all business. "Let's think this through. I am sure this will not spell the end for us."

Rickenbacker was happy to switch back to problem-solving mode.

"Absolutely not. Under no circumstances. By no means is this the end of the line for us. Negative. Most certainly."

"Are you sure?"

"Let's think it through, as you suggested. What harm does it do to our plan if she and Matteo . . . you know? I mean, does it get in the way of the task we need her to perform?"

"You're asking me? I have no more experience with this than you do."

"But her . . . *feelings* for Matteo . . . do they make her hate you less?"

Phoenix puzzled through this. "No, I don't think so. But having said that, it could, I suppose, make her feel so positive and happy about the band that she has more confidence in dealing with me." He gasped and alarm flashed in his eyes. "In fact, it already has. She told me off this morning! Refused to make baklava and threatened to quit! And when *he* entered, she calmed right down! If that's the case, then," he frowned, "she might not do it." He dropped his face into his hands. "Oh no, oh no, oh no! And the deadline is too close! We don't have time to fix this, Rickenbacker."

"Oh, I think we do. We have another couple of days to make some changes." Rickenbacker shrugged. "Perhaps if we just have him tone things down a little. That would keep the focus where it should be."

Phoenix stood up again, tapping the desk with his fingers. "Good idea. She needs to hate me with no distractions. What if she doesn't do it?"

"It's the Big Day. For us and for her. As I understand it, these can be stressful times. Tense. What better time to augment the pressure?"

"How can you be so calm? If she doesn't do it, then we lose. I don't want to lose."

"I don't want to lose either," Rickenbacker confessed. "We will tone down the MGC's positive influence. You maximize your assoholic tendencies. I will make some adjustments to the Prankster to add a wee bit of extra stress to her life and beyond that? We will see what we will see."

Rickenbacker's confidence rose a few notches from where it had been moments before. He stood and circled around the desk. "We've got this." He put his arm across Phoenix's shoulders and walked him toward the door. "Trust me."

17

Friday, May 18

Friday. Our final rehearsal before the gig. I was a bit of a rebel and didn't even go into the kitchen. (Take *that*, Phoenix!) As for the knife, I had stabbed it into a cantaloupe and put it in the fridge. There was very little doubt in my mind it would not stay there, but it had never appeared in the rehearsal studio; if I stayed out of the kitchen, there might be a chance of my not seeing it.

The band sequestered ourselves in the studio and went through the entire three sets, paying particular attention to openings and endings, making sure they were tight as a duck's arse. We made a few changes to the order, based on flow of energy as well as tempo and key signatures. All in all, it was terrific, and I was absolutely stoked about the gig. I thought I might even invite Calvin.

I reminded the group I would be out of town the next day, but I'd be here in plenty of time on Sunday for the gig.

"I hope your day goes great tomorrow." Matteo smiled. "Hey, listen," he said as I packed up. "Here's a song I heard the other day, and thought I'd like to learn it; not for this gig, but . . . you know."

He was so sweet when he blushed like that. The other three chatted quietly to each other in the corner. They never seemed to include themselves in anything but when we were actually practising. Whatever.

The song he played was a Lightfoot tune. *Beautiful.* He had a voice like honey, and his guitar playing rivalled Bruce Cockburn. Well, or Lightfoot. He'd like to learn it? It sure sounded to me like he'd already mastered it. I was so afraid to imagine he was singing that song for me, I just clenched my teeth and tried not to smile like an idiot.

I had always loved the song. Its melody, hanging over chords that switched between major and minor, had a haunting quality. When Matteo finished playing, he strummed the last chord and swung his arm up the way he had the first time I ever heard him play. Then he didn't look at me but waited for a reaction first.

I didn't do anything so cliché as clap, but I said, "Nice. Very nice."

He looked up then, grinning. "Thanks. It's for someone kinda special."

I smiled back. "They're going to be really pleased."

Oh my god, did he mean *me*? My legs wanted nothing more than to jump up and down. I couldn't bring myself to believe it. He had sure given me all kinds of reasons to think I might be that special person. But I didn't want to assume anything. Matteo could have been singing about his mother, for all I knew.

I was damn sure I wasn't going to ask.

May 18 for a While Longer

Still, on the way home, one of the happiest, jolliest songs *ever* played over and over in my mind. I bounced in my seat on the train, hearing Jeff Lynne's voice singing about the blue sky hiding away for a long time. I wanted to dance up and down the aisle of the train, I was that elated.

As a result, I was a bit unprepared for the drunk who boarded the train and hollered obscenities at my fellow passengers. I didn't even notice him at first, I was so lost in my own world, but then he startled me by bumping into me. When he grabbed a woman's purse and flung it at her, the song in my head changed to *Crazy Train*. Someone pressed the yellow strip under the window, and when the train pulled into the next station, some security people boarded and removed him.

I had to jostle awkwardly with my guitars around a few people to disembark at my station, only to be greeted by two RCMP officers.

"Griffin Trowbridge?" the tall, male one said.

"Umm," I said. "Yeah?"

"We understand you were on the train when the crazy drunk man boarded?"

How irregular. Did cops always refer to perpetrators that way? "Yeah, I was, but he didn't talk to me."

"Fine, fine. We're here to drive you the rest of the way home to make sure you aren't accosted."

"But I wasn't accosted. I witnessed it, kind of, but I didn't have much to do with it."

The shorter, female officer spoke. "Nevertheless, it is important to us that you remain safe."

It wasn't that I objected to being driven home, nor to the concern of whomever had called the cops to insist I be protected. But I was pretty sure it was not standard procedure for police to escort someone home from the train when she's perfectly capable of taking the bus.

I told them so. "What about all the other people who take the train? I'm sure there's someone else who needs help right now. Listen, I take the bus all the time, and I'm totally cool doing that."

"You refuse our assistance?" the tall officer said. "Are you getting this, Walker?"

"Yes," said Walker, who was apparently taking shorthand and writing down my every word. Then she leaned forward and peered at me and jotted down some notes. "Looks flushed, somewhat excited."

"What?" I looked around for whoever was playing this joke on me. "I just got off the train. It was warm in there. I'm not flushed." As soon as I said the words, I recognised a weight in my pocket, and my hand followed it. Yes indeedy, the knife had made its way into a prominent place again. Shit. If the cops asked me to empty my pockets, I was hooped. I slipped my hand out.

"So you're rejecting our offer of a ride up the hill?" the tall one confirmed.

"Yes. I mean, thanks and all, but it's really not necessary."

A bus came around the corner. "There's my bus. Can I go now?" I took a couple of tentative steps.

"Wait!" Walker said. She finished writing . . . and it looked like . . . sketching me. Then she looked up at her partner. "Can she go now, Hendrix?" Walker asked.

My bus approached the stop, slowing down. It would stay for no more than a moment. My heart raced. "Please?"

Hendrix glared at me through shrewd cop eyes. Finally he nodded. "Fine. But be careful. It's a jungle out there."

"Of course." I walked. "Thanks."

I had lost track of the number of times I'd muttered the words "That was weird" to myself over the past couple of weeks.

With *People Are Strange* running vaguely through my mind, I boarded the bus. It pulled away and carried me up the hill and past the park to my apartment.

As soon as I turned my key in the lock, I knew something was wrong. My hair got to its feet, and an awful eddy of heebie-jeebies billowed up from my gut, through my chest, and restricted my throat.

Isn't there some sort of medical condition that occurs when a person experiences too many abrupt changes in mood in a short period of time? Was it only forty-five minutes ago I was bouncing around the train—figuratively speaking—to ELO because Matteo sang a song that might have been directed at me? And now I was at my own doorstep, where it was clear someone had broken into my apartment.

Peter Gabriel started singing about an intruder's skill at sneaking around someone else's home and where to find valuables. (Damn it *where* was that music coming from?) Some of my furniture had been tipped over. Some of it had been moved around, as if the intruder had experimented with redecorating my living room. My books were all over the floor in heaps, and the bookshelf had moved about three feet closer to the window. One framed print on the wall was busted, by which I mean both the glass of the frame and the print itself were split diagonally across. It was of Doune Castle in Scotland. *Starry Night* had been swapped with my grandmother's watercolour. Worse, half of my record collection was spread out on the floor, many of them looking like they'd been purposely folded in half. Leo Kottke had a crease down the centre of his face, and Tuck and Patti had severed their relationship. I felt sick to my stomach.

All the drawers in my living room and bedroom had been dumped out. Some of my decorative things were broken: a couple of vases, the clock on the wall by my dining table, a floor lamp, and—oh, rats—my music box, shaped like a grand piano, which played *Clair de Lune*. Ouch, that hurt. I failed at preventing tears from welling, and overflowing. It had been a birthday present from Calvin.

I looked through without touching, just to see if anything was conspicuously missing. I didn't own much of real value, only sentimental. My guitars were with me, which were the things I cared most about.

I called the cops.

"Hi, I'd like to report a break-in."

I gave her my name and address, and answered all her questions. She told me I'd have to wait just a little while and she'd send an officer. I thanked her and hung up. Then I poured myself a glass of wine.

To my astonishment, yet not really, the officers at my door were my pals Walker and Hendrix. It will come as no surprise that they declared this wouldn't have happened if I'd accepted a ride from them. I didn't think it would be wise to tell them I doubted it, so I kept my mouth shut.

"Has anything been taken?"

I looked around me again. "It's hard to tell; nothing obvious. A few things have been wrecked, though."

"Like what?" Walker was busy with her notebook again, sketching the scene.

"My clock, my music box, that picture— Wait a second; it's not broken." The picture of Doune was fine. I scratched my head. "I thought that print was broken before."

Walker and Hendrix looked at me doubtfully. "Anything else?" Hendrix said.

"Well, in here," I beckoned them to follow me into my room. "See? All the drawers have been—shit."

Hendrix looked shocked.

"Please refrain from swearing," Walker cautioned.

I apologised. "But you see, when I got home, all this stuff had been dumped out all over."

Hendrix leaned against the doorframe. "Yes, I see how disgracefully messy it is in here."

"You know you can't blame your own mess on a crime and expect the cops to come and clean it up for you." Walker was madly taking notes.

I had a bad feeling about returning to the living room.

Sure enough. Although the furniture that had been switched around was still switched around, the books were back up on the shelves, and anything that had been broken or dumped was where it should be. Even the records were perfectly tidy. I pulled out Tuck and Patti, who had patched things up. The theme from *The Twilight Zone* was loud and clear.

"For cryin' out loud," I muttered. "You were in here a moment ago; you saw all the stuff lying broken on the carpet."

The cops tossed frowns at each other.

My guts roiled with rage. This sort of nonsense was getting tired. These cops were already so suspicious of me, I was in danger of being hauled away in a straitjacket. I had to remain calm. "Look, I'm really sorry to have troubled you. This makes no sense. I swear upon my life—"

"What did I tell you about swearing?"

"I know!" I half-yelled, and then instantly pulled myself together. "I *mean* . . . I promise you the place was all messed up and wrecked when I walked in." I spread my arms out. "I don't understand it."

"Well now," Hendrix said in a fatherly tone, "you did have a rough time getting home. I would advise you to have a nice, hot bath and relax."

Seriously? This cop was telling me to have a freakin' *bath*?

"I'm afraid I'm going to have to write you up for wasting police time." Walker scribbled furiously in her ticket book or whatever it was. "Now, may I use your washroom?"

"Sure, it's right down the hall."

"Meanwhile, I suggest you cut down on your drinking, young lady," Hendrix said. "Do we need to call your parents?"

I snapped my jaw shut and unwrinkled my nose so he wouldn't guess how cross I was. "Umm, no. Thank you very much, but I am twenty-seven years old, and I don't need anyone to 'tell' on me to my folks. I'm sorry for wasting your time, but . . . I guess I'm good now."

Hendrix continued to scrutinise all my belongings, picking up each item and turning it over and setting it down. Several minutes passed before I noticed an unexpected sound. I made sure Hendrix wasn't paying attention to me and took a few surreptitious steps down the hall. Sure enough, that wasn't just the running water sound of Walker washing her hands in the sink. I returned to the living room, where Hendrix was trying to balance a book on his head like a debutante.

"Is Walker taking a *shower*?" I demanded.

The book dropped off Hendrix's head onto the floor. "Now look what you made me do." He picked it up and shook it at me like an extension of his index finger.

What I had made him do? "Why are you even doing that during a police . . . investigation or whatever this is? Why is a police officer taking a shower in my apartment?"

Hendrix took several books off my shelf and started standing them up on end, setting them up like a domino track. "Do you prefer people not to bathe in general?"

"Well, no, but—" I shut my mouth. No matter what I said, he would have an answer, and it would not help any of this make sense. I sat in my armchair and did not drink my wine, though it called to me to down it like a church bell summoning parishioners to worship.

Eventually Walker came back to the living room, clothed and, presumably, clean, towel-drying her hair.

"These towels are so soft and smell so fresh!"

"I'm glad you, umm, like it."

She dumped it on the floor and sketched it in her notebook like a piece of found art.

Hendrix tipped the first book, which knocked the second, and when the whole row—about fifteen books—had fallen over, he yelled, "Yes!" and pumped his fist like he'd scored the winning goal in game seven of the Stanley Cup final.

The two cops left shortly thereafter. Walker had admired my little knick-knack of a tiny wooden doll on a swing, so I gave it to her. She cooed over it as they left.

They're Coming to Take Me Away blared through the ceiling. I looked up at it and frowned. I was pretty much sick of this craziness. *Was* I crazy? I mean, that picture had definitely been broken, and then it was suddenly not. I paced the floor. Somebody was toying with me. I didn't know who or how they were doing it, but *somebody* had it in for me. Where would it lead? Did this somebody have a goal in mind? I took a gulp of wine, now that I wasn't being judged, and set it down. I reached into my pocket.

The knife twinkled in the light of the no-longer-broken lamp. "All this has *something* to do with you," I told it. "I don't know what it is or what you want from me, but you are *in* this."

My cell phone rang.

My hand shook as I reached for it. It said *Unknown number*. "Hello?"

Silence.

"Hello?" I demanded.

I heard quiet breathing.

The skin on my back crinkled.

Click.

My hand trembled so I had trouble putting my phone in my pocket. The knife, with its steadfast commitment to my life, steadied me. I tossed both it and my phone on a chair. Heedless of the cops' warning, I refilled my wine glass and took a few more turns around my apartment. I tossed Walker's towel in the laundry hamper, then went back into my bedroom, where most of the drawers had returned to their places. Had I been mistaken? I closed my eyes and counted to ten. I was being gaslighted by sources unknown.

I turned to leave the room but stopped short. The crinkling of my skin spread up my neck. I set down my wine glass on the dresser and picked up my music box. My guitarist's calloused fingers slid over the wooden keyboard and inspected the tiny stick that held up the lid of the piano. Not a mark, not a scratch, not a single bit of evidence that mere moments ago, the little instrument had been in pieces on the floor. I turned the key and fought back tears as the little *plink-plink* sounds replaced the disturbing stillness with Debussy.

On the other hand, maybe the source of the gaslighting wasn't so unknown after all.

"I don't know how you're doing this, Phoenix," I said aloud, "but I have just about had it." My breaths came short and shallow, and I was getting dizzy. My trembling fingers set the precious item back on the dresser. I took a moment to calm my breathing before returning to the living room.

Seated in my favourite armchair—I didn't mind its new position on the other side of the room, as it happened—I practised *Gotta Have You* on my guitar until my cell phone *pinged*. There was a notification of two missed calls. What the heck?

Calvin had left a message in the afternoon, which said, "All right, just letting you know I'm leaving to catch the ferry, so . . . I'll see you at the wedding. Thanks again for doing this, Griffin."

And one from my mother. "Griffin, since I'll probably never see you again, I might as well tell you the business barely has enough to replace my stock. I'm low on everything, and I probably won't make it through the summer. All your little jet-setter friends from the Snifter wedding have done their best to ruin me. I'm sure you're not quite satisfied with abandoning—"

I heard my father's voice in the background, "Adele, is that Griffin?"

Mom's hand "covering" the receiver as she stage-whispered, "She needs to know the damage she's done to my poor nerves." Then, back at me, "Well, *think* of your family on Sunday nights, at least." A pause during which I was pretty sure I heard a forced sob. "Good-bye, darling."

While running over my schedule for Saturday, I sipped my wine. I didn't know how much more of this I could take. I was now really wishing I had told Brian I couldn't teach Liam's students this week. He would have understood. I had been too ambitious. Trying to please too many people. This would have been an easy fix, but it was too late now. Thank goodness I had booked a co-op car again; that would make things a lot easier. It occurred to me then to go print off my plane ticket and boarding pass. One less thing to do in the morning.

I would be staying overnight in Victoria, so I packed my little backpack with pyjamas and a change of clothes for Sunday. I would wear my outfit for the wedding on the plane to save time. Hanging out with Calvin and his family at the reception and so forth would be a good time. Then I'd come home late Sunday morning. It would give me a chance to sleep in, and I would still get home in plenty of time for The Spurious Correlations gig in the evening.

Everything was working out perfectly.

18

Saturday, May 19: The Big Day

I got up on Saturday morning with lots of energy and hustled in my preparations, determined that everything was going to go smoothly. I mean, why shouldn't it? I had four lessons to teach before coming home to grab my things and leave for Teresa's wedding. I took the quick bus trip to the mall to pick up the car I'd reserved and drove to the music store, telling myself over and over that I just needed to take the day one step at a time. Unbidden, my fingers drummed on the steering wheel in time to *I'm So Excited* on the radio, as if that would keep me calm.

When I got to the store, Brian informed me that my 11:00, my last lesson of the day, had cancelled because she was sick, buying me an extra half hour in my stressful day! How perfect was that? Then, to my joy, believe it or not, the lessons went as I might have expected before all the nuttiness began, unless you count all three students playing way above the level they'd been at the week before, but I decided not to overthink it. Obviously they were learning from me. That's what I told myself. Melissa didn't barf and Markus had actually learned the three chords I had taught him. I began to think my suspicions about being somehow set up had been paranoid imaginings resulting from a stressful week.

I raced out at eleven and drove home as speedily as I could get away with. I would grab my backpack and be off again.

The local paper had been shoved through the mail slot, and the flyers were scattered all over the floor. I gathered them up, and underneath the papers I found a letter. It was in a business envelope labelled with the logo of my apartment's management company and had been hand-delivered, which explained its arriving on a Saturday. I sliced it open with a letter opener and shrieked.

It wasn't a letter opener in my hand. I didn't even own a letter opener. I had subconsciously reached into my back pocket and pulled out the knife. The knife which had not been in my pocket while I was at work because that was where I had tucked my cell phone during lessons. As bugs crawled up my back, I set it on the table where I could keep an eye on it.

I unfolded the letter. It was on management letterhead.

Ms. Trowbridge,

Please be advised that your entire rent is due on the first of each month. You are presently in arrears in the amount of $675.00. Please submit payment immediately. Failure to do so will result in management having to take further steps.

At the bottom was a handwritten note from Mrs. Kingsley. *Goodness dear, this has never happened before. I hope you can pay soon. You've always been such a good tenant!*

What the *hell*? My rent had been set up for auto-withdrawal for three years! Besides, why was this only being brought to my attention on the 19th of the month? I had to go, but I had an extra half hour, and this shouldn't take long. I picked up the phone.

"Hi, Mrs. Kingsley? It's Griffin."

"Who?"

"Griffin Trowbridge. In 217. I just got this letter about my rent, and I don't understand why my full payment didn't—"

"Now, see here. I don't know who you are or why you keep phoning this number. I'll bet you're one of those elder abuse jerks who try to get trusting, unsuspecting people to send them money. I'm calling the police as soon as I hang up." The phone banged down, making my ear ring. The line disconnected.

Imagining pastoral and tranquil lake scenes, I sat at my computer and tried to get into my online banking. I failed. Why is it the system is down right when you really, really need it to not be down?

This was an unforeseen obstacle, but I wouldn't have a good time today if I didn't deal with it right away. Given my extra half hour, I could spare a little bit of time and go to the bank on my way to the harbour airport.

I changed into the pants and blouse I would wear to the wedding. There was something in my pants' pocket. That god-damned knife. With a loud exhale that would make any yoga instructor proud, I pitched the thing out a window and slammed it shut. I added toothbrush and toothpaste to my backpack.

I fumbled through retying my shoelaces. Pain forming between my eyes, I jammed my arms into the sleeves of my jacket and gathered up my stuff, including my guitar and my travel mug of coffee. Slamming the door behind me I locked it and ran down the hall and down the stairs. I had just been paid from the music store, so it would be a piece of cake: I'd dash to the bank, get cash, take it to Mrs. Kingsley, get a receipt—oh, and find out why the auto-withdrawal didn't work all of a sudden. Honestly, you pay all these damn bank fees and don't get the services you've paid for. Someone at the bank was going to get an earful.

I joined the queue at the bank machine. One machine was out of order, leaving two machines in use. The person at the machine on the left finished up and walked off, so the next woman stepped up, opening her handbag. The customer at the other machine left, and the dad in front of me moved in, holding his child by the hand. I watched the line-up inside the bank. There were about fifteen people in the queue and only two tellers. I was still happy with my choice to remain out here.

Then I noticed that handbag lady had a list of about twenty-seven transactions to make. She was pushing buttons like a spaceship pilot, and the damn machine was beeping away as if it were communicating in Morse code. The dad, on the other hand, was explaining every little step to his kid as if it were going to be the kid's job to do the banking for the family from now on.

"And now you see here I have three accounts accessible on this card. One is the chequing account, which we use regularly for most of our spending. The second is the savings account. This is where we put money and don't touch it because we want it to earn interest—"

"What's interest?" the kid asked.

Dad explained while I looked at the time and tapped my fingers inside my pockets. The queue inside the bank hadn't moved.

"And the third account is the—"

"Excuse me," I said politely. "I'm in a bit of a hurry, so I wonder if you'd mind, umm, going a little faster today?"

The man huffed at me. "This, young lady, is called 'a teaching moment.' I am teaching my child how things work at the bank. I'm doing this because I believe it's important for children to be curious, to ask questions and receive honest, detailed answers. That's how they learn about life."

"Yes, well, be sure to teach him all about the phases of the moon too, 'cause we're going to go through all of them in the time I'm waiting here."

The man's face went red, and his kid's eyes flitted back and forth between his dad and me.

"I'm done here," said spacewoman and left the other machine.

I said, "Thanks," and glared at the man as I stepped in.

"Never mind," he muttered at the kid. "Some people are just *like* that, which is another thing you need to learn about life."

I thrust my card in, and the thing beeped as I followed the instructions. I keyed in my PIN and asked it to give me $680. I waited, tapping my fingers on the machine as it thought. The dad was now explaining the concept of a line of credit.

A bell sounded and lights flashed all around my machine. A loud computer voice yelled, "Insufficient funds! Insufficient funds!" as if I were a big winner at a slot machine.

"What?!" I yelled back. "I just got paid!"

It spat my card out so it flew across the room and hit the window. I scrambled to pick it up.

"Irresponsible . . ." muttered the dad to his kid. "This is why I'm teaching you these things so you can manage your funds more effectively than *she* does."

I stormed into the bank, where the queue had shortened by a couple of people, but one teller put up her Closed sign. *I am so changing banks!* I had already used twenty minutes of my extra half hour. I finally got my turn.

"The bank machine said insufficient funds, but I know there should be over a thousand dollars in the account."

The teller took my card, clicked away on her computer, and frowned. *Uh-oh.*

"Is it a new account?"

"I've had it for fifteen years. Is that considered new?"

"Hm." She asked my name. I told her. A lump formed in my chest. A tight, trembly feeling crept up the backs of my knees. She clicked. "Is this your home branch?"

"Yes."

"I'm sorry, we have no record of an account in your name." She looked at me as if to say, *I'm done with you. Next, please.*

I picked up my card, summarily dismissed, and floated out of the bank in a haze. There was no point anymore in trying to deal with this problem right now. I had to leave for the airport. It would have to wait until Monday. Nearly crying with anger at myself for not having made that decision half an hour ago, I pulled into the traffic and got stuck at a red light. The song on the radio was *Money*, of course, and I tapped out the rhythm onto the steering wheel. I couldn't bear the thought of asking my mom if I could borrow almost $700 to pay my rent until I could get this bank stuff sorted out. Maybe my dad . . . No, I had worked so hard to show my folks I could be independent, that I could be a musician and still make out fine, even if it meant working some other jobs on the side. If I asked them for money, even though this was a particularly unusual and rare circumstance, I'd still be given the pursed-lip-raised-eyebrow look that triumphantly screamed, "I've been counting the days for this moment."

Boy, this had to be the longest light in the world. I'd been sitting there so long, the radio was playing the tail end of a different song. Was this the same red light, or had I sat through an entire sequence? No, there was no way I could have sat through an entire green light with nobody honking at me. On the contrary, my dad had always defined a "split second" as the length of time between the light turning green and the person behind you honking.

Well, if there was a problem with the light, I could afford to waste no more time. I put my blinker on and shoulder-checked to pull into the right-hand turn lane. No problem; I'd go a different route home. The lane was clear, so I pulled in and drove ahead toward the stop line.

Slam!

A car from out of nowhere hit me from behind.

I sat in my car, hands gripping the wheel, eyes shut, tears squeezing past my lids. I breathed. I took stock of the situation. I had coffee all over me, thanks to the lid being shunted off my travel mug. Was I hurt? I didn't think so. The impact had startled me, but I didn't seem to be in any pain. Just to be sure, I carefully tilted my head from side to side. Still, I knew right away I had to change the plan. Okay. I could deal with that. *I'll phone and change to the 2:30 flight, that's all. It'll be close but I'll make it.* That would give me time to go home and change my clothes. Having made that decision, I was able to breathe more freely. I opened my eyes and looked in the rear-view mirror at the car that had hit me. Not a car. An enormous truck, like a Suburban or something. Tinted windows. Were those legal? I reached over to my backpack and pulled out a notepad and pen. I got out of the car.

Funny how the light was green now and all the traffic was moving. *Thanks, folks, I sure hope I don't need a witness. Thanks for stopping to make sure everyone's all right.* Nobody had emerged from the truck. The back of my co-op car was in bad shape. It had lovely all-new wrinkled convex contours, with a beautiful cobweb for a rear windshield. Presently, the car had a Suburban for a prosthetic. I'd have jotted down the license plate number, but it was obscured by my car.

That the driver hadn't emerged was alarming. I moved around to the door and, though I felt kind of silly, I, umm . . . knocked. No answer. *Holy shit! Are they dead?* I tried the door, which was unlocked, and I flung it open.

"What the . . . ?"

The driver was leaning over, and he and his girlfriend were slobbering all over each other as if it were midnight at the drive-in.

"You're kidding me, right?"

The guy came up for air long enough to say, "Shut the damn door! Can't you see what we're doing here?"

"Can't *you* see you just rear-ended me? My car is probably totalled, and you're back here *making out*?"

"Shut the damn door!" *Slurp slurp.*

There was nothing in the driver's manual about how to behave when you were in a car accident with some people who pretended it hadn't happened. I blinked and shut the door. There were literally no other cars around. I went to the rear of the truck and took down the plate number and the make and model of the vehicle. I also took a couple of photos on my phone. There wasn't much more I could do without the cooperation of the other driver. I would file a claim and let the insurance corporation deal with them. I'd have to call the car co-op and explain as best I could. One thing I could not do was stay here and not get moving.

For a split second, I considered phoning my mother to ask if I could borrow her car, but what would be the point? She'd have a whole bunch of I-told-you-so-type remarks, followed by the If-you-got-a-real-job-you-could-have-your-own-car-to-total-themed speech. I rolled my eyes and got back behind the wheel. Bloody hell, could this day get any worse?

I turned over the engine, and with a little metallic crunch, detached my back end from the front end of the Suburban. With teeth clenched to hold back a scream of frustration, I drove home with the same meticulous care as someone taking her driver's test.

Before even going inside, I called the airline to change my booking to the later flight. I explained to the woman on the phone that I had had some setbacks, including being rear-ended.

"Don't you worry about a thing. Just get here safely, okay?"

I wanted to tell her not to be nice to me or I would cry, but instead I thanked her and went in. I didn't have to race out the door now that I was taking the later flight. I didn't have a ton of time, but I could at least make myself a sandwich. I peeled off my coffee-drenched outfit and threw on a bathrobe so I could eat some lunch without danger of spilling on myself. Prudent! When you get to be my age, you think of these things.

All right, I said to myself as I licked peanut butter off my thumb. *All right*. I could handle this. After all, what was the most important thing? My best friend needed me to sing with him at his sister's wedding in the afternoon, and his happiness was more important than all these setbacks.

I finished eating, picked a new outfit, put it on, brushed my teeth.

Time to get rolling.

The phone rang.

Don't answer it, advised the voice in my head.

I picked it up. "Hello?"

Bad idea, the voice said, and I knew it was shaking its head.

"Griffin, it's Phoenix. How soon can you be here?"

"What do you mean? I'm going to my friend's wedding in Victoria this afternoon, remember? I was supposed to be on a plane already—"

"What?"

I heard a shriek and pulled the phone away from my ear.

"Griffin. Griffin, are you there?"

"Yes, I'm here, but I'm heading out the door."

"Good, you're on your way?"

I spoke pointedly. "To my friend's wedding, yes."

"No! You gotta come here. There's been a change. The gig is tonight."

Told you, said the voice. I told it to shut the hell up.

"What did you say?" said Phoenix.

"Nothing. Look, what do you mean the gig is tonight? I confirmed with Rickenbacker that the gig is tomorrow. I told everybody at the very beginning that I was going to Victoria today for my friend's wedding. You *can't* change the gig to tonight."

"Too late. The client wanted to change it, so we changed it."

"Without making sure the band was available? That's insane! The client doesn't—"

"The band *is* available, Griffin. You signed a contract."

I did? "No, I didn't." I didn't think I had, but I wasn't sure about anything these days. The confidence with which I had told him to get a new guitarist two days ago had deserted me.

Phoenix said, "You will be there. You start at nine."

He rang off and I stared at the phone, sweating and shaking. If I hadn't known better, I'd have thought I was coming down with the flu. "You . . . you *jerk*! *Asshat!*" I slammed the phone down, aware of an army of ninja spiders stealthily floating along my bloodstream, creeping up on me for the ultimate attack. If they reached my heart, it would stop and I'd keel over, dead. Except it wasn't ninja spiders; it was panic. The only thing I could think of to do was to run. I dropped my backpack from my shoulder to the floor and ran to the bedroom to grab my short black skirt and the low-cut top I had planned to wear for the gig. I shoved them into the pack, next to the book I was going to read on the plane. My sweat was a reminder to run to the bathroom and add the deodorant to the pack. I could play the wedding, then ask about a return flight this evening. Salamander's wasn't far from the harbour where the plane would land. I was disappointed not to be able to enjoy the time and stay overnight as I'd— Wait a minute. I wasn't "disappointed," I was "enraged." That was more like it.

I grabbed both guitars and threw everything in the back seat of the wrecked car and gunned it out of the parking lot.

When I saw the flashing lights cruise up behind me, I thought, *Of course*.

I didn't hesitate to pull over. It seemed quite normal that I should be stopped by the cops at this time. I had *not* been speeding, so who knew what they wanted? But shit like this had become synonymous with my life. My back was rigid like concrete, and my face was taut with the effort of holding back the threatening tears. The pain between my eyes had spread to the top of my head.

"License and registration."

I handed it to him with a vibrating hand. "It's a co-op car."

"Seems you've had a bit of an accident."

"Yes, I was rear-ended earlier today. I have an appointment with an adjuster on Monday," I lied.

"Your tail lights are both out, no doubt as a result of the accident. You shouldn't be driving this car."

No no no! I was reaching my limit. I wanted—no, desperately needed—to scream my head off, but it would have landed me in jail. "I have to get to the airport. I'm going to my friend's wedding in Victoria, and I've had a bit of a bad day."

To make a long story short, he gave me a fine and told me to hurry up and get the car off the road. I promised I'd park it at the harbour to harbour terminal and take a cab later. *Sigh.*

By the time I got into the terminal after parking the damn car and paying the $27.75 on my credit card, I had just fifteen minutes before my flight. I ran full tilt with my backpack and guitars to the entrance of the little building that was the harbour to harbour terminal and joined the bloody queue to go through security. I reached into my jacket pocket to see if I had a peppermint or something. I was tense. Anything to help me calm down. I didn't find a peppermint. I found something else.

Shit! Fuck! Crap! What the hell!

The leather sheath containing the knife, which I had thrown out the window, was in my pocket. I would never in this lifetime get through airport security with a knife in my pocket. I yanked it out and without even glancing around to see who might see, I flung it onto the floor, where it slid on the shiny tile and hit the wall.

Phew, dodged that bullet.

I took a few steps forward and set my stuff down again. I was now third in line. I reached into my pocket to pull out my boarding pass.

I shrieked, drawing all kinds of attention.

The knife was in my pocket. I whirled around and looked toward where it had slid across the floor. It was gone.

Oh no, oh no, oh no. There were those ninja spiders again. I was never going to make it through security. Sweat gushed down my body like a garden water feature. My shaking could rival those machines that mix cans of paint. I was looking around furtively. Basically I was displaying every single sign of being a Person of Suspicion. There was no chance in hell any security officer wouldn't believe I wasn't up to something. They would take me into another room, they would strip search me, they would do a complete search of every orifice and cavity—likely orifices and cavities I didn't even know I had.

And suddenly it was my turn. I showed the officer my ticket and boarding pass.

"Off to Victoria, are you? Aren't you a little late? Flight leaves soon."

"Yes. I've had a bad day."

"You'll make it if you hustle. They're boarding now."

I couldn't believe my ears. Words of support and encouragement? A lump formed in my throat. *No, do* not *cry.* I put my backpack in the bin, followed by my boots.

"Remove your jacket, please."

Sure, sure I could remove my jacket. Could I also pretend it belonged to someone else? Another officer opened my guitar cases.

"You seem nervous."

"I'm—I have a fear of flying." I wanted to laugh out loud. They'd never buy it.

"Why are you flying, then?"

"I'm going to my friend's wedding in Victoria, and I didn't have time today to go by ferry."

She smiled at me—*kindly*, if you can believe it. "What a good friend you are, flying there when you have such a fear."

Yeah, she'd believe me until my jacket went through the X-ray machine.

The machine beeped. Of course it did.

My jacket came out the other side.

"Please remove the items from your pockets."

Here it came. My hands were trembling so I could hardly function. Fingers grasping the leather sheath, I shut my eyes and pulled it out. I held it up, hopefully in a nonthreatening manner so they wouldn't attack me and fling me to the floor.

"Open it, please."

I opened it and slid out the—

The *spoons*?

"What are those, ma'am?"

I tried to speak, couldn't, swallowed over a dryness that was akin to sandpaper. "They . . . they're spoons, it seems."

"Spoons?"

"Spoons."

"Ma'am, may I ask why you have . . . spoons in a leather pouch?"

My mind hurtled through a card index of brilliant responses. The ninja spiders had picked up speed. "I'm a musician!" I cried with triumph. "I play guitar, as you can see, and I also play the—the spoons." With an enormous, fake smile of enthusiasm, I drew them out and placed them back to back and began clapping them away onto my knee. My situation depended entirely on how much musical background these security guards possessed. Surely anyone who had even sung in a choir would recognise the shittiness of my performance.

"That's really interesting. Thanks. Move on."

"What?"

"Next please."

Stunned, I was immobile for a moment. The guard's eye contact had shifted completely away from me. Then I gave my head a shake. I had put my jacket back on, shoved my feet in my boots, pocketed the . . . spoons, and picked up my pack and guitars before the person behind me had even removed her jacket. I slammed through the door and ran pell-mell down the gangplank labelled *Departures* and along the dock to the impatiently waiting seaplane just as they were about to close the door.

"Wait! I'm here!" I had to yell over the noise of the propellers.

"Cutting it a little close, aren't you?"

"Sorry. Bad day," I said between huffs of breath.

The flight attendant checked my ticket and boarding pass and ID and waved me up the stairs. As I stepped over the threshold, the flight attendant at the door took my guitars and stowed them for me. I made it down the centre aisle of the plane without giving anyone a concussion with my backpack and dropped into my leather seat. The plane was taxiing through the harbour before I had even done up my seatbelt.

I had intended to read on the plane. I didn't. I shut my eyes and took up meditation.

The flight landed (Do you still call it "landing" when it's on water? I'll have to ask someone that, someday.) only a few minutes late. I checked my cell phone, and it was only 2:50. I weaved around slower walkers and hurried up to the airport to ask about a return flight later and was told it would be no problem to get on a 5:00 or 6:00 flight. I thanked her and ran to the road to grab a cab.

The street was deserted. I started walking. I had looked up the address of the venue to give to a cabbie, so I plugged it into a map on my phone. To my surprise and delight, the place was only a few blocks away. It was 3:15. I could do this.

It didn't take me long to remember that it was the May long weekend, and a long weekend in Victoria means tourists. People crowded the streets, all of them headed in the opposite direction from me, apparently. They also liked to stop and take selfies in front of buildings and pieces of art or to stop suddenly to point at something their friend couldn't possibly see without their help. The late-afternoon sun was warm, and I was wearing a jacket and carrying two guitars and a backpack. By the time I reached the venue, I was drenched in sweat and practically blind with fury and a whole bunch of other emotions. Not a soul was in sight. My skin tightening with dread, I checked the location. I was in the right place. Where the hell was everybody? The wedding was to start at 3:30, and my cell said it was 3:40. *Crap. Double crap.* I didn't think weddings ever started on time; why did this one have to be the exception? *Who has their wedding at 3:30, anyway?* I thought crossly.

I hurried up the steps to the main doors, slinging my Tele higher on my shoulder so I could more easily pull the door open but still knocked the other guitar case on the hard wood. I stepped into an entryway of sorts and held the door behind me so it would close quietly. Straight in front of me was the main door to the hall, and through it I could hear guitar music and a male voice singing.

Apparently I had the time wrong.

Claws grabbed my heart and squeezed it. I opened the door and tried not to clunk my stuff as I entered. A few heads turned to see who was so rude to enter so late. The bride and groom seemed to not notice; they were rather focused on each other. Their attendants glanced in my direction, but were intently listening to the figure at the front of the audience. He did not look up. Pointedly? I didn't know.

Calvin was nearly finished playing the song we were supposed to sing together. He sounded great. It would have been even better with the second guitar part and harmony, though. The music travelled all around the room, Calvin's passionate baritone voice spun in the air along with the guitar notes. He was flawless. The final strum of *Gotta Have You* reached into the rafters and hung there for a moment before being joined by the applause of an enthusiastic audience. Only then did Calvin look up and right into my eyes. I wanted to smile at him, to tell him he'd sounded fantastic. But I was concentrating on holding back tears. His expression didn't change. It was a mixture of appreciation for the applause and a dark hurt I knew I had caused. The claw squeezed and stuck its talons into me.

I slid into a seat at the back as the ceremony proceeded with some uncle doing a reading. Something squeezed my chest so I couldn't breathe; I was drowning in shame and embarrassment. My ears filled with silence like being under water. Why had I bothered coming? I should have just told Calvin I couldn't make it.

No, you've got it wrong, moron. What I ought to have done was get my priorities straight. I *should* have told Brian I wouldn't be able to handle the lessons this week; that I had a prior commitment. I shouldn't have been so arrogant as to think I could give everybody what they wanted, to think I had to be some sort of hero and come through for them, as if I were out to get some kind of award or something.

Instead, I had caused my best friend a whole lot of stress and forced him to perform on his own. Not that he wasn't capable of it, but that wasn't the point.

The wedding officiant went on to the vows, followed by the rings, but I missed what was actually said. I was too busy hating myself.

The reception was a cocktail party with hors d'oeuvres and music. I was a wallflower at the event, afraid to approach anyone. The servers came round with their trays, and I took a glass of white wine and a mushroom cap stuffed with something-or-other. I wasn't all that hungry, even though my peanut butter sandwich was hours ago. My stomach was churning with the stress of the entire day. Teresa and James made the rounds, chatting with each guest. They were only a few people away from me, so I moved to the other side of the room. I didn't see Calvin, but I wasn't sure I wanted to talk to him anyway.

It occurred to me I had spent an awful lot of time in these past two weeks wanting to avoid the people I cared most about.

When I saw Calvin's dad in his wheelchair next to the gift table, a dart of sadness thrust into me, so I went over to him, uncertain if the dementia would allow him to recognize me. I pulled up a chair so I could sit at his eye level.

"Hey, Mr. Sheeley, it's nice to see you."

His face lit up. "Hey-ya, Griffin!" He always said my name so quickly, it was like it was only one syllable. I very nearly burst into tears. Not only because he recognized me through the disease-driven haze of his mind, but that he was happy to see me. Unlike some.

"I like your tie," I said.

"Bow ties are cool." He winked and I laughed at the reference to *Doctor Who*.

"Hey, you know what?" He poked me on the arm. "You're a terrific singer. You should have sung with Calvin!"

Sinking like the *Titanic*, I tried to smile. "Aw, yeah, that's okay. He did great." Agitation tightening my throat, I looked for a way out. I was saved by a couple who stepped up to say hello to him. "Take care, Mr. Sheeley. I'll see you later."

I moved away and tried to recapture that new philosophy from last week, the one I had so easily let slip through my fingers.

A program from the ceremony lay on a table, left there by one of the guests. I picked it up and looked it over. My breath caught in my chest. The order of the ceremony showed that there would be a reading, the vows, our song, and then the rings. I thought about this for a moment, then folded the program and put it in my pocket. I had just laid eyes on Calvin.

A few couples were dancing in the centre of the room, including Calvin, who danced with a very pretty girl who I heard someone refer to as the groom's cousin from the prairies. She had long, dark hair; perfect makeup; and was an excellent dancer. She had a beautiful smile, and Calvin looked at her with admiration that alarmed me in an unfamiliar way. She looked perfect; she probably *was* perfect. She had probably been on time. Probably *early*. She was likely a good guitarist and singer, and cook and probably had a good job and made good money and was terribly organized and never made thoughtless decisions or mistakes. I hated her.

An insane thought had followed the ninja spiders through my bloodstream and had chosen this moment to lodge itself in my heart. Dizzy and out of breath, I knew it was time to do the right thing.

I swallowed the last of my wine, and as the song they were dancing to ended—I don't even know what song it was, I was paying so little attention, which gives you an idea of how agitated I was—I approached Calvin on the dance floor the way a child heads to the principal's office.

He said something to the woman, and she walked away, but not before giving his arm a squeeze. He interrupted me before I even had a chance to say, "Hey."

"Why did you even bother coming?"

His tone was so cold, I was taken aback, even though I was expecting his anger.

I stuttered a bit as I replied. "I said I was coming, so I came. I am so sorry I was late, but all this stuff happened, it was crowded . . . you wouldn't believe the trouble I had—"

"Save it, Griffin."

It could have been the anxious day I'd had, combined with the wine. But I felt sick. Like actual, get-me-a-bucket sick. Some deep-seated instinct stirred in its hiding place in my body's lower mantle layer and told me Calvin's cold anger was not just about the wedding. "What . . . is this . . . about?"

Calvin rolled his eyes at me, an expression not at all in character. "When were you planning on telling me, Griffin?"

Horrible Sinking Feeling.

"'I just need more *time*, I'm so *upset.*' It was all such a load of bullshit, Griffin. Did you wait until the next day before joining another band, or was it that very night after I left?"

Hand up to hair. Staring at floor. Stuck in car that has driven off the end of pier. Cannot get the window open to escape.

"That 'friend of a friend' stuff didn't ring true: if he was a friend of Jillian's, you'd have just said, 'He's a friend of Jillian's.' If I ask Jillian about him, what will she say, Griffin? Good acting job, though, from both of you."

Water rising around the car. Light waning. Cannot open locked door.

"All that crap about teaching extra lessons. All this 'I'll take the harbour to harbour,' trying to show me you're making such a sacrifice, so everyone will admire Griffin. *Look how hard she works! Look at how much effort she put into being here . . . She's* such *a fucking good friend*. So benevolent. Bullshit.

Absolute bullshit. It was about you all the time. How can *Griffin* still do what *Griffin* wants to do, pretending to help Calvin with as little sacrifice to *Griffin* as possible? Well, no thanks. I'm done."

"I was about to tell you—"

"Oh, of course you were. That's pretty easy to say."

"I was. The night we got together. But you started talking about your dad. How was I supposed to tell you then?"

"You had plenty of opportunity to tell me. I'd only called you about seven times since the stupid wedding gig. But no, it was all about self-preservation with you. I got to find out from *Jason*."

Car nearly fully submerged. Try to breathe slowly, so you don't use up the air . . .

"Jason! How—?"

"I stopped by the store yesterday to check in with you. You weren't there. But your ex-boyfriend was. He tells me he even met this new fella of yours, this *Matteo*, the very next night after the wedding. He met this guy *in your apartment*, and apparently you told him you're in this guy's band."

Car completely surrounded by murky water and caught in algae and weeds. I rubbed my head, since I couldn't get the windows open. I would suffocate and die here.

"Lots of big talk about how important our friendship is to you." His voice caught. "When, exactly, were you going to tell me you have a new boyfriend *and* a new band? Oh, forget it. There's really not much you can say at this point. Well, I sure hope this new band of yours is awesome, because the rest of the guys and I are going to carry on without you. And we'll find our own lead guitarist so Matteo can give you his undivided attention."

He walked away, leaving me stranded, feeling completely and utterly alone in the middle of the crowd. Swirling people. Everything dark. People stared at first, and then ignored me altogether, dismissing the cast-off in the centre of the room. I was so invisible, someone bumped right into me and I stumbled. That startled me out of my misery.

I wove through the dancers and found Calvin by the punch table. I hurried over to him.

"Calvin, no. You're wrong. I mean, you're right about some of it. Yes, I should have told you about the band, and about Matteo. But I thought and thought and debated and argued with myself over and over and decided to wait. I mean, I don't even know what's going on with it, and if I can stand to stay with it or not. I *was* about to tell you the night we got together, but then I couldn't bring myself to do it. And then I thought if you guys wanted Matteo in our band it would all be immaterial. Of course I'm sorry you found out the way you did, but I guess I kind of hoped you'd give me the benefit of the doubt, especially when it was Jason you were talking to. I thought we were good enough friends for that at least.

"And if you had any idea, any *fucking idea* what I've been through today, let alone the last two weeks . . . Anyway, you don't know and I'm not going into it right now. But believe me, if this were all about me, I would not have spent $300 to come here at all today. I obviously fucked up, but I'm not the only one." I frantically pulled the program out of my pocket. "Look here," I held it out so he could see. "You told me we were on after the vows. I was here for that."

An auntly woman interrupted just then to speak to Calvin. "It was *so* good of you to volunteer to sing first, so Uncle George could get here in time to do the reading and not miss the crux of the ceremony. *Thank* you." She nodded at me and shuffled off. I stared at my . . . friend.

I didn't care anymore. "If you'll excuse me, I have a plane to catch in order to please everybody telling me what to do. Tell Teresa I'm sorry I single-handedly fucked up her wedding day, and I truly hope she'll have a happy married life in spite of it."

I barely looked at Calvin as I walked away, but I'm pretty sure he resembled a zombie.

If I felt like crap before, I felt like something worse than crap now, maybe puke mixed with crap. Diarrhea. I grabbed my gear and headed to the door. I had to pass the gift table, where Calvin's dad was still sitting.

I set down my acoustic and crouched next to him. "Hey Mr. Sheeley."

He smiled like he hadn't seen me in days. "Heya, Griffin!"

"I umm . . . I—" I hoped he didn't notice my lip trembling.

"You know what?" He took my hand. "You should have sung with Calvin!"

I was so close to absolutely losing it, I looked down at the floor and fought to hold it together. I nodded, and when I spoke my words were barely audible. "Yeah, I agree with you. I should've. Listen, I gotta go, but it was great seeing you."

I squeezed his hand, picked up my guitar and left. Outside, I breathed the sea air and couldn't help but notice that the streets were filled with taxis. I thought, *Screw it*, and walked back to the harbour. Having left the wedding earlier than planned, I had plenty of time to make my flight. I leaned against a railing and stared out at the sunshine's reflection on the water. I was so dejected, I didn't notice right away that the knife was pressing against my ribcage inside my jacket.

I pulled it out. "Are you trying to drive me to the breaking point? Is that it? Am I supposed to end it all? Well, fuck you." I hurled it into the harbour. "Fuck you," I whispered. I wiped tears from my cheeks and continued on my way.

Seated on the plane, I rummaged through my shoulder bag for my book. It was pretty much no surprise at all to find the knife being used as a bookmark.

I looked out the window, unseeing, as the plane taxied through the water.

"I've got the god-damned message," I whispered, gripping the offending utensil. "But you are not going to win."

19

Saturday, May 19 is far from over

The view from the plane should have been breathtaking, but I had no appreciation for the splendour of the Victoria inner harbour, nor the view of the ferry travelling below us between the islands, nor as we approached our landing site. On any other day, I'd be thrilled to be where I was at that moment, and I'd probably be close to weeping with the beauty of it. Instead, I felt like weeping in despair. My preference was to close the blind and not even look out the window.

And my day was nowhere near over yet. *Damn.* I still could not believe Phoenix would change the gig. Who does that? My stomach was roiling with stress, a hasty glass of wine, and nothing to eat but a mushroom cap.

The plane landed and I leapt to my feet to be the first off. But the elderly lady in the seat in front of me made it into the aisle first. I could only do what I could do. I followed her painstaking steps all the way up the gangplank, through the building, and to the road, where she pulled a skateboard out from nowhere, dropped it with a clatter, and stepped on. With a few pushes, she surfed down the sidewalk, and I wasn't even a little bit surprised when she executed a perfect kickturn and vanished from my sight.

It was 6:40. The band didn't play until nine, so I was still fine for time. Even so, I wanted to be able to relax and have a breather before it was time to get ready. I had promised the cop I wouldn't drive the co-op car, so I caught a cab to the restaurant. It was just a five-minute drive. It was worth the few bucks it would cost me.

I chucked all my gear in the back seat and climbed in with it, giving the cabbie the address on Powell Street. He pulled out and turned up Howe

Street. I shut my eyes.

My cell phone rang. It was Jillian, so of course I picked it up right away.

"Hey, Jill. What's up?"

There was a sniff and a choking sound on the other end. I sat up, alarmed.

"Jillian, what's the matter? Jillian!"

"Oh, Griffin, I can't stand it. I'm so sorry."

Shit, what now? "What is it? Take a deep breath."

"Teryn has done it again. God, I *hate* her, Griffin."

Holy crap, I had never, *ever* heard my sister speak of anyone like that. "What now?"

"Have you had the call yet? No, I guess not; you've been in Victoria all day. Snifter has demanded that you, personally, make a public apology for what happened at Teryn's wedding. He's demanded I be suspended from dance until you do it."

I hadn't thought I had any guts left high enough in my body to sink further. I was wrong. "He—" It came out as a whisper, so I tried again. "He can't do that. I have nothing to do with the dance studio. How can he take this out on you? He can't have a legal leg to stand on."

"Mm-mm." I could feel Jillian shaking her head and pictured her long hair swaying. "I'm sure you're right, but he's threatened to put a personal boycott on the show and advertise it in the papers. By the time it gets to any legal action, the run of the ballet will be over. The studio is caving and has agreed to cut me from the show."

She broke down into sobs. Could this day get any worse? "Look, I'll do it. I'll do whatever they want me to. I won't let them do this to you."

"But, Griffin, I don't want you to! It isn't fair. It isn't even true. I can't stand that she's going to get away with this. You should have seen her: She stood there next to him, smiling all prissy and gloating. The other dancers were all standing around. Some of them wanted to kill her, but the others were glaring at me. They want the show to go on so bad, they started pressuring me to tell you, even though it's wrong. They're so selfish."

"Never mind, Jill. It's okay." I'd already been accused of being selfish today. Maybe this was another way I could prove I wasn't. "I'll . . . just do it. You matter to me more than my reputation. I don't even have one, anyway. Now, don't worry about it. I'll take care of it. Hey!"

The cabbie had crossed the Cambie Street bridge, way off course from where I needed to be.

"Jill, honey, I have to go."

I stuck my phone in my backpack. "Where are you going? I have to get to Powell Street; I told you that."

"What? You said Peverill."

"No, I bloody didn't! Will you please turn around?"

He sighed ridiculously heavily, like he was being asked to go way above the call of duty. But he turned around and headed back to the downtown core, where he got stuck in one-way-street hell, and finally dropped me off at Salamander's.

I paid him exactly what I owed him, not a penny more. I suffered his wrath only long enough to slam the door as hard as I could.

I burst through the front door of Salamander House of Music and Pudding at 7:00, my load of backpack and guitars clunking on, well, everything.

The place was packed, and the patrons were banging the tables with their mugs, chanting, "We want the band! We want the band!"

Phoenix saw me and came rushing over. His outfit was grey with about a bejillion yellow ribbons attached to it, which fluttered out behind him like squid tentacles. "Griffin, where the hell have you been?"

"Oh, for cryin' out loud, Phoenix! You know exactly where I've been. Now I want to go relax for a bit before we play."

"There isn't time, you pillock. You start at 7:30."

I wished I hadn't asked if this day could get any worse.

"No, " I insisted. "We start at nine, that's what you told me on the phone this morning."

"And I told you 7:30 when I called you back later."

Wallace

"Why are you doing this? I was at a wedding! I had my phone off." I put my pack down on a table and dug through it for my phone.

"Then you should have got the message once you turned it back on."

"There was no message when I—" Sure enough, the voice mail icon was blinking away. It had *not* been there before. I swore under my breath and started off.

Phoenix grabbed my arm. "You can't go through here. The restaurant is *open*, as you can see, I hope, and you're going to crash into the patrons with all that stuff." He turned to the patrons and yelled, "Nothing to see here!" which of course drew their attention, where they hadn't been paying any before. I really hated Phoenix. "Now go out here and go around to the employee entrance." He gave me a shove, and I found myself out on the street again.

Could this day get any—*No! Stop it. Do* not *finish that thought.*

20

The Answer Is Yes. (Still May 19)

I stood on the street, pressing my lips and eyes shut, and shuddering like an airplane in turbulence. Tears were very close to the surface. I had to hold them off; I couldn't let go. I was already going to be a mess. I had the faintest of hopes that playing music would be a distraction.

Was any of this worth it? All I'd wanted to do was make music. I'd been asked to join this band; I hadn't sought them out. So why were they making it so difficult? Was making music with this particular group, with Matteo MacCallum, really worth all this?

I didn't even know how to get around to the back of the building, so I was forced to use the parkade entrance. I was partway down when a car whizzed by me and I had to flatten myself against the concrete. Tightening up the dam on the emotion reservoir just a while longer, I stuck to the wall, and looked over my shoulder every three seconds. Since I was preoccupied with stress of a different nature, I persevered. I was in a version of the Iron Man competition, all this running around, carrying my backpack and two guitars.

When I reached the level where the door to the building was, it was with the relief of arriving home after a long business trip. But I couldn't relax. I had to get inside and up the stairs to find the rest of the band and get myself ready. Getting through the door was another test of my patience, and as I climbed the stairs, I counted them, breathing deeply. Inhale for four steps; exhale for four steps. It was a good try, but by the time I got to the right level and entered the building, I was so out of breath, I wasn't sure if I'd ever be able to sing again. On the other hand, the exercise had helped me work through my anxiety. I had suppressed it enough that I felt under control. I might have been kidding myself, but it was the best I could do. I was very worried tonight's gig wasn't going to be as good as the first one, but I was experienced enough to know that once we got started, I'd get lost in the tunes and feel much better.

I ran down the corridor, glancing at my phone for the time. It had taken me ten minutes to get this far. No problem. Twenty minutes to change my clothes; I could warm up my voice at the same time. I don't know what the group had done about sound check, but if they had done one at all, it wouldn't be too tricky to add me into the mix. It would all be fine.

I burst through the door into the studio, calling, "I'm here! I didn't know the time had been—" I nearly collided with a stranger. A woman. A buxom brunette wearing knee-high boots with heels that put her at six feet at least. Her fish-netted legs stretching out from under a black leather mini skirt, paired with a bright red bustier to barely cover her ample cleavage, she was showing more than I do when I'm naked. She wore more make-up than an entire clown parade.

"Uh, hi." I sought information from the others as I dumped my stuff and started pulling out my gigging clothes. "Listen, I'll be ready super quick, have no fear. Who have we here?"

The drummer and bassist were warming up in the back of the room. Matteo stepped forward and took the woman by the hand.

"Griffin, I'd like you to meet Priscilla. My girlfriend."

The sound of blood rushing through my head. A stunned expression on my face, I'm sure. My body had pretty much been tasered.

Priscilla rubbed Matteo's arm, turning her nose up a little. "I see what you mean about her."

What?

Girlfriend? He had never said anything about a girlfriend. Had he? No! He *kissed* me, for cryin' out loud. Had I read into that? No, god damn it. How do you *read into* the way he kissed me? He'd kissed me like that more than once.

Phoenix magically appeared, ribbons and all, and told me in a triumphant voice, "We brought Priscilla in because we couldn't be sure you'd make it in time."

"And it's our seven month-iversary," she said cutely.

Couldn't be sure I'd— "I'm here, aren't I? *You* went and changed everything last minute, and I'm still here."

"Ah, but you're clearly not yourself." Phoenix tried to put his arm around me, apparently wishing to guide me away. I squirmed free of him and his tentacles.

"I'm *fine*. I dropped everything to be here. I will change and be ready to go on stage in ten minutes." I was lying; I would not be "ready" by my usual definition. But what else could I do? "We do not need *her*."

Phoenix spoke behind his hand at the rest of the band. "Well, someone's a little touchy."

I snatched up my clothes and ran to the bathroom, where I absolutely could *not* let myself cry. Shaking like a human earthquake, I changed my clothes, squeezed some product into the mess on top of my head, and ran my fingers through it. I observed myself in the mirror, in my black skirt and royal purple top, and couldn't help but compare myself to the leggy woman in the other room.

I was grossly deficient.

Seven months they'd been together? Then what the *hell* was all that about, with the way he had been behaving with me?

What a dunce I was. A tearless sob escaped my lungs. I splashed water on my face and breathed slowly through my mouth so I wouldn't throw up. *Just get through it.* That's all I had to do. I went back to join the others.

Priscilla was sucking Matteo's face off. He had his hands in all kinds of cosy places. I picked up my guitar, tuned, and suddenly it was time to head to the stage. Priscilla walked along, side by side with Matteo. Where I should have been. She didn't have an instrument. Could she sing? Did she know any of the harmony parts? What the hell would she do? Why was I not putting my foot down and refusing to let this happen? Why didn't I just leave and say forget it?

Because all I had been through had been for this. If I left, what would it all have been for?

We took up our positions on the stage. Me on the left, Matteo in the middle, Priscilla the Demon Amazon of Powell Street on the right. Whatshisface the drummer in the rear, flanked by Whosiwhatsit on bass and Whojimafliggit on keyboards. I didn't even register the fact that they clearly knew I was coming because there was a freakin' microphone set up for me. Phoenix stood beside me, as if he was part of the band. To introduce us? I plugged into my amp and adjusted the volume.

The crowd was restless. The servers dashed around, delivering desserts and beverages so everyone would be set for the music to begin. Rickenbacker leaned against the wall, arms folded across his chest. He kept checking his watch, smoothing down his fancy coat, playing with his hair—all the things a person does when he does not wish to appear nervous. What was *he* nervous about? He had everything he wanted.

I plucked my guitar strings to check my tuning and stepped over to the bass player to make sure I was in tune with him. My set list sheet was on the floor under my microphone stand. I noticed the red pen marks where things had been crossed out, just as Phoenix spoke.

"Now, remember, everyone, since Priscilla's here, she's gonna sing the opening number."

Vertigo. One of my tunes. "Since when?" I said. "She's not even in the frickin' band. And since when are you the leader?"

"Griffin, you've never showed such a display of ego before," Phoenix said. "Get over yourself. Priscilla is here so we may as well give her something to do."

"Yeah well, you're the one who invited her, and I'm still trying to figure out why."

"Come now, just play as best you can," he said as if speaking to a nine-year-old about to play her first piano recital. He turned to the microphone. "Ladies and gentlemen, you've been a very patient crowd, an enthusiastic one! I know the band is looking forward to playing for you as much as you're looking forward to hearing them. So I won't stand in your way any longer. Here they are: Priscilla and . . . The Spurious Correlations!"

I was irate. Now she was getting top billing, for fuck's sake? I was at least grateful for the hard rock pounding of an E chord to eat up some of my frustration. The show must go on, and I considered myself professional, if nothing else. But though I thought I'd feel better once I started playing, I did not. I was near breaking point. I kept feeling sobs climbing up my throat and had to shove them down. Maybe it was just as well I wasn't singing lead. Would I have been able to choke out any notes? The warmup of singing harmony was probably good for me. I couldn't even hear Whatsherface; I wasn't listening. I figured it would just upset me. We got through the song, I guess.

There seemed to be electricity in the room. The place was packed, and the air was ever so slightly sparkly . . . effervescent. Intense energy emanated from the crowd like sound waves, and the servers rushed around. Everything felt on edge, as if everyone was waiting for something. But since the band had already started playing, it wasn't that; they were waiting for something else.

Matteo sang lead in *Take It Easy*, and I sang my regular part; it felt good vocally, but it seemed like I couldn't play anything right. I was almost certain the band kept skipping beats every now and again. I had to keep my eyes on Matteo, which ordinarily would make me extraordinarily happy, but not tonight. Every time I made a "mistake"—or rather played it the way we'd rehearsed it instead of the way the band was playing it tonight—Matteo gave me a funny look. And it wasn't the kind, encouraging glance I had gotten used to over the past two weeks. Everything felt wrong. *Just get through it.*

And Priscilla pranced about and shook her cleavage around the stage and made sure the audience could see her clearly. And she sang flat with a lot of downright wrong notes. Her voice was harsh, with no subtlety or dynamics, as much feeling as a bench. The audience cheered and roared. They sounded more like a stadium of sixty thousand people than a crowded restaurant.

Phoenix wouldn't leave the stage. He behaved like a sixties go-go dancer, showing the audience what they ought to be doing down on the floor. He crowded me and he wouldn't go away. I was afraid he would try to share my microphone with me.

The third song was supposed to be *I'm Gonna Be*, but just before I started the intro, Phoenix did step up to my microphone.

"How're you enjoying the music so far?" he cried, and the cheers and feet-stamping were thunderous. "I won't stop these guys any longer, but tonight we have a special surprise!"

He didn't specify who the surprise was for.

"Tonight is a very special night. Our lead guitarist, Matteo—" Tumultuous applause for him. I studied my guitar strings. "—has been dating this fine specimen of a woman, Priscilla—" Hoots and hollers. Classy. "—for seven months. So she's going to sing a song for him."

The crowd was on their feet. I looked to Matteo, to the bass player, to anyone for guidance. The drummer—Kenneth?—counted us in.

"What the hell song are we playing?" I said away from the microphone.

Just as the first notes had to come in, Matteo said, "*At Last.*"

"God damn it, that's *my song!*" I protested. The drum entry came in, and I had to follow or look like an idiot.

I came in on the right chord. I would stake my life that it was the right chord. Certainly the one we'd practised. But my F chord was not even a little bit right in the new key the band had selected without telling me. Flustered, I looked to Matteo, but he was so busy getting ready to be sung to by his cow of a girlfriend that his back was directly to me. The bass player—Marvin?— was watching them. I felt completely invisible. I tried to figure out which key they were in. I have a damn good ear, but I couldn't figure out the interval; I swear it kept changing. No matter which chord I tried, it was off by several notes.

The audience lapped it up. Priscilla butchered my song vocally, while I treated it like a slasher movie. The audience was on their feet and, to my horror, began pointing and laughing at me.

Suddenly, halfway through the song, Matteo stopped playing and turned to me with ice in his eyes.

"Why do you have to go and wreck such a beautiful moment?"

His tone stabbed me through my heart. He might as well have just told me to bugger off then and there.

I held my ground. The world slowed. All day nothing, but *nothing*, had gone right. My rent was screwed up, I'd lost my bank account, I'd smashed a car that didn't even belong to me. My sister was being taken hostage by the most evil businessman in the city. And that was just today. All the crap I'd put up with for the past two weeks: Phoenix's abuse in the kitchen in spite of the effort I'd put into learning, messing up at the music store, all the screwed-up lessons . . . Worst of all, I'd ruined my friendship with my best friend. I did not know if he would ever want to see me again, and in this moment, I finally realized how much that meant to me.

Everything I'd endured in the past two weeks had been because of my desire to play with *this band*. And now everything was going up in flames. The audience was laughing at me. The band was laughing at me. And there, in front of me, was Phoenix, tears of mirth running down his cheeks, gesturing to Rickenbacker off to the side as if to say, "This was all your idea! Good one."

And there was this knife.

The knife felt cool in my hand. It had a nice weight to it, and was well balanced. All this time, it had wanted me to use it. It sparkled and tingled and would not leave me alone. I couldn't take anymore. Phoenix gave Rickenbacker a thumbs-up, gave someone a high-five, and I had the sense he'd planned all this, that for whatever reason it was his design from the start to take me down. The knife sparkled in the stage lights. Matteo's arm was around Priscilla, and they faced me, she looking miffed that I'd ruined her moment, and he . . .

Matteo looked adoringly at her. Then he turned to me, and his smile had a hint of derision in the corner, which he matched with his eyes.

In my head I heard Matteo's whisper: "I don't want to start something I can't finish."

Phoenix took a step toward me, nodding with a gleeful, encouraging smile. I felt again Matteo's kitten-soft lips on mine.

I had been preyed upon this whole time. And I wasn't going to take it anymore. The knife felt good in my hand. The knife that kept reappearing in my possession. The knife was the key. Telling me to use it. To make all this stop, I had to use it. I pushed past Phoenix.

Matteo's expression changed from mirth to shock as I plunged the knife into his chest.

He fell to the stage, and his body crumbled into colourful fragments as I fell on top of him in a cacophony of guitar notes. The fragments hissed and sizzled like those birthday sparklers, and my hands and knees slammed the stage floor. I heard myself screaming my lungs out, all the screaming I had held back all week. The world came back to regular speed, and fireworks shot up out of the stage, and sparkling confetti fell out of the ceiling all over. I glanced up to see the other band members literally go *Poof!* and vanish, including Priscilla, Queen of the Scrags. Beneath me, Matteo's fragments sizzled, and he joined the others in *Poofdom*. I kept screaming.

A marching band had appeared out of nowhere in the middle of the restaurant, playing *It's the End of the World as We Know It*.

Someone else was screaming too. "Nooooo! You did it wrong!"

Rickenbacker ran toward the stage. "No! No!" He waved his arms. "It was supposed to be *Phoenix*. Not the MGC. Phoenix! Why, why, why did you do that? Didn't he make you hate him?"

Phoenix still stood next to me, but now his head was in his hands and his shoulders shook. He whimpered, "We were so close . . . so close . . ." over and over.

My screaming faded and turned into sobbing instead. Heavy, wracking sobs to reflect what had happened to me since the night of the awful wedding gig, since I'd met Rickenbacker. To reflect my recognition that I, Griffin Trowbridge, musician, had just been pushed to the limit so that I had stabbed a person. Never mind that that "person" appeared to not have been . . . quite . . . *real*? I had fallen—hard—in love with him. And he wasn't even real? All the weird shit of my recent life flashed through my mind, and all the pent-up frustration flowed out of me as I curled up on the stage in the place where Matteo had disintegrated, my sides aching as I wept my heart out, my Telecaster in my arms.

When I finally pushed up onto my elbow, my nose stuffy and face drooping from the release of tension, the audience had disappeared. They had been replaced by a small contingent of oddly dressed folk who sat in gilt-edged armchairs on a raised platform. The brass band had assumed a formation around the walls of the now nearly empty dining room. Two men were being escorted from the room in shackles.

A tall, spindly figure, who looked something like a daddy longlegs or maybe a stick insect, approached the stage with urgency in her step. She wore a red-and-gold brocade gown—at least, the top half of a gown. Her bottom half wore gold tights, allowing me to see the spindliness. A large-brimmed hat with an enormous peacock feather had mounds of curly blue hair exploding from beneath it like the billows of cloud produced by a rocket ship taking off.

"Did we see there a series of Magically Generated Characters?" she asked in a high-pitched, operatic voice.

Rickenbacker's face lit up in alarm, and he whirled around. "Why, yes Madam Skeezix, Your Honourable Judgeworthiness." He bowed so low, his head touched his knee. "I assure you I went through the rules with a finglesprot and found no reference to MGCs whatsoever."

The woman halted. She stared at him. Her indignant glare transformed into a suspicious frown. "I shall consult the judges." She pivoted with military precision and walked away. Her bustle looked like a duck's bottom and wobbled as she waddled.

MGC. Magically Generated Character. To have learned what the acronym meant elucidated exactly nothing. "Is anybody going to tell me what this is about?" I asked, utterly spent.

Phoenix sat on the stage steps, weeping and running his fingers through his ribbons. Rickenbacker leaned his arms on the foot of the stage. He was right at my eye level.

"It remains to be seen whether we placed in the competition, but we can be sure that we did not win the championship trophy. Rest assured we are nonetheless very grateful for your contribution."

I stared at him and followed his gaze to survey the scene around me. Somehow, the guitars and bass had all been hung on their stands. I pushed myself up and sat with my legs in a *V* amid a heaping pile of confetti. No human remains, just the contents of a thorough paper shredder. I sat among the detritus of my dream band, my face dripping wet with my own tears and my heart aching. "What . . . what are you talking about?"

"We, Phoenix and I, are former champions of the Quinquennial Inter-Urban Live-Action Role-Playing Game. May I make the assumption that you are familiar with the concept of the role-playing game? Of LARPing?"

I nodded. I'd never played one myself, but my bandmates had—my *real* bandmates. Another little sob escaped me. *Calvin.* Who had found a beautiful, dark-haired woman.

"Phoenix and I are from Salamander—a world other than yours; a parallel world, if you like. I teach Audio/Visual Magic at Salamander University. Phoenix, there, is a clothing designer and shop owner. We are professional LARPers. The challenge for this year's competition was to include someone from the Other World—yours—with the ultimate task of getting you to stab someone—in this case, Phoenix."

I stared at him, slack jawed. "You *wanted* me to *kill* him?" I was too exhausted to feel the resentment I knew I ought to feel at being manipulated to this extreme.

Phoenix lifted his face from his tear-soaked hands long enough to say, "You wouldn't have actually killed me, dummy; you would merely have triggered the end of the competition."

Dummy? "But—" Really, there were just so many questions I could have asked. I gave up and let myself sag.

Rickenbacker looked at Phoenix, who had planted his face in his hands again, and back at me. "Clearly we were successful at one aspect: that of causing you enough aggravation to make you lash out here, at the end."

"Fantastic. Congratu-fucking-lations," I said.

"Having said that," he went on, "we seem to have been mistaken in the direction of your displeasure."

Had I been drinking? If not, I sure as hell needed to.

"Are you telling me this entire last two weeks, from the moment I met you in the hotel, coming here to work, making . . . fucking crème fucking *brûlée* . . . and the god-damned *hose*— all the last-minute changes, everything . . . was part of a—Christ, are you saying that Matteo was part of this *game*?" I was still struggling with the shock of getting so angry, I had stabbed someone, never mind that he wasn't real.

Rickenbacker nodded. "All of it. Everything that happened to you. Matteo, the rest of the band, Priscilla, the music playing in your head, the bizarre occurrences at your music store. Even this restaurant, the other staff and all the patrons. I admit the Matteo part of the plan seemed to have got a bit out of our control. We made some assumptions . . . regrettably."

A horrifying thought struck me, and a new rage awakened my limbs. "What about my sister?" I sat up straighter. "If you're responsible for the hell that she's—"

"No!" Rickenbacker held both hands up. "I give you my word that we have had no involvement whatsoever in your beloved sister's disappointment. That began prior to my connection with you, and the blame for that rests solely on Mr. Snifter. For goodness' sake, Phoenix, pull yourself together," he snapped as my hands unclenched—if he *had* caused my sister's misery I really *would* have stabbed him. "Our star participant is recuperating here; you must stop wallowing."

"But we can't *win*. I wanted to win."

"Nonsense. We may still place first, second, or third, depending on how our competitors fared. We won't win the championship title, you're right, but wouldn't it all be worth it just to say we placed ahead of Blinky and Jethro? Which seems likely, I might add."

Phoenix shook his head back and forth like a four-year-old having a temper tantrum. "No! No! No! No!"

"What about me?" I cried. "I don't care about your stupid competition. I just wanted to play music. What happened to the band?" I clutched my belly, where a lump the size of a softball might make me barf, and searched among the instruments on the stage for something that felt real. "And what happens now? Am I supposed to just go back to my regular life and try to pick up the pieces of the great big mess it's become?"

Rickenbacker crossed his arms on the stage. "Yes, well. I might have to take some—*ahem*—responsibility for that as well. Certainly we won't wipe your memory. Such action would not only be cliché, but it would be a lame ending to a good story. No, we will adjust a few things as necessary and numb certain aspects of what has happened. For instance, your own observation that you were driven to violent behaviour is something I take personal responsibility for. As for the rest, I have heard it said that when one's life is falling apart, the pieces really are falling into place."

The man was mad.

I kind of rolled over onto my hands and knees, manoeuvring my guitar, and pushed myself up to standing the way a toddler would. I brushed confetti off my skirt. "Can I go home now?"

"I highly recommend it."

In a daze, I grabbed my guitars and stumbled back to the rehearsal studio to gather my gear, not too surprised to discover that it was a blank space, a completely empty soundstage. I was reminded of the holodeck from *Star Trek*. My guitar cases and backpack held lonely vigil in a pool of light. I lay my precious instruments in their cases and mindlessly coiled cable. The sleeves of my jacket seemed tighter than usual, I was just so tired. I finally got my jacket on, slung my Tele across my back, my backpack over my shoulder, and picked up my acoustic and twelve-string. I trudged over to the door, which politely opened for me, saving me the hassle of putting anything down to negotiate it.

"Thank you," I said out of habit. Who was I talking to? Ah well, it didn't matter.

I trudged down the corridor and put my back against the door into the dining room. I dreaded seeing what that room looked like, yet I dreaded even more the chilly, mid-May air of the outdoors and a long transit trip home. But we do what we must. I stepped backward to push it open, turned, and entered . . .

21

Late on May 19: After the Party's Over

My apartment.

I sighed deeply and let out a couple of tearless sobs. I stepped into my entryway and put my crap down on the floor, locking the door behind me. I hung my jacket in the closet. Something smelled good. And it was toasty warm.

A gas fireplace I didn't have before radiated glorious warmth.

To my surprise and exhausted delight, a smile was drawn from me by the bottle of red wine already open and aerating on the table. In case I had a preference, a bottle of white was chilling in an ice bucket on a stand next to the table. I felt a whole lot better about things. A glass of red in hand, I went and changed into comfortable pyjamas. Then I filled a plate with the roast beef dinner that still steamed, it had been placed there so recently.

I almost wished I had someone to share this marvellous meal with. Almost.

I sat in front of the fire and let it and the wine purge me of stress and anxiety. The silence was one of the first things I noticed. No music came from my neighbour's place, or anywhere else. The peace and quiet had the same effect as a bowl of chicken soup, warm and healing. The meal was delectable, with perfectly cooked beef (unlike my mother's), mashed potatoes, veggies and Caesar salad. There was even dessert, and to my surprise, I wasn't so sick of dessert that I didn't find the tiramisu mouth watering.

I ate and drank and stared at the fire and evaluated the current situation with much more equanimity than I had been capable of a couple of hours ago.

My sister's entire dance company was being held hostage by an Evil Overlord Businessman until I met his demands. My bank account had unaccountably vanished, leaving me in arrears with my rent. I had smashed up a co-op car, which remained in long-term parking at the harbour airport. My mother wasn't speaking to me.

Worst of all, I no longer had a band. The man I had fallen in love with had gone *poof* in a flash of fireworks when I'd stabbed him—I had *stabbed him!*—with a magical knife, leaving nothing but a pile of confetti. The whole band turned out to have been nonexistent, and they had also gone *poof*. Two weeks of my life had been part of an elaborate game show that made *Just For Laughs: Gags* look like it was for preschoolers.

The ridiculousness of it all started me giggling. It developed into laughing, and soon I was rolling on the floor in a cloud of hysterics. Phoenix's outfits, the crème brûlée, the mountainous mille-feuilles, the yoga, the haiku . . . It was all so outrageous.

After a while, I just lay there, spread eagled, staring at the ceiling.

The only thing I couldn't laugh about was Calvin. My best friend hated me and might never speak to me again. Worse, I had an eerie suspicion that in an Emma-to-Mr.-Knightly kind of way, I had been on the wrong track for a very long time, and if Calvin chose to remove himself from my life, I would be missing more than a best friend and bandmate. Much more. I rolled onto my side and held my head in the crook of my arm. Why had I not seen it before? What if he didn't feel the same? What if he had found more suitable companionship in a perfect, dark-haired beauty he met at a wedding?

Some problems, I reasoned, I could solve. I would apologise to the world about the behaviour of my ex-lead guitarist. I could word it in such a way that anyone listening would know what really happened. And anyhow? In the end, it meant nothing to me to do it. And it would help Jillian so . . . Duh.

My bank account . . . well, that was a bit trickier. But I would go in and speak to someone. I had bank statements to prove what I was saying.

The car? That's what insurance was for. It could not be mistaken for anything but a rear-ender, so it should be a pretty cut-and-dry situation. Especially if they didn't even file a claim because they were so busy snogging.

As for my mother not speaking to me?

Well, I could scratch that one off the list of negatives. As Calvin had once said—on the very night all this had begun—"Thank heaven for small mercies."

See? I'm a glass-half-full kind of person.

But regarding Calvin, now . . . That was very much up to Calvin.

I finally sat up and reached for my guitar. I began plucking my way through *All I Know So Far* until the lyrics made me choke up. I set my guitar aside and picked up my glass of wine from the end table. I stayed on the floor, leaning back against the comfy chair, and observed that when they refer to the heart aching, it's because it actually does ache. So there was an answer to an oft-asked question. Yay. Thank goodness for wine.

Pleasantly stuffed, and somewhat resolved, I continued to stare at the fire as I savoured the wine until I got too drowsy to keep my eyes open any longer. I switched off the fire. What would my landlady think of it? Never mind. I didn't plan on moving any time soon.

My bed had been remade with all kinds of thick, fluffy comforters and fluffy pillows. I sank into the cushiony softness and was asleep instantly.

Sunday, May 20

I woke up feeling the way a fairy-tale princess must feel, all cosy and surrounded by feathery softness. Like sleeping on a cloud, all bundled up in my blankets. The clock said *2:20*, and the sun beamed through the crack between the curtains, yet I felt no sense of alarm or urgency. A pale shadow hung over me, which I connected to Calvin, but since he was still on the Island, there was no sense worrying over something that I couldn't deal with until later. So instead, I smiled contentedly and yawned.

Eventually I dragged myself— No, actually I didn't. To "drag myself" implies "groggy and tired," and I was neither. I hopped out of bed, showered, and felt great. I had already booked today off work because I was supposed to be in Victoria, so I had a bonus day to myself. I'd had enough stress to last me at least a couple of days.

In the kitchen, I discovered the food had all been put away. It hadn't just vanished; it had been tidily packed away in containers in the fridge. The fridge was stocked with more food than I ever usually had for just me, but it was fabulous. It meant I'd be eating well for days.

I fixed myself some eggs with bacon, sausage and fried tomato, and sat down with my cell phone. The ringer had been turned off so I wouldn't be disturbed. That was awfully polite. I pressed buttons to subject myself to voice mail messages. It said there were only two.

"Hey, Griffin," said Brian. "Don't worry, I'm not calling to ask you to come in, I know you booked the day off." He chuckled. "I just wanted to see how you're doing. You've been working really hard lately, it seems; we've all been remarking on how you've looked kind of stressed out, so take it easy today, and of course the store's closed tomorrow. I'll check in with you for Tuesday, but no pressure, okay? Take it easy, Griffin."

Beep.

"Hey. It's me." My breath caught at the sound of Calvin's voice, and I instantly understood how afraid I had been of this call. "Listen, Griffin, I'm calling from Victoria. I'll be back in town later today, like four-ish. Can I— would it be all right if I came by? I need to see you." *Pause.* "Anyway, I'll call you. And I'm sorry." *Click.*

That was it. I figured there'd be seven million messages. So I was left with the freedom to overthink things.

Calvin was sorry? He had very little to be sorry for. I have to admit my mood elevated almost to elation at the basic knowledge that Calvin still wanted to see me. All was not lost. But in the way that one does when one desperately wants a thing, I did a brilliant job of making myself believe that exactly the opposite of that thing would happen.

I did bugger all for the rest of the day. I turned the fireplace on and ate food and drank tea and watched TV. I did everything I could to not worry about what Calvin had to say. The only time I left the armchair was to use the bathroom.

Calvin called around 4:30. Naturally I said he could come over. I paced around the apartment, all nerves, and hit the ceiling when the buzzer went. Then it felt like an eternity before he knocked. I opened the door. We stood watching each other's eyes fill.

"Come here," I said. He stepped forward and we stood there, hugging in my doorway, for a very, very long time.

"You were right." My voice quivered through a wobbly lip and a lump in my throat. I had a very real fear of bawling. "My priorities have been really screwed up lately."

"I'm sorry too," he said.

"I was afraid you wouldn't want to see me again."

He hugged me tighter. He smelled like coriander. "Griffin, I thought of that for about a millisecond, and I knew I could never—" He took a deep breath, came the rest of the way in, and shut the door. He took my hand and pulled me into the living room, where he completely ignored the fireplace as he pushed me onto my little couch and sat next to me.

"Griffin, I'm going to stick my neck out here, because I can't keep watching you."

I didn't know what he meant by that but remained silent, anticipating elucidation. My patience was rewarded.

He took a deep breath again. "Griffin, when I moved back into the neighbourhood and saw you in high school, I didn't see you only as the girl I had had picnics with when we were little. I saw you as the amazing girl who knew all the lyrics to *Spirit of Radio*. Who liked *Doctor Who* and all the same bands I did. Who didn't think I was a geek. At least, if you thought I was a geek, it didn't matter. You were that awesome girl who made me feel like I wasn't alone at school.

"You've seen me at my best and my worst, and you still wanted to be friends with me. It scares the hell out of me to say this because I don't want to lose your friendship, but at the same time, I can't keep watching you with other guys."

Was he saying what I thought he was saying?

"Maybe you see me as 'just friends,' and if that's what this is, then I'll take it. I have no entitlement here. But to me you are way more than 'just a friend,' and if after the way I treated you, you want to put me off, I accept that."

That did it. I couldn't let him go on that way. "The way you treated *me*?" I said. Was he on glue? "Calvin, I have been awful to you lately."

"Yeah! And that's the weird thing."

Geez, did he have to agree with me so easily? He carried on.

"And then you were late, and I was mad as hell at you . . . about a whole bunch of things." My shoulder blades contracted, but I let him continue. "So when my aunt said Uncle George was running late, I suggested we swap places in the program. Teresa asked about it, but I told her it didn't matter, which it did, and she was really disappointed. But I wanted to punish you, and that was really not cool, and you pointed it out, and I saw you talking to my dad, and I knew almost right away that no matter what had happened lately, you not being there—with me—was the worst part." He got up and walked to the middle of the room. "I don't ever want you to not be with me."

The hiss from the gas fireplace was the only sound as we stared at each other, me on the couch and him standing in the middle of the living room with a declaratory stance. I was without words for the longest time. His facial expression kept changing as he waited for me to say something, and ultimately I became fearful that he would take my silence as a response and leave. There was no way I was letting him leave.

"I was worried you'd go off with that hot brunette you were dancing with."

"Who? Oh, her. Well, I'm sure the groom's whole family thought of that, but no. She had never heard of Rush and thinks LEGO is for children."

A chuckle burst from my throat in spite of my efforts to be mature.

He threw his arms out wide. "What do you say? Do you think it's possible that we—?"

He didn't need to finish the sentence.

I rose and grabbed his face in my hands and gave him my answer.

Now, I have kissed quite a few guys in my time, but I have to say that if Rickenbacker's soundtrack were still working? I would expect no less than to hear *Kiss on My List* by Hall & Oates right now; this one was at the top. Soft and warm and with the intensity of being long awaited on one side and a fabulous surprise on the other. It had to end at some point, but neither of us wanted it to. Calvin started humming, then singing, the chorus of *Kiss the Girl* by Chameleon Circuit. Naturally I joined in, because I love that song, and the words fit us perfectly. He said, "I have wanted to sing that for a long time," and he kissed me again.

After, he whispered in my ear. "When the hell did you get a fireplace?"

I laughed then and a whole lot of pent-up emotion released itself, and we held each other and laughed our heads off. "That is a very long story," I said breathlessly, at last.

"I have another question," he said.

"If it is in my power to give you an answer, I will not hesitate to do so," I told him.

Calvin cleared his throat, as if bracing himself. "What about Matteo? Do you still want him in our band?"

I let out a kind of burst of a laugh. "Umm, no. I have to say, I don't."

"Good," Calvin said then seemed to catch himself. "I mean. Why not?"

I looked over at the fire. "He kind of . . . is gone. Look, I have a lot of food. Why don't we eat some, and I will tell you a very long story?"

We ate leftover roast beef dinner—almost as good as it had been the night before—and drank wine. I told him the entire thing. Every last detail.

I'm certain a small part of him thinks I was making it up, but I pointed out that the truth is stranger than fiction.

When I came to the part about Snifter's demand for an apology, he was absolutely incensed.

"But if you do this, I'm coming with you," he said. "Not only was it not your fault, but you were not the only one whose fault it wasn't. I'll get the rest of the guys to come too."

"Are they willing to still talk to me?"

"Griffin, I have to be honest with you. You're the heart of our band. The other day when we were jamming? It wasn't nearly as good. Not as fun either. I was really upset when I heard about this other band thing you were doing but more because I figured it spelled the end of ours, just when we're really starting to cook, y' know? And if I'm completely honest, I was frickin' jealous of Matteo, so yes, the guys still want you around. And this bullshit with Snifter involves them too. Besides, lead guitarists are a dime a dozen. But a solid rhythm player? One in a million."

It was the second-best news I'd heard all day.

The best news was that Calvin had no intention of going home that night.

Monday, May 21

Monday at about noon—Calvin had had to get up and go to work at the record store, gosh darn it—I heard the soft, metallic *flup* of my mail slot. On the carpet I found a letter in a brownish envelope. Its stamp and cancellation mark, though unusual, were familiar.

I pulled a certain knife out of my junk drawer. I noticed it had a nice weight to it, and felt good in my hand. It no longer tingled, but it made an excellent letter opener. I sat in my armchair and withdrew two sheets of high quality paper, and unfolded them. An SD card slipped out of the letter, which was from Rickenbacker, written in a foreign-looking hand.

> *Dear Ms. Trowbridge,*
>
> *Phoenix and I wish to thank you for your participation, albeit unwitting, in our contest. I have taken care of a few of the difficulties to which you were subjected during these two weeks, with some additional contributions to show our indescribable appreciation.*
>
> *As for the tournament, it may be too soon for you to reminisce on this time with any fondness, though I hope that may change. To that end, I have enclosed the unedited audio recording of the entire experience, which I was able to procure with ease: This is my specialty as instructor of Audio/Visual Arts at Salamander University. I hope, in time, you will be able to listen to it and perhaps even regale your friends.*
>
> *You were the best Other Worldly Participant we could have hoped for and we wish you much success.*
>
> *Your servant,*
>
> *Rickenbacker Topiary*

At first I thought this was in poor taste. I was royally pissed off that my emotions had been manipulated, that I had been misused so ridiculously. On the flip side, I was grateful to have confirmation that these things had actually happened to me, and I hadn't lost my mind. I had been worried I'd have trouble recovering from the trauma of what I had done, but my subconscious mind must have been doing some heavy-duty meditation. It was early days yet, but I was pretty sure I wouldn't need years of therapy. Though I don't know if I will ever wish to regale my friends with my humiliation of being covered in pastry muck.

Smiling, I slipped both letter and SD card back in the envelope and tucked it in a drawer.

A little later the buzzer for my apartment door went off, startling me out of a song I was trying to create, plucking away on my guitar. I pressed the intercom button.

"Hello?"

"Griffin, it's me. I have to see you." It was Jillian. Probably here to give me my instructions for "apologising" to the Snifter family. I was ready for it. I'd already started planning my speech. It would involve strong hints at the truth and a fair-sized dollop of sarcasm. In a way, I was kind of looking forward to it.

When she came to my door, I let in a much more chipper person than I had expected.

I was automatically suspicious. "What's up with you?"

"Oh, Griffin, you will *not* believe what's happened."

"Do tell." I pointed her to the couch, which she sat in, then bounced out again.

"Oh, it's just too cool. Snifter has totally recanted about you. Two things: one, Teryn broke her ankle rollerblading yesterday. Two, Paul Webb from the *Society Report* found out about Snifter's threat to pull funding. Snifter tried to *bribe* him not to publish the story, proving once again that he is a total jerk. So Paul basically said, "Screw you," and published the story about the extortion *and* the bribe! It was Markie who told me all this, by the way." She took me by the hands, pulling me up out of my armchair and spinning me round. "Snifter's backed down on the whole thing, of course. I've got the principle role back, and get this—

"He's not only letting the ballet keep the money, but he's adding a twenty-*thousand*-dollar donation. Markie said it's like he's smoothing it all over in hopes everyone'll forget it ever happened."

Jillian broke into peels of laughter. I'd seen her laugh before, but never had she expressed such deliciously malicious mirth. I was prodigiously proud of her.

I told her about Calvin and me, and she shrieked, apparently with delight, as she grabbed me and hugged me.

That night, cuddled in front of the fire with Calvin's arms around me, I drank a toast to Karma for returning my sister's joy.

Tuesday, May 22

Several things happened on Tuesday. I called Brian and told him I'd be in to work but a little late because I had some things to sort out since my bank had been closed on Monday.

My dad phoned after I hung up from Brian.

"Griffin, I was wondering if you could spare some time this week. I know baking isn't your favourite thing to do, but it turns out I'm swamped."

"Really? That sounds good, Dad."

"Yes, it seems word about the little cake mishap has reached the LGBTQ community. I'm scheduled to cater half a dozen gay weddings in the next two weeks, and I have a lot of baking to do."

I had to laugh. "I'd be happy to help wherever I can. It's the least I can do for ruining Mom's business."

Dad snorted. "Are you kidding? She's losing her mind and has to hire another shop clerk."

"But she's been telling me—"

"Has she not been telling you about Mrs. So-and-So bringing in three of her friends, and then they've been bringing in their friends? That she ran out of stock the other day because so many new customers came? Honestly, whatever happened at that wedding of yours has tripled your mom's business. It seems a lot of women are less than friends with Pearl Snifter, so any place she disparages has them all interested."

This was a fascinating turn of events. It did make sense. My mom *had* said she was running out of stock, but she'd let me believe it was all doom and gloom. Come to think of it, the only way that could happen is if people, I dunno, *bought* it, and the only way she could lose money was if she hadn't charged enough. It certainly wasn't my fault.

I told my dad I'd be able to help him the next day. "Oh, and just so you know, Dad, I make a mean puff pastry." Even without Steven and his fast fridge, I was sure I could handle this.

The next item on the list was to call the car co-op and report my accident before calling a tow truck to pick it up from the Harbour Air terminal. The woman on the phone was pleasant.

"Thanks for calling, Ms. Trowbridge, but our records show the car as being returned in perfect condition to the same lot where you picked it up."

"Oh," I said, wondering if this meant I didn't have to make the call to the towing company, let alone the insurance corporation. I wanted to ask if she was sure because it had been pretty beat up, but I realised how goofy it would sound if I insisted that I had wrecked a car that she said had been returned undamaged.

Instead, I thanked her and hung up. I crossed the call to ICBC off my to-do list.

Following that, I went to the bank and asked to speak to someone in accounts so I could sort out the mystery of my missing funds. The woman was happy to help such an esteemed customer and was very confused. Nobody had any recollection of having denied the existence of my account. She asked over and over if there was anything else, anything at all, she could do to help? I appreciated her attention, though I was put off by the obsequiousness. Then I saw the balance of my account.

Dear Rickenbacker.

My account held a balance of $450,000.

Not that I'd jump at the chance to work for Salamander's again, but you might say it was a decent wage.

Apparently my spirit was ready for music again because my favourite "happy" songs were surging through me, begging for escape. As I waited for the bus, on the bus, all the way to the music store, my body bounced with the tunes in my head, *Release Release, Lifting My Heart, the Big Sky, Here Comes the Sun*, and many others. Though I didn't let myself break out into full voice, I did hum, which was enough to draw glances from strangers. But they were nice, nonjudgemental glances. The humming told the strangers I was happy, not that I was insane. There's a big difference.

My elation was infectious, and lots of customers left the store in a better mood than when they'd come in. Brian laughed at me.

"Wow, Griffin, you should take stress breaks more often."

"You won't hear any arguments from me."

When I got home, another letter lay on the carpet below my mail slot. The knife really did work well for this purpose.

I unfolded the letter. It was on management letterhead.

Ms. Trowbridge,

Our records indicate that an error has been made. Although your account is set up for automatic withdrawal, it appears your rent has been overpaid in the amount of $11,310.00. This accounts for six months' rent. We will halt the automatic withdrawals for the next six months.

Wednesday, May 23 and onward

It turns out that when your heart has been broken by somebody who was some sort of hologram, it's way easier to put it behind you than when it's someone real.

This and whatever else Rickenbacker had done to ease my coping with having stabbed someone was working.

Calvin and I did a lot of thinking and talking over the next couple of days. (We also did a lot of not talking too, but that's none of your business.) We lay in my bed, arms around each other, doing our best to make up for what could be perceived as "lost time." I stroked the fine hairs on his chest and thought they were the loveliest chest hairs in the whole wide world.

"Why is it," I said, "Jason could be such a jerk to you and it never bothered me, yet at the audition, when Matteo said, 'Do you need to take a minute?' I was really pissed off that he would be so rude?"

Calvin murmured something into my neck, and it tickled so I squirmed.

"You know what I think?" I went on. "I figure I always knew you would rise above anything Jason had to say."

Calvin raised his head onto his fist and thought for a moment. "I honestly never felt threatened by Jason. I hated that he was an ass to you, but I guess I counted on you getting your shit together eventually."

I laughed. "Oh, thanks!"

"No, seriously. Sticking up for you with you right there was awkward. I tried. I don't know if it changed anything for you when we weren't around, but it didn't seem to have an effect at rehearsal. I figured Jason would always be a jerk, so I was just . . . waiting. He wasn't the first guy you'd been with, and you always came to your senses. You just needed to weed out all the guys who didn't deserve you."

"And you figure you deserve me?"

Calvin rolled me over and stared down at me. "Damn right I do."

I played with his dark curls, tucking them behind his ears. "Why on earth didn't you give up on me?"

"Because you make really good shortbread."

I laughed. We exchanged no words for several minutes.

"But what about Matteo?" I said during a pause. "Why did you suddenly react differently to him? He was just another guy."

"No," Calvin said. "He wasn't. Matteo was more of a threat because he was a whole lot of things: He was gorgeous and you clearly admired him. He was a mind-blowing guitarist, and worst of all, he was obviously a really nice guy."

I didn't get it. "So?"

Calvin rolled onto his back. "I still felt like I was part of your life with Jason around. I never felt like I'd have to, you know, step aside. But Matteo . . . I was afraid I *would* have to step aside for Matteo. You wouldn't need me anymore."

Love is a fucking crazy thing.

In between helping my dad with baking—with which I had some success, I might add—I worked at the store. I continued with my own lessons plus Liam's, and to my joy, nothing weird happened.

On Friday I ran the till, rang in orders, helped customers with instrument rentals, took lesson payments. It was a busy day, and I loved it. It felt like a long time since I'd been truly happy to be at work, thinking about music, all aspects of it. Late in the day, I was rummaging around under the front counter, rearranging the items in the display case, when the bell of the door rang.

A young woman entered. She was a bit taller than me, and had light brown shoulder-length hair. I watched her as she looked around the store a bit. She admired the guitars that hung along the wall, and eventually approached the front counter.

"This is a really nice store." She was about twenty-five, with bright blue eyes.

"Yeah, I like it, too," I said.

"I'm checking out what's around the neighbourhood."

"Are you new here?"

She smiled kind of shyly. "Yeah, I just moved here from Edmonton, so . . ."

"Oh." I believed more words were needed here. "Congratulations."

She laughed. "Petra." She stuck her hand out across the counter, and I shook it.

"Griffin. Are you a musician?"

"Yeah. Guitar."

I brightened. "Me too."

"Yeah? Well, I wonder if you know . . . I'm sort of hoping I can find a band to play with. Do you, maybe, know of any bands that need a lead guitarist?"

Now, there was a coincidence. "As it happens, our lead just quit a couple weeks ago, and we need someone. I play rhythm."

"Sweet."

"Listen, we're rehearsing tomorrow night. I can call the guys; I'm sure you'd be welcome to come jam with us."

22

Three Months Later

My new band waited in the back hall of a hotel corridor. Calvin tapped his drumsticks on the concrete wall. The rest of us hung by the doors listening to the speeching. Cameron wiped his tears on his sleeve. Andy and Petra laughed at him.

Calvin came over and put his arm around my shoulders and kissed the top of my head. "We're gonna be great tonight," he said eagerly.

"Yes," I agreed. "We are."

Mrs. Beckett had brought her full entourage of lady friends into my mom's shop for their dresses. Her daughter, Wendy, was now married to a gorgeous woman named Christine. The cake I'd helped my dad design was on display under beautiful lighting in the corner of the banquet hall. I was wearing a funky top Phoenix had sent me. Splashes of bright colours, and not a single tentacle.

We'd tossed around new names for the band, and though I had shut my eyes with trepidation as I'd made my suggestion, the gang all liked it.

I'd easily paid Brian for my Telecaster, and I had Rickenbacker Topiary, and yes, even Phoenix Reysing, to thank for the way everything in my life had fallen into place. My confidence had gone through the roof, it seemed, so that when a potential client didn't want to pay us what we were worth, I had no trouble saying, "See, when you hire a plumber, you expect to pay for the service. It's the same with musicians. You want us to play three sets and fill an evening? That's how much it costs." If the client didn't want to pay, that was fine.

There'll be other gigs, Griff.

After all I'd been through, I was much more laid back. Nothing I had faced in life since "the codswallop," as it came to be known, had caused me anywhere near the level of stress and anxiety it would have in days gone by. I dare you to toss some sort of obstacle my way. I'll knock it out of the park.

It was weeks before I even noticed I hadn't thought once of *CAPPA*. I went online and deleted my account.

Petra was fantastic and the group gelled better than we ever had with Jason.

Calvin and I arranged a gathering so we could play *Gotta Have You* for Teresa and James the way we had rehearsed it.

I had paid close attention to today's wedding, so I could get ideas for my own. We had six months to prepare. Jillian, (who had been absolutely sensational in the ballet), was so excited to be my maid of honour that she had already started doing crafts and designing centrepieces. The only trouble was that Calvin and I wanted to be the band at our own wedding, and our parents were having none of that. I guess they had a point. They couldn't keep us from singing altogether, though: We had already started working on our duet of *You're My Best Friend* for the ceremony. And he doesn't know it, but I'm writing a song to sing to Calvin at the reception. Shh . . . It's a surprise.

The best day was when we announced our engagement to Calvin's folks. His dad's dementia blocked his memory of the nurses who cared for him. Yet when Calvin told him we were going to be married, he took my hand and, in a beautiful moment of lucidity, said, "Griffin, dear. It's about time." I admit there were tears.

Oh, and I should probably mention that Calvin and I took a drive downtown Vancouver so I could show him where everything had happened. The old brick building where Rickenbacker introduced me to Matteo was a realtor's office, and where Salamander's had been on Powell Street were decades of weeds in an empty lot. Go figure.

The speeches wrapped up, and there came the moment we had waited for.

"And now, ladies and gentlemen... *Griffin and The Spurious Correlations!*"

The first dance was *At Last*, in F, and I must say, I sounded awesome with my band.

Ending Bit

"Seeing Blinky and Jethro taken away in chains for cheating was fun," Rickenbacker pointed out. He uncrossed his ankles on the coffee table and recrossed them the other way.

Phoenix snorted and said nothing. Rickenbacker couldn't be sure Phoenix hadn't merely got some feathers from his black, fluffy sweater up his nose. He looked like a giant crow.

Rickenbacker forced a laugh. "Ha ha ha!" He nudged Phoenix with his elbow. "To think they thought they could get away with their little ploy!"

Phoenix tilted to the side with the nudge and straightened again, like a Weeble. His pout grew more frowny.

Rickenbacker sighed and threw up his hands. "Really, Phoenix, you are just not pleasant to be around when you get like this. What, pray, is the problem?"

Phoenix's head pivoted on his neck, and he directed his glare at his friend. "What is the problem? You ask me what is the problem?"

Rickenbacker folded his hands on his lap. "I do."

"What have I said all along? Since the beginning of this fiasco?"

"Now, Phoenix—"

"The *title*, Rickenbacker. I wanted the championship title."

Rickenbacker rolled his eyes. "Do you think I did not?"

Phoenix pouted again and looked at the small trophy on the coffee table before them.

"My dear fellow, nobody won the title. Isn't that better than Blinky and Jethro winning it? Isn't there just a little bit of joy in knowing their Other World target bolted after only six days?" He shook his head and tutted. "To think they believed the tournament judges wouldn't notice that they resorted to having Jethro stab Blinky! Ha! Doesn't it give you any pleasure to have seen them disqualified and taken away, knowing they will not be allowed to even compete in the tournament for twenty years?"

Phoenix grunted. "I guess so."

"You guess so? Come now, isn't it a happy thing that we avoided disqualification ourselves regarding our use of an MGC?"

Phoenix mewed like a kitten.

"And for goodness' sake, my friend! Madam Skeezix was wearing one of your designs! I cannot imagine you are not overjoyed over that, surely."

Phoenix lifted his head. "We-ell . . ."

"We won first place because we were the only ones to get our participant to stab *somebody*. She didn't stab the right person, that's all."

Phoenix leapt to his feet. "That's the point!" he cried, moving around the table and over to the mirrored desk, where he turned and flung his arms wide. "I was so mean! I worked so hard to make her hate me. And I'd worked myself up to it. I was so scared, but by the time it came down to it, I was ready. And it was such a letdown to me emotionally that she didn't allow me to live up to my expectations of myself. She didn't allow me to realize my full potential!"

Rickenbacker sipped his wine. "Have you been reading self-help books again?"

Phoenix hung his head and nodded.

"Oh, Phoenix, my dear fellow." He put his feet down into the faux-fur rug. "Now listen, it was you who pointed out my error in instruction to our MGC. I was too specific in that instruction and then not specific enough in my instruction to him afterward. Somehow, rather than merely toning down his obvious attraction to our OWP, he went completely the opposite direction. Now, at least Griffin stabbed him. But if you hadn't discovered my error, she likely would not have stabbed anyone at all, and we wouldn't be sitting here with this lovely little first place trophy, nor this fabulous honourable mention prize."

Phoenix looked up with puppy eyes.

"Now, grab the wine off the desk and come and sit back down."

Phoenix did so and once their cups were refilled and their ankles comfortable on the table, they gazed in admiration at their two awards.

"It isn't *the* trophy," Phoenix said. "But it's quite cute."

The first place trophy was about eight inches tall and featured a spindly cactus.

"Yes," agreed Rickenbacker.

"Is it glass?"

Rickenbacker sighed at his friend's total lack of sophistication. "No, Phoenix, it is Bollerian crystal."

"It would have been better to win the title."

Rickenbacker shrugged. "Yes."

"We should have lied to her; told her I was responsible for her sister's problems."

"I do believe you're right, my friend."

"Will we get to be on talk shows?"

It was odd, the things Phoenix cared about. Rickenbacker nodded. "And don't forget the ribbon-cutting ceremonies."

Phoenix cocked his head. "What is that other award supposed to be?" It was black and looked like an upside-down squid whose tentacles curled around so they resembled the spokes of a wheel that wished to be closer friends by forming a sort of sphere. It was about two feet in diameter. In the base was a series of cups.

Rickenbacker was feeling benevolent. "I humbly offer that to you, my friend. It is a state-of-the-art onion ring stand."

Thank you for reading. Reviews mean the world to authors. If you enjoyed *Griffin and the Spurious Correlations*, it would be really cool of you to review it, or give it some stars. Thank you so much!

For more about me and my books, visit my website,
and subscribe to my
Totally Fantastic Email List
for lots of free stuff and exclusive content
https://kristawallace.com

Turn the page for a sneak peek at my traditional fantasy series, which begins with …

Sneak Preview

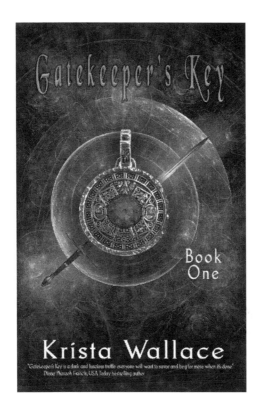

One

One Way to Be Noticed

Another town, another gem of a man who wanted to dazzle her with his "broadsword." All she had done was sit next to him, on one of only two empty stools at the bar. Hadn't even looked at him. Kyer set her beer mug on the bar with a clunk and eyed the cocky bastard as if he were a squashed slug. "What did you say?" *Full tavern. About forty. One third elven. Males and females.*

He nodded at the empty counter before her. "If you're hungry, I got plenty you can feast on. Let's go spend the evening up in my bed." He rested his elbow on the counter, displaying the thickness of his upper arm for her to be roused by.

Kyer wished she could vomit on cue. She stared at him blankly. "Why would I do that?" *Door to the corridor about five paces; exit door about twenty, between tables. Two goblins at the booth behind.*

He shrugged and blinked slowly in that way that was meant to be alluring but wasn't. "No sense you paying for your own room, honey, when Jack and I already took my gear up to my regular room."

"Wow." She nodded, feigning awe. "First-name basis with the stable boy. You've taken my breath away." *Door to the kitchen to the left. Tricky to leap the bar without taking someone out.*

"I'll do more than that, beautiful, given the chance," he said, oblivious to her sarcasm.

"I'll pass." She took another large swallow of beer.

He repeated his fingers-through-the-dark-curls gesture that hadn't impressed her earlier.

After three weeks on the road and two days without food, she didn't have the energy for this. She ignored him with as much threat as she could muster. Honestly, why had Brendow sent her here?

"Name's Simon. Simon Diduck," he said—as if she cared. He edged closer with a salacious sidelong smile. "I'm at your service, darlin'."

"Funny, you seem to think I'm at *yours*."

A low chuckle burst from a black-cloaked man two barstools down. She'd noticed him right away upon entering the tavern at the Burnished Blade. One of those types who is always watching.

Her would-be lover remained unaffected. "Oh, come on. You're such a treasure; only a fool'd let you slip through his fingers." He reached to stroke her cheek, and that was where Kyer drew the line.

She stood up, bristling, itching with the desire to scratch his eyes out. A serving girl stepped in through the door from the corridor and hesitated next to the fireplace. She gestured to someone and a large man joined her, leaning his only arm on the door frame. The silence of the crowded tavern was interrupted by only the crackling of the fire and the jabbering argument of the two goblins behind her. Kyer's shoulders stiffened with the gaze of human and elf alike, some with curiosity, some poised to flee. Diduck was a regular here. Had they seen his tactics before? Nobody seemed eager to offer any assistance. She was on her own. As usual. *Fine.*

"Men like you," she said, "are boring." Her muscles tingled to life, dispelling weariness and hunger. "And you're everywhere. Like rats and cockroaches."

He laughed. "Now that's just plain mean-spirited. Come say, 'sorry.'" His hand stretched out to touch her again but halted because the tip of her stiletto pricked the underside of his chin.

"Can't. I wouldn't want to lie to you." The threat tactic usually worked against bullies; this one was particularly persistent. "Now why don't you go and sit somewhere else, and we'll forget all about this."

The cockroach pushed her weapon aside. "Because rejection doesn't suit me."

Especially in front of an audience. The heat of anger climbing her neck, she raised the knife again. "Brace yourself for disappointment."

His lip curled in a sneer. Apparently he still believed—or was willing to pretend—she was bluffing. "You'd better put that away, darlin'; you might hurt yourself." He sought a favourable reaction from the patrons nearby and found none.

A calm, cold fury draped over her. She couldn't back down now. "Let's settle it."

Though the tightness in his lip betrayed a sudden doubt, he laughed.

Her eyebrows shot up. "So not only are you a boor; you're also a coward," she clarified.

His flash of anger told her she might have struck a nerve. "I'd have thought it cowardly of me to challenge a *girl* to a duel! Hardly honourable." He folded his arms on his chest.

Kyer couldn't help but chuckle. "Isn't it a little late to think about preserving your honour? Besides, I challenged you, not the other way around."

"I must insist we do it properly." He patted the hilt of his broadsword.

With an innocent look as if she were dealing with a child, she sheathed her knife. "Naturally." She brushed back her cloak. Murmurs undulated throughout the tavern. Diduck took one glance at her sullied leather armour and the long sheath of the bastard sword at her belt. His face paled then took on a purplish hue, as if he were angry at her, as if she'd somehow misrepresented herself.

Kyer sighed with frustration. "You can't have thought I'd challenged you to a dagger toss." She gave a quick nod to the publican, who reached under the counter and drew out a book. "With respect to our esteemed proprietor, shall we take this outside? Then he won't have to mop your blood up off his floor." Laughter erupted from many of the patrons. The man in the black cloak two seats away snorted.

"That sounds fine with me," Diduck said.

"If you please." The bartender held the book open with one hand, and a quill in the other.

At the top of the page was written the word *Duel*. Below it was a list of named pairs and dates. Next to one name in each pair was the word *Victor*, and the result, everything ranging from "first blood" to "weapon arm severed." Of the four duels listed on the page, none said, "death," which reflected Kyer's opinion that a dispute between civilized people could be decided without loss of life. She took the quill and signed her name under the date, as written by her host. She passed it back to the publican.

"Kire?" he asked, gesturing to the one-armed man in the doorway.

"No, it's Kee-Air."

"Most unusual."

The one-armed man loomed over her.

"This is Bill," the publican said. "He will be Arbiter." He turned the book around again for Simon to sign. "And the terms?"

Kyer said, "Loss of weapon. If I win, you take your sorry ass to the other inn and I never see you again." She gave him her back and stalked to the door.

"And if *I* win?" Simon called.

She flung the challenge over her shoulder. "If I lose, I'm yours for the night."

"Either way, you're in trouble, boy," a gruff voice said from a nearby table.

Kyer stepped outside into the crisp, late-winter air, shaking tension from her hands. She drew fresh, chilly breaths scented with greenery, filling her lungs, annoyed that it had come to this. When she left home on the advice of her trainer, she was looking for allies, not adversaries. In her three weeks of travelling, she'd had to put up with similar propositions more than once, but usually a few firm words were all that was necessary. Here, she had sat quietly, kept her cloak wrapped about her, her braid pulled around front, minded her own business. Was she supposed to cut her hair off and wear a floppy hat to be left alone? She embraced the sharp chill in her lungs and focussed her concentration.

At the edge of the veranda, she surveyed the yard. Pond to her left, oak tree out front by the road with a bench surrounding it, driveway from the road to the inn's stable at the right. A delineated fighting space. How many times had the area been used this way? Enough that no grass grew. The sun hung just behind the oak tree, casting mottled shade over the area, but it was by no means dim. She crossed the porch and stepped lightly down to the hard-packed dirt ground. The rest of the patrons spilled out the doors and prepared to watch from the veranda and the driveway as if it were a marketplace cock fight.

Bill planted his heavily-booted feet at the top of the stairs. "Before witnesses, Kyer Halidan and Simon Diduck, to the loss of weapon."

The man in black from the bar stood at the end of the veranda, grey eyes piercing from behind shoulder-length black hair. The other patrons gave him his space as they placed wagers with murmurs and shuffling of hands. They became a mere mass of rippling colour in Kyer's vision as she dismissed them.

She circled the yard, scanning the ground for uneven spots or rocks, a meditative procedure, part of her routine that settled her into inner calm. Damn Simon Diduck couldn't possibly have waited to harass her until after she'd eaten. But never mind. She flexed and stretched her hands and arms and focussed on breathing life into all the travel-weary muscles she was about to call on. The clean scent of wood chips and water lilies on the pond seeped in and awakened her senses. The process took no more than a few moments, but when she turned her attention back to her opponent, she wasn't nervous anymore. He approached, watching her uncertainly.

She removed her cloak to lay it on the ground. In that brief moment, she sensed a quick movement behind her and heard a stifled gasp from the crowd. She spun around. The coward had already drawn and was coming at her. Outraged, she tossed her cloak at him, entangling him and buying herself time to back out of his reach.

In one flowing, swift motion, she let her fingers curl around the hilt of her bastard sword and drew. *Okay, you cheat, you just changed the rules.*

One-handed, she automatically parried the level slash flying at her left shoulder. The yard echoed with a ring of steel. Her left hand now joining her right on the hilt she feinted a thrust at his face, and he flinched, and when he overparried from his right to left, she turned her wrist over in a crossing cut to his sword arm. Again steel clashed as he stopped it, barely. He countered with a weak thrust, and she easily stepped out of his line, sending his sword down and out of the way.

Sensing her advantage, she lunged at him, feet dancing forward, and forced him back across the yard toward the pond. He yielded to her thrust, and with a quick flip of his blade, nicked her left shoulder as he passed her.

She winced. The sharp pain vibrated down to her hand, but she dared not react further. *One to him.* But only one. Angry at her carelessness, she regrouped with a deep breath, not taking her eyes off him. His self-congratulatory smile signalled his over-confidence, and she took advantage of his lack of focus to step closer. She charged forward and slashed at his legs, forcing him to stumble to one side in his effort to avoid her blade.

A thrill rushed through her. *This* was what all those arduous hours of training were for. She kept at him, varying her rhythm, tiring him. She parried his every move calmly and precisely, while he became more careless, and fell behind her increasing tempo. Kyer parried a desperate slash with ease and pivoted to the side. Her blade slid along his with a ringing sound. She disengaged and dropped low, slicing into the muscle over his right knee.

With a yell, he clutched his leg and went down. His face twisted with agony from his wound and his humiliating defeat. Instantly she stood over him. A flick of her foot sent his sword flying a few feet away. Blood dribbled through his clenched fingers to pool into a thick, spreading puddle at her feet.

Kyer nodded, satisfied. "Loss of weapon. I'll get a healer over here for you. Have a good sleep . . . somewhere else." She turned to retrieve her cloak.

A shuffling sound and a gasp from the crowd startled her. She whirled around as Simon, on his feet with his boot dagger in hand, flew at her. His dagger bit the flesh of her upper arm. She plunged her blade into his chest, feeling it grind along his ribs, and as he fell, it stopped in the ground underneath him.

Shock in his eyes, his body convulsed and was still. As his blood stirred up the dirt and trickled away in a muddy whorl, so did the red haze lift from around her vision. The magnitude of what she had done hit like a gust of wind and she staggered. *By Guerrin, I killed him.* It was what she had trained to do, and yet she could not have prepared for *this.*

Trembling overtook her from head to toe, and this time it was not from lack of food. Kyer let her sword take some of her weight and gritted her teeth to stop them from chattering. Her rage depleted, exhaustion replaced it. Her knees wobbled and she knelt down next to her victim's body, gulping air to counteract the nausea. Her breath came out in puffs. *I killed him.* Quivering like an aspen leaf, she hissed with pain as she drew his knife out of her arm and let it drop. The flow of blood striped her sleeve.

Bill shrugged. The outcome was too obvious to declare. Murmurs rose like a flock of birds as the spectators filtered back indoors. Some who'd been watching in the yard stepped over and spat on the cheater's body before returning to what they'd been doing. Kyer fought with her conscience. *I didn't mean to k—* No, wait. That kind of thinking had to stop. She was a swordfighter; trained for years. He cheated in a publicly recognized duel. He hadn't waited for the opening salute. She'd bested him in fair combat, and he'd come at her back with a knife. If she'd let him live, what would he have tried later? No, mid-battle was not the time to waver. Diduck had forced her to make a quick decision, and she'd done it.

The difference between this and her last fight, a week before she left home, was not lost on her. This duel had at least been her choice, albeit one she had been forced to make. Better than the surprise attack in an alley by people she knew, with eight-to-one odds. She shook her head, dismissing the memory and the anger it would rekindle.

In the stillness of the yard, she pushed herself up. She braced her feet and yanked her weapon out of its resting place. With trembling hands, she wiped the blood off the blade on his shirt and sheathed it, allowing the steady, automatic movement to restore her equanimity. She unbuttoned his waistcoat and tore a strip of cloth from his sweat-soaked tunic. She fashioned a bandage and tied it, with the help of her teeth, around the arm that had met Simon's dagger. An inspection of her left shoulder showed her only a small amount of blood seeping; that wound could wait.

Kyer steeled herself, uncomfortable with the thought of performing the customary search. But she had killed him, and it had to be done. Bill watched from the top of the stairs. She slipped a tentative hand inside his bloodied waistcoat and found a purse. Her jaw dropped when she found it contained about thirty hexagonal gold nobles. More money than she'd ever seen. Her own depleted purse would be gratefully replenished and then some. In a breast pocket, she found a piece of cloth folded around a tiny key. She transferred it to her pouch. His dagger was nothing special. Even his sword, though serviceable, was not as good as her own. She left it for the benefit of the cleanup crew. He had nothing else she needed. The job done, she washed the blood off her hands in the pond with a shudder, glad to be rid of the metallic smell. She picked up her cloak, dusty from where Diduck had flung it aside. It had a new tear in it thanks to the louse's sword. *Great.*

She stood in the silent yard and stared at the aftermath—the scuffed dirt, the blood, the body—and the responsibility of having begun her life as a fighter settled its weight on her shoulders. One last deep breath, long and slow. She'd made a decision; she'd acted on it. It was time to live with it.

She took three steps back toward the inn and stopped, a flicker of annoyance tingling in her brow. The man in black stood on the veranda, watching her, even though everyone else, including Bill, had gone back inside. He leaned against the railing, cloak wrapped around his shoulders, the worn heel of one scuffed riding boot hooked over the lower rung. His long, stringy hair curtained his profile.

She continued up the steps and regarded him evenly. "If you're the local reeve, I hope that wasn't a personal guest of the magistrate." She walked by him with deliberate, steady steps. Part of her desired to ask the barkeep for the key to Diduck's room—now hers—and go to sleep for three days. The other part had something to prove. The patrons of the Burnished Blade didn't need to know he was the first man she'd killed. She returned to her seat at the bar, laying her cloak on the counter next to her. A few people overtly whispered. One man raised his mug to her. She felt their scrutiny like darts on her back and sat straighter. Her belly was in knots.

Despite the choice of free seats, the man in black sat next to her. Her arm muscles contracted, and her hairs stood up. She was *not* ready for another Simon Diduck.

She opened her mouth to make a snarky remark, but the bartender set a fresh pint before her. "I figure you could use that."

Kyer's dry throat accepted the long, cool drink with gratitude, and her nostrils appreciated the ale's earthy aroma. The liquid calmed the tremor in her hands and began to settle the disquiet in her belly. Her mouth watered, and suddenly she was so hungry a bucketful of dirt might taste good. She finally ordered some food.

She raised her mug again, and the man in black raised his glass of wine at the same time. Was he trying to be funny? The bartender winked at her as he went to the kitchen, and she wondered if there were some sort of joke she was missing. Still, in no mood to be friendly to eccentric strangers, she drank her beer, watching the man in black out of the corner of her eye as he sipped his wine. She was determined to keep her mug to her lips longer and ignore his game of mirroring her actions. But the annoying man seemed bent on his amusement and kept drinking. She kept drinking too. He drained his wine glass and at last placed it on the wood countertop. Kyer set her mug down and also noticed that her knee was bouncing with residual nerves. Sensing a comment from her neighbour approaching, she clenched her teeth and breathed through her nose; she was not inclined to let him draw her into another fight. She turned her torso to close herself off from him and likewise shifted her attention. Maybe the odd man would go away.

Why had Brendow directed her here? After the attack in the alley, he had at last said it was time. She'd asked the old man where she should go.

"Wanaka," he'd said unequivocally. "To an inn called the Burnished Blade. It's in the southwest corner of Shae duchy and should take you about three weeks. Get yourself a job there in the village."

He was right about the timeframe, but he never told her why this was the best place to start her new life and search for answers. All he had added was, "It's a hub of sorts. Things happen there." What was special about Wanaka? *Apparently not its high class of people.* Kyer drank again.

The bartender burst through the door wearing thick gloves and holding a dish of game pie, which he placed before her. He tucked the gloves into his apron and handed her a steaming, wet towel to clean her hands. He also refilled her beer glass, which made him her favourite person. "I confess I was hoping you would return without the, uh, gentleman."

The delicious aroma of the pie assailed her. Her mouth watered again and she felt weak. But another thought struck her, and it ought to be addressed. "Had the 'gentleman' already paid for his 'regular' room?"

"Yes." The publican wiped his hands on his towel and reached under the counter, pulling out a leather-bound book. "Breakfast is included."

Wary of the man next to her repeating Simon's offer, she said, "Perfect."

"Splendid!" He slid the log book over to her--not the same book as the duel list--and she filled in her name underneath Diduck's. His name had already been crossed off.

He replaced the book under the counter. "I'm Maginn Medlicott, here to take care of your every need. Here's the key. I imagine you'll want to, uh, go through . . . things. I'll have Jack take your belongings from the stable up to the room."

Any second now, the Man in Black would offer to join her in her room . . .

At last, she picked up her spoon and caved in the flaky crust of pie, drawing out an enormous scoop. A puff of steam issued from beneath the pastry, carrying with it a heavenly aroma of meat and vegetables. She burned her tongue on the first bite and had to hiss cool air through her teeth, but she still ate so fast, the pie was three quarters gone by the time Maginn came back with her neighbour's dinner. She set down her spoon so she could breathe. Her neighbour stabbed a piece of meat with his knife.

Maginn smiled. "I guess you like it."

She sighed deeply.

But something was wrong. Unfinished. Brendow's presence was vivid in the back of her mind. Sitting together in his front room after a training session, a bottle and two glasses before them. She needed wine. But not just any wine, not for Simon Diduck. Her first.

Drawing Simon's purse into her hand, she opened it and discreetly counted. It was a veritable fortune. And this was the right choice. It mattered. She got Maginn's attention. Just above a whisper, she said, "Do you have any elvish wine in stock?"

His eyebrows went up. "Why, absolutely." He did not move right away but kept his eyes on her with a thoughtful gaze. Then with an almost imperceptible nod, as if in approval of some unvoiced suggestion, he disappeared for about five minutes and returned with a dusty bottle and a glass. He opened it for her and said in a low voice, "I can tell that you're a woman of good taste. That's ten rydals." Kyer observed the depth of his fingerprints in the dust that clung to the bottle. She counted five nobles out of Simon's purse. She still had plenty to get by on for weeks.

Maginn poured a small amount into her glass. It tasted of an ancient melody, plucked delicately on an unfamiliar instrument. It trickled down her throat like a stream from a mountain spring. Ten rydals was a bargain. She'd drunk plenty of elvish wine before, but this was of a whole new quality. Unable to adequately express her appreciation for it, Kyer said, "That will do nicely." Maybe *that* would show the Man in Black she had some sophistication. But whether it did or not, she needed to carry on. She held the bottle in both hands and closed her eyes.

"Is there another bottle like that, Medlicott?" The Man in Black had a warm voice.

"You bet, my lord." The little man trundled off again.

Kyer frowned (he'd been drinking wine before, so surely he wasn't just copying her again). She focussed, mouthing the name of the man whose life she had taken. She poured to fill the glass and set the bottle down. Nonchalantly, in an effort to be inconspicuous, she dipped the fourth finger of her left hand (the weakest finger on her non-dominant hand) into the rich, red wine and traced the rim of the glass, not quite completing a full circle. *Life cut short.* She raised the glass with her right hand, just a bit, not so much as to make a big show of it, and spoke Simon's name to herself again. She took a sip. Dipped the finger and once more around the rim in the opposite direction, a full circle this time. *Completion.* One more raise followed by a sip. She set the glass down and removed her hands.

There. Now things felt right. Like washing dirt from her hands, the tension melted away, leaving her wiped out. Every training session had ended with a glass of wine, always elvish. Brendow had taught her the ritual, and she had run through it countless times. This was the first time she had done it for real, and she finally grasped its import. She picked up her spoon again.

The Man cleared his throat. Kyer refused to acknowledge him. She twisted in her seat, showing more of her back to him, and gazed around the room.

Most people had gone back to their meals and beverages. Some sets of eyes darted at her nervously; that she had intimidated a few people was a lovely reminder of home. Others expressed a less familiar emotion:

admiration. They looked at her and smiled a little as they spoke to their neighbours. She turned away, unused to approval. The goblins in the corner booth appeared not to have let the excitement interrupt their argument. They were snatching a gold coin back and forth between them. The servers had gone back to carrying trays of ale and food. The chatter was as it had been. It was all very pleasant, but *damn it*. Why in hell had Brendow sent her here? And why had he sounded overly relaxed about it?

Maginn returned with the second ancient, dusty bottle and opened it, pouring a taste for the one who'd ordered it. The Man picked up the glass with a heavily scarred hand and sipped, licking his lips in unsophisticated satisfaction. "Marvellous, as always."

Kyer rolled her eyes. *Pretentious git.* She lifted her glass and swirled a sip around her tongue. The Man in Black did the same. Annoyed, she plunked her glass down and spooned up a bite of food.

"Well, Kyer," said the man, "I am impressed by your taste in wine."

So he thought he had the right to use her first name? She chuckled with a scoffing tone. "Too bad I'm not interested in *impressing* you."

He looked surprised. "I certainly wouldn't want to be your enemy." He indicated the door. Was he mocking her?

She did not look at him. "Then I'd advise you not to piss me off."

"Fair enough."

Damn fellow still sounded like he was laughing at her.

"Those were some interesting techniques you were using," he said. "If I'm not mistaken, I recognize some of the more subtle moves."

Nice try. Kyer wasn't about to fall for his bait. He wanted to get her talking to him, but anyone could lie about such a thing. Nobody could truly recognize her *wæpnian* techniques but someone who'd trained with Brendow, and he'd been in Hreth longer than Kyer could remember. Hiding. Anybody who knew Brendow would be someone from his past who did not have his best interests in mind. If this man wanted to avoid being her enemy . . .

"Trained by a stocky short fellow, nasty limp from a bad left knee, has an unusual interest in languages? He taught you the *wasp* manoeuvre."

Kyer leapt from her seat, hand on her hilt. The tension in her throat squeezed so her voice was barely above a whisper. "Why do you know Brendow?" *Shit.* She should never have said his name aloud. And she wouldn't have if this character hadn't tricked her.

Instead of answering, he side-eyed her quizzically and swirled his wine. "Brendow, is it? That's interesting."

"Why?"

His grey eyes pierced her, full of laughter.

Kyer loosened her sword and didn't let go. "Who the hell do you think you are, the bloody Duke of Equart?"

His face lost all expression. Then the corners of his mouth twitched. His left hand eased back along his belt. His movement opened his cloak just enough for her to see his armour, the breast plate intricately enamelled with the rowan tree of Equart over the chest and a tiny sprig of foxglove beneath its left side.

"Shit," she whispered, and the ground fell out from under her. Drowning in embarrassment, she sat down hard on her stool. Mind racing, she connected a profusion of details: the long black hair and moustache, the scars on his hand and the one down the left side of his face, the cloak made of quality fabric . . . He was the only other person in the room drinking *wine,* for the love of Farro, and further—how could she have been so *thick* to have missed it—Maginn had called him *my lord.* She'd heard all the stories countless times; she ought to have at least had a suspicion of who he was, even though his hair concealed his ears. If there was a single person in the entire continent of Rydris she *would* have wanted to impress, this was him. *Shit.* Her heart plummeted to the bottom of her gut.

She drained her glass and tried to think of something to say.

He graciously did not smirk as he said, "Pleased to meet you."

"Kyer." She tentatively put out a hand, which he shook. "Halidan," she added, knowing it wouldn't mean anything to him. "Do you dress in black just to be intimidating?"

"Naw, it's only because my white suit's being cleaned." He did smile then.

She laughed a little but felt slightly sick. He was a dark elf, and about four hundred fifty years old. Stories had been told of this hero since she was a child. Songs in his praise had been sung since the first time she'd stepped into a tavern. And here was she, a nobody from a nowhere place like Hreth, being unforgivably rude to him. Guerrin's fire, she'd killed a man while Valrayker, the Duke of Equart, watched her.

She turned her head to hide her enormous sigh. Following it with a resigned shrug, she poured another glass of wine. For the second time in the space of half an hour, she had a choice to make: If she could have had a second chance at a first encounter with her greatest hero, without a doubt, she would have behaved with aplomb. But as it was, she'd treated him abominably, and whatever his first impression of her was, it was carved in stone. Now she could either slink away to her room and leave town first thing in the morning or she could carry on. Slinking away was not her style. Besides, even if all he gave her was five minutes of his time, she would take it. She'd acted; it was time to live with it.

"Well, now I'm really glad I won that fight." She had a faint hope that he'd tell her she had done the right thing in killing Simon.

"Quite handily too."

"You can't say I didn't warn him."

"No, indeed."

Not reassured by his response, she finished the last few bites of her meal, the whole time aware of Valrayker observing her. She'd been judged and found wanting countless times by people she could easily disregard. Brendow, and her parents of course, she respected. But this time—for the first time—she was being sized up by someone outside her circle whose opinion actually mattered.

"So you trained with . . . Brendow, did you say? Where are you from?"

Well, this answer certainly wouldn't be impressive. "Hreth," she said, biting back a "sorry." "It's a rather backward little village in northwestern Heath." She could tell Valrayker about Brendow's location; Brendow himself would confirm there was probably no one more trustworthy in all of Rydris.

The silence that followed was deeply thoughtful. After a time, he asked, "And what brings you all the way from Hreth to Wanaka?"

"Brendow recommended I look for work here. Didn't seem to be any point in being a swordswoman in a place like Hreth." Even now that she knew his identity, was there a use in telling him she didn't know her own? *I walked out of a cornfield when I was three, and I'd kind of like to know what that was all about* was not likely to raise her in his esteem. Nor was *It's not much fun living in a village where everyone thinks you're a witch.* Instead, she said, "So how do you know Brendow?"

"Knew him," Valrayker corrected. "It was a long time ago."

She wanted to probe further, get him to elaborate, to ask him to explain why he seemed familiar, yet unfamiliar with Brendow's name. But the dark elf's tone had implied finality, and she decided to respect it rather than persist.

Still a bit shaky, she drank more wine to steady her nerves. She knew her reaction wasn't just about making a fool of herself to Valrayker. She had killed a man, and it was not something she could brush off with ease. She drained the bottle into her glass and regretfully set it on the counter. All good things had to come to an end.

Maginn approached and picked up her and Valrayker's dishes. "Will that be all, my lord?"

"For now, thank you." He glanced sidelong at Kyer. "So." Valrayker swirled his wine. "It's . . . lucky I happened to run into you here. I have to be at a meeting in a short time. Would you care to join me?"

Kyer choked on her wine. Could he be serious after she'd shown him how unseasoned she was? When her cough stopped she tried to sound sophisticated and just mildly curious. "What sort of a meeting?"

"All in good time," he said. In spite of the angle, she could still perceive the twinkle in his eye. "You coming or not?"

She hesitated for a fleeting moment. But surely this was what she had been hoping for when she left home. Was this why Brendow— *But how could he have known?* Kyer could not turn down an evening with Valrayker of Equart. With a passing thought of a few people in Hreth and what their reactions would be to this development, she gave him a casual half smile, trying to hide her eagerness. "I have nothing better to do. Do you mind if I go up to my room and take care of this cut first?" Her shoulder still oozed a little.

"I would mind if you didn't."

Kyer grabbed her cloak, brushing the wine glass off the counter where it landed in Valrayker's lap, and he caught it deftly before it could fall to the floor. Her face enflamed, her gaze leapt to his, fearful that he would see her discomposure and change his mind. But instead she was startled at what she saw. His grey eyes smiled softly and showed the wisdom that only four and a half centuries of life experience can bring. As the last remaining dark elf in the known world, there would be no fooling him. The corners of his mouth turned up gently.

"It takes a while to recover after the first one. And unfortunately, it gets easier."

Read more about Kyer Halidan's adventures in *Gatekeeper's Key*

Acknowledgements

"They" keep saying writing is a solitary pursuit. And so it is, to a degree. But when I poke my head out of my closet door I find I am surrounded by countless people supporting me, cheering me on, sharing their opinions, offering suggestions, and pointing out things I missed. I am eternally grateful. I wrote this book during a really dark time in my life, and it was a thing that brought me great joy. You all made it a better story.

To my many friends who read the story and gave me your opinions, thank you! I would like to especially thank my beta readers, Harold Gross, Eve Gordon, Jonathan Lyster and Julie Reeser, for your thoughtful feedback, all of which I took to heart. To Chari Grant and Myst DeVana: you let me read the first three chapters aloud to you and gave me reason to believe it was worth pursuing. Myst, you have been one of my biggest fans from the get-go, and your support and encouragement are priceless. Char, thank you for being a "beta listener," and for sitting with me for hours while I picked your brain. That was above and beyond even though there was wine.

Huge thanks to Stephanie Kwok who not only reads my stuff and gives me feedback, but also is a marvellous webmaven, to Catherine Branch for answering my dance-related questions, and to Jasper Fforde, who gave me exactly the answer I needed about the opening, and assured me I didn't babble. My sincere gratitude goes to my writing peeps (you know who you are!) especially Beth Wagner, Brenda Carre and Laura Kelly. Jonathan Lyster, you get two mentions because you're a gem. I'm so glad we met at SiWC.

As ever and always, my family. Honestly, you four, where would I be??

And finally, to all the musicians who created the music referenced in this book, as well as all the musicians whose songs I couldn't fit in here, thank you for creating.

Also by Krista Wallace

In paperback, ebook and audiobook

The Gatekeeper Series

Gatekeeper's Key
Gatekeeper's Deception I - Deceiver
Gatekeeper's Deception II - Deceived

coming soon: Gatekeeper's Crucible
and
Gatekeeper's Revelation

In audiobook

To Serve and Protect
The Inner Light

Find my work at Books2Read.com/KristaWallace
Learn more about me at kristawallace.com

About Krista Wallace

Krista started out as a singer, studied Theatre and got her degree in Acting at UVic, then eventually added writing to her creative endeavours. She has sung classical, musical theatre, rock, R&B and jazz. She has been the vocalist for FAT Jazz for something like 427 years, and is half of a jazz duo called The Itty Bitty Big Band. She writes primarily fantasy, but dabbles in other genres, in both short and long fiction. Combining all her artistic exploits, she took on audiobook narration, and producing a podcast, [Totally Fantastic Title], which then branched into the production of her own audiobooks. Krista grew up in the Port Coquitlam vortex, and so was naturally pulled back there after her time away.

To be continued. . .

Manufactured by Amazon.ca
Bolton, ON

42236385R00175